Collections *for*
Excellence

Corinne Powers & Ruth Nesse
Endowment Fund
Children's

Praise for *WE ARE NOT FREE*

"A brilliant and intimate portrayal. . . . A beautiful, painful, and necessary work of historical fiction."
—VEERA HIRANANDANI, Newbery Honor–winning author of *The Night Diary*

"These powerful interconnected stories of incarceration during WWII told by Nisei youth will wrap around your heart like barbed wire. With deft touches of humor, heart, pathos, and anger, *We Are Not Free* . . . is the best Japanese-American incarceration novel I've read."
—DEBBI MICHIKO FLORENCE, author of the Jasmine Toguchi series

"Nothing short of a masterpiece. With [Traci Chee's characters], you will blaze with incandescent rage, crumble with internalized shame, and laugh with true, soul-deep joy."
—MISA SUGIURA, author of *This Time Will Be Different* and *It's Not Like It's a Secret,* winner of the 2018 APALA Award for YA Literature

"Powerful, moving, and so incredibly necessary."
—AKEMI DAWN BOWMAN, Morris Award finalist and author of *Starfish*

"With a cast of fully developed and beautifully written characters you love and root for, *We Are Not Free* reminds us of a shameful episode in American history and asks us not to forget. *We Are Not Free* is not only a brave story, it's a necessary one."
—STACEY LEE, award-winning author of *Outrun the Moon*

"Devastating, vital, and deeply human, *We Are Not Free* is a tour de force and should be required reading—for this moment in time and for every future generation."
—KELLY LOY GILBERT, Morris Award finalist and author of *Conviction*

WE ARE NOT FREE

WE
ARE

TRACI CHEE

NOT FREE

Houghton Mifflin Harcourt

Boston   New York

hmhbooks.com

The text was set in Adobe Garamond Pro.
Illustrations on pages 46–47 and 367 © 2020 Julia Kuo
Paper texture © Houghton Mifflin Harcourt
Interior design by Mary Claire Cruz

Library of Congress Cataloging-in-Publication Data
Names: Chee, Traci, author.
Title: We are not free / Traci Chee.
Description: Boston : Houghton Mifflin Harcourt, [2020] | Audience: Ages 12 and up. | Audience: Grades 7–9. | Summary: For fourteen-year-old budding artist Minoru Ito, her two brothers, her friends, and the other members of the Japanese-American community in southern California, the three months since Pearl Harbor was attacked have become a waking nightmare: attacked, spat on, and abused with no way to retaliate—and now things are about to get worse, their lives forever changed by the mass incarcerations in the relocation camps.
Identifiers: LCCN 2019029407 | ISBN 9780358131434 (hardcover) | ISBN 9780358330004 (ebook) | ISBN 9780358343165 | ISBN 9780358343561
Subjects: LCSH: Japanese Americans—Evacuation and relocation, 1942–1945—Juvenile fiction. | Japanese American families—Juvenile fiction. | World War, 1939–1945—Concentration camps—United States—Juvenile fiction. | World War, 1939–1945—Japanese Americans—Juvenile fiction. | Concentration camps—United States—Juvenile fiction. | Prejudices—Juvenile fiction. | California—History—20th century—Juvenile fiction. | CYAC: Japanese Americans—Evacuation and relocation, 1942–1945—Fiction. | World War, 1939–1945—United States—Fiction. | Prejudices—Fiction. | California—History—20th century—Fiction. | LCGFT: Historical fiction.
Classification: LCC PZ7.1.C497 We 2020 | DDC 813.6 [Fic]—dc23
LC record available at https://lccn.loc.gov/2019029407

Manufactured in the United States of America
DOC 10 9 8 7 6 5 4 3 2
4500815634

For my grandparents,
Margaret & Peter Kitagawa and Sachiko & Michio Iwata;

their brothers and sisters,
Kojiro Kawaguchi, Yuki Okuda, Mary Uchiyama, Midori Goto, Jane
Imura, Saburo Kitagawa, Yoshiro Kitagawa, Naomi Ogawa, Mutsuo
Kitagawa, Yoshimi Hamada, Emiko Aoki, Katsuko Kuranaga, Teruko
Hamada, Hiroshi Hamada, Eiko Mayeda, Shinobu Hamada, Mitsuko
Ochoa, Minoru Nakano, Osuye Okano;

and June Kitagawa and Aiji Uchiyama

with love and gratitude

CHARACTER REGISTRY

NAME		OTHER NAMES	FAMILY NUMBER	SEX	AGE AT EVACUATION	PRE-EVACUATION ADDRESS
FUJITA,	Francis	"Frankie"	22585	M	19	San Francisco, Calif.
HARANO,	Tom	"Tommy"	20695	M	16	San Francisco, Calif.
	Aiko	"Ike"	20695	F	13	San Francisco, Calif.
HASHIMOTO,	David	"Twitchy"	22603	M	17	San Francisco, Calif.
ITO,	Masaru	"Mas"	22437	M	20	San Francisco, Calif.
	Shigeo	"Shig"	22437	M	17	San Francisco, Calif.
	Minoru	"Minnow"	22437	M	14	San Francisco, Calif.
KATSUMOTO,	Stanley	"Stan"	20115	M	18	San Francisco, Calif.
	Mary		20115	F	15	San Francisco, Calif.
KIMURA,	Keiko		21744	F	16	San Francisco, Calif.
NAKANO,	Hiromi	"Bette"	22804	F	17	San Francisco, Calif.
	Yuki		22804	F	14	San Francisco, Calif.
OISHI,	Amy	"Yum-yum"	21239	F	16	San Francisco, Calif.
TANI,	Kiyoshi	"Yosh"	10690	M	16	Los Angeles, Calif.

WAR

500 KILLED JA

RESS VOTES W

00 DEAD IN HA

TTLESHIPS SUNK TOK

APANESE BOMB

K OAHU

XTRA

XTRA

S BOMB U.S

R U.S.-JAP WA

WAII JAPAN

DECLARES WAR ON U

WAR

AT WAR

I

WE NEVER LOOK LIKE US

MINNOW, 14
MARCH 1942

It's been over three months since the attack on Pearl Harbor, and my oldest brother, Mas, has told me to come straight home from school each day. *Take the bus,* he says. *No loitering around,* he says. *I mean it, Minnow.*

I used to love walking back to the apartment in the afternoons, seeing all the interesting things going on in the city: bodies being excavated at Calvary Cemetery, buildings going up in empty lots, chattering kids coming out of Kinmon Gakuen, the old Japanese language school.

But that's been closed since last December, when it became the Civil Control Station, because Pearl Harbor changed everything for us. We have a new eight-p.m. curfew. People are starting to talk about involuntary evacuation. And Mas has warned me not to get caught out alone. *Don't do anything that'll make them come down on you,* he says. *Don't give them any excuse.*

And I haven't.

Until today.

I don't know what happened. I was walking out of George Washington High School, headed for the bus stop like always, when I saw the football team practicing on the field, racing back and forth across the grass with the red towers of the Golden Gate Bridge rising beyond the school building like a promise, and before I knew it, I was sitting in the bleachers with my sketchbook in my hands and my butt going numb on the concrete.

Oops.

I'm so panicked, I gather up my sketchpad and bolt right past the bus stop, hoping to make it home before Mas gets back from work.

No matter how many times I try to explain it, he never understands. Sometimes I get so wrapped up in a drawing that I get transported onto the paper, and the charcoal suspension cables and pencil players become more real to me than the bleachers or the grass or the school, and when I come back to my body, it's hours later, everyone's gone, and I'm walking home alone as fog cascades into the bay.

I know it'd be faster if I waited for a bus, but I'm afraid if I hang around at one of the stops, someone will chase me off, or call me "Jap!" or worse. So I keep walking, and buses keep passing me while I'm between stops, and I keep thinking I should just wait at the next one, but . . .

Mas says that's my problem — there's always something going on inside my head, but I never *think*.

My middle brother, Shig, likes to tell him it's because my head's up in the clouds, where it doesn't do me any good.

I'm still walking, trying to decide if I should keep going or try waiting, when I catch sight of a flyer for Sutro Baths in a drugstore window, and I stop cold. For a second, all I can think is, *Mas was right. I* don't *think.*

I should've gone straight home. I should've waited for a bus. I shouldn't be out like this. Because it's dangerous to be hanging around with a face like mine, three months into the war.

It was a Sunday in December, and we were getting ready for lunch when Mas asked Shig to turn on the radio and we all heard the news that Japan had attacked Pearl Harbor.

Mom's face went taut and white as a sheet. If I was going to draw her the way she looked then, I'd draw her with thin lips and frightened eyes, pinned to a clothesline, her body flapping in the wind of a passing Nakajima B5N bomber.

We've never been allowed inside Sutro Baths, but I used to draw it from the park at Lands End (the glass ceilings, the rough water, the tide-eaten cliffs), imagining what it was like inside those glinting cupolas: the smell of salt water and wet concrete, every sound in that echoing space a slap.

Now I kind of wish the whole thing would slide into the Pacific.

The ad says GET IN TRIM FOR FIGHTING HIM! and in the center there's a drawing of a Japanese soldier with diagonal slits for eyes, nostrils like watermelon seeds, and two big square teeth jutting out over his lower lip.

I'm not a great artist or anything, but I'm a better artist than *that*. When I draw the people in my neighborhood, I draw them with eyes like crescent moons and kindness and red bean cakes split down the center. I draw them with real noses and regular-size teeth. If someone is out looking for a Japanese spy and they think a Japanese spy looks like the guy from the Sutro's ad, they'll never find him.

• • •

After the attack, the chimneys in Japantown bloomed with smoke. In the living room, Mom dug into her trunks and began feeding heirlooms into the fireplace, starting with the Japanese flag. I remember her kneeling by the hearth, plump hands folded in her lap, watching the flames obliterate the white sky, the red sun. Next, she burned letters from relatives I'd never met; Jii-chan's Imperial Army uniform, smelling of mothballs; and a woodblock print of ancestral warriors I used to study for hours (the armor, the ferocious eyes, the wild, battle-blown hair). They looked nothing like me, in my denim and button-downs.

Mas tried to stop her (some of the things she was burning belonged to Dad), but she didn't stop.

"I'm not a citizen," she told him. "If they think I'm disloyal, they'll take me away like Oishi-san."

Mr. Oishi, Shig's girl Yum-yum's dad, is a businessman with contacts in Japan. The FBI whisked him away the night of the bombing like a piece of litter.

He and Mom are what the government calls "enemy aliens."

We call them Issei. They're the first generation of Japanese immigrants to come to the United States, but they've never been allowed to become naturalized citizens.

That night, I sat on our stoop and drew the Japantown skyline with storm-colored flowers rising from the rooftops, dispersing ash like seeds on the wind.

Studying my reflection in the drugstore window, I put my fingers to the corners of my eyes, pulling upward to see if I can make myself look like the guy from the flyer. (I can't.) Behind me, there's the sound of heels clicking on the sidewalk, and two white women in polo coats, hats, and little suede gloves pass, staring with round blue eyes like binocular lenses, and I remember to keep walking.

As I pass beneath the Spanish tile roofs and honeycomb windows of the Jewish Community Center, I almost kick myself for forgetting again. I should've waited at the bus stop. In my head, I hear Mas's voice again—*Think, Minnow*—deep and gruff like if he was forced to say a kind word, he'd choke on it.

Mas—that's short for Masaru—is big and handsome and a lot more serious than he should be at twenty years old. If I was going to draw him, I'd draw him as a rectangle of granite with a chisel-cut mouth and stony black eyes. Sometimes I think Mas looks at me with those eyes and sees nothing but the A's I could be getting on my report card if only I "applied myself." He doesn't see *me* (Minoru Ito, solid B student), doesn't see that I'd rather be filling my sketchpad with stick figures than throwing touchdowns or doing geometry proofs.

If he finds out I didn't take the bus directly after school, he'll yell at me for sure.

I'm on the outskirts of Japantown when I pass a store I know almost as well as any place in the neighborhood, a grocery owned by Stan Katsumoto's family. They get fruits and vegetables from their cousins in Sacramento, and if we aren't forced to evacuate, in a couple of months they'll have the best peaches in the city: soft, sweet as candy, with juices that run down your chin. Once, when we were younger, all of us stuffed ourselves on the bruised fruit Mr. Katsumoto couldn't sell. Shig ate so much, he threw it all up again and smiled the whole time, saying it tasted as good coming up as it did going down.

Looking at it now, I kind of feel sick. In addition to the words GROCERY and FRUITS & VEGETABLES, there's a new sign. Over the door on a big white board are the words I AM AN AMERICAN. One of the windows is busted and covered up with plywood.

After Pearl Harbor, it seemed like ketos — white people — were jumping everyone with black hair and brown eyes. It got so out of hand that Chinese guys started pinning badges to their lapels declaring I AM CHINESE, just so the ketos would leave them alone.

Before Christmas, *Life* magazine published an article called "How to Tell Japs from the Chinese." I guess it was supposed to tell ketos which of us to attack, but if you ask me, it wasn't very helpful, because American citizens are still getting jumped all the time, like when the ketos cornered Tommy Harano behind the YMCA. They shoved him around and called him dirty words like "Jap" and "Nip." They said the only good Jap was a dead Jap. They said they were going to do their country a favor and get rid of him right then.

It was lucky Mr. Tanaka, who works at the YMCA, came out for a smoke, because he chased off the ketos and sat with Tommy until he stopped shaking.

That's why Mas doesn't want me or Shig to act out at all. We can't call attention to ourselves in any way.

Except some of the guys, like Shig's best buddy, Twitchy Hashimoto, you can't help but pay attention to. Twitchy's the best-looking guy in our group, the kind of handsome that makes everybody, even ketos, stop and stare. He's tall and slim, with straight white teeth that belong in a toothpaste ad. Of all the guys, I like drawing Twitchy best (even though it's hard because he's constantly moving, running around or playing with that butterfly knife he stole off a Filipino guy, though he had to turn that in because it was considered contraband) because when he moves, you can see every shadow in his forearms, his shoulders, his back.

I'm almost two blocks from Webster Street, the unofficial border of the neighborhood, when I realize I've got four white guys following me.

I think of running for it, but I'm afraid I'll look guilty if I run, and I'm not guilty of anything but being born with this face, so I just lengthen my stride and try to act natural, or as natural as I can when I'm being tailed by a bunch of guys I'm sure want to jump me, but I only get another ten yards by the time the ketos catch up to me.

Think, Minnow. If I'd run for it, maybe I would've already made it to Japantown, where there's always someone hanging around. Maybe I would've found Shig and Twitchy or Stan Katsumoto. Maybe they would've stopped whatever's about to happen.

I swallow, hard. I'm not as small as Tommy Harano, but I'm smaller than Mas and Shig were when they were fourteen, and the ketos outnumber me four to one.

I look around for help and see some guys on the opposite corner —they have black hair and brown eyes like me, but they're wearing big round buttons that say I AM CHINESE.

They catch me staring. I wonder if I should call to them, but my mouth's so dry, I think if I open it, the only thing that'll come out is dust.

While I hesitate, they turn and run the other direction. From behind, they look just like Japanese guys. They could be from my neighborhood. They could be my friends or cousins or brothers.

But they're not.

I back up, clutching my sketchbook, as the ketos surround me.

"Whatcha got there, Jap?"

The word is hard, like a wet palm striking me on the cheek.

I'm so dazed by it, I don't answer, and the guy grabs my sketchpad. I lunge forward, but he's taller than me, and he snatches it out of my reach while the other boys laugh.

The first guy has a gap in his front teeth and a leather jacket that looks brand-new. He riffles through the pages, and I know he's seeing my friends, my family, my Ocean Beach, my cemeteries, my Japan-town chimneys, my many studies of the Golden Gate Bridge, my city, the city that I love.

Rrrrrip. He tears a drawing from the spine, and I cringe. The sketchbook was a present from Dad, before he died.

"You spying on us, Jap?" the gap-toothed guy says, shoving the sketch in my face. "You gonna send these back to the emperor?"

I look at the drawing—it's of the bridge—and the only thing I can think is that I didn't get the perspective right. The tower looks flimsy and out of proportion, like it wouldn't be able to hold up to the weight of all its promises.

Before I can answer, he pulls the bridge back again and draws a knife on me. The blade's over four inches—if he were Japanese, it'd be contraband.

For some reason, I start laughing.

"You think that's funny?" he says, advancing on me. "I'll show you funny."

I stop laughing as the other ketos grab me from behind.

I try to fight them, but the next thing I know, I'm flat on my back and the sidewalk's cold under me. The first guy's on top of me, sneering, and I'm struggling to breathe.

I'm still fighting, or at least I think I am, but suddenly he rears back and then there's three bright blossoms of pain in the right side of my face. For a second, I see blood-red suns against the white San Francisco sky, feel the thin sliver of a knife against my cheek.

"Wanna see what real Americans do to Jap spies?" the gap-toothed guy growls.

I AM AN AMERICAN

I'm seeing Mr. Katsumoto's sign again. I want to write it everywhere: on my forehead — I AM AN AMERICAN — on the white sky — I AM AN AMERICAN — on the windows of Sutro Baths — I AM AN AMERICAN.

But that won't make them see me. That won't stop them from killing me, if they can.

The only good Jap is a dead Jap.

I start bucking and screaming. I shout for Shig, Mas, Twitchy, Stan, Frankie Fujita —

Then the first guy punches me again, and my head lolls to the side. In the gutter, my sketchpad lies face-down, pages wrinkled beneath it.

I can see bits and pieces of my rumpled drawings — a view of the bridge from the Presidio on the north edge of the city, Mas in his football uniform, the Dutch windmills along the shoreline, Twitchy running down Buchanan Street at midnight, going so fast I drew him blurry, like a spirit you see only as you're turning a corner, and when you look again, he's gone.

Ten days ago, President Roosevelt established the War Relocation Authority, a federal agency that's supposed to be in charge of figuring out how to get us out of military zones where the government doesn't want us. We just don't know which of us they'll move. Or how it's going to happen. Or when.

Some people say they'll take only Isseis like Mom. But what about their American-born kids? We'll have to go wherever our parents do. Maybe Shigeo and I could stay in San Francisco with Mas, since he's over eighteen. But none of us would ever leave Mom alone.

Some people say we'll only have to go a little ways inland, but Stan Katsumoto told us his Sacramento family has heard rumors they'll have to evacuate too. They'll have to abandon their farm at the start of the fruit season—no strawberries, no apricots, no candy-sweet peaches dripping juice. Maybe we'll all have to leave California.

I've never been beyond the Sierra Nevada. What would it be like, walking down the block and not smelling sunbei baking in the Shungetsu-do confectionary? Going to school and not seeing the rust-colored tips of the bridge jutting out of the fog? Not tasting the salt air of the Pacific Ocean on every breath?

I don't want to leave. No one else does either, not Mom, who's been here for over twenty years, not Mas or Shig or any of our pals.

Why should we have to, when we're Americans like anyone else?

I know the answer, and I hate the answer: because we're Japs, enemy aliens.

Because we look like us.

The sounds of yelping and shouting reach me as if through a haze. I barely notice until the weight on my chest eases, and suddenly everything is very sharp and very loud. The ketos are flying away like leaves on the wind.

Someone grabs me, and at first I try to struggle, but then I realize it's Mas. He's half dragging, half carrying me across the street while the other guys run after the ketos, hurling rocks and soda bottles. He's strong enough to pick me up, but I'm glad he doesn't. The fellas would never let me live it down if they saw me cradled in Mas's arms like a baby.

Mas has had to grow up fast these past two years. Unlike Shig and me, Mas is a brain. He was in his first semester at UC Berkeley when Dad died. After that, Mas had to drop out and take over Dad's job as a gardener to help Mom with the finances. He tries to be like Dad and keep me and Shig out of trouble, especially now, except Dad was made of warm, soft pine instead of stone.

Finally, we make it across Webster Street, and Mas sets me down on the steps of Mr. Hidekawa's apartment. The FBI picked up Mr. Hidekawa the same night they got Mr. Oishi. One of our community leaders, Mr. Hidekawa served in the military in the First World War, hoping he'd get his citizenship. (He didn't.) When he heard the authorities were coming for him, he dug out his old jacket and trousers, polished his boots, and met them at the door as a uniformed U.S. Army veteran.

They took him all the same.

Mr. Hidekawa's apartment is empty now. His neighbors, the Yamadas and the Tadachis, are looking after his place. Their house is like a lot of the others in Japantown, with decorative cornices and bay windows from the Victorian era. The buildings here are all so similar, but I like the little details that make them different: the fluting on some entryway columns, the ornamented brackets, the turtle-shaped bell over Mr. Hidekawa's door. It's those details I'll miss if we have to leave.

Mas steps back onto the sidewalk, like he needs some distance to really size me up. He must have just gotten back from his job, because he's got dirt on his forearms and the knees of his pants. Normally, he showers and dresses in clean, neatly ironed shirts and trousers as soon as he gets home, even if he's not going out again. That's something Dad used to do—he took a lot of pride in looking tidy. "What happened? Why'd they attack you?" he says.

Trust Mas to blame *me* for getting jumped.

"Nothing. I was walking home and—"

"Why didn't you take a bus?"

I shrug.

I must look more messed up than I think, because Mas doesn't yell at me like I expect him to. Instead, he whips out a handkerchief and begins rubbing my face. "How many times do I have to tell you, Minnow? You have to—"

I was walking! I want to shout. *I was just walking!*

But what comes out is this: "We could do everything right, and they'd still think we were dangerous."

Mas stops. His face kind of cracks, and I see that underneath the layer of anger, he's scared. Really scared. I wish I had my sketchpad right now so I could draw that bright rift of fear that's running through his core like a vein of silver.

But he closes up again as Shig comes over to us and takes the handkerchief. "Jeez, Mas! You're roughing him up worse than the ketos." He plants the sketchbook in my arms. "Here, Minnow."

The covers are bent, and the pages are damp with gutter water. "Thanks," I whisper.

He plops down on the stoop beside me and dabs gently at my cheekbone.

Shig's not as handsome as Twitchy or Mas, but I think he's the most well-liked fella in our group. It's all in his manner—he's got an easy, crooked smile, and an easy way of talking, like there's no place in the world he'd rather be than right here, with you. He's not good at school or sports or anything, but Shigeo is good at *people*. He could walk down any street in Japantown, greet everybody by name, and ask after every one of their kids, grandkids, gardens, and hobbies.

"You didn't bleed on him, did you?" Shig asks me, glancing sidelong at Mas with his heavily lidded eyes. "I got blood on his favorite shirt once and he nearly flipped his wig."

Mas crosses his arms. "Blood, huh? I could've sworn it was paint, because *you* thought it would be funny to change the color of my outfit right before the Senior Ball."

"Oh yeah." Shigeo grins. "That *was* funny."

Before Mas can reply, the rest of the guys come sauntering back across Webster Street. They're all between sixteen and twenty years old, and, except for Frankie Fujita, who moved here when he was ten, they all grew up together in Japantown.

"Got this for you, Minnow." Twitchy Hashimoto unfolds the crumpled drawing of the Golden Gate Bridge, smoothing it a couple of times on his thigh, and hands it back to me.

"Thanks." As I take it, I notice that the other side is filled with sketches of him doing tricks with his butterfly knife. I guess I draw Twitchy a lot.

Blushing, I slide the page into the sketchbook and clap the covers closed.

"That's a nice shiner you got," Twitchy says.

Gingerly, I touch the side of my face, where the skin is warm and swollen. "You think so?"

He just laughs, ruffles my hair, and skips up a couple of Mr. Hidekawa's steps before sliding down the banister again.

"You're all right now, Minnow," says Tommy with a small grin. "We've got you."

Seeing Tommy smile cheers me up a bit. Tommy's sixteen, but looking at him, you wouldn't know it. He's small and nervous, with round eyes that are too big for his face. If he can smile at a time like this, so can I. "How'd you guys know I was in trouble?" I ask.

"Some Chinese guys came running over, saying the white boys were at it again," Mas answers.

I remember their buttons—I AM CHINESE—and the backs of their heads. I guess they didn't abandon me after all.

Frankie Fujita strolls up then, hands jammed in his pockets. I've got a few drawings of Frankie, and in them he always looks like he's spoiling for a fight: blazing comets for eyes, high cheekbones, hair he wears long and messy like the guys in Mom's woodblock prints. Sometimes I think he should've been born into another era, when he could've made fighting his whole life. That boy likes fighting more than almost anything. He'll fight ketos, Chinese, Mexicans, Blacks, anybody. He's nineteen, and after Pearl Harbor, he wanted to sign up to fight the Japanese and the Germans and the Italians, but the government reclassified us from A-1 to C-4, making us all "enemy aliens" (even though people like Frankie and me and the guys are Nisei, second-generation Japanese-American citizens), so he couldn't fight anybody.

Before moving here, Frankie grew up in New York, where he was getting into so much trouble that his parents sent him out West to live with his uncle, hoping California life would tame him some. He could've gone back to New York when President Roosevelt signed

Executive Order 9066 back in February and all those rumors about evacuation started, but he didn't. He stayed with the boys.

I don't like him much, but you can't say he's not loyal.

He crosses his arms, and his anger flares in his eyes. "Goddamn ketos."

"But thank God for Chinese guys, huh?" Shig winks at me.

Stan Katsumoto clasps his hands in front of him like he's in the front pew at Sunday services. Behind his glasses, his smart black eyes shine like a crow's. "Dear Heavenly Father," he intones, "we thank you for this day, all the blessings you have given us, and Chinese guys."

Twitchy laughs. He's got a great laugh. It shakes you a little at first, and then you feel all the restless bits of your soul settle like grains of rice in a washing pot. "I've got half a mind to steal a few of those buttons," he says, "just so the ketos'll leave us alone."

Tommy frowns. "We don't look Chinese."

In *PM Magazine,* Dr. Seuss, the kids' book author, has been drawing us with pig noses and wiry mustaches, queuing up for boxes of TNT. There are all sorts of cartoons like that. Sometimes we look like pigs, sometimes monkeys, sometimes rats.

We never look like us.

Stan leans back against the banister, spinning one finger like it's a roulette wheel. "Chinese, Japanese, Korean, Filipino . . . Who wants to guess who the ketos are going after next week?"

Stan's smart, maybe even smarter than Mas, and he uses his smarts to make jokes, skipping along the surfaces of things like a stone over water, so they barely touch him. But he wasn't joking the day he helped his father hang the sign at Katsumoto Co.: I AM AN AMERICAN.

"Next week?" Frankie grunts. "There won't be a 'next week' for much longer if they kick us outta here."

And just like that, the conversation turns, as it always does these days, to the evacuation.

"I heard the Bainbridge Japanese only got six days to pack," Tommy says.

Bainbridge is this little island in Washington. Last Saturday, their Japanese got the first exclusion order, telling them they'd have to leave their homes.

Their homes.

Our homes.

"What hard-working nihonjin *can't* pack up their whole life in six days?" Stan clicks his tongue. "Bad Asians."

"Maybe we won't . . ." Tommy doesn't finish his sentence. We all know we're going to get that exclusion order one day, even though, at the same time, we hope that day never comes.

"Anybody know where they're going?" Mas asks.

"Owens Valley got some 'volunteers' last weekend." Twitchy makes quotation marks with his fingers when he says the word "volunteers."

The Owens Valley Reception Center is near Kings Canyon National Park. I've never been there, but at least it's still in California.

I hate myself a little bit for thinking that. For trying to convince myself the situation isn't as bad as it is.

Because it *is* bad. Really bad. That's why Mas is so angry and so scared. It's so bad that being an American won't protect you when you have faces like ours.

I was walking!

I was just *walking*.

I've never broken the law. I'm a pretty good student, despite what Mas will tell you. I keep to myself. I mind my own business.

I'm a *good* Japanese.

I'm a good *American*.

But that won't be enough, will it? To keep me here? To make them leave me alone?

"Think we'll go to Owens Valley too?" Tommy asks. "That's not far."

"It's far enough," Stan says.

A silence falls over us, and in my head, I do a sketch of the guys. We're on Mr. Hidekawa's steps, and all around us, our eight-p.m. curfew approaches in dark clouds of charcoal.

"Come on." Mas gestures to Shig and me. "You two have homework to do." Then he smacks me on the back, harder than he needs to, but now I know it's not because he's angry with me.

It's because the ketos could come back for us.

It's because we could all be rounded up, no matter how many laws we obey or what grades we have. It doesn't matter how good we are, because they see only what they want to see, and when they look at us, all they see are Japs.

"Why bother?" Shig laughs. "Where they're sending us, maybe there's no school."

Mas gives him a hard look. "Because we won't be there forever."

As we head down the street, we take in the neighborhood: the hotels with lighted signs buzzing in the fog, the churches advertising next Sunday's services like we won't be herded off any day now, the smells of hot sesame oil and grilled fish wafting from the nearest restaurants.

Frankie stuffs his hands into his pockets. "Sure gonna miss this place when Uncle Sam kicks us out."

That night, after Mom, Mas, and Shig have gone to bed, I stand in front of the bathroom mirror, studying my reflection. The skin around my right eye's purple as an eggplant. It's so swollen, my eye's turned into a slit I can hardly see through.

If you cover the left side of my face, I look like the guy from the Sutro's ad.

When I leave the bathroom, I don't go back to the room Shig and I share. I sit in the living room, open my sketchbook to a blank page, and begin to draw.

The paper's wrinkled with water damage, but that doesn't stop me.

I draw myself, today, on March 26, 1942. It's an ugly portrait, cobbled together out of scraps: I'm a Seussian sketch; I'm a woodblock samurai; I'm the bruised kid in the mirror.

I draw Japantown, the dry-goods stores, the restaurants, the dentists and beauty salons, the lamps dangling like teardrops in the fog.

I draw Mas, and he looks tired.

I draw the bombing of Pearl Harbor and a burning Hinomaru.

I draw Frankie in his father's WWI 82nd Infantry uniform, the double-A "All-American" patch sewn onto the left shoulder, fighting boys who could be his brothers.

I draw Twitchy—he's racing barefoot across Ocean Beach with seagulls flying before him.

I draw my favorite places in this city I call home: the George Washington High School bleachers, Lands End, Katsumoto Co., the Victorians, the Golden Gate . . .

And when I'm done, I tear my self-portrait from my sketchbook and light a match. I set fire to the page and stuff it into the fireplace, where the flames blacken the edges, consuming my Jap skin, my Jap eyes, my family, my friends, my city, my bridge . . . and we all go up in smoke.

NOTICE

Headquarters
Western Defense Command
and Fourth Army

Presidio of San Francisco, California
April 24, 1942

Civilian Exclusion Order No. 20

1. Pursuant to the provisions of Public Proclamations Nos. 1 and 2, this Headquarters, dated March 2, 1942, and March 16, 1942, respectively, it is hereby ordered that from and after 12 o'clock noon, P. W. T., of Friday, May 1, 1942, all persons of Japanese ancestry, both alien and non-alien, be excluded from that portion of Military Area No. 1 described as follows:

All of that portion of the City and County of San Francisco, State of California, bounded on the north by California Street, bounded on the east by Van Ness Avenue, bounded on the south by Sutter Street, and bounded on the west by Presidio Avenue.

2. A responsible member of each family, and each individual living alone, in the above described area will report between the hours of 8:00 A. M. and 5:00 P. M., Saturday, April 25, 1942, or during the same hours on Sunday, April 26, 1942, to the Civil Control Station located at:

> Japanese American Citizens' League Auditorium,
> 2031 Bush Street,
> San Francisco, California.

3. Any person subject to this order who fails to comply with any of its provisions or with the provisions of published instructions pertaining hereto or who is found in the above area after 12 o'clock noon, P. W. T., of Friday, May 1, 1942, will be liable to the criminal penalties provided by Public Law No. 503, 77th Congress, approved March 21, 1942, entitled "An Act to Provide a Penalty for Violation of Restrictions or Orders with Respect to Persons Entering, Remaining in, Leaving, or Committing Any Act in Military Areas or Zones," and alien Japanese will be subject to immediate apprehension and internment.

J. L. DeWITT
Lieutenant General, U. S. Army
Commanding

II

WHAT STAYS, WHAT GIVES, WHAT GOES

SHIG, 17
APRIL–MAY 1942

It's a Friday in April, and me and Twitchy are on our way to school when we see the crowd in front of the Civil Control Station. The building and the Japanese school in it used to belong to the Japanese American Citizens League, but last month they just rolled over and handed it to the War Relocation Authority, the government agency in charge of rounding us up, neat as you please.

You'd think the JACL would've put up a fight or something, but they've been doing all sorts of wacky stuff to help Roosevelt and his cronies. After the attack, they helped arrest Issei leaders like Mr. Hidekawa and Yum-yum's dad, Mr. Oishi. They told us all to cooperate when the WRA started packing us off to desert camps. I bet they'd bend over and kiss their own asses if Washington asked them to.

"You see this?" I elbow Twitchy as we head toward the crowd. "What's the government want now, our used underwear?"

"No one wants your dirty drawers, Shigeo." Twitchy elbows me back. "Maybe Mike Masaoka's resigning in disgrace or something."

Mike Masaoka's the JACL executive secretary. What d'you wanna bet a big shot like him isn't going into camp with the rest of us?

I scoff. "Nah, I checked the weather report. Hell's showing no signs of freezing over."

We shoulder our way through the wall of hats and backs toward some official-looking notices pasted to the Civil Control Station walls. I end up sandwiched between Mr. Inouye, who always wears a flat cap because he's embarrassed about losing his hair, and Mrs. Mayeda, who always smells like coffee breath and Chantilly perfume.

Through the crowd, I catch a glimpse of the notices—CIVILIAN EXCLUSION ORDER NO. 20—and I know. I know even before I read the rest of it.

Mike Masaoka's not resigning.

The JACL's not protesting.

The evacuation has come to Japantown.

Halfway down the page, there's a paragraph describing the borders of the evacuation area—it's the whole north half of the neighborhood, only missing my apartment by a block.

"Tommy's family lives up there," Twitchy mutters.

"And Stan's," I add. Two of our best friends in the world are going to be torn from their homes, and no one's doing a damn thing about it.

Between my teeth, I can feel a low buzz, like a power line inside me is busted and I'm going to start breathing sparks if I open my mouth.

I shake my head, and the humming subsides—you can't fight the federal government, not unless you want to end up in prison—and I glance back at Twitchy with a lopsided grin. "You know, all of a sudden I don't feel like going to school."

He chuckles. "You never feel like going to school."

"Yeah, but why bother now?" There's that buzzing again. I taste electricity on my tongue. "They're going to kick us all out in a couple weeks anyway."

When no one's looking, we climb the fire escape three stories to the roof of the Toyo Hotel, where we always go when we ditch because no one will find us up there. It's even got a couple bottles of soda and a bunch of comic books we stashed in a box near the ledge overlooking the intersection at Post and Buchanan.

Below, people are milling about like ants. All those people who're gonna be gone.

There's my girl, Yum-yum, and her friend Hiromi, who's wearing a blond wig, on their way to school. There's Mr. Tanaka, who works at the YMCA—he's trailing a cloud of smoke because he wants to get in one last cigarette before he clocks in. There's Jim Kitano and his brother, Shuji, those bullies who used to pick on Minnow in elementary school. There's Tommy Harano—you can recognize Tommy anywhere, he's so short. The kids used to call him ebi—you know, like "shrimp"—but that was before me and Mas adopted him into our group. No one's called him that in years because they all know they'd have to answer to us.

"Hey, Tommy!" Twitchy jumps up, waving his arms like he's bringing a plane in to land. *"Tommy!"*

Tommy looks around, but so do Yum-yum and Hiromi and Mr. Tanaka and the Kitano brothers. Yum-yum frowns up at us, and I blow her a kiss before I pull Twitchy back down. "You wanna get us caught?"

"Nah, but Tommy—"

"You got anything to throw?" I turn out my pockets. I'm carrying: the homework I won't be turning in, my student ID, thirty-eight cents, a candy-bar wrapper, and the key to our apartment, which won't be our apartment soon, I guess.

Together, we peer over the edge of the roof. Below, Tommy's already crossing the street.

Twitchy wads up some of my homework and hurls it at Tommy's back. It falls short by a yard.

Quickly, I take the first page of an English essay and fold it in half lengthwise. The paper's crisp. The creases are clean.

"Hurry up, Shig." Twitchy jiggles my shoulder. "He's getting away!"

"Quit shaking me!" I make a couple diagonal folds and bend the flaps into the shapes of wings.

Then, standing, I let it fly.

The paper airplane soars out over the street, turning and wheeling almost like it's alive. It strikes Tommy in the neck before he's even made it to the other side of the road.

"Direct hit!" Twitchy laughs.

Tommy turns again, rubbing the back of his neck, and this time he sees us beckoning him up to the rooftop. His big eyes widen, and he beams up at us, waving, as he runs back toward the Toyo Hotel fire escape.

"What're you doing up here?" he asks as he scrambles onto the roof. "Aren't you going to school?"

Twitchy and I glance at each other. Tommy always takes things harder than the rest of us. How do we break the news that he's getting kicked out of the only place he's ever lived?

We sit him down between us and tell him about the exclusion order. "Your family's in the first group," I say as gently as I can, because right now, Tommy looks like someone's kicked him in the teeth.

"At least this way, you don't have to go to school either," Twitchy adds.

Tommy just stares down at the rooftop between his sneakers.

Gently, I crumple the second page of my essay and press it into his hands. "Here," I say, pointing at Bob Tomioka, who's standing on the street corner in those oxford shoes he keeps shined up like mirrors. "Bet you can't hit Bob over there."

Tommy's hand closes around the ball of paper, and he gives me a weak smile. "How much?"

The rest of the morning, we throw things at passersby, laughing when they spin around, trying to find us.

Goodbye, student ID. It's not like I'm gonna need you anyway.

Goodbye, last three pages of my English essay.

Goodbye, candy-bar wrapper.

Goodbye, biology notes I was supposed to study.

Goodbye, goodbye, goodbye.

That night, Mas tells me and Minnow to start making lists. The evacuees can take only two suitcases each, he says, so we've got to be smart about what to bring when it's our turn to go.

"Smart?" I laugh. "Have you met me? 'Smart' isn't in my vocabulary."

He fixes me with one of those stares, you know, the ones where he tries to act like our dad instead of our older brother. "You'd better study up, then," he says.

So here goes, I guess.

THINGS TO BRING
WHEN IT'S OUR TURN TO LEAVE

money

clothes

more money

Over the weekend, signs pop up all around the neighborhood. EVACU-
ATION SALE. FURNITURE SALE. CLOSING OUT SALE. BIG SALE. PRICES
SMASHED. Some are printed, but most are handwritten in squashed
block letters.

Me, Mas, Minnow, Twitchy, and Frankie get together to help out
the guys who have to leave. At Stan Katsumoto's family grocery, we
sort through the shelves, marking down prices on rice and kombu
and tea. When Mas isn't paying attention, I tag him with a 50% OFF
sticker, and Twitchy adds a 5¢ tag to the seat of his pants. One of the
other fellas snickers. Mary, Stan's younger sister, glowers at us. Me and
Twitchy smother our laughter and stick Mas with six more tags before
Mrs. Katsumoto looks up from the counter and goes, "Aiya, what are
you doing? Masaru's a handsome boy—we can get at least a dollar for
him!"

I wish I could tell you what Mas's face looks like, but me and
Twitchy are already out the door, running down the block as Mas
roars after us.

When we break for lunch, Mrs. Katsumoto posts a note on the
door beneath the words, I AM AN AMERICAN. It's a message to
their customers, thanking them for twenty years of patronage.

Stan stares at it for a second, then cocks his eyebrow. "You sure
about this, Ma? We don't want them to get the wrong idea about us."

"What wrong idea?" Mrs. Katsumoto asks.

"That we're decent people or something."

"What's wrong with that?"

"Decent people don't kick out other decent people, so if *we're* decent, they *can't* be decent." He fans out his hands. "You're going to cause an existential crisis, Ma! If white people aren't *decent*, are they *anything?*"

She sighs and presses down a bit of tape with her thumbnail. "It's the right thing to do," she says, "for us."

For *us?* The buzzing returns, sharp and metallic. You thank other people to make *them* feel good, and *good* is the last thing anyone should feel about what's happening to us.

Mr. Katsumoto says nothing. He lowers his head over the counter, silently marking down packages of umeboshi.

After lunch, we go to help Tommy's family lay out their belongings on the sidewalk: dishes they brought from Japan when they immigrated, kitchen appliances, extra towels, desks, Tommy's record player and all his beloved records, their washing machine, lamps, rugs, books.

The bargain hunters descend before we've even got half the Haranos' things out of the apartment. They come with pinched faces and tight fists, offering ten cents to every dollar's worth of stuff.

For a while, we try to entertain Tommy's three younger sisters. We let Aiko, who's thirteen, hop and chatter around us as we move pieces of furniture onto the ketos' trucks. Twitchy makes faces behind the bargain hunters' backs for the littlest ones, Fumi and Frannie, who laugh and clap. But things get harder as the day wears on. Aiko accidentally drops a lamp and has to sit out the rest of the afternoon on the stoop. The twins start crying when their kokeshi dolls are sold, and nothing us or Tommy or their mom does can make them stop. Mr. Harano is stonefaced when their sofa goes for three bucks; their beds, for two each.

At the end of the day, they're left with a few hundred dollars. A few hundred dollars for a lifetime of things that can't go with them.

THINGS YOU CAN'T PUT A PRICE ON
the most perfect sand dollar I ever found at Ocean Beach,
wrapped in a handkerchief Yum-yum gave me on our third date

The first families move out on Tuesday, April 28. They line up in front of the Civil Control Station in their Sunday best—the men in suits, the women in veiled hats and gloves—like they're going to church instead of an internment camp. I wonder why they bother.

From the stoop across the street, me and Twitchy watch the bags stack up on the curb: first the steamer trunks, then the suitcases, and the canvas bundles expertly knotted at the top. The piles grow so high in places, you can't see over them to the keto guard and his Springfield rifle posted by the doors of the Civil Control Station.

We say goodbye to Tommy, who promises to write, and to the rest of the Haranos. As they board their Greyhound bus, Fumi and Frannie start crying and grabbing at Mrs. Harano's hair, and she shoves one of the twins at Tommy, who bounces her gently in his arms.

We can still hear them wailing as they drive away.

When the day's over, there's still bits of baggage left on the sidewalk: duffle bags, crates tied with rope, trunks painted with English and Japanese names. Relatives and friends are lugging away what they can, but there are people without relatives or friends, and their things are still on the pavement when the street lamps go on.

• • •

The night the last families are evacuated from the north side of Japantown, me and Frankie Fujita walk through the neighborhood together.

The deserted streets.

The abandoned businesses.

The boarded windows.

The darkened homes.

Half of this community amputated, the people I've grown up with shipped off to who-knows-where.

There's hardly anyone around now—just me and Frankie and the shadows and the streetlights haloed in fog. We walk down the middle of the road like the kings of a hollow kingdom.

He's practically humming with anger. I can feel it like a current coming off him.

Hell, I can feel it coming off me, too, growing stronger with every vacant house we pass.

My fists are electric.

We break into a noodle house. There's not much left. The tables and chairs have all been sold off. There are a few blank spaces on the walls where wood carvings used to hang, but the rest is papered with menus in kanji and hiragana and English, peeling at the corners.

We rip it apart. We tear the daily specials from the walls. We throw napkin dispensers and empty tubs. Frankie shreds a string of paper cranes, sending them limply into the air like confetti. In the kitchen, I find a maneki-neko, a ceramic good-luck cat—big eyes and calico spots—and drop-kick it into the dining room, where it shatters.

One of the neko's red ears skids to a stop in front of Frankie. He stares at it for a second. Then he laughs. It's a horrible, humorless laugh, and his open mouth looks desperate and hungry, like he wants to devour the whole world.

When we make our way outside again, we find the Kitano brothers, Jim and Shuji, smoking on the corner of Bush and Laguna. Beside me, Frankie picks up the pace. He's practically running at them, shouting, "Hey, Jimmy, you ugly son of a bitch, where's that two dollars you owe me?"

I don't remember Jim owing Frankie money, but he *is* a son of a bitch, and I'm itching for a fight, and who the hell cares anyway?

Before either of the Kitano brothers can say anything, Frankie slugs Jim in the jaw. Not hard. I've seen Frankie hit like a hammer, and this is nothing. This is a love tap.

He wants Jimmy to fight back.

And he does. Jim comes up swinging, and then they're grunting and grappling on the curb, stumbling into the street.

Before Shuji can do anything, I clobber him. It feels good to hit something. To make something hurt.

We're throwing punches. We're getting bloody. The Kitano brothers are yelling, but me and Frankie are stern and fierce and the only sound we make is our breathing. Exhaling anger.

Shuji gets me good in the mouth, but I hardly feel it. No, I welcome it. I eat up the pain like breakfast.

Lights go on down the street. Someone's shouting at us. Sirens wail in the distance.

We scatter into the night—Jimmy and Shuji in one direction, me and Frankie in the other—swallowed up by the empty street.

We finally come to a stop in an alley. We're doubled over, breathing hard. When he stands, I see he's got a black eye and a bloody nose—backlit from the street, he looks like a young samurai, glowing and wrathful.

"Goddamn it all," he says.

I straighten, tonguing my split lip.

Yeah.

I spit blood.

Goddamn it all.

THINGS I'M HOLDING ON TO

my anger

When I get home, Mom's waiting up for me. She's wearing her old robe, fraying at the cuffs, as she kneels in the living room, sorting our things into piles.

What stays behind: the carpets, the coffee table, boxes of Dad's old clothes I didn't know she'd kept.

What goes with us: sheets, blankets, cups and bowls and silverware for each of us, a hot plate, a kettle.

She looks up at me, pursing her lips, and for a second, I think she's going to scold me. But she doesn't. She just pats the bare floor until I sit next to her. "What happened to you, Shigeo?" she asks, turning my chin to the light.

I don't meet her gaze. "Got in a fight."

"With who?"

"The Kitano brothers."

She clicks her tongue. "Those bad boys."

I laugh—quietly, because Mas and Minnow are sleeping.

"You shouldn't be fighting."

"I know, Mom." I sneak the last of Mas's yearbooks from the "stay" pile. It's filled with notes from his friends: Chinese friends, hakujin —white—friends, friends who have been evacuated. "But I wanted to fight *something*."

She sighs. "You can't change our situation with your fists."

"But it has to change, Mom. Doesn't it?"

She tugs at a stray thread on her sleeve. It unravels. "No, Shigeo, it doesn't."

Angry tears fall onto the pages of Mas's yearbook, and I wipe my eyes with the back of my hand. "Then what do we do?"

She puts her hand on my shoulder and squeezes once. "Gaman."

The word means something like *persevere* or *endure*. It's a word for when you can't do anything to change your situation, so you bear it patiently . . . or as patiently as you can, I guess.

I think of Mrs. Katsumoto and her thank-you note. I think of the people dressed in their best for their own eviction.

But I can't do it. I can't suffer nobly while we're displaced. I can't not feel this electricity inside me. I can't not be hurt and angry and want to wrench things from the walls.

I don't think "gaman" is in my vocabulary, either.

When Civilian Exclusion Order No. 41 tells us we're being forced to leave, Twitchy steals one of the flyers. We sit behind the YMCA, where we know Mr. Tanaka won't come chase us off, because Mr. Tanaka's gone. Together, we read the instructions over and over, like the next time we read them, the words will be different.

We won't have to evacuate.

We'll be allowed to stay.

But nothing changes.

"I bet we're going to Tanforan," Twitchy says finally.

The Tanforan Assembly Center's an old racetrack fifteen miles south of the city. That's where Tommy and Stan ended up.

I don't say anything as I tear the evacuation order into a square, ripping away the signature at the bottom—J. L. DeWitt of the Western Defense Command. He's convinced we're all a bunch of Jap spies, and I guess he's convinced everyone else of it too, because, well . . . here we are.

I toss his name in the trash, where it belongs.

"That wouldn't be so bad," Twitchy continues. "It's not that far from home, and at least we'd be together . . ."

I'm hardly listening. I'm creasing and pleating and bending the notice into something different, something other than what it is: the piece of paper that's going to uproot us.

Under my hands, it becomes a square, a diamond, a crane with a long neck, a sharp beak, and the words "alien and non-alien" visible on one wing.

They can't even use the word *citizen* for us Nisei, can they?

I want to crush the paper bird in my palm, like that would unmake every sentence of the exclusion order and all the men who wrote it.

"Hey, where'd you learn to do origami?" Twitchy asks, interrupting my thoughts.

I twirl the paper bird by its pointed tail. "Kinmon Gakuen," I lie.

He makes a disbelieving sound. "Where was I that day?"

"In time-out," I tell him with a smirk, "like usual."

"Ha ha." He eyes me like he knows I'm fibbing, but he doesn't push me.

We don't stay out, not like last time, because now we're the ones who're leaving. We have to go home. We have to help our families pack.

On the step next to me are black smudges where Mr. Tanaka used to stub out his cigarettes. I leave the crane perched next to them like a temple offering.

THINGS NO ONE KNOWS I HAVE
one of Dad's hats

Don't tell anyone, but Dad's the one who got me into paper folding. He used to do it when he was happy, or when he was working through something he wasn't ready to tell Mom about, but mostly when he was happy. I can remember Sundays when we went to Ocean Beach to fly kites and look for shells, and he'd be sitting in the sand, folding a piece of newspaper.

He didn't make a fuss about it, either. You'd see him toying with a candy-bar wrapper or something, but you'd never see it take shape. He might leave it somewhere for you to find, if he was especially proud of it, but usually, it would just be gone. I don't know if he threw them away or what.

Now I do it too, even though no one really knows about it, not even Twitchy. It's kind of private, you know? It's something just between me and Dad, even though he's gone, too.

On Wednesday, Mas comes home with a fistful of ID tags. We have to mark all our luggage, and on the day of the evacuation, we have to wear them. Like we can't be trusted to remember our own names.

I'm *Ito, Shigeo*.

No. *22437.*

<small>INSTRUCTED TO REPORT READY TO TRAVEL ON:</small> *Saturday 5/9, 11:30.*

That's five days. Five days to pack up our entire lives.

They couldn't even give us a week.

THINGS THAT HAVE TO STAY

the tin canister of marbles and baseball cards we buried somewhere in the backyard

the dent in the wall where Mas's shoulder hit it when we were wrestling

the names we carved into the baseboard: MAS, SHIG, and a little fish for Minnow

Vultures.

The white people come around again, sniffing out bargains.

The Kitanos' whole dry-cleaning business, equipment and all, goes for fifty dollars. I know because you can hear the ketos crowing about it as they head back to their Cadillac. Across the street, Jim Kitano steps out onto the sidewalk, and I meet his gaze. He's got a greenish-yellow bruise on his jaw where Frankie punched him last Friday.

I nod at him.

He nods back, lighting a cigarette, and leans against the door of the pool hall, where Frankie used to dupe guys out of their money when he got bored. It's abandoned now, its windows papered over.

Next to me, a couple of ketos are haggling over the American flag Dad used to fly from our stoop every day. One of Mas's eyelids is twitching the way it does when he's trying not to cry. He loves that flag almost as much as Dad did, kept flying it after Dad died.

Gaman, I remind myself.

Grin and bear it.

Bend over and kiss your own ass.

But ever since that night out with Frankie, my anger's been filling me up. Every day, it's there inside me, buzzing louder and louder like a malfunctioning transformer until sometimes it's all I can hear or feel.

"No deal," I say suddenly. "Get outta here!" I wave my arms at them, and they hop away like irritated gulls.

"Shigeo!" Mom says.

"What?" Buzzing. "That's *Dad's* flag. It's worth more than a quarter."

She combs my hair with her fingers, like she used to when I was little, but even that doesn't quiet my anger. "It's not about what it's worth," she says. "It's not about what we deserve. It's about what they're willing to give us."

"Shit," Minnow says, looking up from his sketchpad. "All they're willing to give us is shit."

"Watch your mouth, Minoru," Mas snaps. He looks like he's about to crack in half like a brick in an earthquake.

But he doesn't. Not even when Dad's flag goes for fifteen cents an hour later.

No, it's Mom who breaks, that afternoon.

She's wrapping a set of red-and-black lacquerware, placing tissue paper between each dish to protect it, and she just starts crying. It was her grandmother's lacquer set, you know? One of the nicest things she brought over from Japan when she married Dad.

She never let us or Dad touch it, not even to clean it. She displayed it on the highest shelf in the living room and dusted it herself with a soft brush. It was *hers,* and it was precious.

Now some hakujin strangers are going to take it. They don't want our alien faces in their neighborhoods, but they don't mind our lacquerware in their homes.

Inside me, the buzzing is so loud, I can barely hear Mom crying in my arms.

The vulture shifts uncomfortably as Mas passes her the lacquer set, but she doesn't do anything, at first. Guilt and pity pool behind her glasses.

After what seems like a full minute, she tries to hand him another dollar. A whole goddamn *dollar*. It hangs limply from her fingers like a dead thing.

He doesn't take it. "We already agreed on a price," he says flatly.

"But—"

Mas crosses his arms. He's almost six feet tall with the build of an Olympic wrestler. He can be real intimidating when he wants to be. "Thank you for your business," he says, and she scurries off, the dollar flapping uselessly in her hand.

In one of the trash piles, I find a shoebox full of origami: frogs and birds and balloons, pinwheels and boats and even a potbellied pig.

I guess Mom knew the whole time. She must have been collecting all those little things Dad was making.

And we can't keep them. We don't have the space.

THINGS THEY'VE TAKEN

my home
my friends
my community

I'm with Yum-yum when her mom sells her piano.

Lucky for them, they own the building, so they can rent it out while they're gone. Or, technically, Yum-yum owns it. It's in her name, because the California Alien Land Law doesn't allow Issei to own property here.

But, homeowners or not, they're as Japanese as the rest of us, so they still have to move. They still have to store or get rid of the things they can't rent or take with them.

We would've lent them a hand even if Mr. Oishi hadn't been arrested, but me and the guys make an extra effort to help Yum-yum's family. Together, we heave the piano down the stairs and onto the sidewalk to be picked up by a Bekins Moving and Storage truck.

Don't tell her, but we all hated hearing her play at first. The piano was already old when she got it, beat up and out of tune, and you could hear every swampy note as she banged out her scales, up and down the keys.

But she's good now, and we all lean in when she sits at the piano bench and lays her hands on the keyboard one last time.

Yum-yum's always been pretty, but today she's beautiful, and strong, too, sitting there, fingers still, like she's saying goodbye with her silence.

She begins—loud, then real soft. The music is heavy as fog crawling down the San Francisco streets, heavy as the footsteps of two guys out at night, wanting to break things.

It builds and builds, getting darker and darker, when all of a sudden it speeds up, and the notes are sparks, they're catching things on fire, the whole street is filled with them. They're explosions. All the buildings collapse, crashing into the road in heaps of luggage-shaped rubble. If she could, I bet Yum-yum would tear down the whole city with her music.

But by the end, it's soft again, and her face doesn't betray any of the violence and turmoil inside her. Standing, she walks into my arms, and I hold her until the truck comes to take her piano away. She doesn't cry.

And I get it, finally. Gaman.

The ability to hold your pain and bitterness inside you and not let them destroy you. To make something beautiful through your anger, or *with* your anger, and neither erase it nor let it define you. To suffer. And to rage. And to persevere.

When I get home, I find out we got a letter from Tommy.

> *Dear Mas, Shig, and Minnow,*
>
> *Well, we're all settled in at Tanforan now. The house, or horse stall, has two rooms. Mom, Dad, and the twins sleep in the back; Aiko and I sleep in the front. They do a head count every morning at six thirty (and again in the evening), and since I'm the oldest, and the only boy, in the front, it's my job to tell them we're all here.*
>
> *I don't know if you've gotten your evacuation notice yet, but wherever you go, bring your saw, hammer, and sockets. There's no furniture anywhere except the army cots, so everyone's having to make chairs and tables out of scrap wood. If you find out you're coming here, I'll try to save some for you.*
>
> *The food is pretty bad. Yesterday we had potatoes, meat innards, and bread. It's served by hakujin workers they hire from outside, and they touch everything with their bare hands. When we eat, there's a line two or three blocks long, so you better get in line early!*

Mas, some men in camp are driving instead of taking the buses. They load their cars with all sorts of things, like canned fruit and handmade soap. Maybe you can pack up the Chevrolet and bring in some food from outside. I'll take a chocolate bar as a thank-you.

Take care of yourselves,
Tommy

P.S. Say hello to Twitchy and Frankie.
P.P.S. I'm sorry for writing in pencil, but I'm trying to economize on ink.

THINGS WE HAVE TO FIND SPACE FOR

tools
food
gaman

It's the night before we have to leave, and me and Minnow are lying on the floor of our bedroom. The walls are bare. The mattresses have been sold off. All we've got are our suitcases and the things Mas is going to pack into the Chevy.

And the shoebox of origami I rescued from the trash. Mom must not have thought anyone would pay for it.

There's the buzzing again. A hot electric current running under my skin. If I'm not careful, I'm going to ignite every paper creature between my hands just because I want something to burn.

"What's that?" Minnow says, propping himself up on his elbows.

"Dad's."

"What is it, though?"

"None of your business," I say, and regret it immediately. I don't usually snap at my little brother—that's Masaru's deal. "Sorry, Minnow."

He looks at me, and even though he's almost as small as Tommy, he seems older than fourteen all of a sudden. He's been everywhere these past couple weeks: drawing the mountains of luggage, doing portraits of the families waiting for the Greyhound buses, sketching the army soldiers and hakujin photographers the government sent in, his fingertips black with charcoal.

He's always drawn a lot, but there's something different about him lately. He used to disappear into the background like he was part of it. Now when he draws, you can't miss him. He's there in the middle of things, with this new ferocity, like if he doesn't capture this moment, he'll never get the chance.

That's how it is these days. You hesitate, and your neighbors have vanished. You look away, and your friends have been stolen from you. You blink, and you're gone.

I open the box.

"I always wondered where these went," Minnow says, holding up butterflies and stars so the overhead light shines through them, making them glow.

I guess Minnow noticed Dad doing origami too. It shouldn't surprise me. Minnow notices a lot of things—that's what makes him such a good artist.

"Should we give it to Mas?" he asks. "I bet he could find space in the Chevrolet."

I shake my head.

"We could carry it. I don't think anyone would notice."

But that doesn't feel right to me either. I want to do something good with these scraps nobody would pay for. I want to change things, the way Dad changed all these old envelopes and ticket stubs and potato-chip bags. I want to do what Yum-yum did with her piano, what Mrs. Katsumoto did with her thank-you note.

I want to show they haven't beaten me.

"I'll tell you what," I say. "I've got a plan. You wanna help?"

After Mas loads up the Chevrolet and drives off, me, Minnow, and Ma report to the Civil Control Station, where we weave between the curbside luggage, the army guards, the lines of weary people waiting to board the Greyhound buses.

Under one arm, I've got the box of origami.

Twitchy comes to see us off, and he doesn't bat an eye when me and Minnow tell him the plan — you gotta love Twitchy for that — he just takes some of the paper figures as carefully as he'd handle his old butterfly knife and gives us a smile.

While we wait for our turn to go, we put on party hats me and Minnow made out of newspaper and, with big, flashy smiles, we march through the crowd, distributing Dad's origami to the kids. We're not evacuees today — we're kings in a parade, we're cheerleaders at a pep rally, we're three beardless Japanese Santa Clauses, and Christmas has come early this year!

I give Jeannie Kitano, Jim and Shuji's sister, a crane that flaps its wings when you pull its tail, and baby Don Morita a box he instantly crushes in one of his chubby fists. The Abe sisters get a ball they can blow up and bat around. Minnow hands Toshie Nishino a fox. Twitchy tosses her brother a cat. Every kid gets something on Evacuation Day!

When it's almost 11:30 a.m., I turn to Twitchy, who's not leaving until tomorrow, and press forty-five cents into his hand. It's all the change me and Minnow could find in the apartment last night. "Get some candy for tomorrow's evacuation," I tell him as me and Minnow stuff our pockets with the last of the origami. "To give to the kids."

"We were thinking malt balls or something," Minnow adds, tossing the empty shoebox onto a mound of baggage.

Twitchy frowns, jingling the coins in his palm. "Your mom would want you to save this for a rainy day or something," he says.

"C'mon, Twitch—"

"But I'm fine blowing it on chocolate!" He grins.

Me and Minnow grin back. We're standing on a street corner with everything we've ever known about to come crashing down around us.

And we're angry.

And we're smiling.

And we aren't broken.

<u>THINGS THAT DON'T TAKE UP
ANY SPACE AT ALL</u>

my humor

my courage

my joy

When our group is finally called, we're the last people to board, and as me and Minnow follow Mom to the back of the bus, we fish into our pockets for dogs, koi, turtles, and gulls, passing them out to the other families.

The Greyhound becomes a menagerie on wheels, a circus, a traveling zoo of paper animals, filled with the kids' delighted shrieking and the imagined sounds of elephants and zebras and monkeys.

As we drive away, I see Twitchy standing on the steps where we watched the first families leave Japantown, waving like he's trying to bring a plane in to land.

It doesn't take long to get to Tanforan, but it feels like hours. I spend the ride unfolding and refolding the last piece of origami, following the creases Dad made years ago, a rabbit appearing and disappearing in my hands like a magic trick.

There and gone.

There and gone.

We see the barbed wire first. The chatter in the bus quiets. The fence seems ten feet tall, with guard towers at regular intervals, like it's a prison.

Like we're criminals.

Then the grandstand, the muddy racetrack, the tarpaper barracks, and now no one's speaking.

You will not beat me, I think.

There are things you can't take.

Mom reaches for my hand. She's already holding Minnow's.

I turn Dad's origami rabbit in my fingers. It's already starting to split along the creases, gaps opening up at the corners.

Gaman, I think.

We drive through the gates.

III

I AM NOT FREE

YUM-YUM, 16
MAY–JUNE 1942

DAY 1

It's a shock at first. One minute, Mom, Fred, and I are traversing the roads of San Bruno, California, like we're on a road trip down Highway 101, headed for Los Angeles. The next, we're being ordered off the buses between guard towers and armed soldiers, a barbed-wire fence separating us from the rest of the city—its streets, its schools, its citizens, wandering free.

As we're herded toward the nearest buildings, I wonder if we'll ever be allowed to wander again.

Between Mom and me, my younger brother, Fred, fidgets and tugs at our hands. At nine years old, he's small for his age, with a cowlick at the back of his head that won't stay flat, no matter how much you comb it. Mom likes to say it's as unruly as he is.

I pull him closer.

Ahead, the crowd splits. Men are shuffling into one building; women, into another. Medical examinations, someone says. They want to make sure we're not diseased.

Bowing, Mom approaches one of the soldiers. "My son is only nine years old," she says in Japanese, clinging to Fred like the rush of people will take him from her the same way the FBI took my father last December—swiftly, almost soundlessly, so quick we barely had time for last words. "He has no one to accompany him."

Sensing the soldier's impatience, I translate quickly.

"What about her husband?" the soldier asks.

"Missoula," I tell him. Montana. My father is a good man—he's always done right by us. But now he's in a prisoner-of-war camp almost a thousand miles away, and he looks to me to do what he cannot.

The soldier shrugs. "These are the rules."

My mother doesn't need to be fluent in English to understand his indifference. Her grip on Fred tightens.

I waver. We can't be separated. *I* can't let us be separated.

"Beishi!" Fred squeals suddenly, wriggling out of Mom's grasp as he chases one of his friends from Japantown into the men's line.

Mom tries to cry out, but she doubles over, coughing.

So I'm the one who acts. I have to be. I dive after him, but a soldier shoves me back. "Men this way. Women that way."

"But—"

"These are the rules."

Standing on tiptoe, I catch a glimpse of Fred's cowlick as he squeezes into the men's building. For a moment, I wish for my father, and for my father's advice. He'd know what to say. He'd know how to keep us together.

But then I remember how docilely he went with the FBI agents that night: the hollow *clop-clop-clop* of his heels on the sidewalk, the stoop of his shoulders, the moonlight on the back of his bowed head.

And I know he would have done the same as I do now—the same as we all do.

Obey.

The examination room has curtained cubicles to undress in, but the hakujin nurses are careless with the partitions, and the women cover their chests and bellies as best they can with their hands, avoiding one another's eyes.

"Here? In front of everyone?" Mom coughs—a delicate sound, hastily smothered, like a secret.

"The faster we do it, the sooner we can find Fred," I assure her, though I feel anything but sure.

In the cowed quiet, every noise is as loud as a landslide: sniffles, shifting feet, shame. Somewhere nearby, one of the Issei women begins weeping.

A few cubicles down is Hiromi Nakano in her blond wig. The day she wore it home, her father was *furious,* thinking she'd dyed her hair. He raged at her for almost ten minutes, his face turning red as a plum, before she finally took it off, laughing and waving it in his face. She still wears it when she's feeling rebellious.

Today, she removes it when she's ordered to, the wig dangling limply from her hand as a nurse inspects her scalp for lice.

In the cubicle, I disrobe beneath the impersonal stare of my nurse. As I look away, embarrassed, I spy Keiko Kimura across from me. Her parents were teachers at Soko Gakuen, one of the Japanese schools, before they were taken by the FBI the same night as my father.

She and I are the same age, but we went to different schools, joined different clubs, had different friends. I'd see her around, of course, but we rarely spoke to each other. Through a gap in the curtains, I can see her bare shoulder, her hip, the length of her thigh.

Unlike with Hiromi, or anyone else in the examination room, we lock eyes. For a second, her gaze flicks over me, almost carelessly, and she grins, mouthing something I cannot hear even in the stifled quiet.

"What?" I whisper.

She does it again, but her words are still unintelligible.

"What?"

Exasperated, Keiko rolls her eyes. *"I said, 'Nice kabochas'!"*

I gasp. Everyone — the women, the nurses, the guards — they all turn to glare at me.

"Keiko!" someone says sharply.

"Shitsueri!" *Rude!*

"Sukebe!"

Then Hiromi Nakano snorts. Someone else starts giggling. Mortified, I try to cover my breasts, my face, my everything. I bury my face in my shoulder, but there's nowhere to hide.

Nowhere to run.

After our examinations, we're reunited with Fred and assigned to our new home.

Except it isn't home.

I lean against the splintering doorframe. *Home* was our San Francisco apartment — its carved banisters, Mom's fine china, the worn velvet cushion where I used to practice at my piano for hours, the music drifting out over the busy street below. *Home* smelled of wood polish and fermenting tsukemono and Dad's cigars.

This is a horse stable — a twenty-by-nine-foot stall stinking of manure, sweat, and lime. Besides our army-issue cots, there's no other furniture, no running water, no source of heat. Fred and I are to share the front half of our stall; Mom will have the back.

A stable meant for a single horse will now house a family of three.

It would have housed four, if Dad had been with us.

If he had been with us, I think, he would have tried to find hope in the cobwebs and the dirty floors. He would have looked around and said, *Adversity is the crucible of the spirit.*

So I try to do as he would have done. I cajole Fred into sweeping while I fetch straw for our mattresses. We spend the day cleaning and dusting and trying to appear chipper, but as soon as evening roll call is over, we climb into our cots, cold and weary and heartsick.

Still, I can't sleep.

I try playing one of Chopin's nocturnes on the edge of my blanket, but I stop after twelve measures. The sounds here are all wrong: I should be hearing cars passing on the street and foghorns in the distance, not our new neighbor snoring next door and worried snippets of Japanese from the far end of the stables.

Sighing, I turn onto my side. In the light from our narrow window, I can see shapes whitewashed into the wall: protruding nails, bits of straw, petrified carcasses of spiders, trapped before they could run away.

Mom shifts in her cot, coughing. The last time she was sick, she had to be hospitalized. Dad and I barely held it together the month she was gone, and I'll be the only one left if she falls ill again.

Please, not here. Not now.

As if in response, she coughs again.

Abruptly, I get up. Across the room, Fred is curled under his covers with his teddy bear, Kuma. The stuffed animal took up half his suitcase, but Kuma is Fred's most precious possession, and he'd never leave him behind.

Shoving my feet into my boots, I sneak into the open air, toward the bathrooms. At this hour, the latrines are empty. Bare electric bulbs illuminate our toilets—a long board with a row of circular holes cut into it.

I decide I don't have to go after all.

Turning away, I find Keiko Kimura sitting on the stoop of a barrack. My cheeks grow hot again. "Oh," I say, as coolly as I can. "It's you."

"Well, if it isn't Kabochas." Her voice is low and velvety, like a viola.

Defensively, I pull my coat closer around my chest. "My name's Amy," I correct her, "but my friends call me Yum-yum."

She smirks. "I'm Keiko . . . and my friends call me Keiko." After a moment, her expression softens. "They took your dad too, right?"

I nod.

She pats the stair next to her, and I sit. "You know the last thing my dad said to me before they took him?" she asks. "He told me to be a good girl."

"How's that going?"

She winks. "It isn't."

I can't help but smile.

Keiko is staying with her aunt and uncle here in Tanforan—it was that, or go with the other orphans to Manzanar. But Keiko isn't an orphan—her parents would be with her now, if our government hadn't imprisoned them.

I wonder if she still feels like an orphan, though. If she still feels alone.

For a moment, we're silent. Overhead, the moon flits in and out of the clouds. "Mine told me to look after the family," I say finally.

No *I love you*. No *I'll miss you*. No *goodbye*. Just, *Take care of them, Amy.*

And I will, I promise myself. Because he believes in me. Because he's counting on me.

Because they're all counting on me.

DAY 4

We're finally settling in, learning the new addresses of our old friends and neighbors, when we get a letter from our father, who tells us he's taking a carpentry class from another of the Missoula inmates. *Self-edification is important,* he reminds us, *especially in these uncertain times.*

He asks how we are, but I don't know what to tell him.

Dear Father, I wish you could make us some furniture.

Signs of construction are everywhere in camp: work crews, half-finished barracks, piles of leftover lumber continually scavenged to make tables and shelves for the bare stalls. We need something to put our belongings in so we don't have to keep living out of our suitcases, but we don't have any tools, and even if we did, I wouldn't know where to begin.

"How hard can it be?" Keiko says one morning while I sift through Fred's clothes, trying to determine which are dirty and which are clean. "Saw, saw, hammer, hammer. Just borrow some tools and figure it out."

"*Yum-yum?*" Hiromi laughs and fluffs her blond wig. "Make *furniture?* Your dad wouldn't like it."

No, he wouldn't. He would tell me he didn't pay for a piano and ten years' worth of lessons for me to ruin my hands with woodworking.

54

But he's not here.

And with my mother's cough worsening every day, it falls to me to do it. So I trek across the infield to my boyfriend Shig's barrack to ask if he'll teach me to make some furniture. He smiles crookedly when he says hello, his gaze falling briefly to my lips before lifting back up to my eyes.

I blush and clear my throat. "You can use a hammer, right?"

He grins. "Yeah, you hit stuff with it."

I roll my eyes and explain my dilemma to him. Of course, he agrees to help. I've seen him carry groceries for his neighbors, fix our fence when my dad was away on business, wash a dirty word from a Japanese business without anyone asking. That's the kind of guy Shig is.

When I leave, and no one's looking, I give him a quick peck on the cheek.

An hour later, Shig and his older brother, Mas, arrive with tools and discarded planks. While Mom lies in the back room, resting, the boys show Keiko and me how to draw up a plan, how to use a saw, how to fasten two boards together.

Eventually, Fred wanders back from wherever he's been, bearing new scratches on his knees. Seeing Keiko, he darts up to her. "Tickle me, Keiko! Tickle me!"

With a cry, she abandons her tools to chase him around the front room. When she catches him, she pins him to the floor, tickling him until he's shrieking with laughter.

For a while, he joins us, and the boys let him hammer in a couple of nails, but he quickly grows bored. "Can I go play with my new friends?" he asks me.

"What new friends?"

"From Barrack Twelve."

"What are their—"

"Thanks. Bye!" Before I can stop him, he scampers off.

Shig glances up from the table he's sanding. "Want me to go after him?"

I almost say yes. Dad would want Fred to learn. Dad would want me to know exactly where Fred is at all times.

But Dad isn't here, and if Fred's stuck with us, moping and complaining that he's bored, it will only slow down our progress, so I just sigh and pick up a saw. "He knows to come back before dinner."

Through the open door, I can see Dad's letter sitting unanswered on my cot. *Dear Father, do you really want to know how we are?* I drive the blade into a piece of wood. *Fred is wilder than ever.*

Mom is sick again.

I wouldn't have to do this alone if you were here.

DAY 12

For a while, I try to be the daughter my father wants me to be.

I brush my teeth in a horse trough and tell myself I'm "roughing it" like we did on our vacation to Yosemite last year.

I walk the perimeter with Keiko and Fred, watching the cars on El Camino Real. To pass the time, we invent lives for the motorists: jobs as bank tellers and shipping clerks, trips to Monterey. Sometimes I picture myself driving down Highway 1, surrounded by the whisper of the tires, the purr of the engine, the hiss of the wind . . . until Fred starts pestering me again, and I realize I'm not going anywhere.

I finish up my studies of chemistry and civics with Hiromi, who's determined not to be left behind whenever school starts up again.

From an old textbook, we learn how wonderful we are, how lucky, how endowed by our Creator with certain inalienable rights.

Because we're American citizens.

Because *we're free people.*

Not like my father, or Keiko's parents. They're not wonderful, lucky, endowed Americans like me, here behind the barbed wire.

The days pass. I stand in line for the mess hall, for the canteen, for the post office, where I collect letters from Dad. He writes to us about his victory garden, his Bible study, his work thinning sugar beets, his instructions for us to *keep busy* and *be good.*

For him, for all of us, I try to hold it together as best I can: I help Mom to the latrine. I bring her soup and warm compresses. I do the laundry at four a.m. before the hot water is all gone. I try to keep track of where Fred is when he's not at home, which is more and more often as our mother's condition worsens.

At mealtimes, I glare at Fred while he pushes cubes of liver around his plate.

"Eat it," I tell him.

He sticks his tongue out. "*You* eat it."

"I did."

It made me gag. They've fed us beef innards for three days in a row —our last passable meal was watered-down stew from a can, a special feast the white administrators held to prove to the International Red Cross how good we have it here. But it's my job to set a good example for Fred, even if it makes me sick.

"Liver-eater! Liver-eater!" he chants, his voice growing louder and louder in the crowded hall. "Liver-eater!"

People turn to glare at us. Nearby, one of the Issei bachelors mutters, "Gasa-gasa." I look away, red-faced with shame.

"Liver-eater!"

The days pass. My composure flakes. I yell at Fred for spilling his juice. I threaten to throw Kuma in the garbage if Fred leaves him on the floor *one more time.*

Screaming, he snatches the bear from my hands. "I hate you!"

From the back room comes Mom's faint voice—"Fred, listen to your sister"—followed by a long spell of thorny, hacking coughs.

Suddenly quiet, Fred sits down on the edge of his cot, clutching Kuma to his chest. I sit down opposite him, head in my hands. Between my feet, I can see streaks of dirt on the linoleum floor I just swept yesterday.

I imagine my father's disapproval.

I hate my father's disapproval.

Or maybe, I think, *I'm just beginning to hate my father.*

DAY 19

On May 24, we get a letter from Dad, addressed to all of us, as usual. He writes that he's proud of me, that I'm a good girl, and I almost laugh.

I almost cry.

I want to say, *It's been over five months since you've seen me. You don't know me at all.*

For the first time, I don't write back.

DAY 26

One night while I'm with Fred at dinner, one of our neighbors checks our mother into the camp hospital. When we arrive, she's lying beneath the blankets, skeletal and pale. In the harsh infirmary lights, her eyes seem sunken; her skin, fragile as paper.

As soon as he sees her, Fred backs away, clinging to the waistband of my pants.

Mom tries not to look hurt, but I know she is. While I stand awkwardly at her bedside, she coaxes Fred into a nearby chair, where he sits, squirming, as she combs his cowlick with her fingers until he turns to me and says, "Can we go home now?"

This isn't home, I think as I tuck Kuma under the blanket beside Fred later that night. I try to ignore the darkness and the silence in the back of the stall, where my parents should be.

"Does Dad know about Mom?" Fred asks, interrupting my thoughts.

"How could he? She just checked into the hospital today, and he's all the way in Montana." I try to mask the sour note in my voice. "Someone needs to write to him."

Someone who isn't me.

"Can you show me where Montana is again?"

I sigh. How do you explain three states and a thousand miles to someone who's never been out of California? After digging out a textbook I never bothered to return to the camp library, I flip to a map of the United States. "We're here." Pointing to the San Francisco Peninsula, I begin tracing a diagonal line across the page. "If you go northeast, over the Sierras, you reach Nevada . . . then Idaho . . ."

He watches my finger intently, like it's really traveling the mountain roads, the high, flat desert, to our father.

". . . then Montana."

"That's far," Fred says.

"It took him three days to get there by train."

He frowns. "There are train tracks outside the fence."

I nod. Sometimes, when Keiko and I walk by, I imagine I'm sitting on the velvet cushions of a luxury car, with the plaintive sounds of a string quartet playing in the background. There are no mess-hall lines, no stinking latrines, no one to tell me they hate me. Just me, the rhythm of the rails, and amber waves of grain rolling past the windows.

"But we can't get to them," I say. This time, I can't keep the bitterness out of my words.

When Fred finally falls asleep, I climb into my cot and try to play Chopin on the edge of my blanket, but it's like I've forgotten the notes, the music drained out of me in Mom's absence.

Take care of them, Amy.

In the darkness, the walls seem to close in around me. The smell of horse grows fouler. I'm being pressed, gasping, into my cot by an invisible weight, and if I don't do anything, I'm going to be crushed.

Lurching to my feet, I grab my boots and stumble for the door, staggering out into the night air, where I collapse, shivering.

I don't know how long I sit there, but eventually I hear a voice: "Is that you, Kabochas?"

I blink. "Keiko? What are you doing out here?"

"Nothing good." Winking, she sits beside me. "What's the matter?"

I tell her everything. How Mom is in the infirmary. How I stopped writing to Dad. How I'm the only one left.

"I'm sorry." She puts her arm around me. "You want to get out of here?"

I draw back. *"What?"*

"Not beyond the fences or anything." She grins. "But who wants to be cooped up in the barrack all night?"

"Won't we get in trouble?"

"Not if they don't catch us."

I hesitate even as she pulls me to my feet. I shouldn't leave the stall. I shouldn't leave Fred. I should be good, *obedient*.

But what did obedience ever do for me?

Someone should have told me. Breaking the rules is *wonderful*. We're sneaking between the barracks and the showers and the recreation centers, and at any moment we could be caught.

But we aren't.

Out here, darkness shrouds the fences and the sentries with their rifles, watching the perimeter, and if you don't look closely, you can pretend you're somewhere else. Some*one* else.

I laugh as we reach the edge of the racetrack. I'm sprinting across the infield, unchecked, the wind cool in my hair and the grass wet on my ankles, and I'm dancing, twirling under a black, star-spangled sky.

Then I trip. A man grunts. I tumble forward and feel flesh, warm and moist, under my hands. A woman squeaks in surprise.

And I'm me again, obedient and meek. My cheeks go hot as I realize what they're doing out here together. "Sumimasen!" I gasp. *Excuse me!*

I don't hear if the couple answers. Keiko's fumbling for my elbow, hauling me up. We're tearing across the field, the hems of our night-gowns wet with dew.

We don't stop until we reach my barrack, where she doubles over, laughing.

"Shhh!" I whisper. "That was so embarrassing!"

"For who? They don't care. *I* wouldn't, if I were . . ." She waggles her eyebrows.

"You—" For an instant, I imagine her on the infield with a boy on top of her. "You mean you would—"

"I said *if!*" She waves me off, rolling her eyes. "I didn't say I'd do it."

"Well, I wouldn't either!"

Would I?

Not if I was Amy Oishi.

But if I was who I was tonight, uninhibited, jubilant, *free?*

Keiko grins, like she can read my thoughts, and saunters off, singing, *"Good night, Kabochas."*

But I don't go inside yet.

I sit outside my stall, watching the sky. Would Shig meet me out there, under the stars, if I asked him to? Would he fondle my hair and kiss me in the darkness, lips roving down my neck, over my collarbone?

I blush again. Amy Oishi would never think such scandalous thoughts.

But I don't want to be Amy Oishi anymore.

Amy Oishi is compliant. Her mother is sick and her father is a prisoner and they've left her alone to care for her shrinking family.

Amy Oishi is trapped.

I don't want to be her. I want to be different. I *need* to be different. I can't be the same girl I was on the outside. If that girl is in a detention center, an American citizen imprisoned without trial or even charges, then the world doesn't make sense.

But if I'm someone else, then it's easier to accept that the world now operates by different rules.

Up is down.

Wrong is right.

Captivity is freedom.

DAY 27

After that night, things change.

During the day, I am myself. I am the obedient daughter, the dutiful sister, the high-strung disciplinarian. While Mom is in the hospital, I make sure Fred is bathed and clothed and fed. I pick up the toys he always leaves on the floor. I weather his tantrums. I put him to bed.

But at night, I am someone else.

I sneak out after he's fallen asleep, and I wander the camp. Sometimes Keiko joins me. Sometimes we meet up with Shig and the boys and Hiromi in her blond wig.

Sometimes we're out for hours. Sometimes minutes.

But for those hours, those minutes, we pretend there is no roll call, there is no barbed wire, there is just darkness and rebellion and laughter ringing out into the night.

We're young, we're reckless, and we're just like anyone else. We're not Japanese-Americans, we're just *Americans*. This isn't a detention center; it's just another neighborhood in San Bruno. My father isn't in prison for suspected espionage; he's just working late. My mother isn't in the hospital; she's just back home — *we have a home* — padding through the hallways in her slippers, peeking into Fred's room while he sleeps soundly inside.

DAY 32

After we defeat the Japanese at the Battle of Midway, Twitchy steals us a cask of sake, and we celebrate on the infield once the rest of the camp has gone to bed, toasting the brave men of the U.S. Navy. The liquor is sweet on our tongues, and we drink until our skin is hot and our eyes are bright as stars.

Shig puts his arm around my shoulders, and I lean into him,

pressing my mouth to the tender area at the corner of his jaw. He tastes like the ocean.

In the sake-slick darkness, I am blurry and happy and warm. Around us, Twitchy and Keiko turn cartwheels in the grass, competing to see how many they can do before they collapse in a giggling heap. Hiromi, Frankie Fujita, and Stan Katsumoto are arguing about their favorite films. Tommy and Minnow lie on their backs, connecting stars with the tips of their fingers, creating new constellations, constellations that look like us. "It's Frankie, see? He's fighting a couple of ketos."

Frankie chuckles. "And beating their asses, right?"

"Right!"

"And there's Yum-yum."

I squint, blearily, at the sky. "Where?"

"There," Minnow says, pointing. "You're playing a piano."

I imagine keys of starlight under my fingers, melodies like the singing of distant galaxies.

"Ooh, there's Mas!"

"That's a square, Minnow."

"I know!" Minnow laughs like it's the funniest thing he's ever heard, but he yelps and scrambles to his feet as Mas charges him. They race circles around us until Mas finally tackles him. When Mas gets up, he raises both fists in the air like he used to when he threw a winning touchdown. On the ground, Minnow is still laughing.

There, in the dewy grass, with the guard towers nearly indistinguishable against the foothills of the Santa Cruz Mountains, the war seems almost over.

We're almost victorious.

Almost free.

DAY 36

But the war doesn't end. And we're still here.

When I visit my mother in the infirmary, she doesn't seem to be getting any better. In fact, she seems to be getting weaker. "Are you eating?" I ask.

"Never mind me. Are you getting enough sleep?" She reaches up to brush a lock of hair from my forehead, and I resist the urge to lean away. "You look so tired."

"I'm fine, Mom."

"What about Fred? Where is he?"

"Playing baseball."

"*Tsk.* Tell him to come visit his mother."

"Yes, Mom," I say, though I know he won't. He'll do almost anything to avoid seeing her like this, including picking fights with me.

In Dad's letters, he continues exhorting us to *be good* and *take care of your mother*. There's no sign that he even cares I've stopped responding.

Fred keeps writing, though. He's pinned the map of the United States to the wall above his cot, Missoula, Montana, circled in red. Around it are crude drawings of trains, his latest fascination.

When he asks me why I don't write, I tell him, "I just don't have anything to say."

Dear Father, I got so drunk the other night I threw up in my hair.

Dear Father, sometimes I think you wouldn't recognize me if you saw me now.

Sometimes I'm glad.

After that, I stop reading my father's letters, leaving every one unopened on Mom's bedside table.

DAY 40

Nights with Fred are the worst. He doesn't want to go to bed. He doesn't want to put away his toys. He doesn't want me telling him what to do.

Tonight, I'm chasing him around the stall with a washcloth while he throws things at me, screaming like I want to murder him instead of just wipe his face.

Maybe I should *murder him,* I think as I dodge the book he hurls at my head. The next one hits me in the shins, and I cry out as I stumble on the wooden train he keeps leaving out. *Then I'd never have to wipe his face again.*

Taking a flying leap, I wrestle him, flailing and shrieking, to the linoleum. "Ha!"

From the other side of the stables, someone shouts at us to be quiet.

"It's cold!" Fred kicks at me. One of his feet catches me in the stomach.

I grunt, scrubbing his cheeks with the damp cloth. "It would've been warm if you'd let me do it sooner!"

When I finally let him up, he stomps to his cot. "I hate you!"

"I hate you too!" I shout.

I don't mean it. Of course I don't.

But I say it.

The shock of it brings tears to his eyes. He dives into his cot, curled toward the map on his wall. "I wish I was with Dad!"

"So do I," I snap.

Buried in his covers, Fred doesn't reply.

• • •

That night, when the others retire, I ask Shig to stay. We're standing in the eucalyptus grove, and above us, the moon is a bright disc through the sickle-shaped leaves.

"Want me to walk you home?" he asks.

"That's not home," I say.

"Yeah." He traces the inner curve of my wrist. "Want me to walk you back?"

He tries to lead me away again, but I'm not going back—not there, not tonight, not yet—and I tug him to me, swiftly, hard.

Beneath the eucalyptus trees, I kiss him. I've been wanting to kiss him like this for weeks—urgently and wrapped in shadow.

His tongue grazes my lower lip, touching the edge of my teeth, and I moan. I want to breathe his breath. I want to devour him. I want to be changed.

He leans into me, hands sliding up my neck, into my hair, pulling me closer. Briefly, I wonder if he can feel my heart thrumming in my chest.

He chuckles, his mouth moving along mine. *"Oishii,"* he murmurs. *Yum.*

Laughing, I swat at him and pull back.

In the moonlight, I can see his lopsided grin, the faint gleam of sweat along his hairline. "You're full of surprises." His voice is huskier than I've ever heard it, dark with want.

I grin and throw myself back into his arms.

We kiss for hours, long and slow and hard, until I can taste him in every tender corner of my mouth. We kiss all night, until the skies turn gray and the camp begins to stir.

"Shit," Shig says. "We're going to miss roll call."

Hand in hand, we race back to the barracks, where, in front of my door, he pauses, breathless, and kisses me again. "See you soon," he whispers.

Then he's gone, and the sun is breaking over the rooftops. This time, I stayed out until dawn. This time, I was alone with a boy. This time, for the first time since we entered camp, I breathe in the day and feel *different*.

Hopeful.

New.

DAY 41

As soon as I enter the stall, I know something is wrong.

Fred's suitcase is missing, as is Kuma. Above his cot, the map of the United States has disappeared. My head spins.

Fred's gone.

He's gone to find our father in Montana.

Or, at least, he's going to try.

Someone knocks at the stable door.

Roll call.

I freeze. *What do I say? What do I do?*

I think of the soldiers combing the camp for a little boy.

I think of their guns.

"All here!" My voice is taut and hoarse.

There's a pause, and for a second, I'm sure they know I'm lying. They're going to burst through the door, brandishing their rifles.

But then there's another knock, not on our door but on our neighbors'. "All here," he calls.

I sink to my knees.

Fred must still be in camp, right? If they'd caught him trying to squeeze under the barbed wire, we would have heard a siren.

Or a gunshot.

Unless he got out without them noticing. I imagine him walking along the highway with his suitcase and teddy bear. I imagine the police, the army, the National Guard, the manhunt.

No. He's still here. And I have to find him.

I race to Shig's barrack, where he dispatches Minnow to fetch Keiko and the rest of the group, and it's not long before everyone's assembled: Tommy, Frankie, Stan and Mary Katsumoto, Hiromi and her younger sister, Yuki, who's almost as fast as Twitchy, bouncing lightly from foot to foot in the dust.

"Don't worry; we'll find him," Keiko says. "We would've known if he'd tried to get out."

"Twitch, Yuki." Shig's voice is as level as ever. "Can you check the fences?"

Nodding, Twitchy flicks us a salute and sprints toward the perimeter with Yuki hot on his heels.

"Let's try the usual places. The Okimuras, the Aoyagis . . ." To my surprise, Shig begins ticking off a list of Fred's old friends from Japantown, sending Minnow and Tommy off to knock on doors.

I tell the others about Fred's new friends, his favorite mess halls, how he might be at one of the recreation centers, the baseball field, the pond, the grandstand. One by one, the others race away.

Then it hits me.

Fred and his obsession with trains.

I turn to Hiromi. "Stay here in case he comes back."

And I run.

I run past the eucalyptus trees, past the infield, past people stumbling to the latrines in their handmade zoris, past the breakfast lines, until I reach the gate near the train tracks.

But Fred isn't there.

The dust isn't even disturbed where he might have crawled under the fence.

I haven't cried since we got here, but I cry now. I collapse against the back of the nearest tarpaper building, sobbing. I was so stupid, staying out all night, pretending that everything was okay, that I didn't have a brother to watch, that my parents were here and well, that *here* wasn't a racetrack-turned-prison because our own government was afraid of us.

Hated us.

Beyond the barbed wire, the city of San Bruno is stirring. Cars drive by, windows flashing in the dawn light. People are going to work, the grocery store, the beach. They avert their eyes from the fences, from the guard towers, from me, like if they pretend hard enough, we'll disappear.

But *I* know pretending doesn't change things. I'm still here, still trapped as I was when my father was taken, when my mother got sick, when my brother—

I look up suddenly, blinking tears from my eyes. There's still one place I didn't think to check.

Standing, I turn my back on the world beyond the fence and race to the infirmary.

I find Fred curled up on the end of Mom's bed like a cat, Kuma pillowed under his head.

"Fred!" I launch myself at him, pinning him to the mattress.

"Hey! Get off!"

But I just hold tighter. "I'm sorry," I mutter into his cowlick. "I don't hate you. I could never hate you."

At my words, he relaxes. After a moment, he whispers, "I don't hate you either."

"I thought you'd gone to find Dad."

"I did. But I got scared."

"I was scared too. I'm scared a lot." *I'm scared that Dad will never come back. I'm scared that Mom will die in this hospital. I'm scared we'll be deported. I'm scared we'll be shot. I'm scared of failing. I'm scared of being trapped.*

"Really?"

"All the time."

"Is that why you're so mean to me?"

I laugh, but before I can answer, Mom stirs. "Amy? Fred? What are you doing here so early?"

Fred looks at me. I shrug.

"Nothing," we say in unison.

He grins at me, like he used to when we were keeping something from our parents. A popsicle we shared before dinner. A fight he got in with one of the neighborhood boys.

I grin back.

Mom glances at his suitcase, sitting in the corner. Then she says, "Amy, you look tired. There are bags under your eyes." She takes a hand mirror from her bedside table, but she doesn't show me my face. In the reflection, I see a kiss-shaped bruise on the side of my neck.

My hand goes to my throat. My cheeks burn.

"What's that?" Fred asks.

Our mother ignores him. "I left a case of powder in my top drawer," she says to me. "It worked wonders for me when I was your age."

I blink. *Mom?* How many love bites did she have to cover up when she was younger? How many nights did she sneak out of her parents' farmhouse back in Japan?

Before I can thank her, she leans over again, selecting one of my father's letters from the bedside table. "This is for you."

I shake my head. "No, I—" But I stop when I see the salutation.

Dear Amy,

This is the first time he's written to me—*only* to me. Maybe he did care, after all.

I tuck it into my pocket. "I guess we'd better get going, then." Out of habit, I almost grab for Fred's arm before he can run away, but I stop. "Ready to go home, Fred?" I extend my hand to him.

After a moment, he takes it.

They're all there when we get back, crammed into our stall—Keiko, Shig, Minnow, Tommy, Twitchy, Frankie, Hiromi, Yuki, Stan Katsumoto, Mary—shoulder to shoulder on the cots, leaning back in chairs I made myself, filling both the tiny rooms.

With a cry, Keiko races up to Fred, twirling him around and around as he throws his head back and laughs. On my cot, Hiromi is making Mary try on her blond wig, saying things like, "This color suits you!" Mary looks furious.

Dashing forward, Twitchy takes Fred's suitcase. Plopping down, he opens it. "What's this? Canned sausages? Where's the chocolate bars? The M&M's?" Looking up, he shakes his head. "Freddy, you better talk to me before you run away next time. I'll—"

"There won't be a next time," I interrupt.

"Of course not." Twitchy winks at Fred, who clumsily tries to wink back.

Gently, Shig takes my hand. "You okay, Yum-yum?"

"No." Taking Dad's letter from my pocket, I place it on my dresser until I can read it. *Dear Amy.* "But we will be."

All around me, my friends are making tea, tuning a Silvertone radio I recognize as Mas's, shuffling a deck of playing cards, talking, joking, laughing. Outside is the camp, the barbed wire, the guard towers, the city, the country that hates us. But in here, we are together.

We are not free.

But we are not alone.

Topaz, Utah

IV

THE INDOMITABLE BETTE NAKANO

HIROMI "BETTE," 17
SEPTEMBER–DECEMBER 1942

SEPTEMBER

By September, the evacuation from the assembly center at Tanforan to our new camp in Utah is well under way as we pack our suitcases and prepare to ship our scrap-wood furniture by train. It's a curious feeling, saying goodbye to Tanforan. The camp may have smelled, been poorly constructed, and had repulsive food, but it was only twenty minutes from home, and some of us had dared to hope we wouldn't have to leave California after all.

As for me, after four months of the same dusty racetrack, I am looking forward to another adventure, particularly aboard a train, although I must confess I'm a tad disappointed with the railcars that screech to a stop next to the Tanforan fence. I know it's silly — my younger sister, Yuki, likes to say I've seen too many movies — but I was picturing a sleek locomotive with state-of-the-art brass fixtures and polished beverage carts pushed by waiters in bellboy caps. Instead, what we get is an old coal train with steel siding and hardwood seats I know Bachan will be complaining about within the hour.

As we settle in for the ride, I quarrel with Yuki over who gets the window seat, but I lose our game of Jon-Ken-Po and have to make do with the aisle . . . However, I feel particularly mollified when the captain of our train car announces that the shades must be drawn until we reach the Sierra Nevada mountains, which means that Yuki will have no view at all, while I, at least, can content myself with spying on the other people in our car.

Then the whistle blows, a long, mournful sound like you might hear if you were a lost princess aboard the Trans-Siberian Railway, the train lurches forward, and I sit up eagerly as my first railroad adventure begins.

An hour later, Bachan is using Mother's knitting bag as a cushion, while Mother dozes on Father's shoulder as he attempts to read the newspaper under the flickering gaslights. Yuki halfheartedly tosses a softball into the air and catches it in her dirty leather mitt, tosses it and catches it, again and again.

As the train hits a particularly rough section of track, someone stumbles against the back of our seat. "Sumimasen," he murmurs.

Looking up, I lock gazes with a tall boy with slicked-back hair and sparkling wide-set eyes.

How is it possible that I've never seen him before? I know Tanforan housed almost eight thousand people, but how outrageous to have missed a boy this handsome!

He grins. "Nice hair."

Blushing, I run my hands over my blond wig. "You think so? My sister says it's dumb."

Yuki rolls her eyes and *thwacks* the ball deep into her mitt. I don't think I'll ever understand her—she's fifteen! You'd think she'd recognize a handsome boy when she saw one, but her disinterest is *palpable.*

"Nah." The boy smiles wider, revealing a crooked front tooth. "You look like a Japanese Lana Turner."

I beam at him.

"Your name's Hiromi, right? I'm Joe. Tanaka." He says it just like that. Joe — pause — Tanaka. Like Clark — pause — Gable.

I extend my hand. "Actually," I say in my best Vivien Leigh impression, "I go by my middle name, Bette, now."

Yuki scoffs. "Since *when?*"

I shoot her a look. "Since *now.*"

To tell you the truth, I've been thinking about changing my name for some time. "Hiromi" is so old-fashioned and so hard to pronounce — I can't count the number of times I've been called "Hye-romi" or "Her-omee" — and "Bette" is so much more appropriate for a modern American girl like me.

"Like Bette Davis." Of course, Joe pronounces it correctly, like "Bet-*tee*," and takes my hand, grinning.

"Exactly!"

The rest of the train ride is like something out of a dream. Other people complain about the heat, or the stuffiness, or the water running out, but Joe and I are in a world of our own. He's from San Leandro, across the bay. His favorite song is "Harbor Lights" by Frances Langford, and when he sings a few bars under his breath, I think I might die of happiness.

The first night, coal dust drifts through the cracks as we rattle through the mountain tunnels, and hardly anyone gets any sleep, but in the morning, during our single stop in Nevada, Joe and I stroll past the armed soldiers like we're in a park instead of a desert depot.

After two days in Joe's company, I'm in such high spirits when we leave the train in the charming town of Delta, Utah, that I don't even fight Yuki for a window seat on the bus that will take us the rest of the way to Topaz City.

Gradually, the picket fences and carefully tended flower beds of Delta give way to a broad, flat desert where the earth is so dry, it's crackled and fragmented like a mosaic.

Where are we going? There's absolutely nothing but gnarled greasewood bushes for miles and miles. Taking a steadying breath, I close my eyes, imagining how I'll describe Joe to Yum-yum and Keiko when I see them next.

So funny! So kind! With such long eyelashes!

When the bus halts, I open my eyes again, hoping for an oasis fit for an out-of-the-way romance like in *Morocco* or *Casablanca*.

Topaz is nothing like that, however. Here, there are no exotic gardens or pavilions where lovers can meet. There isn't even a tree in sight.

A barbed-wire fence stretches around an enormous compound—the fence is short, made of three strands, as if it were for cattle. Inside, row after row of long, tarpaper barracks stretches into the distance, each one looking squat and grim and the same as the last. With all the buildings lined up so neatly, I bet Topaz could hold eight thousand people or even more, all in a single square mile!

From the nearby buildings rises a steel smokestack that dwarfs the rest of camp, even the guard towers that line the perimeter. Those are only a couple of stories tall, but there's no mistaking them or the Caucasian soldiers surveying the Main Gate area from their observation decks.

I sigh. *Okay, so it's a* mite *bleak.*

But with no tall buildings or forests, one can see clear to the Prussian blue mountains ascending in the distance, and I can just picture Joe kissing me for the first time with those majestic ridges behind us.

Frankie Fujita, one of the Japantown boys, is behind me with his uncle, who seems bewildered in his rumpled overcoat and fedora. Tugging a stray thread on his father's old WWI jacket, Frankie makes a disgusted sound as we approach the door. "What a dump."

"I think it's marvelous!" Tossing my hair, I step from the bus in what I hope is a dignified maneuver, but as soon as I touch the ground, my shoe sinks two inches into the dust, and I pitch forward gracelessly.

Frankie catches my elbow, steadying me with his hard grip. "Yeah?" he says. "You oughta get your eyes checked, Nakano."

I don't bother telling him I prefer "Bette" now. Frankie calls everyone by their last name.

Straightening my skirt, I take another unsteady step as the Boy Scout Drum and Bugle Corps begins to play a lively marching tune, giving our arrival a festive air.

This is where it will happen, I think, memorizing the pale sand, the unvarying barracks, and the barbed wire that hems my new city. *This is where Joe and I will fall in love.*

OCTOBER

I'm so excited for the school year to *finally* begin that even the unfinished classrooms and dearth of supplies can't dampen my spirits. My senior year! Even though we're not in San Francisco anymore, there will still be clubs, sports (I hear Joe Tanaka is a star basketball player, and I can't wait to cheer him on, although we don't have a gymnasium yet), and, best of all, *dances!* There's already a "Halloween Spook-tacular" planned for this Saturday in Dining Hall 1, provided the administration can engage a band for the evening, and although Joe hasn't asked me for a dance yet, I'm saving room on my dance card just for him.

On Monday morning, Yum-yum, Keiko, and I cram into our classroom, which, if I had to guess, is even colder than it is outside . . . and it's freezing outside! The hospital is the only area with central heating—that's what the steel smokestack is for—so most of the buildings will rely on stoves for warmth and Sheetrock for insulation. Unfortunately, construction of the camp still hasn't finished, so there's a hole in the roof of the classroom where the stove and chimney will eventually be. For now, we huddle at our desks in our military-issue coats, blowing on our hands to warm them.

I already know a lot of the other students from Japantown, like Shig and Tommy, who are drawing stick figures on the condensation-fogged windows, but there's one Caucasian girl among us too.

You wouldn't have guessed it, but there are a lot of Caucasians in camp, and not just guards, although we have those, too, on the watchtowers and at the gates. They work as doctors, administrative staff, teachers, and the chiefs of the different sectors, overseeing nihonjin workers. Some of them live in Delta, the nearest town, or a special section of Caucasian housing that's separate from the rest of the camp, although it's still inside the fence.

The girl's name, I find out, is Gail Johnson, the blond-haired, blue-eyed daughter of the Agricultural Division Chief, and she's the only one of us in a Sears, Roebuck polo coat of beautiful novelty tweed instead of the navy wool the rest of us have to wear.

"She's so pretty," I whisper to Yum-yum and Keiko. "I wish I was as pretty as her."

Yum-yum glances at Gail. "I guess she's all right."

"For a hakujin girl," Keiko adds with a smirk.

Quickly, I run my hands over my wig. For a moment, I entertain the idea of purchasing another, but with even the doctors and teachers earning less than a private in the army, no one in camp has the money for something like that. Even if I could scrape together some odd jobs, it would take me over a year to save up enough to look like Gail Johnson.

I'm pinching the bridge of my nose to see if I can make it appear less flat when, to my surprise, our teacher announces that we're dismissed. The high desert mornings are so cold that until the high school rooms are winterized, classes will take place only in the afternoons. Shig leaps up from his chair with a whoop and leads the charge from the classroom, followed by Tommy and the others.

Gathering her things, Gail follows, her hair flashing like gold in the chilly sunlight.

On Wednesday, much to my disappointment, an announcement in the *Topaz Times,* the camp newspaper, declares that the "Halloween Spook-tacular" has been canceled due to lack of a band. I'm complaining about it to Frankie as we leave the mess hall for the high school, where he's kind enough to accompany me every weekday afternoon.

Dining hall, I think belatedly, remembering to use the correct expression from the booklets we received on Topaz terminology. Frankie hates it, but I think using words like "dining hall" instead of "mess hall" makes everything seem a little more civilized.

"Bet the ketos didn't want to play for a bunch of enemy Japs," Frankie grumbles.

Every block has a dining hall and an H-shaped latrines-and-laundry, with six barracks arranged on each side and an extra building for things like churches, libraries, and recreation centers. There are forty-two blocks in all, but not all of them are for housing—two have baseball diamonds, and the four in the center of camp are still waiting for construction.

This means that the Japantown boys and girls are spread out over a mile, which is farther apart than we've ever been before, but Frankie and I are on the same block, so we often see each other at meals, and despite his penchant for cynicism, I have to admit I quite enjoy his company. Even the sourest of his moods reminds me of being back in San Francisco.

"It's more likely they couldn't afford the travel expense," I say delicately. "Topaz City isn't exactly a hot spot for nightlife, you know."

"You're tellin' me, Nakano. They couldn't've exiled us any farther from civilization if they'd sent us to Alaska." Disgusted, Frankie kicks at the frozen ground. Although it's past noon, the entire camp is still covered in a glittering veil of frost the likes of which I could have only dreamed when I still lived in San Francisco. Lifting my chin, I pretend I am not a Nisei girl picking her way along a dusty lane but a Russian empress floating over a floor of crystal.

"I was *so* hoping for a dance with Joe, though!" I say.

"But the guy hadn't even asked for a dance yet."

"*Yet!*" I say. Frankie has always been kind of a dolt when it comes to romance, so I'm in the middle of explaining the many rules of courtship, including the game of cat-and-mouse Joe and I are currently playing, when the horizon darkens in a sinister, familiar way.

My eyes water as a cold wind rises, screaming over the barracks.

"Shit!" Frankie grabs my hand as a dust storm explodes down the street. "C'mon, Nakano, move your ass!"

Hand in hand, we race to the shelter of the nearest building. Tempests like this have been plaguing us since our arrival, but this one is bigger than any I've yet seen. It's like something out of the vast Sahara, sending a child's wagon careening into the barracks and scattering coal from the coal piles. Coughing, we run through the storm as the winds buffet us this way and that, the sand stinging our eyes and cheeks.

Throwing open the laundry, Frankie shoves me inside and leaps in after, slamming the door as a gust of air reaches us, rattling the walls. Plunking down on the edge of the laundry tub, I shudder. Outside, it sounds as if the world is going to shake apart.

Frankie kicks the door, cracking it. A thin stream of sand pours across the floor. "Goddamn it!"

Frowning, I brush dust from my wig. It wafts from between my fingers, pale as clouds and fine as powder. "Cool it, Frankie. That door never did anything to you."

He begins pacing the laundry room as dust accumulates under the door and windows in soft piles. He reminds me of a wild horse I once saw at the San Francisco Zoo. "How can you stand it, Nakano?" he asks. "Don't you hate it here?"

I try to sniff, but the dust is so thick that it makes me sneeze instead. "We have food, shelter, jobs . . . We have each other," I say. "What's there to hate?"

He stops by the door, staring at me with those eyes that Minnow says look like embers. "What are you, stupid, Nakano? Can't you see shit when your face is rubbed in it?"

My retort dies on my tongue. Frankie's always been distrustful and angry, but he's never been *cruel*. Not to us.

Standing, I draw myself up to my full height, even though the top of my head only reaches Frankie's shoulder. "You shut your mouth, Francis Fujita," I say, advancing on him. "I see a lot more than you give me credit for. In fact, I see *you,* and if you let your anger continue to fester like that, it's going to destroy you and anyone who gets too close, and you'll have only yourself to blame."

His jaw drops. I've surprised him. *Good.* Let him think twice before insulting me again. Before he can collect himself, I draw my scarf over my wig, fling open the door, and step out into the raging winds.

The next day, I'm still fuming as I walk to school, alone. I *do* see where we are. I see the sewer pipes breaking every week. I see the dust coming in through the cracks in the barracks. I see the armed soldiers in their guard towers. But unlike that oaf Frankie, I choose to see the good where he chooses to see only the bad.

Being an optimist does not make me stupid.

When the first snowflakes begin to fall, however, all thoughts of Frankie fly right out of my mind. Perfect six-branched stars drift silently over the camp, alighting on my hair and shoulders as I dash into the dirt lane, throwing my arms wide.

What a wonder!

Snow fills the air, dense as the Milky Way on the darkest of nights. I twirl, my skirts flying out around my knees, like I'm a ballerina in a glass globe. All around me, children and adults fling themselves to the ground, creating dusty white angels.

In the road, Mas is being dogpiled in the slush by his students from the junior high school. Since he has a little college education and there weren't enough Caucasian teachers, he was hired to teach the seventh-graders, who shriek and laugh as he heaves himself upright, one or two of them hanging off his biceps.

I'm a little surprised to see Keiko giggling with Yum-yum, their heads thrown back to catch the cold flakes on their tongues. Keiko always seems a little cooler, a little more detached, a little more grown-up; it's easy to forget that she's just a kid like the rest of us, even if, like Yum-yum, she had to grow up faster because her parents were taken by the FBI after Pearl Harbor.

"Bette! Can you believe it?" someone cries, startling me. "Snow!" Joe races up behind me, grabbing my mittened hands and swinging me around, laughing. We spin in the snow as the barracks flash past us, blending in with the powdery sky, until he is the only thing in focus: his slick hair, his smile, his fingers on mine.

We're surrounded by kids on their way to school and adults without jobs stumbling from games of Go, but I truly believe at this moment that Joe and I are the only two people in the entire desert, the entire universe, even, whirling at the center while all of creation revolves around us.

Gradually, we slow, but the world continues to turn dizzily. He chuckles, steadying me in his arms as I lean against him, breathless.

"Too bad the 'Halloween Spook-tacular' is canceled," he says. "We could've done this properly, on the dance floor."

Looking up at him, I bat my eyelashes. "You'll have to *ask* me properly next time, Joe. Without your name on my dance card, I couldn't guarantee that we'd even speak to each other the whole night."

"Well, I can't let that happen, can I?" He smiles. "Next ti—"

Splat! Something wet and cold smacks right into my bottom, utterly ruining my moment with Joe. Aghast, I turn, feeling my skirt, which is now covered in dirty, dripping sleet.

Across the road, Shig, Twitchy, and Keiko—*How could she?*—are laughing and pointing, balling up new handfuls of snow.

My eyes narrow.

I could be disappointed.

I could be angry, like Frankie.

But I am Bette Nakano, and Bette Nakano doesn't get disappointed. She doesn't get angry. She takes matters into her own hands.

I lean down, scooping up a pile of slush, and run at them. Yelping, Shig and Twitchy scatter, but they're too late. My first snowball hits Shig in the neck. My second strikes Twitchy in the back.

"Nice arm, Bette!" Joe races up beside me, flinging snowballs of his own. We're all laughing, shoveling dust and snow at one another with both hands, shrieking as it runs down our necks into our collars.

In the midst of it all, I glance over at Joe, who grins at me through a shower of white sparkles. It's our first snow in Topaz—the first snow of our lives—and we get to share it together.

NOVEMBER

After the disappointing cancellation of the "Halloween Spook-tacular," it takes almost a month for the Community Activities Section to accumulate a campwide record collection so we'll no longer have to rely on a band for dance music, and by the time Thanksgiving—and the Thanksgiving Dance—arrives, I am *more* than ready to swing and jive.

On Thursday, the dining halls serve roast turkey and walnut dressing with jiggling slices of cranberry sauce that still bear impressions from the inside of the can. It smells of the holidays back home in San Francisco, when my whole family would spend days in the kitchen, baking and brining and boiling, before digging in to fresh Dungeness crab and somen salad along with our turkey and mashed potatoes.

The cafeteria-style dining hall with its raw wood beams, picnic tables, serving counter, and dishwashing station may be a far cry from home, but we're still together, and in true American tradition, I know I have a lot to be grateful for.

While our block manager makes a particularly long-winded speech at the front of the dining hall, Yuki and I pick the candied topping from our sweet potatoes, sneaking bites when Mother and Father aren't looking. Bachan sees us, but she simply winks and pops a scoop of pumpkin-pie filling into her mouth.

I wolf down my meal in the most unladylike manner, especially the bread and *real butter*—none of that oleomargarine tonight!—and get a second heaping helping of turkey and gravy.

At the dishwashing station, I encounter Frankie, who still hasn't apologized for his nasty remarks last month.

I regard him coolly as I rinse my plate. "Francis."

"Nakano." He nods. "You look like you're having fun over there."

"I am."

"Wish they'd had real gravy instead of that walnut stuff," he says. "I couldn't eat it."

"I thought it was nice." I wait for him to apologize, but he simply dips his fork and knife in the soapy water, looking as if he'd rather swallow a toad than say he was sorry for anything, so I place my dishes in the drying rack with a clatter. "Well, I hope you and your uncle have a happy Thanksgiving."

That night, in preparation for the dance, I hang up my dress, a beautiful white rayon splashed with flowers, and polish the dust from my pumps.

Because we're a family of five or more, we have two connected apartments instead of one, which means that Bachan, Yuki, and I share one room while Mother and Father have the other. The ceiling, walls, and floors are all covered in Masonite, with exposed nail heads shining around the perimeter of each square board. It's not the coziest of accommodations, I'll give you that, but, with a few improvements, we've managed to make it homey enough.

There are the curtains Mother sewed from empty rice sacks, and the tables, chairs, and dressers Father shipped from Tanforan. He's also built a wardrobe for our clothes and shelves to display photographs or hold necessities like toiletries and cups.

By the cast-iron stove are pegs for our towels to dry, along with coal and kindling buckets that, as the eldest, it's my duty to keep filled. Bachan's cot is closest to the stove, where it's warmest, then Yuki's, then mine, where I've hung a curtain for a little privacy.

Now Yuki and her friend Mary, Stan Katsumoto's sister, who's also on the softball team, sit on my cot, reviewing my dance card.

It's nearly full, with Shig, Twitchy, Tommy, and Stan having signed up, but there's only one name that matters to me.

1. JOE TANAKA

9. JOE TANAKA

16. JOE TANAKA

True to his word, Joe has called not once but *three times* to ask me for a dance. I think I'm in heaven!

"Do you think he's going to kiss you?" Yuki asks.

Mary scowls. She'd be much prettier if she weren't scowling so much of the time, but it's not my place to say.

With a laugh, I swipe the last of the dust from my heels. "The question is, 'Will I let him?'"

"*Well?*"

"Well, I haven't decided!" I plop down on the cot between them. Mary leans away uncomfortably. "If he's a gentleman, then—"

My stomach lets out an embarrassingly loud gurgle, momentarily silencing me. In the back of my throat, I taste bile. Quickly, I clap my hands over my mouth.

Mary is already reaching for the waste bin. "You okay?"

I shake my head. "I think it must have been something I ate—"

"You didn't eat the walnuts, did you? Mom refused to serve them in our mess hall."

Yuki's stomach growls, even louder than mine, and she jumps up, grimacing. "I knew that gravy was off!"

As one, she and I scramble for our zoris and fly toward the door, doubled over in pain. Outside, it seems like the whole block is fleeing for the latrines, filling the air with groans and the stench of sickness.

I'm so ill with food poisoning that I spend all night in bed with a bucket on the floor beside me.

I miss the dance.

Worst of all, I miss my dances with Joe.

By the next morning, however, I'm feeling almost as good as new, if a little tired, when who should knock at my door but Joe Tanaka himself! *"Hi-ro-miii!"* Yuki screams, though I'm only behind my curtain. "It's for *you-uuu!*"

Flustered, I tighten my wig band over my hair and pull on my blond curls, peeking frantically at my hand mirror to ensure that none of my black hair shows.

"Hiromi!"

"For the last time, it's *Bette* now!" Pinching my cheeks to put a little color in them, I check my expression once more and throw back my curtain, appearing in what I hope is a dramatic fashion.

Huffing, Yuki goes to sulk at the table. "Your hair is crooked."

Mortified, I tug my wig straight as I sashay to the door, where Joe Tanaka is standing on the doorstep, his breath clouding in the morning air. "We missed you at the dance," he says, offering me a crepe-paper flower. "Everyone was there, even that Caucasian girl, Gail. I didn't think she'd want to party with a bunch of nihonjin kids, but you should've seen —"

"Oh, Joe, you shouldn't have!" I interrupt. The flower is a red camellia with rippled petals and a riot of yellow stamens in the center — in Japan, red camellias are a symbol of love. "It's wonderful!"

Bashfully, he stuffs his hands into his coat pockets. "Well, I thought it was the least I could do, since you couldn't make it out last night."

"I can make it out today," I say brightly. "Are you going to the volleyball game this afternoon?"

"Haven't thought about it yet. Maybe I'll see you there?"

"Maybe!" Shrugging, I do my best Scarlett O'Hara impression, pretending indifference, even though I'd love nothing more than to sit by him on the high school field, shoulder to shoulder and thigh to thigh. "If something more interesting doesn't come up."

He smiles, and I nearly collapse against the doorframe, swooning. "You make everything more interesting, Bette."

I wink. "Then I suppose you'd better be wherever I am, Joe."

DECEMBER

Unfortunately, after what seemed like such a promising start the day after Thanksgiving, my romance with Joe has stalled. Although he's no less kind, I feel as if when we talk, he's more distracted than usual. I suppose he's busy with school, where we've finally resumed our morning classes, and basketball, because the Topaz Rams are already trouncing neighboring schools. He still has a place on my dance card for the "Holiday Jitter-Hop," but only one: the fourteenth, as unremarkable a dance as you can get.

My worries, however, are eclipsed by the Christmas festivities. On the morning of the twenty-fifth, we wake to a fresh inch of snow that ices all of Topaz City like a delicious buttercream cake. Icicles drip from the eaves like crystals, smoke drifts from the chimneys, and we stand in our doorways as carolers march through the streets, singing "O Come, All Ye Faithful." In the brittle winter air, their voices are clear and bright as bells.

Inside, next to Bachan's cot, our stove burns merrily, our concerns about coal rationing forgotten for the moment. On the table are presents wrapped in brown paper and twine. A few of Yuki's—donations from the Quakers at the American Friends Service—even glisten with tinsel.

As we open our gifts, we find fruitcakes from hakujin friends in San Francisco and manju from our older brother and his wife in New York, where they were living when we got the exclusion order. He offered to come back to be with the family, but Mother and Father wouldn't hear of it. Of course he and his wife had to stay back East. Why would you come here if you could be in New York City?

Among my presents is a brand-new Tangee Satin-Finish Lipstick in Theatrical Red that I've been coveting for months. "Oh, Yuki, thank you!" I cry, flinging myself at her. "You're my favorite sister; did you know that?"

She flops in my arms, although I can hear her smiling when she says, "I'm your *only* sister!"

I try on the lipstick the next night while I'm getting ready for the dance with Keiko and Yum-yum, who is positively *glowing,* she's so happy. Her father was released from Missoula—he should arrive any day now.

Puckering and pouting, I examine my reflection in my hand mirror. "Does this shade suit me?" I ask.

"You look good in everything, Bette," Yum-yum says.

"I don't know." I flip to the Tangee advertisement in *Vogue* magazine, where Constance Luft Huhn, head of the House of Tangee, is reclining on a pea-green divan, bedecked in pearls and sapphires that gleam against her creamy skin. I squint at her lips and rouged cheeks, her sky-blue eyes and perfectly arched brows. "It looks different in the ad."

"Yeah." Keiko rolls her eyes. "Because she's *Caucasian.*"

I frown at my reflection—my round cheeks, my flat nose—feeling like a dumpling compared to the likes of Constance Luft Huhn, Gail Johnson, and the pretty white women in my favorite films and magazines.

"She's not even real," Keiko says, tapping the ad. "That's a drawing, not a photograph. In real life, she's probably got acne and a double chin like the rest of us."

"Oh." For a moment, I feel silly. Naturally, I can't look like this illustrated woman, nor should I want to. What a bore, to be two-dimensional.

Yum-yum tucks the red-paper camellia behind my ear. "You're real, though, and beautiful."

"Aren't we all?" Keiko laughs, fluffing her hair in what's clearly an imitation of me.

With a smile, I throw my arms around Yum-yum and Keiko, squeezing them so tightly, our cheeks squish. "Absolutely."

The "Holiday Jitter-Hop" dance is in Dining Hall 32, and I can hear the music even before I enter, the strains of a Mills Brothers song filtering through the walls. Standing before the steps, I brush out my skirt and look up at the door—the unvarnished wood is plain, even unsightly, spattered with mud from the slushy December days, but I want to memorize every nail, every splinter, every moment of anticipation.

Joe's inside.

My dance is inside.

The rest of my life is inside.

"Are we going in, or are we going to stand out here all night like dunces?" Keiko asks, cocking an eyebrow at me.

"Of course we're going in!" I flash her a smile. As I check my dress and wig one last time, the red camellia crackles in my hair.

I'm ready, I think. Twining my arm in Keiko's, I take the steps up to the dining hall.

Inside, the building has been transformed into a true Christmas wonderland for the decorating contest. Fragrant juniper and pine boughs from Mount Topaz adorn the walls, and the beams are festooned with streamers and poinsettias made from back issues of the *Topaz Times.* Atop a table, a tree strung with garlands stands in one corner. Cardboard snowflakes dangle from the ceiling, turning beautifully around a small bunch of mistletoe suspended over the center of the dance floor.

"Looks like a kids' craft project in here," Keiko says, crossing her arms and leaning against the doorframe.

I blink back tears. "I think it's perfect," I breathe.

And it is.

Beneath the hot dining-hall lights, the evening passes like a flurry of snow. I dance with Tommy, Shig, Stan, Mas. Twitchy takes me out to swing, spinning me around the dance floor, our heels kicking up, our faces sweaty and glorious. He's a *marvelous* dancer, all that buoyant energy going into every twirl, every lift, every dip.

All too soon, and not soon enough, it's the fourteenth song of the night. I glance down at my dance card, even though I already know who my partner will be.

14. Joe Tanaka

Couples are quickly dissolving and pairing off again like shapes in a kaleidoscope, whirling away in spirals of multicolored skirts as the music starts.

It's "Harbor Lights" by Frances Langford—Joe's favorite song—the same song he sang to me as we rode the train from Tanforan three months ago. It couldn't be more perfect.

I search the crowded mess hall for a glimpse of Joe's slicked-back hair, his sparkling, wide-set eyes, but he's nowhere to be found.

"Have you seen Joe?" I ask Yum-yum, who's dancing with Stan Katsumoto.

"No. Do you want me to help you look?"

I shake my head, twining my hands in my dress. The seconds keep slipping away!

"He ducked outside." Stan nods at the door. "The guy was red as a keto sunburn."

"It *is* hot in here," Yum-yum says.

Biting my lip, I hurry from the dining hall as Frances Langford begins to sing. Without my coat, the outdoor air is chilly on my skin, and I hug my arms as I search the empty street.

"Joe?" I call, descending the stairs.

There's no answer.

Shivering, I turn the corner.

And there he is, on the dark side of the building. Breaking out in a smile, I take a step forward.

But my joy freezes in my chest as I near him.

He's not alone. There's a girl in his arms, almost as tall as he is, with golden hair like summer sunshine in the dining-hall shadows.

It's Gail Johnson, and they're *kissing,* lips locked, pressed against the wall, like they're the only two people in the entire universe.

No, no, no, this can't be right.

This was *my* dance.

That was *my* kiss.

Tears fill my eyes. A sob catches in my throat.

And I flee. I run into the darkness, crying, until one of my heels catches in the slush, and I go tumbling forward onto my hands and knees. Dirty water spatters my arms, my legs, my white flowered dress.

The red camellia tumbles from behind my ear, landing petals-down in the mud.

"Whoa, whoa, Nakano," someone says, hoisting me up. In an

instant, I recognize the "All-American" patch on the sleeve—*Frankie*. "Are you okay?"

Covered in mud, with tears running down my face, I know I've never looked worse, but at this moment, I couldn't care less. I fling myself into Frankie's arms as he sets me on my feet. "No, I'm not."

He pats my shoulder. "That Tanaka boy break your heart?"

With a wail, I bury my face in Frankie's shoulder.

He sighs, and through the haze of my anguish, I feel his arms go around me. "Want me to hit him for you?" he asks.

I let out a sound that's supposed to be a laugh, but it comes out more like a hiccup. "Oh, Frankie." Leaning back, I smack him lightly in the chest. "That wouldn't do any good."

He smirks.

"But thanks for offering."

As we stand in the ice and mud, the last notes of "Harbor Lights" drift over the empty street. My eyes well up again.

"C'mon, Nakano, don't cry." Gently, Frankie takes my hand, swaying with me as the next song begins. "What happened?"

"He was kissing Gail Johnson." I hiccup again. "During *our song!*"

"That keto girl?" He has the audacity to laugh—a big, bellowing laugh that would sound harsh if it didn't have such warmth to it. "Shit, Nakano, you're twice the girl she is. Dumb boy doesn't know what he's missing."

I sniff. In his arms, I feel the chill beginning to ease from my bones. "You really think so?"

"Yeah."

"But she's—" I stop myself from adding *so pretty*. I'm pretty too, after all. Instead, I frown at Frankie. "Why are you being so nice to me?"

"You're a nice gal. You deserve nice things." His gaze flicks to the icy road and mud-splattered barracks, and his eyes harden for a moment. "Nicer than this, at least."

Blinking away the last of my tears, I lay my head on his shoulder. "You too, Frankie," I murmur.

We dance outside under the orange lamps. We dance while Joe Tanaka kisses Gail Johnson in the shadows. We dance while the song changes to Count Basie, and the mess-hall floorboards thunder with footsteps.

At last, Frankie kisses me on the forehead and takes a step back. He smiles. "Your wig's crooked."

"Oh no!" I blush, but Frankie just shakes his head.

"Cut it out, Nakano. You make a big deal of seeing the good in everything, but you're a dunce if you can't see how good you look tonight."

He extends his hand then, but I don't take it right away.

I suppose it's true. I choose to see the bright side of any situation, no matter how dim. I saw the good in that God-awful train ride from California. I see the good in Topaz, despite the dust, the plumbing, and the cold. I even see the good in Frankie. This should be no different. *I* should be no different, and it should be easy, because as of tonight, I've decided to think of myself as gorgeous, and not once in my life have I been *dim*.

But if Frankie Fujita is right about something, he's not going to hear it from me.

"I'm no dunce," I say primly, taking his hand.

"I know." Grinning, he walks me back to the dining hall, where the dance has gotten hotter and louder and more joyous. In the crowd, Twitchy and Stan are teaching Tommy some kind of complicated step pattern, and Keiko and Yum-yum are swinging together, skirts swirling out around them like flower petals. Seeing Frankie and me by the entrance, Shig beams and beckons us over. "There you are!"

I feel Frankie starting to slide out of my grasp, so I tighten my grip.

He raises an eyebrow. "I'm not on your dance card, Nakano."

I lift my head proudly, crooked wig and all. "Forget the dance card!" I say, and, laughing, I pull him into the crowd.

TOPAZ TIMES
News Daily

EXTRA   EXTRA   EXTRA

Vol. II Extra   TOPAZ, UTAH   Friday, January 29, 1943

TO RECRUIT NISEI

MYER PLEASED BY ARMY PLAN

Expressing his gratification over the War Department's decision to recruit a combat team from the nisei, Dillon S. Myer, national WRA head, sent the following message to Topaz:

"I find deep satisfaction in the announcement by Secretary of War Henry L. Stimson that a combat team composed of American citizens of Japanese ancestry is to be recruited by the United States Army for active service in a theater of war. This announcement makes January 28, 1943, the most significant date of the last 10 months for persons of Japanese ancestry in the United States.

"Many have told me in conversations and letters of their desire for active service in the armed forces of this country. For many months I have been looking forward with them to the time when their desire might be realized.

"All facilities of the WRA, both at the relocation centers and in Washington, will immediately be placed at the disposal of the War Department to speed the formation of the combat team announced by Mr. Stimson."

SIX RESIDENTS GIVE TO JACL NATIONAL FUND

Contributions to the National JACL fund from 6 Topaz residents were acknowledged this week by Mito Okada, treasurer, of Salt Lake City.

WAR DEPARTMENT PLANS TO ORGANIZE JAPANESE AMERICAN COMBAT TEAM

WASHINGTON, D.C., Jan. 29--At a press conference in his office yesterday morning, Secretary of War Henry L. Stimson issued the following press release:

"The War Department announced today that plans have been completed for the admission of a substantial number of American citizens of Japanese ancestry to the Army of the United States.

"This action was taken following study by the War Department of many earnest requests by loyal American citizens of Japanese extraction for the organization of a special unit of the Army in which they could have their share in the fight against the nation's enemies."

The initial procedure in the formation of the unit authorized by Secretary Stimson will be voluntary induction, the War Department announced. Facilities for this will be nation-wide, including the Hawaiian Islands and the War Relocation centers in this country. No individual will be inducted if doubt exists as to his loyalty upon induction.

The nisei will begin training as a combat team for service in an active theater. This combat team will include the customary elements of infantry, artillery, engineer and medical personnel. No effort will be spared in developing it into an efficient, well-rounded, hard-hitting unit.

The new unit will be trained separately from the battalion of Americans of Japanese extraction--originally a Hawaiian National Guard organization

PRINCIPLE OF ACTION GIVEN

The basic principle prompting the War Department's latest action was given by Secretary Stimson in a statement released with the Department announcement as follows:

"It is the inherent right of every faithful citizen, regardless of ancestry, to bear arms in the nation's battle. When obstacles to the free expression of that right are imposed by emergency considerations, those barriers should be removed as soon as humanly possible.

"Loyalty to country is a voice that must be heard, and I am glad that I am now able to give active proof that this basic American belief is not a casualty of war."

--which is already a component of the Army.

The War Department's action, it was announced, is part of a larger program which will enable all loyal American citizens of Japanese ancestry to make their proper contribution toward winning the war--through employment in war production as well as military service.

V

WILD BOY

FRANKIE, 19
JANUARY–FEBRUARY 1943

Me and Stan Katsumoto are hanging around by 1-9-E, so-called "City Hall," when the army jeep comes roaring toward camp, and I'm not gonna lie, the sight of the tires kicking up a dust cloud in the cold January morning makes me wanna hit something.

The army guys are here to recruit volunteers for Roosevelt's new combat team. See, we don't got liberty, we don't got property, but you better believe we've got the Great American Right to die for a country that doesn't want us.

The gates open. The jeep rolls into camp.

Out on the greasewood flats, the dust cloud rears up like a buckskin stallion. For a second, I can see laid-back ears and bared teeth and sharp hooves pumping the air. Then it collapses into nothing.

I dunno why, but it feels like a punch in the gut.

Four ketos get out of the jeep, followed by a nihonjin guy. That's why we're here, see. Last Thursday, the newspaper listed the army guys who were coming—Lieutenant Something-or-Another, a couple sergeants, and a technician with a Japanese name—and we wanted to know what kind of asshole would walk into a camp filled with his own people and ask us to enlist.

Little fella looks shocked, to tell you the truth, like it's the first time he's laid eyes on a relocation center.

Stan smirks. "He doesn't walk like he's got balls of steel. But I guess looks can be deceiving."

I laugh. Stan's always been twice as smart as anyone I know, with a smart mouth to match. He should've been in college or something by now—he coulda been sponsored by the Quakers, who've been helping kids get settled in all sorts of places in the Midwest—but for some reason, he stayed in camp with the rest of us.

The army guys are headed into the Camp Director's office across the street, filing up the steps like good little soldiers. The nihonjin guy's last, of course, and when he turns to get the door, we lock eyes.

The shocked expression on his face turns to something else. Something like pity.

He can shove his pity up his ass.

I'm not close enough to spit at his feet, but I spit as far as I can into the road, raising a puff of dust in the middle of the lane like the explosion of a tiny bomb.

The guy grimaces and closes the door, and me and Stan are left alone on the street.

You know, my pop fought for this country thirty years ago? He was on the front lines with the 82nd in France. Loves horses, that guy. When I was seven, he took me to a horserace. I remember the excitement, the starting bell, the animals charging around the track, the most beautiful sight I'd ever seen.

Then it all went wrong. One of the horses got hurt somehow. He was on the ground, screaming, and all these guys started jumping out from nowhere. I thought for sure they were gonna help him, get him a stretcher or something.

Pop had gone gray. He kept tugging me toward the exit, saying things like, "You don't wanna see this, Frank."

I remember the gunshot, how the horse stopped screaming, but I don't remember much after that.

My vision going white at the edges. That asshole with the gun. I remember pulling away from my pop, barreling down the steps like I was gonna murder someone. Like I was gonna pummel them into the dirt for destroying something so beautiful.

But I was just a goddamn kid, and they caught me before I reached the track. They hauled me away, kicking and shrieking, and that was the last time we ever went to the races.

After dinner one night, me and the boys are on the edge of camp, tossing rocks over the barbed wire. There's plenty to throw. Rocks are maybe the only thing that's plentiful here besides dust and anger.

For maybe the hundredth time, I think about leaping that fence. It's only about three feet high, and kids like Yum-yum's brother, Fred, sneak through all the time to catch scorpions in the desert. I could go running out there, out with the wild horses they say roam this part of Utah, free as the goddamn wind.

But I'd never abandon Mas and the boys, or my uncle Yas, who took me in when my parents shipped me out to California.

The whole camp's buzzing with the news today. Everyone seventeen and up has gotta do this questionnaire to see who's loyal and who's not. If you're loyal, you can volunteer for Roosevelt's combat unit. It's Nisei-only, which is a shit idea, if you ask me. If Uncle Sam sends 'em to the Pacific, the other battalions are gonna mistake them for the enemy.

"They won't get sent to the Pacific," Mas says, pitching a stone so far into the desert, it disappears from sight. He's got a good arm, that guy. That's why he was a star quarterback in high school.

Me, I was a delinquent. I would've dropped out of school, too, if Mas hadn't made me go to class, if he hadn't made me sit down with Shig and Minnow at their kitchen table, answering questions about algebra and history no one gives a shit about now.

"Oh yeah." Stan kicks around in the dust for another rock. "Let us too close to the Empire, and we'll be pulled back to Hirohito like magnets. We won't be able to help ourselves! It's science!"

We laugh, but Stan's right. The government's got a few Military Intelligence guys training to do translation over there, but no way they're gonna let five thousand of us into the Pacific, where we can give away America's game to the enemy.

"Isn't that what the questionnaire is for?" Tommy asks in that namby-pamby way of his. "To make sure everyone who volunteers is loyal?"

Sometimes I dunno why Mas and the others let Tommy hang around. He's so small and scared all the time, and he's not even related to them, like Minnow. Tommy's scrappy kid sister Aiko is always trying to tag along with us too, and to be honest with you, sometimes I'd rather she came than Tommy. At least she can handle herself in a fight.

Reaching over, I rough Tommy up a little to teach him not to ask stupid questions. I go easy on him, though, and let him squirm out of my grasp. He's one of us, after all. "Bottom line is this," I say as he tries to comb his hair straight again. "To them, we'll always be Japs."

"That's what the combat unit's for, though," Twitchy says. "To prove to everyone we're not." He throws two stones, one after the other, so fast they let out a loud *clack* as they collide in midair.

Damn. Is there anything Twitchy isn't good at?

Minnow's jaw drops like he's thinking the same thing. I swear to God, that boy would follow Twitchy Hashimoto to the ends of the earth without even being asked.

"You thinking of volunteering, Hashimoto?" I ask.

But it's not Twitchy who answers.

"I am," Mas says.

We all stop what we're doing to stare at him. His kid brothers, Shig and Minnow, exchange a sick glance like they already knew. Wonder if they already tried to talk him out of it, not that you can talk Masaru out of anything once he's made up his mind.

I feel like he's socked me in the gut, and if you've seen Mas, you know how much that'd hurt. How can he do this to us? To me? The U.S. government put us here, and he's going to go fight for them? I mean, I knew Mas fancied himself an all-American boy, but I didn't think he'd betray the rest of us for a country that clearly doesn't give a shit about him.

"Really?" Tommy asks.

"GI Ito." Stan starts whistling "Yankee Doodle Dandy."

Mas glares at him for a second, and then he looks at me like he's asking me to understand, even though I could never understand, never in a million years. "I still believe in this country."

"Plus, it pays better than any job you could get around here," Twitchy adds, breaking the tension.

"What about you, Frankie?" Shig asks, nudging me. Good ol'

Shig, he's always the one to notice when someone's being left out. "You gonna do it?"

I try to laugh, but it comes out kind of strangled. "Already tried, remember?" I wanted to enlist right after Pearl Harbor, but they wouldn't let me. 4-C. Enemy alien. Ineligible to fight for my own damn country. "They wouldn't take me then, so why should they have me now?"

I pick up a rock and hurl it as hard as I can into the darkening sky, hoping it'll break on impact, hoping it'll make a crater, hoping for *something,* but it lands on the other side of the fence without a sound.

Sometimes I get so angry, I can't see straight. My vision tunnels, and all I can see is my anger: bright, blinding, white. White as this keto bastard standing in our gymnasium, telling us we've got to make sacrifices for the greater good. White as a baby's ass, this guy is. Lieutenant What's-His-Face. Who cares? He's gonna be gone in a week or two, and we'll still be here, eating the same shit, shitting in the same holes. It's no skin off *his* nose whether we join up or not, whether we fight or not, whether we kiss Uncle Sam's ass or not. It's not *his* family, *his* freedom, on the line.

Lieutenant Whatever is describing the new unit now. He says, "All-Japanese."

He means, "All-expendable."

Who d'you think is gonna get the most dangerous missions? The jobs nobody else wants 'cause they're too risky? *The Japs.* Line us up so we'll get picked off—*pop! pop! pop!* That's five thousand less of us they have to deal with.

Lieutenant So-and-So says the combat team is gonna show the

ketos how American we are, how wrong they were to lock us up. Like it's *our* job to fix the prejudice in this country.

As soon as the questions are done, I explode out of the meeting. I want to hit something. I want something to hit back.

Twitchy, Stan, and Mas are on my heels. We stand there as the rest of the crowd floods around us, chattering excitedly, and some piece of shit starts up a chorus of "God Bless America." Soon, more and more voices join him, like if they sing loud enough, they'll turn their yellow faces white.

I can't stand it. Don't they see how backward this all is? How insulting? I run at the nearest singer—I don't give a shit who it is; they better cut out that goddamn racket. I take a swing. My fist connects with someone's stomach.

I hear the *whoosh* of air leaving him.

I grin.

I'm fighting. I'm grappling and punching and grunting. I don't even know why; I just want to fight. I want to fight the soldiers on the watchtowers and the project director and Lieutenant What's-His-Name. I want to fight the fucking president of the United States. I want to fight every pasty senator who voted to put us here. I want their noses to bleed.

I'm going down in a storm of fists. I'm catching kicks in the ribs. They're dogpiling me, hitting me as hard as they can.

Let 'em.

I'm no good for much of anything, but at least I can take a hit.

People are shouting, hauling bodies off me, and all of a sudden, I can breathe again. Stan Katsumoto and Twitchy have got me by the arms and they're dragging me out of the fray while Mas comes between me and those government stooges.

He's one of the good ones, that boy. He's the one who stuck up for me in that street fight with the Italians just after I moved from New York. He's the one who let me in with the Japantown boys. He's the one who straightened me out when nobody else could. Without Mas, I'd have been knifed or jumped or maybe I would've just drifted away, no ties to anybody.

"Walk away," he tells the crowd in that deep voice of his. In the lamplight, he's all shoulders and a silhouette that belongs on a recruitment poster.

GI Ito.

Japanese Captain America.

He's the kinda guy who speaks, and you listen. He's the kinda guy who says to walk away, and you do.

So they do. They mutter and disperse and, thank Christ, no one's singing anymore.

"What the hell, Frankie?" Mas whirls on me as the last of them go. "What's the matter with you?"

I shrug off Twitchy and Stan. "I don't know, okay? I don't know. The whole thing just makes me so mad—"

"Everything makes you mad," Mas says.

"Because everything is fucked!"

He comes at me then, and for a second, I think he's gonna hit me. But that isn't Mas's way. He just gets right up in my face. He's got a good three inches on me, that boy, and he says, real low, "Yeah, it is. But you can't fight everything, Frankie. You've got to pick something to fight *for*, or you'll wear yourself out trying to fight the world."

When I wake up the next morning, Uncle Yas is sitting by the fire, sewing the patch back onto Pop's WWI jacket. Yas was a tailor back in Japantown. Best in the neighborhood, if you ask me. But he can't see so well anymore. Got joints that hurt in the cold. He's the reason I stayed, you know, instead of heading back to New York. He needs someone to take care of him.

"You don't have to do that." I swing my legs over the edge of my cot and pull on a sweater.

"*Tch,*" Yas says. "Did you get in a fight again?"

I touch my lip, which is painful and swollen where it's been split, and grin. "You should see the other guy."

He squints at me. "I don't know why you went to that meeting in the first place. You already said you weren't going to volunteer."

I get up, taking the jacket out of his gnarled hands. "I dunno."

"So you just went to get riled up."

"I guess."

As I sit down across from him and start sewing, he leans over and cups my face. His palms are smooth but hard. "You're a wild boy, Frankie," he says. "You aren't meant to be penned up in a place like this. If you stay here, you're going to get yourself into trouble not even your friends will be able to get you out of."

I glare down at the red double-*A* of Pop's "All-American" patch and jab the needle through the fabric. "I'll be all right, Uncle Yas," I say, even though I don't know if I believe it.

Pop says thousands of horses died in the war. Killed by machine guns and poison gas and starvation and a hundred other things. He says there's so much wrong with the world that it makes you wanna tear it down to the foundations.

I think about that a lot, you know, those foundations. And some-times I think that if I just rammed my head into them hard enough, for long enough, all the backward frameworks and rotten girders of the world would crumble. And maybe then we could build something better.

It's the last citizens' meeting before they start administering the questionnaire, and here I am again, standing at the back of the room, grinding my teeth, because Mas is in front of the crowd talking all kinds of nonsense. He's got to fight for democracy everywhere, he's got to oppose tyranny wherever he finds it, bullshit like that. Tell you the truth, I stop listening after the first few minutes because all I can think is, *Tyranny is locking us up. Tyranny is taking our freedom. Tyranny is right here. Tyranny is American.*

I'm so mad, I could hit him. What's he thinking, trying to recruit us? Mas is supposed to be smarter than this.

About half the crowd is eating it up. He's got them slobbering at his feet, ready to throw themselves on the Germans' bayonets in the name of the red, white, and blue.

The other half is as pissed as I am. A lot of them are Kibei — you know, guys who were born here but got sent back to Japan to be educated — but not all of them. Some of them are guys like Stan Katsumoto, who lost his family's store in the evacuation. That little store his mom and pop worked so hard for, sold off piece by piece to the lowest bidder. You'd be a sucker not to be pissed about that.

But I'm the only guy who *hates* Mas for this. For betraying us like this. For abandoning me like this. Because I don't want to put my life on the line for this goddamn country, and that means while he's off playing soldier boy for Uncle Sam, I'm gonna be rotting in this fucking camp without him.

I want to scream at him. I want to beat some sense into him. *Don't go, Mas. They don't give a shit about you.* We *give a shit about you. We're your family. I'm—*

I'm so mad, I stalk the Topaz streets after the meeting, getting madder with every step. How could he do this to me? How could he leave me? He was supposed to be the guy we could all rely on.

I'm ready to pummel someone. Just give me an excuse. *C'mon.*

And all of a sudden, I'm on Mas's block.

They all look the same, these barracks, but Mrs. Ito's got a neat little rock garden in the plot outside the front door. I'd recognize those stones anywhere because I helped haul 'em here.

My fists curl.

Mas.

C'mon.

My feet are carrying me forward. I'm seeing white.

But before I make it there, a couple guys sneak out of the shadows. I can't see their faces because it's dark and the streetlights aren't so good, but one of them picks up a rock from Mrs. Ito's garden, hefts it, and draws his arm back like he's Bob Feller pitching for the Indians.

The fuckers are going to smash Mas's windows.

I forget I was ever mad at Mas. I forget I was ever mad at anyone except these spineless bastards. I charge them, barreling straight into the one with the rock. It falls from his hand as we stagger into the street, grunting.

He's hitting me over the back of the head, but I'm so mad, I barely feel it. I get in a few good punches, and the breath goes out of him as he stumbles back, wheezing.

The other guy tries to grab me, but I shove him off and hit the first guy again. My knuckles split on something, maybe his nose, I dunno. I don't give a damn. I just hope it hurts.

But before I can hit him again, they run. I spit after them, tasting blood on my tongue.

Then I turn back to the Itos' apartment. Through the curtains, I watch Mas's silhouette cross to the window.

I duck into the shadow of another barrack as he peers through the curtains. From behind, he's lit with this glow, like he's Superman coming out of the clouds, and for a second, I'm sure he can see me, out here in the dark, me and my stupid anger.

What was I thinking?

Was I really going to fight Mas? The guy who brought me into the group? The guy who's always stood up for me, no matter how bad I messed up?

He lets the curtain fall closed again.

Shaking, I pick up the rock from Mrs. Ito's garden and place it back where it belongs before slinking away like the coward I am.

That night, I dream about horses, the wild ones, with shaggy black manes and mud-spattered coats and flashing eyes. I dream about jumping the fence and running so hard, my hooves tear up the earth. Me and the horses and the stars.

The next morning, when I stride into Dining Hall 1 to fill out my questionnaire, I'm sporting a shiner to match my split lip. I can feel myself sneering at all the stooges, some of them keto, some of them nihonjin, sitting at the long tables to log everyone's answers.

Loyal or not.

Volunteering or not.

I must look a mess, because the guy who's supposed to help me with the questionnaire kinda recoils when I sit down across from him, but I just grin.

Uncle Yas was right. I can't stay here. I can't be locked up with my anger like this. If I stay here, my anger's gonna eat me up from the inside, like a white-hot fire, and if I don't get it out somehow, I'm gonna turn on everyone who ever loved me.

And I'll die before I let that happen.

"Sign me up," I say. "I wanna fight."

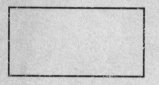

FORM APPROVED

BUDGET BUREAU No. 33-R04l-43

STATEMENT OF UNITED STATES CITIZEN OF JAPANESE ANCESTRY

27. Are you willing to serve in the armed forces of the United States on combat duty, wherever ordered? _____

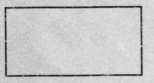

FORM APPROVED

BUDGET BUREAU No. 33-R04l-43

STATEMENT OF UNITED STATES CITIZEN OF JAPANESE ANCESTRY

---

28. Will you swear unqualified allegiance to the United States of America and faithfully defend the United States from any or all attack by foreign or domestic forces, and forswear any form of allegiance or obedience to the Japanese emperor, or any other foreign government, power, or organization? _____

VI

THE INFINITE INDECISIONS OF A DEWY-EYED IDIOT

STAN, 18
FEBRUARY 1943

Once, when I was younger, my dad let me hold the Katsumoto Co. deposit bag for six full minutes. We had closed the store and were walking toward the bank when he leaned over, plopped the leather envelope into my hands, and said, "Here, Stan, you take it."

Can you imagine? A whole day's revenue steaming in my hot little hands. I couldn't stop thinking of all the things I could do with that money. I could buy a truck or a hundred books or a swimming pool full of Jell-O. I could visit Egypt or send my little sister to a convent or buy a house for my buddy Shig so his family wouldn't have to rent anymore. The possibilities were endless!

No, the possibilities *were* endless, and that was a *lot* of money. What if I misplaced it on our three-block walk to the bank? What if someone drove by while we were on the corner and snatched it right out of my arms? What if Bonnie and Clyde rode up with their Thompsons and opened fire?

Convinced I was going to lose the deposit bag somehow, I tried tucking it under my armpit. I tried clasping it to my chest. I tried swinging it between my thumb and forefinger like nothing bad would happen as long as I pretended not to care about it, and it nearly slipped out of my grasp.

That's when Dad smacked me in the back of the head and snatched the bag back.

It was only six minutes, but I still remember how good it felt to hold all that money and how fucking scary it was to know it could all be taken away.

Ten years later, and it happened anyway: We lost the store. We lost our freedom. Sometimes, it feels like we're losing even more than that.

As I pass Dining Hall 1 on my way to the post office, I watch people from Block 8 queue up for the registration, which is what the WRA is calling this stuff with the loyalty questionnaire. It's barely ten a.m., but the line's already starting to wrap around the building. The administration's going to have a hell of a time if they don't step up the pace—for every person who trickles out of the mess hall, two more join the end of the line.

But I guess it wouldn't be Topaz without a wait.

"Hey, Katsumoto!"

I turn to find Frankie Fujita coming out of the mess hall, sporting what looks like a new black eye. Dumb kid just can't keep his hands to himself, can he? He slouches toward me with his fists in his pockets. "What d'you got there?" he says, nodding at the letters in my hands.

I look down, frowning. Damn, I was trying not to think of them.

"Nothing," I lie. Nervously, I shuffle the envelopes—*one, two, three, four, five, six*—and almost drop them. "Letters to my sweethearts."

Frankie snorts. "What sweethearts?"

"Your mom, for one."

"Say something else about my mom, Katsumoto, and you won't be talking for a month."

We both drop the subject. I stuff the envelopes in my back pocket and pat them twice to make sure they won't fall out. "Did you fill out your questionnaire?" I ask.

He nods.

"What was on it?"

"I don't know." He shrugs. "I said I wanted to fight, and they said okay."

I laugh. And they're going to put a gun in this guy's hands? God bless America, I guess.

Look, I didn't want to tell Frankie, but sometimes you want things so bad, you're scared to even say it. I wanted to stay in San Francisco. I wanted to be treated like an American citizen.

But maybe this time will be different. Maybe if I say it, it'll come true.

I'm going to college. Hopefully.

I was supposed to go last year, after I graduated—I had the grades for it, anyway—but most universities weren't accepting Nisei students at the time, so I didn't bother applying. Sure, I could've gotten help from the Quakers or the National Japanese American Student Relocation Council, who were getting kids set up at religious places like BYU and St. Olaf's, but here's the thing: *Why should I have to?*

We've been in camps for almost a year, and no one's been found guilty of espionage. With background checks, people are getting resettled all the time in cities like Denver and Detroit. After the loyalty questionnaire, that process is going to go even faster. They have to accept me now. They've got no reason not to.

So I'm writing letters to a bunch of universities, requesting application forms. I'll just fill them out, tell them I'm loyal, and *poof!* I'll be out of here in time for summer classes, a dewy-eyed freshman just like the rest.

But it's never that easy, is it? They couldn't just ask, *Are you loyal to the United States of America? Yes or no?* and be done with it. Not *this* government, who said last year that there was no way to measure the loyalty of the Japanese in America. At least not until *after* they put us in camps.

I guess asking for things to "be simple" and "make sense" was kind of a high bar.

Of course, we're all curious to see what kind of white nonsense we have to deal with this time, so Twitchy nabs us a copy of the questionnaire, and we crowd onto the steps of the Itos' barrack with Shig and Tommy to pore over the pages.

Don't call it stealing. Call it "test prep." I learned a long time ago that the secret to academic success isn't smarts. It's knowing what they want from you and giving it to them with a smile.

"'Statement of United States Citizen of Japanese Ancestry,'" Twitchy begins.

"Yeah, yeah, let's get to the good stuff." Impatiently, Shig flips through the pages. After a second, he laughs. "'Number nineteen: Sports and hobbies'!"

Twitchy drums the stair with his palms. "What do they care what sports we play?"

"Maybe they want us to have played American sports like football?" Tommy asks.

"Nah." I snort. "They're scared of us doing shit like judo and karate. They want to know if we're forming a secret ninja army or something." Snatching the questionnaire, I flip to the front again.

It's from the Selective Service System. You know, the guys in charge of the draft. No wonder they're so obsessed with armies.

Shig scoffs and takes the pages back from me. "'Number twenty-two: Give details on any foreign investments.' What do they think we are, rich?"

"Yeah." I roll my eyes. "Rich ninjas."

We laugh, but no one really finds this funny. Four pages of the government trying to trick us into revealing that, oh shit, we really are spies? We didn't even know! Damn, shouldn't have visited those grandparents in Fukuoka, huh? Shouldn't have joined that Japanese theater club. Whoopsy-daisy, guess I'm a traitor now? Good to know!

Eventually, of course, we find them, Questions 27 and 28, the questions that are causing so much trouble, the questions that are *actually* about loyalty and not about whether we macramé in the evenings or crochet.

"What the fuck?" I say.

"What?" Twitchy glances at the questions again, then back to me. "What's wrong with them, Stan?"

I stare at the bottom of the last page, blinking, like the words are going to cha-cha into new arrangements while I'm not looking.

But they don't.

27. Are you willing to serve in the armed forces of the United States on combat duty, wherever ordered? _____

28. Will you swear unqualified allegiance to the United States of America and faithfully defend the United States from any or all attack by foreign or domestic forces, and forswear any form of allegiance or obedience to the Japanese emperor, or any other foreign government, power, or organization? _____

Shig leans back on the steps, shrugging. "What's so hard about that?" he says. "'No' and 'Yeah.'"

"Why 'No'?" I ask.

It's a nifty trick, playing dumb. You ask the right questions, and people magically come around to your way of thinking. Dad hates it, but I tell him to blame Socrates.

"Can you picture me in the army?" Shig chuckles. "They'd kick me out for folding my socks wrong or something."

Twitchy laughs. "Since when do you fold your socks?"

"But this isn't asking you to volunteer." I flick the paper. It snaps against my fingernail, making Tommy jump.

"It isn't?" Shig asks.

"Nah." I smirk. "But it *is* asking you to give up your loyalty to Hirohito."

"What loyalty to Hirohito?"

"Exactly."

Tommy's brow furrows. "So they're wanting us to say we *were* loyal to Hirohito, but we're not anymore?"

I make finger guns at him. "Bingo."

Shig groans, like he's just been sucker punched. I guess we all have. "You were right, Stan. What the fuck."

Turns out, Shig couldn't answer "No" and "Yeah" even if he wanted to. The following day, the *Topaz Times* announces that Questions 27 and 28 must be answered the same. A "No" to one is a "No" to both, no room for exceptions or explanations. You're loyal and a true American patriot, or you're not and you're a filthy goddamn traitor! Go back to Japan if you don't like it!

I slide the stolen questionnaire out from under my mattress, where I've hidden it like a dirty magazine. *Are you willing . . . Will you swear . . .* I've got the rest of the month until I have to report for registration, and I need to figure out how I'm going to answer.

If I say "Yes" and "Yes," I get to leave camp. I get to go to school. I get a shot at my education.

If I say "No" and "No," I give all that up, but at least I'll keep my self-respect.

I check the post office every day to see if my applications have come in, but it isn't until a week later that I finally get a reply.

I open it right there at the counter, ignoring the way Bette, who's behind me, huffs and tosses her hair. She already waited an hour to get in here. She can wait a few seconds longer.

Surprise twist! It's not an application at all. It's a letter describing all the hoops I'll have to jump through, some of them flaming, if I want to attend their undergraduate program. Given these prerequisites, if I'd still like an application form, they'll be happy to supply one.

They want me to be the acrobat, but they're the ones bending over backwards to reject me without *really* having to reject me. I wonder if they've got a manual or something, some step-by-step instructions on how to keep undesirables out of their hallowed alabaster institutions.

Part I: Salutations

Call the subject "my dear." At all times, you must cultivate an air of gentility, so in the event that you are unfairly accused of bigotry, you will have your respectability as your defense. Bigots are not well-mannered, but you, my dear, are a paragon of propriety. Ergo, you cannot be a bigot!

Bette's at the counter now, picking up the new camera she ordered by mail. "Get anything good today, Stan?" she asks.

I crumple the envelope and toss it toward the trash, where it hits the rim and falls to the floor, uncurling like a cramped fist. "Oh, you know," I say, "the usual."

Since we graduated last year, Twitchy and I have gotten jobs with the commissary. Every morning, we load up the truck from the iceboxes and warehouses to deliver food to the mess halls. It's a job a trained monkey could do, but hey, it's a paycheck, which is more than my dad brings in right now.

Sometimes, when we're done, we swing by to pick up Shig and Tommy after school, and we go joyriding around camp for a while.

Sometimes we return the truck with our heads spinning because Twitchy thought it would be funny to turn circles in the firebreak.

Whiplash. Hilarious.

Today, we're lounging around in the truck bed while Shig tells us he said "Yes" and "Yes," like Frankie, Bette, Mas, and Yum-yum, although he didn't volunteer. "I just want to graduate and work at the commissary with you guys," he says, folding a random page of the *Topaz Times*. "Can't do that if I'm getting my toes shot off in Europe."

"You could've kept your toes if you'd said 'No,'" I point out.

He's silent for a second as he fiddles with that piece of paper. I think he's turning it into some kind of bird. A seagull, maybe, like the ones we used to chase around the playground, almost convinced we could catch them. Then he says, "Yeah, I know. But it's what my dad would've wanted."

That's five of my friends who've declared "Yes" and "Yes" for this country. Five out of nine. More than half. I think of the questionnaire and that pre-rejection rejection stuffed under my mattress, the paper crimping from the bed springs.

I'm still waiting on five colleges. I could still get out of here if I say "Yes-Yes" too.

I sigh. It's a weekend afternoon, so the barrack is pretty quiet. Mom's at work at the dining hall, and my younger brother, Paul, is out, probably caterwauling on the other side of the barbed-wire fence with his friends. The guards on the watchtowers must see them, but it must not matter, because they're just kids, I guess. The most harm they can do is pulling the legs off of scorpions to watch them wriggle in the dust.

Dad, as usual, is in his chair by the stove, reading his newspaper.

"What would you say?" I ask Mary, who's reading. "If you had to answer the questionnaire?"

She glances over the edge of her book and back down again, like I'm a gnat she can't be bothered to swat.

Thanks, Mary. I love you, too.

"I'm not seventeen yet," she says. "I don't *get* a say."

And that's the conversation. What a victory! I should run around camp with my fists in the air and the American flag draped over my shoulders.

Mom likes to say Mary's a woman of few words, but really she's just a grouch. I reach over to ruffle her hair, but she ducks out from under my hand, rolling her eyes.

At the table, Dad doesn't look up. Honestly, I don't even know if he knows we're here. He turns the page of his paper. Smoke curls from his pipe like the mustache of a cartoon villain.

Before the evacuation, Dad was always in motion. He was restless and impatient, an earthquake of a man. He was insistent that we work harder, move faster, bring home better grades, sweep the floors, restock the shelves, learn to take inventory. At the store it was always "Do it again, Stan," and "Hurry up, Stan." On family outings, it was "Keep up or be left behind."

Then there's Dad after the evacuation: Every day, he sits by the stove with a weak cup of coffee and the most current edition of the newspaper. He reads that thing every day, page by page, skipping nothing, not even the ads. It takes him hours, because his English isn't great and he won't be caught dead taking Americanization classes with

Mom. When he finishes, he flips the whole thing over and starts again from the beginning.

You could look through our windows and think nothing's wrong. He's healthy, I guess. He's tidy. His mustache is trimmed. But he's like a wax figure. If I sat him too close to the stove, he'd melt.

I get my second and third responses from colleges on the same day, and I swear they could've been written by the same prim white secretary for the same prim white dean. The only difference is that one calls me "Mr. Kistumoto." It's nice to have a little variety in your rejections, like extra fiber.

Part II: Requirements

List requirements that at first glance seem reasonable but are in fact nearly impossible to meet. For your convenience, examples are provided below.

Example A.

Knowing that the applicant, being from an alien family, is likely one of the working class and therefore lacking adequate savings for either tuition or room and board, DO make it agonizingly clear that out-of-state tuition is due in full <u>before</u> the beginning of the first semester but that searching for lodging or employment will not be permitted until <u>after</u> the applicant has arrived. Money is the key to many

doors, fellow white person, and one's inferiors must always
be reminded that without it, all of those doors are closed.

If this had been before the evacuation, Dad would've yelled at me. "Not good enough, Stan," or "You spent money on a stamp for this, Stan?" He would've yelled at the university, the heavens, the Director of Admissions, the guys at the post office. I don't know a lot of Issei who yell, but Dad used to love it. I think it was one of the most American things about him, how he seized upon the freedom to be loud, to be heard, to claim his own space, even if his space encroached on everyone else in earshot.

I mean, if throwing your freedom around like that isn't quintessentially American, I don't know what is.

Now he just sits at the table, staring at his paper, and I quietly pile the letters with the questionnaire and shove them under my mattress.

When Twitchy announces that he's volunteered for the army, like Frankie and Mas, everybody congratulates him, because Twitchy's the kind of guy who can make enlisting seem like the war's already won. With a laugh, Bette turns up Mas's Silvertone radio, proclaiming, "This calls for a party!"

They all leap up, except for Tommy and me, who sit off to the side.

"Mom and Dad are going to say 'No' to the questionnaire." Tommy's voice is nearly drowned out by the music. "They're tired of the way America's treated them."

I shrug. "Aren't we all?"

In the middle of the barrack, our friends are dancing, singing along to the radio, and I probably know the song, but I don't hear the words. All I hear is "Yes" and "Yes" and "Yes" and "Yes."

"I'm going to say 'No' too," Tommy says.

I put my arm around him.

Tommy's been chasing after his parents' approval for as long as we've known him. Maybe if he proves he's a "No-No" too, he'll finally get it.

But I doubt it.

Another pre-rejection, another white-gloved, backhanded slap in the face.

Part II: Requirements
(continued)

Example B.

Ambiguity over specificity. DO limit the academic courses that the applicant has access to, but DO NOT provide details that he or she may contest. DO instruct the applicant that his or her activities will be under surveillance and jurisdiction of the Federal Bureau of Investigation, which, at its discretion, may remove him or her from your institution. DO cite "national security concerns" to allay any of the applicant's objections. It's a matter of national security! One wants one's country to be safe, doesn't one? If the applicant is a "good" nonwhite person, he or she will be happy to comply with your demands.

• • •

With only a week left to decide whether I'm a "Yes-Yes" or a "No-No," I stop by the mess hall one day while Mom's peeling ginger for the pot of teriyaki sauce she's preparing. Except for a few of the staff who are washing rice or sweeping the kitchen at one end of the large wood-beamed room, the place is empty, benches stacked upside down on the tables. Picking up a nearby towel, I start wiping down the serving counter, like I would've done at Katsumoto Co. My hands come away smelling of mildew.

Nothing says "clean" like nasty old towel, I guess.

Mom shrugs when I ask her how she's going to answer the questionnaire. "I don't know . . ." Lifting her cutting board, she flicks slices of ginger into the saucepot. "I've been in this country since I was a little girl, you know. I don't see why I shouldn't make my loyalty official."

"What about Japan?"

"What about it? *I've* never met the emperor." Serenely, she pours a few glugs of shoyu into the pot.

"Oh yeah, and Roosevelt's your best buddy, right?"

She laughs and adds a sprinkle of government-rationed sugar. "You never know," she says good-naturedly. "Did you hear the First Lady might be visiting the camps soon? What if he goes with her? What if he eats some of my saba shioyaki? How embarrassing if I was a No-No."

I grin at her. "So you want to say 'Yes' just in case the president comes to eat at your mess hall?"

"Don't you listen, Stanley? I told you, I'm not sure." Glancing over her shoulder, she sneaks a bottle of sake from under her apron and pours some into the pot.

I laugh. "But Mom! FDR!"

She sighs, capping the bottle. "Have you talked to your father yet?"

Part III: Closings

End your letter with a heartfelt sentiment such as "Very truly yours." DO be genteel. How could anyone be angry with you when you were so polite?

Only one more college left to hear from now. I can already feel the boot kicking me out on my ass.

There were a lot of incidents at Katsumoto Co., particularly in the 1930s when Japan started annexing parts of China and Russia. It was the solemn duty of all true Americans to fight the Yellow Peril wherever they found it, and there was always a new threat to scrub from the door, glass to sweep from the sidewalk, a cracked window to tape or board over with plywood.

But I was only there once when it happened.

I was thirteen, and it was winter, so the dark came early, and when the lights were on inside, we couldn't see out the windows to the street. I used to like that, just Dad and me in our little world of aisles, shelves, bags of rice, boxes of tea. I liked the feeling of the store shutting down, the calm that followed the after-work rush.

We closed out the register. We turned out the lights. We were at the door, all ready to go, both of us thinking of the chicken karaage Mom had promised us for dinner, when someone slammed into the glass with the flat of their hand — *crack!*

"Goddamn Nips!"

Pale faces swam into view outside the windows.

"This is a white man's neighborhood!"

Dad grabbed my shoulder. I swear he was going to rip off my arm or something. "Stan," he said. I'd never heard my dad's voice like that —high and tight and shallow—like it wasn't his voice at all, like he was some high-voiced, arm-ripping stranger. "Go to the back room."

"This is a white man's country!"

They were laughing at us. I could hear them as we slunk toward the storeroom, where they couldn't see us, where they couldn't say those things to our faces and laugh.

Crack! Someone struck the window, not with a hand this time, but with a brick.

What a dunce. Even I, at thirteen, knew that blunt force wasn't a good way to shatter a window.

You need something sharp. Like an ice pick.

Picking up the crowbar he used to pry open shipping crates, Dad shoved me behind him and crouched by the door of the back room, ready to swing.

Peering past him, I watched the letters appear on the windows in white paint, backward but unmistakable:

JAPS GO HOME

After they left, Dad telephoned the police. He filed a statement. He did some yelling. We scrubbed the paint and replaced the windows and went on as if nothing had happened, at least on the outside.

• • •

The day before I have to report for registration, the sixth and last university sends me a response. I'm sitting on the edge of my cot as I open it, the paper crackling like fire in the thick silence of the barrack.

By the stove, Dad doesn't look up.

This is it, I think. *This is the last one. The last rejection. I'm not going to college after all. At least after this, I'll know. Good fucking riddance.*

Except it's not a rejection. It's an application.

No hoops. No flames. No bigotry with a smile. I have to read it twice to be sure.

It's just the form.

I exhale slowly. What a thing. What a beautiful thing, getting the chance to be rejected like anybody else.

What a shitty thing that I'd almost forgotten what it felt like.

Carefully, I tuck the application back into the envelope, hardly daring to touch it in case it disintegrates.

"Dad," I say, "they sent me an application."

At first, I don't think he's heard me. He doesn't turn. He doesn't move. Wax Dad. Evacuation Dad. Maybe some things there's just no coming back from.

But then he folds his newspaper and lays it on the table by his elbow. His chair scrapes along the Masonite floor.

Dad's up. Dad's walking toward me. "One out of six," he says. His voice is softer than I remember. "Sixteen percent."

"I know, I know." I smirk. "If this were a test, I'd have failed."

He takes me by the shoulders, and his eyes are serious and wounded and alive. "I don't think this was a test for you."

That evening, Dad invites me on a walk. People are always stretching their legs or searching for arrowheads after dinner, and we join them in the firebreak that runs along the edge of camp, between the barracks and the fences.

For a while, Dad putters along. He must be trying to hide how out of shape he is or something, because even after the evacuation, he always moved with precision and purpose: making the coffee, packing his pipe, turning the page of his newspaper. He's not the kind of man who *dawdles*.

But when we pass a couple of Issei grandmas shuffling through the dust, he says loudly, "My son Stan was invited to apply to a university."

And I realize he's not puttering. He just wants to brag.

"Dad!" I say.

"Stan is going to college," he says to the grandmas. He's not quite yelling, but close enough.

I roll my eyes and leave him behind to bask in their congratulations, but I can't help putting my hand to my chest pocket to make sure the application is still there.

I guess I could've left it in the barrack, but a dozen things could've happened to it there. What if Mary accidentally threw it the trash? What if someone in the barrack left their hot plate on and started a fire? What if someone left the door open and the wind just kind of swept it away?

No, I want my hope right here, where I can hold it.

Every few minutes, Dad stops to tell someone else, and soon I'm twenty yards ahead of him. The sun's almost gone now, but there's still that last sliver of red on the horizon, steeping the camp in a fiery glow.

Nearby, Mr. Uyeda, one of the bachelors from Block 8, is tossing a stick for his dog. Every time he throws the stick, the little mutt runs after it, yelping, and doesn't stop until she's got the stick in her mouth. Then she brings it back, drops it at Mr. Uyeda's feet, and starts barking again. It's a wonder he can think with all that racket, but I guess he's old and hard of hearing, so maybe it doesn't bother him.

I don't know where these pets keep coming from, because we weren't allowed to bring any from home, but—

Crack!

I jump.

For some reason, I think of a white hand—*Japs go home.*

By the fence, Mr. Uyeda collapses.

A gunshot, I think. It was a gunshot. Someone *shot* him. There he is, groaning, wriggling in the dust.

He might be dying.

There might be shouting. Someone might be screaming.

It might be me.

I dash forward. Someone's got to help him. Someone's got to do something. I can't leave him there. I can't let him die.

I haven't gone two steps when I'm tackled. My glasses are knocked from my face. The world blurs.

I try to fight, but someone wrestles me to the dirt. My arm is being grabbed. It's going to be ripped right out of its socket.

Dad. It's Dad. He was twenty yards behind me. How did he move so fast?

Against my ear, his voice is high and taut. "Don't, Stan. Don't. No, *no.*"

I'm still scrabbling at the dust, trying to get to Mr. Uyeda. Kids break out of the camp all the time. *All the time.* To catch snakes and pull the legs off scorpions. They don't do any harm. Mr. Uyeda couldn't do any harm. He was too old. He was hard of hearing. Did someone tell him to stop? Before they shot him? Did they warn him before they killed him?

He's still squirming on the ground, but his movements are getting smaller and smaller. It's so dark out here now. I can't see. Where's his dog? Did they shoot his fucking dog?

They hold us for interrogation in one of the administrative offices. What did we see? Was Mr. Uyeda trying to escape? What was he doing by the fence?

Nothing, we tell them. *Nothing.*

For hours, they question us. What do we know? Was Mr. Uyeda part of a conspiracy against the United States? What was he trying to do, so close to the barbed wire?

Nothing.

Nothing.

He was a Yes-Yes. He was one of the first to answer the loyalty questionnaire. He was playing with his dog.

For maybe the hundredth time, I take out the envelope with my college application inside it and begin turning it over and over in my hands. The corners are bent now. The crisp white paper, smudged with fingerprints. I'm going to tear the thing to pieces if I keep messing with it, but I can't stop.

"What's going to happen to the killer?" I say suddenly.

Dad squeezes my hand, as if in warning. His knuckles are dirty and cut up from wrestling me to the ground. He saved me, I think. I would've run over to Mr. Uyeda. I would've been shot too. I would've been dead or in a hospital, and they'd be asking Dad if it was me who was trying to escape.

Never mind the fact that I wouldn't have needed to. Never mind the college application. Never mind the resettlement. Never mind the one hundred thousand people who haven't been found guilty of a single traitorous thing. Never mind that as of tomorrow, I could've been a Yes-Yes too.

One of our interrogators blinks. "Killer?" He looks dumbfounded.

"Yeah, *killer*," I say. "That's what you call someone who *kills* people."

The man says nothing.

For a second, I think I'm going to puke.

"Can you at least tell me what happened to his dog?" I say.

"Stan . . ." Dad's eyes are bloodshot and swollen from lack of sleep.

But how can we sleep? How can we go back now, or go on? "Yes" and "Yes"? A dewy-eyed freshman just like the rest? Whistling on my way to some ivy-laden lecture hall, far from the fences, while Dad brags up and down the firebreak where Mr. Uyeda was shot for playing fetch with his dog? How can we do it? How can we do anything, after this?

They tell me no one's seen the dog.

WORDS FROM AN OLD ISSEI

In this time of turmoil, there are those among us who wish to retaliate against the W.R.A. for the death of Mr. Uyeda. These disgruntled fools will pretend to stage an insurrection, but when they are faced with the consequences of their agitations, they will reveal their duplicitous nature, groveling and begging for mercy.

These are the same people who cry for their pitiful condition, who bemoan the loss of their homes and household goods, and call first for the restitution of their civil rights before they declare themselves loyal to this, their homeland.

But I say it is they who have made themselves pitiful with their spineless demands! These are not the virtues of the Japanese people. Let us silence the words of those who seek the pity of others, for they should be ashamed to share their weakness openly.

For there are those who, at this time for patriotism, publicly pledge their allegiance to America, though they have borne the same afflictions. There are those who, even now, are bravely standing on the battlefield, ready to fight for their nation. Put aside your personal feelings. Commit yourself to serving your country. These are the long-cherished tenets of the Japanese people. Moreover, they are the privilege of those who live in these great United States.

Exile those who would shirk and run away! These scoundrels who claim there is no future or security in the U.S. do not deserve the blessings of this nation. Cast aside these troublemakers! We must live life in the essence of the Japanese spirit, burning with love and obligation to America, our homeland.

Awaken, descendants of Japan! You, within whom the Japanese spirit burns! Come together and demonstrate the beauty of our people to the world, rejecting the humiliation of these shameful disloyals and malcontents!

That is all I have to say.

VII

TEAM PLAYER

AIKO, 14
MARCH–SEPTEMBER 1943

The day after the shooting, they don't just cancel school, they cancel *everything*. No work, no co-op, no nothing! All the normal camp stuff screeches to a halt, and what's left is this sudden turn, like everything has gone sideways.

Peeking through the curtains, I watch people running through the streets with shovels and pieces of lumber. It's like they grabbed whatever they could get their hands on and thought, *This'll do some damage.*

"Aiko!" my mom cries. "Get away from there!"

I ignore her. I do that a lot. It's my older brother, Tommy, who's the obedient one, even if our parents never give him credit for it, just like it's Tommy who draws me away from the window.

At the back of the barrack, our mom grabs my wrist and yanks me down to the floor where she's sitting with my younger sisters, Fumi and Frannie. She doesn't thank Tommy for bringing me over, *of course,* but no one expects her to. She and our dad demand a lot from Tommy because he's the oldest and a boy, but no matter what he does, it never pleases them.

I plop down cross-legged, pouting.

Our dad takes my baseball bat from the stand near the coat rack. Okay, if you want to twist my arm about it, it's *technically* Tommy's bat—our dad gave it to him when he was ten and I was seven, to try to make him more active, I guess. But Tommy never did anything with it, so it's mine now, or at least *I* think so.

Our dad turns away from us. Sometimes when I think of our dad, all I can picture is the back of him: shiny black hair, thick neck, hunched shoulders.

"Stay here," he tells us. Our mom cries out again in protest, but that doesn't stop him from walking out the door.

For a while, we huddle on the barrack floor. Mom tries to keep Fumi and Frannie occupied with their dolls, and I flip through an issue of *Captain America* I've read so many times, I could describe each panel with my eyes closed.

But it's hard to concentrate with the crowds roaming the streets outside. Every so often, we hear someone cry for justice for Mr. Uyeda.

There's a knock at the door.

Our mom squeaks. Tommy jumps.

I'm already on my feet when our mom catches my wrist again. "Let your brother get it."

I tap my foot impatiently as Tommy creeps toward the door. "Who is it?"

"It's Mas."

I brighten immediately.

I know it's stupid, but for a long time, I was sure Mas Ito was a superhero in disguise. I mean, just look at him, there in the doorway: broad shoulders, big chest, more muscles than I know the names of.

He looks like Superman. Put a cape on him, and I'm telling you, he'd be able to fly.

"It's getting bad out there," he says to Tommy. "We're going to see if we can calm things down a bit. Want to come?"

Tommy glances back at our mom, who shrugs.

It stings, the way she doesn't care about Tommy, but not bad enough to stop me from raising my hand and saying, "I do!"

Mas smiles at me. That's another thing I like about him: he never treats me like I'm just Tommy's kid sister. "Someone's got to stay behind to look after the family," he tells me.

I straighten at that, even though I know it's just a nice way of telling me I can't come. Like always.

Sometimes, I wish me and Tommy could trade places. Then our mom and dad wouldn't give him such a hard time, and I'd get to hang around with the Japantown guys without them always telling me to go home.

Through the doorway, I see a group of people run past, yelling in Japanese.

"Don't worry, Mrs. Harano," Mas says, even though all of us know she never worries about Tommy unless he's doing something she thinks will reflect poorly on her, "we'll bring him back safe and sound."

As soon as they close the door, I squirm out of our mom's grasp and shove my feet into my shoes. I'm *always* the one who has to stay behind. I'm *always* the one who gets left out.

Not this time.

This time, I'm not a kid anymore. I'm fourteen. Plus, no one's around to stop me.

"Aiko!" my mom snaps. "Don't you—"

"I'll be back soon!" I race out of the barrack after Tommy and Mas. From a distance, I watch them join up with Shig, Frankie, Twitchy, and Stan Katsumoto, and they head into the furor, breaking up fights and stopping acts of vandalism. Boy, I wish I could be up there with them!

But I trail behind, far enough that they won't notice me and tell me to go away.

Actually, no one seems to notice me at all. They're too busy yelling and getting in each other's faces. It's like I'm invisible, slipping past grown men with their rakes and makeshift clubs.

I lose track of the guys in the big crowd by City Hall. It's noisy and people are crammed together like tsukemono in a jar, turning sour in their own anger. I hang around by some steps in the back, searching for Mas's superhero silhouette.

But before I can spot him, the gates open, and the military police flood into camp. They take up positions in front of the administration buildings, yelling at everyone to disperse. The barrels of their Tommy guns make black arcs in the February air.

The crowd panics.

I try to run, like the Flash, but I'm too slow. People charge past me—they're loud and they smell like fear and sweat—and suddenly someone rams into me from behind. I hit the ground, hard, and someone tramples my hand. There's this pain in my fingers, sharp as the crack of a bat. Everyone is so much bigger than me. They can't even see me, down here in the dust. I'm too small, too invisible.

I'm going to be crushed.

Then someone shouts, "Aiko!" and I look up.

Mas Ito is barreling toward me, flanked by the Japantown boys. He scoops me up in his arms, and all of a sudden, the roar of the crowd gets really, really quiet, and I hear Tommy shouting, "Aiko! Ike, are you okay?"

I look around. Above me, Mas is breathing hard, but he's carrying me so carefully, I'm not even being jostled. Next to us, the other guys are pushing people out of our way, Frankie laughing like he's having the time of his life. I smile. "I am now."

The military alert is called off the next day, so the soldiers can't have riot weapons anymore. But they keep their side arms, and a lot of men in camp still carry around wrenches and clubs for protection.

Topaz City simmers with fear and anger. Our dad goes out early, and he takes *my* baseball bat with him. School remains closed, and the work stoppage continues, so no one goes out to the fields.

But people have still got to be taken care of, so the hospital and dining-hall staffs report in as usual.

I wonder if Twitchy and Stan will, too, since they're in charge of delivering the food for the dining halls. All morning, I wait by the window to see if they'll drive past, and when the truck comes, I run after them, ignoring my mom when she tells me to come back.

When I arrive, panting, there's a crowd already there, and at first I think they want to help too, but then I realize they're shouting while the boys jump out of the truck.

They're calling Stan and Twitchy "traitors" and "strikebreakers." As the dining-hall employees come out to help bring in the food, the crowd yells at them, too, shaking their fists.

I screw up my face the way our mom hates and start forward to help.

Someone catches me by the arm.

Tommy. He must have come after me. He's out of breath as he says, "No, Ike."

I tug away from him, disgusted. "Come on, Tommy. Those are *your* friends out there. What would Mas do if he were here?"

He swallows. After a moment, he nods.

Before anyone can stop us, we grab one of the potato sacks. The hand that got stepped on yesterday spasms, and I almost drop my side of it before I get my grip again.

"Aiko? Tommy?" Stan Katsumoto says. Behind his glasses, his eyebrows go way up into his hairline. "What—"

"*Tommy!*" someone snaps.

I know that voice. Eyes wide, Tommy and I turn, still clutching the potatoes.

It's our dad. He's standing there, his jaw tight like it gets sometimes, and he's holding my baseball bat. It looks scary in his hands, like it's not something you use to play games, but something else, something used to hurt people.

"Put that *down*," he says.

Tommy flinches.

"We just want to help?" I say. It sounds like a question, even though I don't mean it to be. The potatoes are getting heavier in my arms, and my injured hand is starting to throb.

"You shouldn't be helping *them*."

"Morning, Mr. Harano," Stan Katsumoto says, coming to stand beside me. "Looks like you're having a productive morning."

Twitchy snickers. None of the guys like my dad very much because of the way he treats Tommy. I don't really like him for that either, but, well . . . he's my dad.

I look up at Stan. Tommy said he was there when Mr. Uyeda was shot. The internal police held him and Mr. K. all night for questioning and didn't let them go until it was time for them to register.

Now the Katsumotos are No-Nos, like us.

Like our dad. And probably the rest of the crowd too.

But Stan's still here, with his friends. So is Tommy. And so am I.

My dad's eyes narrow at Stan. "The ketos are never going to listen to us if we're not united."

"So you're harassing the cooks." Stan's words are pleasant, but his tone cuts. "Great strategy, Mr. Harano. I feel more united already."

My dad glares at him, but it's me and Tommy he barks at: "Tommy, Aiko, *go home.*"

"But Dad—" Tommy begins. There are tears in his eyes and a waver in his voice.

Don't cry, I think. *Dad hates it when you cry. Especially in front of people.*

"*Now!*" our dad shouts.

But Tommy doesn't move, the tendons in his neck sticking out with his effort to hold back the tears, until Twitchy nudges him gently. "We've got this, Tommy. It's okay."

The sack of potatoes makes a scraping sound as we slide it back onto the truck.

Tommy's fists are tight at his sides as we walk away from the crowd. Tears make streaks down his face, but he doesn't bother trying to hide them now.

I take his hand, which, after a moment, relaxes into mine.

• • •

The tenth day after the shooting, all the military police except one guard at the gate are withdrawn, and for a while, it seems like things are going to return to normal.

Except it's like the shooting broke something in camp, and nothing can fix it.

Some people return to their jobs after a while, but for others, Mr. Uyeda's murder was the last straw, and they're finished cooperating with the Caucasians. For months, our dad doesn't go to work at the hog farm. Instead, he meets with other No-Nos to talk about how they can protect themselves. In the streets, there are arguments between "loyals" and "disloyals." They say we're troublemakers. They say we're ungrateful for all the things America has given us. There's talk of shipping us off to another camp, maybe a prison camp like Santa Fe, which is run by the Department of Justice, not the WRA.

One Sunday in April, a reverend is attacked for being a No-No. A couple days later, some people find the guys who jumped him and chase them down with two-by-fours whittled into clubs.

Some people stop talking to me because I'm from a No-No family. I feel their cold stares on me at school and in the dining halls.

More and more, the camp separates. We're being wedged apart by the Caucasians and their questionnaires, by guys like "Old Issei," who wrote that editorial saying all the No-Nos should be shunned, and guys like my dad, who say the Yes-Yeses are sniveling cowards.

But us Japantown kids stick together.

We walk to school as a group, No-Nos and Yes-Yeses both. We eat dinner on the same block, usually the Katsumotos', because Mrs. K. works there, and she knows how to turn the limited rations the administration gives us into nice Japanese meals.

Mas organizes basketball games on the weekends. When Yum-yum hears I'm failing math, she offers to tutor me, and my parents actually agree, because one thing they hate more than Yes-Yeses is bad grades. One Friday night, Bette invites all the girls to her barrack, where she makes us try on lipsticks and rouges and talk about who we have a thing for.

I don't really like it—I don't think anyone does, except Bette—but everyone humors her. Luckily, Mary Katsumoto is there too, and she's so grumpy and annoyed that it makes the rest of us laugh.

I like it better when Twitchy teaches me and Keiko to pick the locks on the iceboxes where the commissary keeps its produce and cheeses. I can hardly believe he lets me tag along, but when I say I want to come, he just winks at me and ruffles my hair. "Delinquent in the making, huh? Don't tell your brother."

At the beginning of May, the night before Mas, Frankie, and Twitchy leave for basic training with the 442nd Regimental Combat Team, Shig throws a party. Mrs. Ito clears out of the barrack to spend the evening with her knitting club, and the boys have the whole place to themselves. They mix up some punch from water, dissolved jellies, and slices of fresh fruit I bet Twitchy stole from the commissary. They stack the beds against the walls and set out chairs for the wallflowers.

Best of all, they let me come.

I'm the youngest kid here, but I don't mind. I sit off to the side with Minnow, who's got his sketchbook in his lap.

I've always resented Minnow—a little bit, at least—because he got to hang around with the Japantown guys, even though he's only a year older than me and can't even help them out in a brawl.

Since they've started inviting me to stuff, though, I've started hating him a little less.

Now he's drawing the dancers, legs kicking, skirts flying. Everyone's just a few squiggles, but somehow, he's getting down every leap, every dip.

"Say, you're really good," I tell him.

He glances at me, smiling shyly.

"You should be on the *Rambler* staff or something," I continue. "I bet they could use a guy like you on the school newspaper."

Mary Katsumoto slumps down between us, arms crossed like she isn't having any fun at all.

"What's the matter?" I ask.

She glares at me, even though I know she's not mad . . . not at me, anyway. "Stan didn't let me bring a book."

By nine o'clock, the apartment is so full, you can barely hear the sound of Mas's Silvertone radio playing in the corner. People are laughing and talking and dancing, and when someone complains how hot it is, I get up to wrestle open the windows while Twitchy sidles over to the punch bowl with a flask in his hands.

When I sit back down again, Tommy won't let me have any more to drink, so I watch the others.

Keiko stands in the doorway, flapping the back of her shirt in the cool night air, while Twitchy stands next to her, close but not touching. He's always real careful around Keiko, I've noticed, like she's a queen and if he touched her by accident, he'd have to chop off his own hand for offending her.

. . . Except when they return to the dance floor, and their hands are all over each other.

I look around for Mary, trying to catch her eye, but she's curled up in the corner, reading one of Mas's books.

"—thinking of applying for resettlement," Shig is saying on the other side of the room. "It's time to get outta here. Maybe I'll go to Chicago, the City of Light!"

Bette fluffs her blond wig. "That's New York, you dolt."

"New York's the City That Never Sleeps." Yum-yum laughs.

Bette looks dismayed. "But it has all those lights!"

Frankie chuckles, but he's watching Bette like he'd still adore her, no matter what she said. I don't think she notices.

"Having fun, Aiko?" Mas sits down next to me. His shoulders are so wide, he has to scoot over so he doesn't crowd me.

I nod so hard, I'm afraid my head's going to topple right off my neck. "It's a great party!" I say a little too enthusiastically. "Are you excited? About leaving tomorrow?"

He shrugs. For a second, I think he's going to do that thing boys do when they try to act tough, but he doesn't. Mas doesn't need to *act* tough, because he *is* tough. "More nervous than excited, I think."

Nervous? Mas Ito? "Why?" I ask.

He laces his fingers together and stares at the floor for a second before looking back at me. "You know how, after Pearl Harbor, it felt like everyone in America was watching us? And it felt like we had to be extra careful not to give anyone the idea that we still had ties to Japan? Because if we slipped up, it didn't just mean that *we* were un-American, it meant that *everyone*—our family, our friends, *everyone* —was un-American and didn't belong here?"

I nod solemnly. It makes me think about how our mom and dad treat Tommy, too, how they act like everything he does or doesn't do represents *them* somehow, even though Tommy's his own person.

"It's going to be like that, I think," Mas says. "But . . . more."

"Don't worry," I say loyally. "You're going to be the best soldiers the army's ever had."

He smiles, but it's strained at the corners. "We'd better be."

Before I can say anything else, Bette calls him over. She's corralling the guys off to one side so she can take a photo with the camera she ordered back in February. Frankie glares at her. Stan Katsumoto's wearing a smirk like it's an old comfortable jacket. Mas stands at the center of them all, beaming, with each of his brothers under one arm. Shig's laughing, but if you're paying attention, you can see he's gripping Mas so tight, it's like he doesn't ever want to let go. Minnow's hand is out, trying to pass a folded piece of paper to Twitchy, who's pulling faces at the camera.

Tommy's in the foreground, smiling like he never smiles when he's with the family, because here, no one expects him to be something he isn't. Here, he's accepted just as he is.

Just as we all are.

Have you ever noticed how cranky people get in the heat? It's like the hotter it is, the meaner they get. In June, two guys get in a fight with rocks and razors. A week later, there's a brawl in one of the rec centers. People are taking bets on where the government is going to send the No-Nos.

Heart Mountain, in Wyoming?

Amache, in Colorado?

Jerome, in Arkansas?

I don't think it matters where we're sent. They just want us gone, even kids like me who weren't old enough to answer the loyalty questionnaire for ourselves.

To make matters worse, without Mas, the group just kind of dissolves. First, Shig takes over Twitchy's job driving the commissary truck, but my parents won't let Tommy join them. Then Yum-yum starts working at the summer camp my dad won't allow me to go to, and Keiko gets a job at the commissary office, so hardly anyone's around anyway. There are no more basketball games, no more girls' nights, at least not that I'm invited to.

It's only Yuki who keeps some of us together. She wants to improve her batting average for next season, so she ropes me and Mary into practicing with her.

As much as I love softball, though, I can't really get excited about it. I'm going to be in tenth grade, which means I'll be old enough to play with them on the new high school team . . . if the government hasn't sent us No-Nos to another camp by then.

Plus, Dad still has my bat.

The adults and boys usually take up the baseball diamonds on Blocks 15 and 21, and they never let us play, so we have to use the recreation area between Block 36 and the fence.

"That's where Mr. Uyeda got shot," Mary points out.

"I know." Yuki bites her lip. "But where else can we go?"

By July, though, we're tired of drills. We want to play a real game.

And I want the group back together.

It takes some wheedling, but I convince everybody to meet on the Block 15 baseball diamond. With nine of the Japantown kids left in Topaz, we've got a team, and Yuki's bossy enough to make the boys who are already there agree to play us.

I mean, it's not like we'll win. Bette's chatting with a couple boys in the outfield. Tommy's dropped every ball that's come his way.

Minnow couldn't hit the broad side of a barn. At third base, Shig's not even that great, even though he makes up for it in trash talk.

It's lucky we've got Yuki behind home plate in the catching gear we borrowed from the rec center. And Mary, who's playing shortstop like usual, fields everything between second and third.

Keiko's the biggest surprise, playing first base. She just has to stretch out her glove, and the ball goes straight into it, like it's effortless. She doesn't even have to look.

But me, Yuki, Mary, and Keiko aren't enough to carry the team. By the fifth inning, we're down seven to two. At third, Shig's smacking his mitt and chattering, "*Hey,* batter-batter-batter, *swing,* batter-batter—"

He stops abruptly at a commotion behind him in the barracks. Someone's *shrieking.*

It's a man, I realize, as a figure comes scrabbling out from behind the recreation building. He's off-balance, clawing at the dust.

Seconds later, two guys come running after him. They're kicking him into the dirt. This far off, I can't hear him grunt, but his body makes a sharp angle like the wind's gone out of him.

I'm thinking a million things at once.

Is he a No-No?

Are they?

Does it matter?

What would Mas do?

I take off before anyone can stop me. I race past Mary, who's watching me, dumbfounded, the ball still clasped in her throwing hand.

"Ike, wait!" Shig cries.

I ignore him.

The attackers don't notice me coming up behind them, which I guess gives me the advantage of surprise, but what am I going to do? They're grown men, and I'm just a girl.

But before I reach them, the ball comes whizzing past me. *Thwock!* It strikes one of the attackers' shoulders, making him crumple.

I glance behind me. Mary's thrown down her glove, and she's running for them now, her face set like she's going to bowl them both over if they get in her way.

Everyone else is with her too. Shig's closest, but Keiko and Stan aren't far behind, and even Bette's running in from right field, her black hair flying out behind her.

Then I'm there in the attackers' faces, my lips peeled back from my teeth in a snarl as mean as Frankie's, yelling at them to back off.

It's a good thing Twitchy taught me how to punch. Maybe I can hit one of them hard enough to knock him out of the fight.

The men hesitate. Maybe they're wondering if they can beat up a girl.

But I'm not just a girl anymore.

I'm all of us. Shig and Mary are right there beside me. And Stan and Keiko and Tommy and Minnow and Bette and Yuki, who's got a *bat!*

She's screaming, "Leave him alone!" Bette's trying to calm her down, but she just raises the bat like she'll crack them good if they try to cross her.

I thought I'd get a kick out of seeing us together ready to brawl, but I don't. I mean, we're just *kids*. We should be playing the game. Why can't they just let us *play the game?*

The attackers turn and run. We watch their retreating forms turn the corner of the rec center.

Tommy and Minnow help the guy on the ground to his feet. There's blood coming from his nose, speckling his shirt.

"That was pretty stupid, Ike," Shig says, but he's grinning. "Frankie would be proud."

Stan rolls his eyes. "'Cause we should all be worried about what *Frankie Fujita* thinks."

His remark doesn't bother me, though, because we *do* care what Frankie would think, just like we care what Twitchy or Mas or any of us thinks.

I smile, but it doesn't feel like a real smile, because the game is over. Shig and Stan help the beat-up guy to the hospital. Everyone else just kind of drifts off until only Yuki and I are left.

"You okay, Ike?" she asks.

Not looking at her, I grind the tip of the bat into the dust. "We lost."

The next day, we get the news. We know for sure. Segregation's going to start in September, and all the No-Nos are going to be shipped off to Tule Lake in California.

All through August, we pack. Our dad and Tommy take lumber from the scrap piles and refashion it into crates. Our mom goes through the barrack, tagging items for Tule Lake, for friends we want to leave them to, for the trash.

It reminds me of the days before we left San Francisco, only this time, we have less. We don't have Tommy's phonograph or his record collection. We don't have a decade of comic books. We don't have Fumi and Frannie's kokeshi dolls or our mom's shamisen she brought from Japan.

But it still hurts. It's like we're pulling up our roots, coming out of the dry soil, all our fragile threads breaking.

Snap! There goes the softball team I could've belonged to.

Pop! That's Tommy's hopes of getting into college.

Worst of all, the next time we're all together in the dining hall, Bette announces that she's going to apply for resettlement.

"I just have to fill out a form," Bette says with a shrug that looks like she practiced it in the mirror. "Since the WRA's set up field offices all over the country, I don't have to have a sponsor or a job or anything. I don't even have to wait for a background check like they used to."

Like they used to before the loyalty questionnaire, she means.

I clench my fists.

She can do this because *she* said "Yes" and "Yes."

"Just one form," she repeats gaily, "a photo ID, and, Bob's your uncle, I'm a free woman!"

"How *could* you?" I shout.

Bette blinks. "Aiko, I don't—"

"You could have *waited!*" I explode out of my seat, towering over her, fists shaking. I don't know when I've been this mad. "You could have *waited* for us to leave before you broke us up!"

"Aiko," Shig says in that easy, reasonable voice of his, "c'mon, you know she didn't—"

I shrug him off angrily. "But you just couldn't *wait* for us to be gone, could you? You just *had* to get out of here sooner than that!" She's staring at me. There are tears in her eyes, but I don't care. "Well, we don't *need* you!"

I storm out.

The wind swirls around me, blowing me back a few steps before I charge forward again.

I don't know where I'm going. I just want to go somewhere.

No, a little voice inside me says. *I want to stay. I want everyone to stay.*

I don't make it very far when someone catches up to me. It's Keiko. I can tell from how she kind of sways when she walks, but not in an annoying way like Bette. I let her walk with me.

The sun sets. Overhead, the sky is a blaze of reds and oranges, like the world is burning down around us.

"Everyone's leaving," I say.

I'm not looking at her, but I think she shrugs. "Everyone always does."

I remember belatedly that her mom and dad are still gone. And Twitchy. For a second, I feel guilty and stupid, but then I'm angry again, and I stop in the middle of the street. "But it's not *fair,*" I say.

One of her eyebrows goes up, and she flicks her fingers like she's brushing away a bit of lint. "Life's not fair, Ike. Haven't you figured that out by now?"

My face twists again in the way that Mom hates, but I can't help it. I don't want to cry in front of Keiko.

I just . . . want things to be *fair,* and they're *not,* and I can't stop them.

I couldn't stop Japan from attacking Hawaii. I couldn't stop the U.S. from locking us up and pitting us against each other. I couldn't stop Mas and Frankie and Twitchy from leaving.

Or Bette.

Or anybody.

I want to believe that if I were bigger, or older, or stronger, or a boy, or a superhero from one of my comic books, I'd have been able to do something. Stop something. Punch a bad guy. Storm into the

White House. Shield Mr. Uyeda. Stand up to my dad. Snap the fences. *Something.*

But I don't think that's true either. I want to believe in superheroes, but I think some things are just too big for one person, even a super one.

And that's *not* fair. That's *not fair.* That's *not fair.*

Keiko keeps walking, and I trail after her, hiccupping, trying not to let the tears fall, trying not to let her see that I'm not as tough as her.

Because Keiko is *really* tough. Not in the way that Frankie's tough. Not in the way that Mary or Bette is tough.

She's kind of *weathered,* if you know what I mean. She's like one of those bonsai trees Mr. Hidekawa used to collect from the Sierras, all curved and windblown and beaten down by snow, but graceful and *strong.* Life's not fair, but she doesn't need it to be fair, because she can take anything life throws at her, and she won't break.

A little over three weeks after Bette submits her resettlement paperwork, she gets her indefinite leave clearance.

Indefinite leave. That means she doesn't have to come back. Ever.

She says goodbye to us at the Main Gate. "I'll write," she says, tweaking my chin gently.

Then, without a party or anything to mark the departure of yet another of us, she hops on a bus to Delta, where she'll board a train to New York.

I hope she's happy there in the big city, under the bright lights.

The night before we leave, I can't sleep. Even when I close my eyes, all I see is the barren apartment. The empty shelves. The hungry closet.

For hours, I flop and turn, curling and uncurling, my cot creaking under me.

I don't know what time it is when my dad gets up, but the light through the windows, which no longer have curtains, is blue and cold as he walks across the floor. He's standing in the doorway, and all I can see is the back of him. Tight shoulders. And my baseball bat in his hand.

I sit up. I don't know where he's going. There hasn't been an attack in days. There's no one to retaliate against. No one to hurt.

But maybe he's like me.

Maybe he wants to do *something*. Break something. Make a statement. Say, *This isn't right.* Say, *I'm not okay.* Say, *Goddamn you for all of this.*

"Dad," I say.

He freezes, one hand on the doorknob. "Go back to sleep, Aiko."

I stand, ignoring him. The Masonite is cold and smooth under my bare soles. "Give me the bat," I say.

He almost turns. I almost see his face. "What?"

I advance on him, padding slowly across the blue-tinged floor. "It's mine. It's for baseball. It's for *games*. It's not for . . . for whatever you're planning." I extend my hand, fingers trembling. "Give it to me."

I don't say "please." I don't need to.

He owes me this.

Or, well, *someone* owes me *something*, and if it can't be any of the other things that would bring us back together in this stupid world, then it might as well be my baseball bat.

He doesn't hand it over, though—he drops it, and it lands on the floor with a clatter, bouncing a little from knob to end cap.

Frannie and Fumi start crying.

Our dad walks out the door.

As Mom and Tommy get up to comfort the twins, I collect my bat and crawl back into bed, leaning the bat against the side of the cot, where I grip it tight.

Slowly, the barrack quiets down again, and everyone drifts back to sleep.

Except for me. I stay awake for a long time, clutching that baseball bat. Under my fingers, the wood has been worn smooth from all the times we played pickup games or Three Flies Up, from all those hands that have touched it, and I wonder if they've left their mark somehow, soaked into the grain like sweat or blood or love—Mas's hands, Frankie's hands, Twitchy's, Bette's, Yuki's, Yum-yum's, Keiko's, Shig's and Minnow's and Stan's and Mary's hands.

And my hands.

And Tommy's hands.

I fall asleep like that, one hand closed around my bat, and I'm still holding on when I wake.

POST CARD

CORRESPONDENCE

ADDRESS

Dearest Sister,

   Alas! I'm still sleeping on
our brother's couch. Today, when
I inquired about a flat on the
West Side, the landlady took one
look at me and said, "No dogs . . .
or Japs!" and slammed the door
in my face. The nerve! Just wait
till I'm rich and famous and
buy the building right out from
under her — ha! Then she'll see.
But enough dreaming for now.
Miss you always.

                              xoxo,
                              Bette

NEW YORK, NEW YORK
OCT 15
4-PM
1943

2 CENTS UNITED STATES POSTAGE

NATIONS UNITED FOR VICTORY

Yuki Nakano
19—2—CD
Topaz, UT

VIII

WITH A CHERRY ON TOP

YUKI, 16
OCTOBER 1943

I'm waiting at the Main Gate with the other girls as the bus drives in. I'm so excited, I can't stop smiling, even when my cheeks start to hurt.

It's our first away game since we arrived in Topaz, and I am *ready*. Last year, things were too disorganized, everyone was still too scared of us, and no one cared enough about girls' sports to give us a proper team. But this year, we've taken our destiny into our own hands. Not only have we organized a girls' high school softball team, but we're also playing in a real league like anybody else.

What a wonder, I think, to be like anybody else! Overhead, the nearby watchtower is empty. In fact, since the No-Nos left camp, every one of the watchtowers is empty. The gates are left unlocked all day and night, with only one guard on duty at the Main Gate after sunset. Best of all, we can come and go as we please. I squeeze through the strands of barbed wire on my daily conditioning runs. Last weekend, Mother and Father even took Bachan and me on a family picnic in the desert. Bette would have hated it—Sitting on the ground! All those bugs!—but Bette's in New York now, and it just felt so *normal*. Like,

160

after all the restrictions and the evacuation and the questionnaire and everything, we were finally regular Americans again.

Now we get to play Delta High, the closest school to ours, and show them that we're just as good at the old American pastime too.

Since they're basically our neighbors, the Delta Rabbits are our de facto rivals, but the Topaz teams love playing *any* Caucasians. We like beating them. We like hearing about *other* teams beating them in the news briefs from the other WRA camps. It's like we've got something to prove, since we're shorter and smaller and under-equipped and all that.

Not that I hate Caucasians or anything. I don't hate anyone. Like, our coach, Miss Jenkins, is great. She's one of the elementary school teachers who lives in the staff housing on the south side of camp. She has mousy-brown hair and porcelain skin Bette used to complain about all the time. *How does she do it? Does she have no pores?* Miss J. is also probably one of the nicest people ever, although she's probably *too* nice, if you know what I mean. She's lucky she's a good coach, or no one would ever listen to her.

We clamber onto the bus, laughing and gabbing, and our bus driver, Mr. Gregson, nods at each of us as we board. "Afternoon, young ladies."

"Hiya, Mr. G." I flash him a grin and slump into the second seat, behind Miss J.

"Feeling good about the game today?" he asks.

I like Mr. Gregson, too. He lives in Delta, but he does a lot of the driving and work on the buses for the camp, so he's here all the time. If you aren't paying attention, he looks like he's always cross, because there are all these lines on his forehead, and his mouth is always turned down at the corners like an upside-down melon rind, but his blue eyes are always twinkling with humor. I know he's got kids at Delta Junior High, but I like to think he's secretly rooting for us.

I nod as he starts the engine. "You bet!"

We rumble through the Main Gate, onto the dirt road that leads to Delta, and the girls let out a cheer. Across from me, Aki "Mori" Morikawa, our star chucker, pops her gum and winks at me.

I laugh. I like a lot of things about softball, but my favorite is that *zing* in the air before a game, like the other girls and I are electric, and sparks are flying from our feet and fingertips, and no matter what else is going on in school or camp or whatever, I'm *sure,* at that moment, that we just can't lose.

Most of the team is fixing their hair for the game, because we can't show up looking like a bunch of slobs, but every so often, someone starts up a cheer to teach the new girls, the ones who have only just gotten to senior high school or the ones we had to get to replace our No-Nos, like Mary Katsumoto.

"Hey, Rams!" Jane "Abunai" Inai calls, half standing in her seat. *"What's that sound in the air, I wonder?"*

The rest of us start chanting, *"It's the Rams, 'cause we hit like thunder!"*

"What's that flash in the sky so frightening?"

We're stomping on the floor now, our cries echoing off the metal ceiling, and good old Mr. Gregson is just tapping his hand on the steering wheel. *"It's the Rams, 'cause we run like lightning!"*

"Boom! Rabbits, you're gonna get beat!"

"Aki Morikawa's bringing the heat!"

Then it starts all over again for a different girl, until we've gone through the whole lineup, and we all go back to talking and fixing our hair as we pass the chicken and hog farms that line the road to Delta.

● ● ●

Delta's a sleepy little town, at least compared to San Francisco, but to us, who've been cooped up in camp for so long, the main drag is like a metropolitan paradise, even though I don't think Bette would agree. There's a deli, a secondhand store, a Bank of America, and Smith Grocery and Fountain, and everything closes at six p.m. As we roll down Main Street, I watch the Smith Grocery shop clerk serving up ice cream cones to a couple of blond-haired, pigtailed girls.

Boy, do I miss real ice cream. The prepackaged Eskimo Pies and Good Humor bars at the co-op store just aren't the same—and that's if you can get them, because even if you wait in line for an hour, they still might sell out.

By the time we reach the high school, the whole team's buzzing with excitement. Quickly, we grab our gear from under the bus and start trotting toward the visitor dugout.

Except for me. I stop at the edge of the diamond with my chest protector and shin guards dangling from one hand, my mitt and helmet from the other, and I take a long, deep breath.

Mary and I used to do this before each game, just take it all in. The blue of the sky. The *crack* of the bat. I used to joke that this should be one of our inalienable rights: life, liberty, and softball. She used to roll her eyes.

The other girls are beginning to warm up. I guess our replacements aren't bad, but our infield could've been better, I think, with Mary and Aiko, but they're in Tule Lake by now. I wonder if they're playing ball out there.

I hope so. I hope they're showing those Tuleans how Topaz does things.

I kneel in the grass—it's real grass here, not Topaz dust—and touch the ground. The blades scratch my palm, prickly as Mary herself. "Wish you were here," I say.

My fingers catch on something smooth and cool. It's a nickel, half-overgrown with grass. I pick it up, rubbing dirt from its faces. It feels like a sign.

Standing, I flick the coin into the air and catch it again before jogging off toward the rest of the team. *Here we go,* I think. *Can't lose.*

Aki and I throw the ball around a bit to loosen up before we really get into it, and then it's *thwack! thwack! thwack!* Ball after ball strikes my mitt. It feels good. It feels right.

Once it's game time, we all stand for the national anthem, and as we salute the flag, I wonder how often Mas and the boys hear this song at Camp Shelby. I picture them on the parade grounds in perfect rows, except for Twitchy, who probably fidgets and makes faces at Frankie through the whole thing.

Then the Delta girls trot out onto the field, and we gather in the dugout, ready to take our turns at bat.

Thanks to Mary and Aiko's help, I'm batting cleanup this year, which is pretty great, if I do say so myself. I worked my butt off all summer, and it's nice to have something to show for it.

Boy, are the Rabbits going to be surprised.

I take my place on the bench as our leadoff hitter, Jane "Abunai" Inai goes up to bat.

"Abunai!" we shout. "Abunaaaaaai!" *Danger! Daaaaanger!*

She looks so glamorous in the on-deck circle, with long eyelashes, big hips, and a swagger like one of the boys. Before she steps into the batter's box, she glances over her shoulder and gives us a wink.

We start cheering and whistling, howling up a storm.

There's that feeling again, like we're lightning about to fork down out of the sky, like we're going to leave scorch marks in our tracks.

I touch the nickel in my pocket for extra luck. *Can't lose.*

I lied. My favorite thing about softball is the feeling *after* the game, when you know you've held nothing back—you've obliterated the competition, and you're on top of the world because you gave it everything you had, and everything you had was more than good enough.

We *destroy* the Rabbits. We beat them *seventeen* to *three*. We're better on defense. We're quicker to the ball. Aki strikes out one after another, the Delta girls swinging and missing every trick pitch. Jane lives up to her nickname and gets on base every time she's at bat. I hit a grand slam in the third inning—my first ever!—and they shout my nickname as I round the bases, blowing kisses to my teammates.

"Yeah, Whitey!"

We're like queens out there. No, like *goddesses.* We dominate the diamond.

When we get back, I plan on telling Minnow all about it. The *Topaz Times* never really cares about girls' sports, but Minnow's on the staff of the high school *Rambler* this year, doing drawings for them, and I'm going to make sure the camp hears about this, one way or another!

The sun is setting by the time we all scramble back onto the bus, sweaty and victorious and loud. "Good job, young ladies," Mr. Gregson says with one of his slim smiles.

I climb into my seat near the front and congratulate the rest of the team as they pass.

"You did great today, Yuki," Miss Jenkins says, taking her usual place in front of me as Mr. Gregson drives off.

"Thanks, Miss J.!"

"If you keep this up, you could play for the All-American Girls Professional Baseball League one day."

"Me? Not a chance," I say, laughing. "Those girls are the greats."

I read about the AAGPBL in Father's newspapers over the summer: the Belles, the Blue Sox, the Comets, the Peaches, Helen "Nickie" Nicol, Dorothy "Kammie" Kamenshek, Gladys "Terrie" Davis.

Miss Jenkins tilts her head. "Who knows? You could be one of the greats too."

Grinning, I lean back, imagining myself in a Peaches uniform. *Yuki "Whitey" Nakano,* because my first name means "snow" in Japanese. Through the windows, there's another one of those blazing Utah sunsets, the colors melting together like sherbet.

Like ice cream.

"It's almost six o'clock!" I cry, bolting upright.

Miss Jenkins glances back at me, one thin eyebrow arched quizzically. "So?"

"So it's almost closing time at Smith Grocery! What d'you say we make a stop for some ice cream, Miss J.?"

"Yeah!" Aki cries. She begins pounding on the seatback, chanting, "Ice cream! Ice cream!"

The rest of the team joins her. *"Ice cream! Ice cream!"*

Miss Jenkins looks flustered, her pale face turning pink. "Girls!" she cries.

"Don't you think we deserve a *little* treat for our hard work?" I ask in my most reasonable *Don't be unreasonable, Miss Jenkins* voice. "It was a good day, right? We won—no, we *crushed*—our first away game—"

There's a chorus of whoops from the girls.

Miss Jenkins bites her lip, but I can tell she's starting to cave. "I don't know . . ."

"Please?" I ask, doing my best impression of Bette, who can charm anyone into anything. "Pretty please? With a cherry on top?"

She glances at Mr. Gregson in the rearview mirror. He shrugs, though his eyes are smiling.

"All right!" she says at last. "All right, you've convinced me!"

We cheer.

"But you're not all going in," she adds, attempting to be stern. "Smith Grocery doesn't need you girls invading its aisles ten minutes before closing."

We groan.

"Except for *you,* Yuki." Miss Jenkins points at me. "You want to be the ringleader; you can come with me and carry the ice cream back for the rest of the team. What do you girls want?"

In a sudden flurry, everyone begins combing through coin purses and calling out orders. I grin as Miss Jenkins frantically scribbles everything on the back of our lineup.

We pull up alongside Smith Grocery with seven minutes to spare. From outside, the shop seems to glow with this yellow light, like a paper lantern or something. Inside, past the weekly deals and mark-down notices, I can see the clerk in his white apron, wiping down the counter. He has a ruddy face and a few wisps of brownish-gray hair sticking out from under his paper soda-jerk hat, with blue eyes like Mr. Gregson's.

Miss Jenkins and I hop off the bus. I'm so excited, I can barely keep from skipping into the store and doing a pirouette in the middle of the checkered floor.

The bell above us jingles as we enter the shop. The clerk looks over at us, but I only have eyes for the ice cream case: luscious chocolate, pale-pink strawberry, creamy butter pecan . . .

But when I glance up again, I recoil.

The man behind the counter is glaring at me, his eyes hard as chips of glass.

I glance over my shoulder. He's probably seen the bus outside and doesn't want to serve anyone so near closing time, I guess. But I don't think seventeen scoops of ice cream — because we're getting one for Mr. Gregson, too, obviously — is really all that bad, is it?

I let Miss Jenkins do the talking, since she's a pretty white lady, and stand with my hands behind my back as we approach the counter, like I can make myself less intimidating that way.

"Good evening," Miss Jenkins says brightly, even though the man doesn't seem to hear her. "I hope it's not too late to get some ice cream. The girls just won their game, and . . ."

Her voice kind of peters out at the end as she realizes the man isn't even looking at her.

He's looking at me.

I'm already pretty small — in the AAGPBL, they could call me Yuki "Shorty" Nakano — but as the man glares at me, I wish I could make myself smaller. I take a step back.

"Um . . ." Miss Jenkins clears her throat and glances at the slip of paper with our orders on it. "One strawberry on a sugar cone, please, two fudge ripples in cups, one chocolate on a waffle cone . . ."

The clerk's face is getting red now, redder and redder with every second, his eyes turning sharp and dangerous.

Abunai, I think.

I try to stop her, tugging her sleeve. "C'mon, Miss J., let's just go, okay?"

But she ignores me, or doesn't hear me, or doesn't want to, because she keeps going, "One chocolate chip with a cherry on—"

"WE DON'T SERVE JAPS HERE!" he bellows, like he can't hold it in anymore. His voice is so loud, it echoes in my head.

JAPS

JAPS

JAPS

Unlike an echo, it doesn't get any softer.

I stagger backwards a little, blinking. This isn't the big city, where Bette gets called "Jap" by strangers. The Deltans *know* us. They work alongside us. They've played on our baseball diamonds. They've performed talent pageants for us, same as we've done for them. They know we've never done anything wrong.

How can they *still* hate us?

Miss Jenkins stiffens like she's the one who's been called a dirty word. She grabs my hand so tight that at first I think I've done something wrong.

But then I see her teary, scared-looking face, and I know I haven't done anything. Angrily, I jerk out of her grasp and storm outside. Overhead, the bell jingles dissonantly in my ears.

Miss Jenkins is sobbing as we walk back to the curb. It's fully dark now, the sky a sort of mulberry purple. Behind us, I hear the door lock with an audible *click*. I don't turn around. I don't want to see his blood-filled face, his hateful eyes.

"That man!" Miss Jenkins is saying, her voice weepy. "That horrible man! I'm so sorry, Yuki—"

I cut her off. "Stop crying, Miss Jenkins." Like I'm the adult and she's the kid. Like I'm scolding her for something she should've known. Because shouldn't she have known? "Let's just get back to camp, okay?" I try to soften my voice, like she's the one who needs protecting, even though she's the one who's older.

And white.

I don't know why, but I kind of hate her for that. For being white. For putting me in that position. For not standing up for me. For being so weak that *I* have to be the strong one.

I kind of hate her the way I hate the clerk. And the girls of the All-American League, because I know now I'll never play with them. And I hate myself a little bit too, for thinking it could've been any other way.

Nodding, Miss Jenkins hiccups a few times and wipes her eyes. I glare at the back of her head as she boards the bus in silence.

Mr. Gregson watches me solemnly as I climb the steps. "I'm sorry, young lady," he says.

"Yeah." I don't look him in the eyes when I say it. He's got blue eyes, like the man behind the counter. Without a word, I sink as low as I can into my seat, where I can't be seen.

I thought things were normal again. I thought I couldn't lose.

But maybe it's my fault, because it took me until now to realize it —as long as *this* is our normal, people like me can *always* lose.

The sky has been drained of all color now, and in the darkness, the only sign that we're nearing camp is the sour miasma of livestock. Through the window, I see the silhouette of the Main Gate watchtower.

Laying my forehead against the glass, I stare at the camp grounds as the bus stops and the engine dies.

The guards may be gone, but the towers and the cattle fences haven't been torn down. The camp hasn't been dismantled. We may have said "Yes" and "Yes" to the questionnaire, but we're still *here*.

I collect my gear, shivering. If they still treat *us* like this, what is it going to be like for Mary and Aiko, in the segregation camp with all the *Japs* who refused to say they were loyal to this country?

Tule Lake Segregation Center, California

IX

HUNKY-DORY WHATEVER

MARY, 16
OCTOBER 1943

Tule Lake doesn't even have proper buses to take us from the train depot to the Segregation Center. Instead, we're prodded onto army trucks, where we shiver under the canvas canopies as armed soldiers slam the tailgates behind us, slapping the siding to let the drivers know we're ready for shipment.

Mom jumps.

If this had been a bus, I would be slumped against the window, watching the barren scenery go by, but I have to settle for slouching, legs spread like a boy.

Dad makes a disapproving sound, but I don't care what he thinks.

"You think Mas rides a truck like this at Camp Shelby?" my brother Paul, who's eleven, asks as we begin to rattle and jolt down the road.

"Yeah," says our older brother, Stan, "and so do POWs."

"What's a POW?"

"A prisoner of war."

I don't think the irony of Stan's comment is lost on anyone, even Paul, whose enthusiasm wilts into silence. The other families in the truck shift uncomfortably as the road unravels behind us like a loose gray ribbon, flapping aimlessly in our wake.

As we pull into Tule Lake, someone in the back of the truck lets out a whimper of dismay.

The fences here are three times as tall as the ones at Topaz, made of chain links and topped with barbed wire, in case someone wants to try escaping, I guess, and the guard towers are even taller than that.

Oh yeah, and there are tanks. I count six of them before we've even left the trucks: squat, greenish-gray things with machine guns mounted on top.

"Can someone say 'overkill'?" Stan mutters to me.

Mom shushes him.

Before, I would've laughed. Now I ignore him and jump from the truck before anyone else can get out. The ground is swampy with rain, and the mud splatters my pants when I land.

Tule Lake is composed of the same tarpaper barracks as Topaz, but as I walk toward one of the firebreaks, away from my family, who are gabbling and trying to count our luggage, the buildings seem to stretch even farther into the distance than they did in Utah.

Topaz used to hold eight thousand people. How many disloyals are they expecting here? Ten thousand? Fifteen?

It starts to drizzle, and in the subdued *pat-pat-pat* of the rain, I realize it's eerily quiet. When we arrived at Topaz, the Boy Scouts were playing marching tunes, but here, the only sounds are of slamming doors and strained voices. If you were a cheerful person like Yuki, you could appreciate Tule Lake's total lack of pretense.

But I am not cheerful.

"Mary," Dad says, interrupting my thoughts, "come help your mother."

I glance over my shoulder just long enough for him to know I heard him. Dad's mustache is in need of trimming, I notice. Over the past couple days on the train, it's grown over the edge of his upper lip, making him appear unkempt and wild.

I turn my back, ignoring him when he calls my name again.

Throughout the afternoon, the rest of the family unpacks their suitcases and settles into the new apartments the administration has assigned us.

I take one look inside and want to curl my lip in disgust. It's got the same shitty coal-burning stove, but I guess they couldn't be bothered to install any Sheetrock, because the floors are bare wood and the walls don't reach the rafters, so we can hear every sound in the whole barrack. Add the smell of manure, and we could be back in Tanforan.

I set up my cot in one corner and flop down on the lumpy army mattress, burying my face in the book I brought from Utah.

I already read it twice on the train ride here, but it's better than having to deal with my family.

"Don't bother getting up," Stan says, helping Dad sweep cobwebs from the ceiling. "We've got this."

I don't respond.

Stan doesn't have the right to complain about anything that happens in Tule Lake. It's his fault—his and Dad's—that we're here at all. Mom wanted to say "Yes" and "Yes" to the questionnaire, but *they* had an axe to grind. *They* wanted to prove something. *They* made us come here.

"Get up," Dad says.

I peer over the edge of my book. He and Stan have finished setting the table next to the stove, and he's staring at me, teeth gritted like he's trying to stop himself from shouting. Wouldn't want the neighbors to know he can't control his own daughter, I guess.

I hop off the cot and walk out the door.

"Hey, why does *she* get to leave?" Paul says.

"Mary!" Mom's voice follows me outside.

But I don't answer, and I don't stop.

When I get back, it's after dinner, and Dad's sitting at the table, smoking a pipe. While I take off my shoes at the door, Paul hops around me, asking where I've been.

"Nowhere," I say.

I'm halfway back to my cot when Dad snaps, "Clean that up."

Turning, I see a couple flecks of mud on the grimy floorboards. With a sullen look, I grab a rag from where Mom's folded them in the corner. Stan does too, and he kneels beside me. Like that'll make me forgive him for being a No-No and making us come here.

"Easy," Stan says after a moment. "You're gonna wear a hole right through the boards. What're you gonna do when Dad makes you replace the whole floor?"

I just scrub harder.

"Aiko and Tommy came by," he adds. "Ike says there's a softball team."

"Good for her," I grunt.

We finish cleaning the floor in silence, under Dad's baleful stare.

• • •

I was right. Tule Lake *is* bigger than Topaz. It's got seventy-four blocks to Topaz's thirty-six, divided into eight wards. The first seven wards are in regular formation, like the blocks at Topaz, but the eighth ward sticks out on its own at the far southeast end of camp. It's still under construction, because more No-Nos are arriving every day, but the Tuleans are already calling it "Alaska" because it's so isolated.

Tule Lake already has double the population of Topaz, and the numbers are still climbing. People say they're expecting eighteen thousand by the time the segregation is complete. *Eighteen thousand* to Topaz's eight. That's a lot of "troublemakers" in one place, if you ask me. What genius came up with that one?

The WRA has canceled school while the loyal Tuleans move out and the No-Nos move in, but Dad enrolls me in one of the ad hoc schools the Japanese cultural organizations have set up in the rec centers. "It'll be good for you," he says. "Maybe you'll learn some manners."

Every day, we speak Japanese, learn Japanese customs, do Japanese arts and crafts. It's supposed to prepare us to return to Japan, I guess, and some of the other girls love it, but I spend most of my time reading books under the table and fantasizing about putting a pair of hashi through my eyes.

I don't want to go back to Japan. I didn't even want to come to Tule Lake in the first place, only I was a few months too young to have any choice in the matter.

One day, I'm reading a novel I borrowed from the camp's English library and pretending to practice my kanji when the door at the back of the room opens and a set of footsteps echoes loudly down the center aisle. *Clop-clop-clop.* They come to a stop near my desk, and out of the corner of my eye, I spy worn leather work boots and laces that have been taped at the ends to prevent them from fraying.

Annoyed, I look up.

The interruption is a boy my age. He has wavy hair and a red-and-black plaid shirt, so neatly tucked, it's clear he's trying too hard.

As if he can sense me judging him, he glances down.

I glare at him and shove my book farther under the table.

"Yes, Mr. Tani?" the teacher asks.

But before he can answer, someone starts up. "Does anyone else smell smoke?"

The rest of us straighten, sniffing. The kids sitting by the dingy windows peer outside.

"There's a fire by the gym!" one shouts.

We charge out of the classroom, ignoring the teacher's plea for us to retain order. A bunch of boys have built a bonfire between the newly constructed gymnasium and the Induction Center, where new No-Nos are processed every day. Clutching their luggage, the arrivals blink and stare dumbly at the blaze while the administrative staff try to hurry them inside.

"Banzai!"

Laughing, the boys heave a bench onto the flaming pile.

Crash!

The crowd gasps and steps back. Sparks fly upward like butterflies.

I laugh too. Some people glare at me, but I don't care. "Banzai" is a Japanese battle cry. Stan and his friends used to say it while they were jumping out of trees or sliding down the sand dunes in old fruit crates. I don't know if these guys are trying to prove something or if they're just being dumb kids, but sure, whatever. Let's burn this place down.

"What's so funny?" someone asks.

It's the boy with the loud boots. I glower at him, hoping he'll take the hint and leave me alone.

"Mary!" From my left, Aiko appears among the other students, elbowing them aside the same way she'd wrestle to the front of a crowd at the Topaz co-op on ice cream day. Her cheeks are flushed with excitement.

I turn my back on Boots Boy. "Hey," I say to her. Aiko's just about the only person I can stand in this whole damn camp, maybe in this whole damn state. I mean, at least *she* didn't choose to be here either.

"Should we do something?" she asks.

Maybe if we'd still been in Topaz. Maybe if we had the rest of the group to back us up. But we're in *Tule Lake* now, and Stan and Tommy are both out of school. It's just Aiko and me.

So I shrug. "Why bother?"

She blinks, and I try to ignore the hurt and disappointment in her face. After a second, she says, "What about the fire department?"

Boots Boy answers from behind me: "The fire truck's been having trouble."

I scowl at him. "No one asked you."

He blinks, surprised.

"Jeez, Mary!" Aiko says. "You don't have to be so rude."

I bite back a retort.

"Banzai!"

Crash!

In the center of the yard, another bench lands in the bonfire.

Dad and I fight all the time now. It always starts out quiet: Dad hissing at me for stomping around the apartment, for not tucking in the corners of my sheets. Because God forbid any of our nosy neighbors hear that Katsumoto-san's daughter doesn't make her bed properly.

But it doesn't take long for things to escalate to Dad snapping at me for not helping around the barrack enough. I should be sweeping the floor. I should be doing the laundry. I should be giving my mother a break.

"You made me go to Japanese school, remember?" I grumble. "What's your excuse?"

Dad's face contorts into something ugly and mean. Here it comes.

"I am the head of this family!" he roars. *"You will listen to me when I—"*

What about Stan? I want to say. *I don't see you yelling at him.*

But I shut my mouth. Let Dad yell.

I don't know what Stan does—I don't even know where he is right now—but he doesn't have a job either, because the WRA cut back on jobs to save money, and Dad's not always harping at *him* about refilling the kettle or mopping the floors or whatever.

Since we've come to Tule Lake, no one's been able to find work. Mom *should* be working in the mess hall, because the food they serve stinks, literally, and there's hardly any rice because one of the cooks is stealing it for his sake still, but the old Tuleans have all the good jobs, and with the work shortage, there's no way they're giving them up to us.

"—if you don't change your attitude—" Dad's still shouting. He slams his fist on the table. *Something something.* *"—intolerable—"* *Something something.* *"—ungrateful—"*

I throw down the coal bucket. *Grateful?* There's a leak in the ceiling, and we have to put a cup under it to collect the water when it rains. *For this?*

He's still yelling at me as I jam my arms into my coat and my feet into my shoes and storm out the door. Surreptitiously, our neighbors peer through their windows. They want to see Katsumoto-san's ungrateful daughter, I guess. But I'm too mad to care, and soon I'm too far away for them to spy on me anymore.

Outside, the camp is gray. Everything is gray here. The gunmetal gray of the tanks. The gray of the silt from the old shallow lakebed where the camp now stands. The gray of smoke from the coal stoves. Primitive street lamps buzz and flicker from their brackets on the sides of the barracks, illuminating gray streets and gray walls and nothing else.

In San Francisco, you'd be able to see every street lit up like it was Christmas, crossing signals flashing red and yellow and green, windows glowing with life from within. There'd be the sounds of cable-car bells, the foghorns in the distance, people yelling and moaning and listening to *Your Hit Parade*.

Here, there's nothing. *Because* we're *nothing*, I think.

Bang. Somewhere nearby, there's a sound like something dull striking something hard. Like a fist against a door, maybe.

I look around, frowning.

Bang. It's regular, not like that beating we saw back at Topaz, punching and kicking and yelps of pain. *Bang.*

Fisting my hands in my pockets, I follow the sound to the next block. There's a girl tossing a baseball against the side of a rec center and catching it as it bounces back again.

Bang.

It's Aiko.

"Oh, hi, Mary," she says. She sounds more tired than I've ever heard her. Tired and sad.

Bang.

"You're going to piss off the neighbors."

"Yeah." *Bang.* "Well, I gotta practice somehow."

The next time she throws the ball, I catch it. It stings my palm a little without a mitt, but she didn't throw it that hard.

"What d'you mean?" I ask, tossing it back to her.

She smacks the ball into her mitt a couple times. "Dad won't let me play on the Tule Lake team. He says it's not Japanese."

I snort. "Bullshit."

"I know." She lobs the ball at me, and we start a game of catch —Aiko to me to Aiko to me—the ball floating back and forth between us.

After a while, she says, "I'm gonna be out of practice." She stares at the ground, her voice wavering. "Yuki's gonna be so mad at me."

"What?"

"When we get back to San Francisco."

I turn the ball in my hands, tracing the red stitches. "You still think you're going back to San Francisco?" I ask, throwing it back.

She snatches it out of the air and shrugs.

Her parents haven't requested repatriation back to Japan, but we both know they don't want to be Americans anymore. Not that they were ever really allowed to be.

The ball comes at me high. I have to jump for it.

I mean, good for the Haranos, I guess. For acknowledging the unfairness of it. For being fed up with everyone saying, *God bless America! Land of the free!* and then locking us up in a place like this, a prison that no one wants to admit is a prison, even the prisoners.

But their *kids* are American—technically, anyway—which makes it worse. I don't know about Tommy, but Aiko's an all-American kid.

She loves baseball, comic books, and Charleston Chews. What's she going to do in Japan?

"I'll practice with you," I say.

She sniffs loudly. If I were closer, I bet I'd see tears on her face. But I don't go to her. I just toss her the ball.

The next weekend, Aiko, Tommy, and Stan drag me to a basketball game, which I hate. Worse, they bring Boots Boy, too.

They tell me his name is Kiyoshi, but whatever, I'm still going to think of him as Boots Boy. At the concession stand, he buys a bag of peanuts, carefully counting each coin the way I've seen Mom do at the co-op because, without any income, all we've got is our dwindling savings.

Tommy and Aiko seem to like him, I guess, so that's probably a point in his favor. He and Tommy talk about music as we climb to the top part of the stands. You can hear the wistfulness in Tommy's voice when he talks about his old records, the ones he had to sell when we left San Francisco. He talks about musicians like they're old friends he hasn't seen in years: Bing, the Duke, ol' Benny, Billie, the Count.

Boots Boy says he wishes he could hear some of them live.

"Come to San Francisco," says Tommy. "I'll take you to the Golden Gate. All the greats play there."

I cross my arms and slump into my seat as the referee blows the whistle and the ball goes soaring into the air. From here, you can't see the fences, the barracks, the soldiers, the tanks. Inside the gym, it's like everyone's trying to pretend we're kids at any other high school.

But how can they forget that the government has packed so many of us in here, it's overloading the plumbing? How can they forget the work accidents or the food shortages? How can they forget the administration isn't giving the coal workers enough breaks? Or protective gear?

I grimace as Aiko, Tommy, and Boots Boy cheer. I kind of hate them for being able to forget, for being stupid and happy, but I kind of envy them too. Sometimes I think it'd be easier to be stupid, because then at least I wouldn't be miserable all the time.

On Tommy's other side, Stan just sits there, miserable as me.

I finally found out where he's been going. Since he and Tommy can't find work, they've been hanging out in the camp's English library. Tommy's been teaching himself to read music. Stan's reading law books and following cases like Fred Korematsu's. Korematsu was arrested and convicted for defying the exclusion order last year, but he's been appealing his case, and Stan's been following every news article about it.

That's the thing about Stan. He knows what's going on here, even if he won't say it.

It makes me want to take him by the collar and shake him until he admits this place is awful. This place is worse than Topaz. I don't know what I would've said to the questionnaire if I'd been old enough to answer it, but I know that if *I'd* brought us here, if *I'd* done this to us, *I* wouldn't be sitting there pretending everything was hunky-dory.

Crack!

From outside, something hits the window above us. The glass splits but doesn't shatter.

Someone screams. Aiko, Tommy, and Stan jump to their feet, but Boots Boy is rooted to the spot, his soft eyes wide, the bag of peanuts clenched tight in his hand.

Crack!

Another window, ten feet away, breaks.

People are running for the exits. Some of the basketball players are stumbling around like they don't know what to do with themselves if there's not a ball to chase.

"Let's get out of here." Stan reaches for my arm, but I jerk out of his reach. He looks hurt, but whatever.

Boots Boy still hasn't moved. He seems like he's frozen in place.

"Come *on*, Kiyoshi!" Aiko cries, tugging his arm.

That seems to snap him out of the spell he was under. His face reddens—I'm not sure if he's angry or embarrassed or what—and he nods at Aiko gratefully.

We scramble down the bleachers, stepping on peanut shells and candy-bar wrappers. My shoe slips in someone's spilled drink.

Outside, a crowd is forming near the side of the building, where people are pushing and shouting at one another. As I run into the darkness with the others, I glance over my shoulder. The broken windows of the gymnasium are lit up from behind like giant, glowing eyes, always keeping watch on us.

Aiko and I normally walk back to the barracks together, but one day in mid-October, she has to stay behind for some reason, so I'm trudging alone through the light snow when a fire truck goes roaring past the next intersection, its sides painted a blazing red.

Two seconds later, there's a screech.

A crash.

People start yelling. All around me, they're flinging open their doors and racing for the intersection.

Lowering my head, I turn and stalk away in the opposite direction.

I haven't made it a block when someone shouts behind me, "Hey, Mary! Wait up!"

Glancing over my shoulder, I see Boots Boy jogging toward me. He's got on the same red-and-black plaid shirt he was wearing the day of the bonfire.

I keep walking, but he catches up to me anyway.

"Did you hear the crash?" he asks.

I shrug.

"Was anyone hurt?"

This guy can't take a hint, can he? "How should I know?" I say.

"It wasn't like this in my old camp," he continues as if I'm not being rude to him. I wonder if he's dumb or just nice. "Gila River was the camp they showed to the public, you know. It wasn't like—"

A WRA warden races past us, and Boots Boy's voice trails off as we watch the man run toward the site of the accident.

In Topaz, after Mr. Uyeda was shot and the camp almost rioted, most of the guards were removed. But here, there are military police; wardens, most of whom are nihonjin; internal security officers, most of whom are white; and Immigration and Naturalization Service officers, too. They all wear different hats and different uniforms, but they're all there to do the same thing: contain us.

"Anyway," Boots Boy says, "there weren't any fences at Gila River, except for these little white picket ones in front of the barrack—"

I was determined to ignore him until he went away, but that gets my attention. "You didn't have fences?" I interrupt.

He shrugs.

"And you didn't run away?"

"Where to? They put us in the middle of the desert for a reason, and barbed wire would've made it look bad for the First Lady and the cameras that came with her. That's what I told her, anyway . . ."

I stop for a second. I mean, I knew Eleanor Roosevelt visited Gila

River in April, but I didn't think she'd really talked to any of the people who had to live there. Boots Boy is still walking, so I have to jog to catch up. Normally I'd be annoyed, but right now he's too interesting to be annoyed at. "Wait," I say. "You met Eleanor Roosevelt?"

"Yeah. She was saying we had to be in camps because we hadn't been integrated into the rest of American society like the Germans and the Italians, and I told her we hadn't been integrated because we weren't allowed to buy or move anywhere except into neighborhoods that were already Japanese, so whose fault was it that we couldn't integrate?"

I smile, even though I decided weeks ago that I wasn't going to like him. But Boots Boy seems smarter than I thought.

"It was still nice, though," he says, "compared to this."

I shrug. "Why'd you leave? 'Cause you wanted to be a No-No so bad?"

Now it's his turn to be silent, although he doesn't stop walking with me. Our footsteps make soft impressions in the dirt: my saddle shoes and his old boots, frayed laces tapping lightly against the leather.

"To get away from my stepdad," he says finally.

I glance at him again. What did Kiyoshi's stepdad do that was so bad, Kiyoshi had to change camps to get away from him? I mean, I hate my dad, but it must have been really, really bad for Kiyoshi to have to come here.

"Shit," is all I can think to say.

"Yeah."

"I'm sorry, Kiyoshi."

Huh, I guess I've started thinking of him as Kiyoshi, then.

He glances sideways at me, a sad little smile tugging at the corners of his mouth. "I just hope he doesn't follow us here."

We walk the rest of the way to my barrack in silence, but it's not my usual stewing, fuming silence. It's like for the first time in months, I've been entrusted with something important, something true, and it's been so long since that's happened that all I want to do is hold on to it.

For once, Dad doesn't yell at me the whole afternoon and evening. I get the water for the kettle without being asked. I fetch coal for the fire before Stan has to. It almost feels like old times when I used to help Mom and Dad around the store: counting stock, replacing fruits and vegetables in the crates, always making sure the oldest produce was in front, even though all the Issei ladies went through every single pear or melon to make sure they got the best one.

But when Dad says, "You're being so helpful tonight, Mary," like it's a surprise, like I wasn't a good, dutiful daughter who looked up to him for *years,* I remember that he could never admit when he was wrong then, either. I remember that he'd go charging onward even if he'd made a mistake, too bullheaded to ever change course or say he was sorry.

Stan shoots him a look. "Couldn't just leave it alone, could you, Dad?"

"Whatever." Grabbing my mitt, I leave the barrack to find some empty building to throw a ball against and hope that something breaks.

Two days later, we hear sirens again. Outside the fence, police cars and ambulances roar down the new road to the farms, where the harvesters have been at work all week, picking potatoes.

Later, we learn one of the farm trucks turned over. Twenty-nine people are injured.

One dies.

The farm workers go on strike for safer working conditions. Agitators take to the streets. Small groups stand under the guard towers, singing the Japanese national anthem.

We're troublemakers, all right, and trouble is coming. You can feel it simmering in the mess halls and in the firebreaks, and it's just a matter of time before the camp erupts.

That night, Dad and I argue about something—I don't even know what—and when I come home from school the next day, my ball and mitt are gone. I'm confined to the barrack, he says, until I earn the privilege of freedom.

I want to say, *What freedom?* But I just bury my face in my book until he prowls to the other room, fists clenched at his sides.

They want me here? Well, I'm here, and I hate it, and I make sure they know it. For a week, I throw my books down when I get back from school. I whack the doorframe with the coal bucket when I refill it. I am the seething, sullen presence they wish they could forget, only I won't let them.

It gets so bad, I don't even have to say anything to piss Dad off. I turn a page of my book, and he's yelling at me about my attitude, my disrespect, the expression on my face. I don't even think he cares if the neighbors know our business now. Mary Katsumoto's a bad egg or Katsumoto-san can't keep his temper or *whatever.* As long as he gets to yell at me, I guess it doesn't matter.

One night, we're standing in the center of the apartment, where Mom and Stan and Paul can see us. Paul is covering his ears as he stares at a comic book he must have borrowed from Aiko. Mom is folding undershirts, pretending she can't hear us.

"What happened to you?" Dad shouts. "You used to be such a good girl!"

"And you used to be a good parent," I snap. "Things change!"

Mom slaps me. It bursts across my cheek, hot and sharp.

Suddenly, all the sound in our neighbors' apartments cuts out.

I'm too stunned to even react. I didn't even notice her get up.

"Do not speak to your father like that." She doesn't yell like he does, but she doesn't have to. Her voice will slice right through you.

I stare at her. I haven't moved to cup my cheek, even though I can feel it stinging the whole right side of my face. I stare at her so long, she folds her hand awkwardly, as if she's ashamed of what it's done.

Clenching my jaw, I spin on my heel and stalk out into the dark, slamming the door so hard, it pops back open again.

I find myself in the administration area, near the Housing Office, this nice, quiet whitewashed building, all its nice, quiet employees gone home for the night, all its windows dark.

Damn it.

I pick up a stone and pitch it through the pane closest to me. It shatters, fragments of glass falling to the ground and shattering again.

Grabbing a new rock, I break another window.

Damn it all.

Why won't anybody admit they were wrong? Why won't they just call this what it is? Why does *everyone* keep *lying?*

They said we were citizens. They said we were "dangerous." They told us they were being considerate of our needs. They said it was an "evacuation" and a "migration," not an incarceration.

They said the camps were full of opportunity.

They said they weren't violating our rights.

I run out of rocks before I run out of windows.

And for what? So they can save face? So they can go on thinking they were right? *Dad* was right? This is *fine?*

I need something else to throw. I put my head down, scanning the ground for another stone. A brick. *Something.* I feel like I should be scared of getting caught—someone might have heard the breaking glass; someone might have called internal security—but I don't even care at this point.

I don't see any more stones, but I do see a pair of shoes. Men's shoes.

Stan's shoes.

Looking up, I glare at him for a moment. His glasses are speckled with rain—I guess it's raining; I didn't even notice—and he has my coat under one arm, but that's not what he's offering me. He's offering me a rock. A good one. Just smaller than fist-size.

I jerk my head at him. A challenge.

You do it.

Smirking, he winds up and pitches the stone at the Housing Office. Together, we smash the remaining windows until there are no more panes to break.

We stand there together amid the broken glass, glittering like frost in the dim light. "Feel better?" Stan asks, holding out my coat to me.

I snatch it from him. "Hardly."

He backs away, hands raised like I'm going to bite.

I roll my eyes. But I'm smiling when I stalk past him, and I don't bother trying to hide it.

Dad and I are the only ones in the barrack the next day when a young guy comes to the door. He's wearing all white, and he speaks in lightly accented English, like maybe he's Kibei or something: "Your presence is requested at the funeral service for Mr. Shimomura."

The guy who died in the farm-truck accident last week.

"Why?" I say.

The Kibei guy looks annoyed. Who is this guy? He's not from our block, or I would've seen him in the mess hall or something. Beyond him, I see an elderly couple being escorted from their apartment by another guy in white.

I don't recognize him, either.

"It's a show of support for the widow," the Kibei guy says.

"Don't know her, either." I'm starting to close the door when Dad comes up behind me.

"We'll go," he says. "Let us put on our shoes and coats."

I'm turning to glare at him when I notice his voice. It's not loud, like it usually is when he's pissed off. Instead, it's even, almost placid, like he's afraid of his own volume.

That's when I see the billy club in the Kibei's hand. *Jesus.*

"Whatever," I say.

When we leave the apartment, Dad and I are caught up in a crowd being herded toward the funeral parlor. People are being turned away from the mess hall and the latrines, forced to walk with the others by young guys with truncheons.

Dad's gripping my arm hard, like he's sure I'm going to twist away from him, so I march alongside him, kicking up silt with every step.

There are so many people in the streets, we don't even get close to the funeral parlor. We're at the back edge of the crowd, and behind us, more guys in white are pacing back and forth like guards.

Just what we need, I think. *More guards.*

Dad mutters a curse in Japanese. "This is a show of something, all right, but it's not for the *widow*."

The funeral parlor's at the corner of Ward 5, near the cemetery. It's not in front of the administration building or anything, but a crowd of Japanese this size is going to get their attention, no matter where it is.

This is a statement from some camp faction to the WRA, and I'm caught in the middle of it.

I'm always caught in the middle of everything.

I yank my arm out of Dad's grasp, ignoring him when he cries out in alarm. I shove through the crowd, trying to find a way out, but everywhere I look, there are guys with clubs blocking my way.

Stubbornly, I try to push through them, but they shove me back into the crowd. My ankle twists underneath me. I stumble.

From behind, Dad grabs my arm, steadying me. "Watch who you're pushing around," he snaps. "That's my daughter."

One of them shrugs. "Keep your daughter in line."

Overhead, the camp loudspeakers crackle to life: "HONORED GUESTS . . ."

Dad stares at the men, one eyelid twitching, fingers curling and uncurling at his sides. I've seen him angry, but I've never seen him like this. "Get out of our way," he growls.

For a second, I'm afraid for him. For us. We've already lost so much.

"Dad," I say, tugging his sleeve.

He doesn't move. I don't think he even breathes.

But before the men can do anything, the loudspeaker dies overhead. There's a sudden squeal, and the scratchy voice cuts out.

The administration has killed the power.

A ripple of anger runs through the crowd, and one of the club guys nods at the others. Like a bunch of stooges, they trot past us into the crowd, toward the funeral parlor.

Dad collapses on the stoop of the nearest apartment. He looks deflated, like a paper balloon that's been struck one too many times.

"I'm sorry," he says.

I'm about to snap at him when I pull back, blinking.

He's *sorry?*

I must have heard wrong. Dad's never apologized for anything in his life.

But then he continues, "I had to choose from a list of bad options, and I don't know that I chose right."

I feel like I should be gloating. I should at least be smug. But honestly, all I feel is tired. Maybe I've been tired for a long time, only I was so angry, I didn't even know it.

I sit beside him. "Okay," I say softly.

He nods. Without looking at me, he pats the back of my hand. "We're going to be all right, Mary."

I sigh. Somewhere in the distance, someone's shouting. Maybe they're trying to give the funeral sermon. Maybe they're trying to calm down the mass of people who have started grumbling and shifting their feet. Maybe they're trying to rile everyone up. In the crowd, there's an undercurrent of something hot and dense, like pressure building in the dark.

For a moment, I allow myself to lean on Dad's shoulder, and for a moment, I feel him lean back. "I hope so," I say.

JAP UPRISING AT TULE LAKE

Hostages Taken, Doctor Beaten

TULE LAKE, Nov. 2—Ten employees of the Tule Lake Segregation Center were held hostage yesterday by 5,000 Jap internees, sources report. Among the hostages were project director Ray Best and head of the War Relocation Authority, Dillon Myer, who was visiting the site.

While Best and Myer met with project officials, a mob of disloyal Japanese surrounded their offices in a blatant display of force, compelling administrators to meet with a Jap committee. After a few hours during which the committee presented its demands, the hostages were released, and the Japs dispersed.

The hostage situation occurred simultaneously with two additional incidents, when Chief Medical Officer Dr. Reece M. Pedicord was severely beaten by a gang of Japs and when several automobiles belonging to white civilians were vandalized in the parking lot. No suspects in either the beating or the vandalism have been apprehended.

In case of future insurrections, a battalion of military police under the command of Lieut. Col. Verne Austin is situated outside the camp.

THE SNAP

KIYOSHI, 17
NOVEMBER–DECEMBER 1943

THURS., NOV. 4

The movie is almost over when Aiko shakes the bag of popcorn, and it rattles like there are only kernels left.

"Aw, man." She starts to crumple it between her hands, the paper crinkling loudly in the crowded mess hall, the noise audible even over the ticking of the film projector and the actors onscreen.

"Shhh," Mary hisses.

I lean forward, trying not to get in Mary's way. I am always trying not to get in Mary's way, even though sometimes, that's the only way to get her to notice me. "I'll take it," I whisper to Aiko.

Mary glares at me, but I don't mind. I know now that she doesn't mean it. If she really hated me, she wouldn't be sitting next to me. She leans back as Aiko passes the bag to Tommy, who passes it across Mary's lap to me.

Carefully, I place a half-popped kernel in my mouth and bite down where the soft inside is showing, splitting it neatly apart. It isn't much, but food is food, and growing up poor taught me never to turn it down when I can get it.

Most of us Japanese are poor, but Mother, my older sister, Kimi, and I were *really* poor. Sometimes, to help pay for rent or food, I had to leave school to help the family pick strawberries, or asparagus, or mikans. I'd miss exams; I'd fall behind in my classes. I got held back a year. My teachers would tell me I was stupid, lazy, a delinquent, useless.

But I didn't want to tell them the truth, which was that sometimes, even the extra money wasn't enough to feed us.

I guess we were eating fine at Gila River, but since we've been at Tule Lake, the portions have been shrinking. It doesn't make sense, if you think about it, because Tule Lake has a pig farm and hundreds of acres of produce. Where's all that food going?

"Hey, Yosh," Stan mutters, "can you eat any louder? I don't think the guys in back can hear you."

"Sorry." I eat another kernel, trying not to chew too loudly.

Tonight, they fed us canned peaches at dinner, which was a treat, but Stan thinks they're just trying to make up for the hubbub on Monday, when the head of the War Relocation Authority was here. Five thousand people showed up to hear him talk about the food shortage, and the labor strikes, and the strikebreakers the Tule Lake project director bused in from the other camps, but they all went away again when the WRA man didn't have anything to say. I guess some of the Caucasian staff got spooked by the assembly, though, because a bunch of them quit.

Things just keep getting worse here, which is why I'm glad for nights like this, when I can see a movie with my friends, eat some popcorn, and pretend that we're normal teenagers who aren't caught up in the tensions of Tule Lake.

• • •

When the film ends and the lights turn on, leaving us squinting and blinking as we pull on our coats and hats, we file out of the mess hall, our heads filled with images of snowy ski resorts and our bellies filled with popcorn. Mary, Stan, Tommy, and I walk four abreast, our breaths puffing in the chill air, while Aiko traipses ahead, belting out the words to "Chattanooga Choo Choo."

Her voice is sweet and clear in the cold, and beside me, I can hear Tommy humming under his breath, smooth and dark as syrup. You wouldn't expect a sound like that to come from him, from Tommy Harano—who's so frail, it looks like a good wind could knock him over—but it does.

There is something so beautiful about this, I think: us, together, in the middle of the dusty road, with the hulking shadows of the barracks looming around us.

But under it, there's an unsettling vibrating in the air, a dull roar that's felt as much as it is heard.

"Are those trucks?" Mary says.

Ahead, Aiko comes to a stop. Her voice dies in her throat.

We look at one another. The rumble of engines is clearly audible now. There must be at least a dozen of them, by the sound of it.

Stan sighs. "We just can't catch a break, can we?"

"I think we should—" I begin.

But before I can finish, people come skidding around the corner from the warehouse area, running full tilt down the street. Headlights flash on the buildings one street over.

"Internal police!" someone shouts. *"Run!"*

Men armed with shovels and wooden clubs are sprinting past us. Their mouths are open, and their eyes are wide, and one's bright-red blood stains the side of his face.

I am rooted to the spot, blinking. I know I should be running too, but I can't seem to make my legs move.

Someone, I don't know who, seizes my hand, pulling me along behind.

A truck screeches to a stop ahead of us. It is dark with yellow eyes. Half a dozen internal police officers spill out, swarming the street.

"Halt!" someone shouts. "Don't move!"

They are knocking down bodies. People are being hauled toward the truck by their ankles, like carcasses. Someone is screaming as he's wrestled to the ground.

I freeze again.

I can't help it. I remember this feeling, this sense that everything around me is thin, and sharp, and brittle, and if I make a move, if I make *any* move, something is going to crack, someone is going to crack, someone is going to get hurt.

"Yosh, come on!"

I hear Stan yelling, but I can't do anything. I am drifting out of my body. I am leaving my legs, and arms, and chest behind. I am a bird, or I am a puff of smoke, and the things that happen to my body aren't happening to me.

"Kiyoshi, move!" he shouts.

I stumble, confused. I am back in my own head, my own feet. Did he push me? Stan's face swims into focus: the hair falling over his forehead, his thick brows, the rims of his glasses, and his black, panicked eyes. Mary and Tommy and Aiko are there too; their lips are moving; they are begging me to move, to run, to come with them. All around us, the internal security men are throwing people into the barrack walls or hogtying them in the dirt.

"Get them out of here!" Stan gives me another shove.

I finally come to my senses. My face burns with shame. What was I doing, waiting for so long? When my friends were counting on me? Quickly, I grab Mary's hand, and her fingers clamp around mine as we take off with Tommy and Aiko. Behind us are the thunder of footsteps, cries for us to halt.

But we don't.

I can't.

Stan told me to get them out of here. Stan trusted me to take care of them.

Stan—

Too late, I realize he isn't with us. As we reach the nearest fire-break, I turn back in time to see two big men in black-billed caps force Stan to his knees.

"Hey, what's the big idea?" he's saying, and I am thinking, *Shut up. Don't move. Don't say anything. Don't move, Stan.* But he is too far away, he is not in my head, he cannot hear me, and he continues, "I didn't do anyth—"

Crack! One of the policemen strikes him across the jaw. His glasses fly from his face as he hits the dirt.

"Stan!" Mary is running at them. Mary is a locomotive. Mary is screaming black smoke.

No, no. Not Mary, too. I want to reach for her, I want to yank her back, I want to protect her the way I can't protect Stan, but I am too scared, or I am too small, too frozen, too stupid, too weak.

Instead, it's Aiko who grabs her. Aiko is saying something in Mary's ear. Aiko is getting her to run.

For a second, I think they're going to leave me; I think they would be right to leave me, but then they take me by the hands, and they drag me after them into the firebreak, away, away, with the sounds of clubs on bodies, the muffled, fleshy impacts, fading quickly into the dark.

FRI., NOV. 5

The next morning, as soon as the dark weight begins to lift from the sky, I walk to the Katsumotos'. I don't know if I slept last night, but if I slept, it wasn't much. I couldn't stop thinking about Stan, kept hearing the *crack* of his jaw and the burn in his voice, shouting, *Get them out of here!*

I heard what happened last night was that a bunch of men tried to stop the trucks from delivering food to the strikebreakers brought in for the farm work. The men surrounded the project director's house, eighty guys, someone said, although another said thirty. No one knows what really happened.

In their barrack, the Katsumotos are already awake. Mary and Paul are at the table with Mr. K., who is sucking on a pipe as if it's lit, although it isn't, and glowering at yesterday's newspaper as if he's reading it, although he isn't, while Mrs. K. paces from the coal stove to the window, peeking through the curtains, then back to the stove, where she lifts the lid on a pot, and the apartment fills with the scent of miso soup.

They haven't heard any news about Stan. They don't know if he was charged, or if he was injured, or where he's being held.

Crack!

His glasses sailing through the darkness.

"I'm sorry," I say, though I know the words are inadequate. They cannot bring their boy back to them; I cannot undo what I did not do; I did not act fast enough; I could not act at all.

"It's not your fault," Mrs. K. says, pointing to the table, where there is a bowl of miso soup for me. "Please, sit."

It's Stan's bowl.

I look away.

His arms being wrenched behind his back, and his face being pushed into the dirt. *My fault,* I think.

Too small, too stupid, too weak.

I wasn't always like this, or at least, I don't think I was.

I know I started freezing up when my stepfather, Mr. Tani, would hit me, but I don't remember the first time it happened.

I remember one time, though, not long after my mother married Mr. Tani, we were in the orchards for the orange harvest, when I'd climb the trees with the fruit picker to collect the oranges the men couldn't reach from the ground. I remember the bark, rough against my palms, and the leaves of the tree flashing green and yellow, with shards of blue sky beyond, and I remember finding a bird's nest: four perfect speckled eggs cradled in twigs and feathers of cloudy gray.

I remember Mr. Tani yelling at me. It was time to go home, or it was time to move to the next tree, or he had been fired because he was drunk on the job again.

I don't know if I moved, or if I moved too quickly, or too slow.

Did he grab my ankle? Did the branch snap beneath me?

The next thing I knew, I was on the ground, and so was the nest. Inside, the eggs were cracked, the mottled shells laced with fractures. I remember looking at those breaks and knowing, *knowing* that they meant death, and stillness, and cold, those baby birds slowly dying within, and maybe not even knowing it.

Because of me.

Mr. Tani was knocking me around by then, shouting at me to get up, but I couldn't move anymore. I was immobile, frozen, petrified, staring at that nest, at those eggs, at those breaks, so delicate; I swear I could hear them crack as they spread across the shells.

And those baby birds dying inside.

There's a knock at the door, and Mrs. K. rushes to answer it, but it isn't Stan, or an internal security officer with news of Stan.

It's Tommy and Aiko. They don't know any more than we do about what happened to Stan, but they tell us they heard on the way over here that the Caucasian staff showed up at the administrative offices this morning, and they found a broken baseball bat. They found blood on the walls and on the bat, and black hairs amid the blood.

Were they Stan's?

My fault.

I stare down at my bowl, watching the green ribbons of wakame churn in the broth. My stomach churns, too, as I force myself to take another bite.

"A *bat?*" Mary slams down her empty bowl.

"*Mary,*" Mr. K. says, "please."

I admire her for her bravery, and for her ferocity. Mary is the kind of person who acts, heedless of danger. She is the kind of person who would never freeze.

As Mary and her father start arguing, I finish my soup, get up so Aiko can sit at the table, and peer out the front window. On the street, groups of people are on their way to work or school, huddled together like clumps of dandelion seeds floating over an overgrown ditch.

As I watch them, I hear a voice crackle in the distance: "DISPERSE."

Then screams.

At the end of the street, shapes appear in the fog—military police in their helmets and gas masks. They're storming down the road, monstrous, boots thudding on the ground. Behind them, a column of armored vehicles crawls along the street.

"Disperse." The loudspeaker crackles again. "Return to your homes."

People are already running, but the soldiers don't give them a chance to clear the roads. One of them flings a gas grenade into the middle of the street.

People shriek and scatter as noxious white smoke hisses from the canister. They are coughing, they can't breathe, they are—

I should help them. I should do something. But I can't.

Mr. K. is already at the door, throwing it open; he is motioning someone inside. They are trying to wash her eyes with water; she is retching and crying—

Outside, the army trucks roll past, blaring commandments from the loudspeaker:

"Residents are confined to their barracks. Only essential personnel are to report to work. School is canceled until further notice. All outdoor gatherings are prohibited.

"Tule Lake is under martial law."

WED., NOV. 17

Stan writes that he is in the stockade, the 250-by-350-square-foot area beyond the motor pool at the southwestern edge of camp. He says he's being fed well, and he asks for a change of clothes, a shaving razor, and maybe one of those law books from the library, if we can get it. He doesn't mention any mistreatment, but the mail is being censored through the military police, so we can't be certain of anything.

We've been permitted to leave our barracks, but school is still canceled, so Mary, Aiko, Tommy, and I loiter by the motor-pool fences, which is the closest we can get to the stockade, hoping to get a glimpse of Stan. To pass the time, we play catch, or we sit and talk, or we watch the coal crew or the farmers filing onto the work trucks at bayonet point.

One day, Aiko brings a stack of comic books for Mary to give to Paul. They look well cared for, no wear on the spines, no creased pages. Tommy has told me Aiko loves comics almost as much as she loves softball and one of the guys from their old camp, Mas Ito, who's now in basic training at Camp Shelby, Mississippi.

Gingerly, I leaf through the comic book at the top of the pile. When I was younger, I used to borrow comic books from the boys at school and read them at lunchtime, devouring every page, as if by memorizing it or loving it enough, I could somehow make it mine.

Mary frowns. "Why're you giving these up?"

"I don't want them anymore," Aiko says with a small, sad shrug.

"Yeah, but *why?*"

Aiko scowls, which is an expression I think she must have learned from Mary, because for a moment, they look like they could be sisters. "Because they fight *Japs,*" she says.

We all glance at the soldiers stationed at the nearby guardhouse with their submachine guns.

"I'll see if Paul wants these," Mary says.

Sometimes, when the guards get bored, they demand to see our identification cards, which have been issued to everyone aged twelve and older. We always have them, because people who are discovered without them are immediately arrested.

Some come back. Some don't.

That's the way it is in Tule Lake now. They say the army is here to retain order, but there's no order. Every day, I hear about more people being arrested—for curfew violation, or for making wisecracks about the internal security officers, or for having the same name as one of the so-called agitators. They say they're here for our safety, but no one feels safe when they've got a gun pointed at them. People disappear. People are held without charges or trial.

And still, we wait by the motor-pool gate, and look, and hope. What else can we do, when we have so little power?

One night, I wake up sweating. Somewhere, someone's shouting. *Bang!* Something crashes against the floor.

I'm half-asleep still, half dreaming. I must be. He's not here. He can't be here.

Mr. Tani.

My stepfather. He's found us. He's come to Tule Lake. I can hear his voice again. He's going to hit me. He's going to haul me out of bed, calling me stupid, calling me slow, calling me weak, over and over, so many times, I start to believe him.

Thud, thud, thud! someone knocks.

I stare up at the ceiling, my blood roaring in my ears like distant truck engines. For a second, I am bound in my blankets, pinned here, frozen, waiting.

Mr. Tani.

Except I realize it can't be Mr. Tani, because Mr. Tani never knocked. He just barged in, smelling of sake, and started throwing me around.

"Get up, Japs!" someone shouts. "Surprise inspection! Get out here!"

I blink as the feeling returns to my body, and I carefully peel back the covers, swinging my legs over the edge of the cot. My limbs feel shaky with fear, or relief, or both.

It's not Mr. Tani.

It's the army.

Sporadic lights shine through the windows as Mother, Kimi, and I pull on our coats and boots.

"Hurry up!"

Mother is trembling, so Kimi and I help her out of the barrack and into the street. Outside, our neighbors are lined up with their hands behind their heads.

The sight of it stops me in my tracks. We look like criminals.

We aren't criminals.

"Get over there," one of the soldiers says, jabbing at Mother with a Tommy gun.

Mother freezes. In the floodlights, she looks like a cornered animal, barely daring to breathe.

There is that feeling again, that feeling as if the world is a sheet of ice, as if it will shatter, as if there will be a *snap!* and we will be on the ground as gunfire rains over our heads.

"Move!"

Carefully, Kimi and I each take one of Mother's arms and guide her toward our neighbors. The frosted ground crackles with every step.

We stand by, immobile, as they charge into our homes. Through the open doors, we hear the sounds of our belongings being ransacked: cots being overturned, drawers being thrown to the floor, chests being kicked over. Up and down the block, they're hauling away radios, and kitchen knives, and a Japanese printing press.

Suddenly, there's a cry from one of the barracks and the sound of a scuffle, and a Japanese man is frogmarched down the steps. Despite being in nothing but his underclothes, he looks proud: his back straight, his chin held high.

How does he do it? How does he look so serene?

"Who is that?" I whisper to Kimi.

"One of the judo teachers," she says. "They say he's one of the instigators of the incident at the director's house, but—"

"Shut it!" one of the MPs—military police—barks, prodding her with a bayonet.

She snaps her mouth shut with an audible *click*.

Mr. Tani never hit Kimi or Mother the way he hit me, but I know it affected them, having to listen to it, or to watch it, if they weren't pretending to be asleep.

Sometimes I think I should be angry at them, and sometimes I am, for letting it happen, but then I think about how if things had been different, if Mr. Tani had knocked one of them around instead, I think I would have frozen, the way I froze when they took Stan. I would have let something bad happen to Mother, or Kimi, or both, and I already hate myself for letting it happen to me; I don't think I could live with it if it had happened to them.

When the judo teacher is loaded into a truck with the rest of the contraband, one of the children starts crying. I can't tell where the sound is coming from, because there's a spotlight mounted to one of the jeeps, and it keeps crossing and recrossing us: bright and dark, bright and dark, bright and dark.

Soldiers are emerging from our barrack now, carrying Mom's rice barrel, a couple of jars of tsukemono she's been saving, and canned goods we bought from the co-op when we could.

"That's our food," Mom says in a panicked whisper. Her face is taut with fear. "What are we going to eat, Yoshi? They're not feeding us enough in the mess halls anymore. That food is all we have—"

On the back of my head, my hands are starting to shake. I should do something. I should try to stop them, or reason with them, or plead.

But I can't, and neither can she, and neither can any of us. What can any of us do? They are armed, and there are more of them, and I am just one person, one boy, one stupid boy, one useless boy, who can't even protect himself.

Bright and dark, bright and dark.

The child is still crying.

SUN., NOV. 28

A few days after Thanksgiving, I'm on my way to the Katsumotos' barrack to help them make tsukemono for Stan and the other prisoners. Each ward is sending something in preparation for the holidays, and although Mother, Kimi, and I don't have enough to spare, the least I can do is help.

As I'm passing one of the mess halls, an army truck drives up, laden with food: eggs, cans, bread, rice, wilted bunches of chard. The soldiers on the back of the truck don't bother getting off to unload, however. They simply check their clipboard and heave the food onto the ground. Crates shatter. I flinch. It actually hurts, seeing the cartons of eggs break, the sacks of rice split, spilling thousands of white grains into the dirt like miniature avalanches.

As the soldiers drive off, the mess-hall staff rush to save what they can. Kneeling, I help them scoop up broken pieces of spaghetti, bruised apples, and mackerel that smells as if it's already turned.

They scurry back to the mess hall, leaving me in the road,

surrounded by scattered grains of rice, which I begin to pick up, one by one, filling my handkerchief with them.

They can be washed; they can be eaten. We won't even know the difference.

I still remember the taste of dirt on my tongue. We'd have nothing to eat, and Kimi would take me out to the weed patch behind our apartment, where she'd put a pinch of soil in my palm.

"Just swallow," she used to say. "It tastes bad, but when it gets to your stomach, you'll forget you were hungry."

With a handful of rice in my handkerchief, I walk the rest of the way to the Katsumotos', where Mary, Mrs. K., and I spend the evening slicing daikon, napa cabbage, beets, and turnips that are only slightly bad. We cut off the ruined parts and toss the rest into jars with salt and garlic, or turmeric, sugar, and vinegar, and soon, the whole apartment smells of pickling liquid.

I like working with Mary. Her hair, which is normally in her face, is pulled back, so you can see her eyes, which are shaped like dark seeds. It also means you can *really* see her scowl at you when you mess up.

She eyes my knifework, frowning. "Don't cut yourself."

Sheepishly, I move the paring knife, the only kind of knife they've left us after the raids, away from my thumb. "Thanks."

She rolls her eyes.

Tommy and Aiko were supposed to have been here too, but Mr. Harano wouldn't let them come. He's strict, their father, and I don't think he treats either one of them very well, because it seems like they'll take any excuse to be away from their apartment when they can.

It's nearing curfew, so Mrs. K. wraps a jar of each batch of tsukemono in a furoshiki and ties it neatly, handing it to me with a little bow. "For your mother and sister," she says.

I take it, bowing back. "Thank you, Mrs. Katsumoto."

"Did you give him the one he bled in?" Mary asks from the table, where she's wiping down the cutting boards.

Mrs. K. looks horrified. I can see her almost reach for the furoshiki, then hold herself back. "He did *what?*"

Mary laughs. I love her laugh. It's loud and brash, and I don't get to hear it often—I don't think anybody does—but now it fills the barrack, following me as I bow again and step out into the night.

When I get home, Mother claps her hands as I unwrap the furoshiki. "This is so kind," she says, holding each of the jars to the light. Some of the colors are pale still, but the daikon is already turning sunbeam yellow in the turmeric.

"We must find a way to thank them," she says, patting the top of each jar, as if blessing them.

I reach into my back pocket for the handkerchief of rice. "I also got—"

I'm interrupted by a sharp rapping at the door.

We freeze, staring at each other, wide-eyed. It's after seven p.m. No Japanese person should be knocking right now. Which means . . .

"Internal security," someone says. "Open up."

The air feels fragile, as if breathing it will fracture something. Cautiously, Kimi lays the book she was reading on her cot and gets up, padding across the floor in her slippers.

As soon as she opens the door, the internal security officers barge inside. There are two of them, their faces pale, their hands hard and grabbing; they're coming for me, and I—

It's like Mr. Tani all over again. The lights are too bright; I'm bewildered and blinking. I'm being seized by the arms.

"That's him," one of them says.

"You're under arrest," says the other.

I blink slowly. *I am?*

"What for?" Kimi demands. Her hands are on her hips.

"Curfew violation."

Mother is motionless, clutching the jar of takuan to her chest like it's the only thing she can hold on to. *It's okay, Mother,* I think.

"It's only five minutes past seven!" Kimi snaps. She's small, slender, her head sometimes seeming too big for her neck, like a doll's, but now she gets into the officers' faces, her eyes narrowed, her canines sharp.

I've never seen Kimi stand up to anyone before.

It is kind of magnificent.

"Five minutes past curfew is past curfew," one of them says.

"But he—"

The other one cuts her off: "You'd better pack a bag. Quick, now."

She glares at them for a second, her eyes brimming with tears, before she spins around, stuffing my clothes into a suitcase. Trouser legs and shirtsleeves flying like kites in the pale yellow light of our single bulb.

Mom still hasn't moved, and neither have I.

"What's this?" one of them says, lifting my closed fist. "Contraband? Let go."

I try. I want to tell him I try.

For some reason, I'm thinking of the eggs in the road, the cartons of eggs, the yolks oozing out, into the mud, yellow as melted butter.

"Come on, you Jap—"

He has to pry open my fingers, wrenching them back one by one, and it *hurts,* I want to tell him it *hurts,* until the handkerchief drops.

Dirty, uncooked rice spills all over the floor. I hear the grains rattle, but I can't look down. Tears form in my eyes, blurring my vision.

The internal security officers laugh.

Then one of them is at the door, and the other one has my suitcase. "Move," he says, prodding me.

I trip, banging my knee into the edge of my cot.

He grabs me again, shaking me. "Don't try anything funny, now." I'm being marched toward the door, but my legs aren't working. I fall; I hit the floor; there are grains of rice beneath my fingers.

Mother finally finds her voice: "Kiyoshi!"

"What's the big idea?" one asks. "D'you think this is a joke?"

I am trying to get to my knees when he smacks me across the head, and then I really start crying. The tears come hot and fast and large, burning down my cheeks. I don't mean to; I don't even know why I'm doing it. I've been knocked around worse than this, but—

I think of that judo teacher who walked down those steps with grace. I don't want to be uncooperative, or slow, or weak . . . but I am. Mr. Tani knew it, and Mother and Kimi knew it, and I know it, and now these men know it too.

They're seizing me now, they're roughing me up, but I am soaring out of my body, I am untethered from my own bones, from the grip of their hands, from my tears. I am safe, even though they are hurting me.

Kimi is screaming at them as they shove me down the steps. My tongue splits as I accidentally bite down on it. I am in the dirt, tasting blood and dust.

I think of the smell of oranges, sunlight flashing in the leaves.

Then I'm being pulled toward a truck, I'm being arrested, and I don't know if I'm coming back.

The last I see of Mother and Kimi, they're standing in the doorway, Mother still holding the jar of takuan, and the light behind them is the color of egg yolks.

They don't tell me how long I'll be here. They don't tell me if there's going to be a trial. They just throw me in the stockade and leave me.

The stockade barracks are like the ones in the rest of camp, but they're crammed wall-to-wall with cots. The men in here are like sardines, jam-packed so close together, there's hardly enough space to walk between beds.

The room smells like body odor and cigarettes, with the faint hint of vomit.

But *Stan* is here.

I hardly recognize him when I see him, because his head's been shaved, poorly, I think, with uneven patches here and there, and he's lost so much weight in the last twenty-four days, he looks like you could snap him in half.

"Look what the cat dragged in," he says, struggling to sit up. I think he's sick. His skin is moist and pale, and there's a sour smell about him, like bile.

"Don't get up," I say, helping him back under the covers. "You look terrible."

"Gee, you sure know how to flatter a guy." He grins. One of his teeth is missing.

I think of his legs being knocked out from under him, of his face being mashed into the dirt. *My fault.*

"Stan, I'm—"

He squints at me, putting on his glasses, which have been broken and taped back together. "Ouch. You could crack a mirror with a face like that. Here." He tosses me a rag. "What'd they get you for?"

Gently, I touch the rag to my swollen lip. "I was out five minutes past curfew."

To my surprise, Stan laughs. "At least you know what you did! Some guys get hauled in with no explanation at all." He looks a little wild, laughing like that, with his uneven hair, his missing tooth, that shine of sweat on his forehead.

I try to smile, but it's hard to smile when I want to cry again. I sniff, trying not to meet his gaze. "What happened to your hair?" I say.

"It's a good look, right? I call it 'Buddhist chic.'" He rubs his stubbled head, and his gaze turns solemn, despite his light tone. "Some of the guys jumped me. They wanted everyone to have the same haircut. Solidarity in baldness, I guess."

I glance around the room, where men are lying on their cots, sleeping, or reading, or smoking and talking in small groups. Against one wall, someone plays a ukulele. Most of them are wearing knit caps to cover their shaven heads, but I spy the judo teacher who was arrested during the night raid, playing a game of Go. He looks like that statue *The Thinker*, his chin resting atop his fist, a paragon of stillness amid the stinking chaos of the barrack.

"That guy has hair," I say, pointing.

"That's Mr. Morimoto. They respect him too much to jump him." Stan leans back against the pillow with a sigh. "You'd think it's the judo, but in reality, he bites."

"Really?"

"Nah, it's the judo. And the whole leader-in-the-community thing." Stan chuckles. "How's Mary and the rest of the family?"

"They're doing fine. You don't need to worry," I tell him. "How are you?"

"Stir-crazy and mad as hell. No matter how many times I tell them I was at the movies that night, they still think I'm one of the guys who threatened the project director. They haven't questioned me in a while, though. What d'you wanna bet they've forgotten I'm here?"

I keep thinking of him falling, of his body hitting the ground.

"I'm sorry," I blurt out.

Stan blinks, his mouth half-open in surprise. "Huh?"

My hands knot in his blanket. "For getting you arrested."

He laughs again. "Those goddamn ketos arrested me." He pats me on the arm. "Come on, don't look like that, Yosh. It's not *your* fault I'm in here. You didn't do anything wrong. None of us did."

I get him a cup of water, which I make him drink. "I wish I could believe you."

THURS., DEC. 30

The stockade is no joke.

For more than a hundred prisoners, there are only five toilets, and three of them aren't working. There's no hot water and only one tub, so we wash our faces and clothes in the sinks, shivering in the winter chill. Most of the time, we stink.

In another part of the camp is a tent called the "bullpen" where Lieutenant Swinson, the Police and Prisoner Officer, puts anyone who looks at him funny. It's guarded day and night by an MP with a rifle and bayonet, which means the prisoners have to sleep out there on the frozen ground with only a bit of canvas and a little stove to protect them from the cold.

I haven't been to the bullpen yet, and neither has Stan, and we go out of our way to stay out of trouble.

He's on his way to being healthy again, but because of the poor conditions, illnesses sweep through the barrack in waves. Someone is always coughing, or vomiting, or running a fever. To pass the time, I think, and to distract themselves, the stockade prisoners decorate the walls with pictures of pinup girls and family photographs. Someone's always playing guitar or the ukulele, and there's always a game of hanafuda going so the guys can gamble for cigarettes and oranges.

Stan and I keep to ourselves mostly, talking, or reading letters we receive from camp:

> *Dear Stan and Yosh,*
>
> *Do you know about Radio Tokyo? It's a broadcast from Japan, and some of the men in camp can pick it up with their radios. (Don't ask me which men, because I don't know.) I haven't heard it myself, but sometimes I see these flyers with highlights from the broadcast. Can you believe it? They're saying Japan is winning the war in the Pacific. They talk about these big American casualties, all these warships sunk and everything. The numbers don't make any sense at all, but people in camp eat it up.*
>
> *They've convinced my parents, anyhow. They're talking about trying to get on the next prisoner exchange ship, even though I tell them our governments have their own agendas in who they want to send back. I suppose I can't blame them—they only want to return to Japan as soon as possible.*

I don't know what I'm going to do if that happens. I've never been to Japan, and you know how bad my Japanese is, Stan. I can barely say こんにちは. *But I don't want to keep disappointing them.*

I'm enclosing a pack of gum. Hopefully it won't be confiscated.

Take care of yourselves,

Tommy

P.S. Aiko sends her love. Mary gives you the finger.

P.P.S. No, Mary gave <u>me</u> the finger. To you, she says, "Don't let the bastards grind you down."

We don't receive the pack of gum, of course. Sometimes we don't even receive our letters. It's like that here. Random. Every so often, someone is taken away for questioning, or someone is locked in the bullpen or returns from the bullpen. Someone new is arrested, or someone is released. There's no logic to it, no reason we're here, and no end in sight.

And under the jokes, and the songs, and the laughter, there's that feeling like the air is being stretched tighter and tighter and tighter, and soon, all it will take is one move, one step, one breath, for it to snap.

On December 30, Lieutenant Swinson takes two prisoners from our barrack and puts them in the bullpen. He gives no explanation.

In protest, we don't leave the barrack for roll call. The men have done things like this before, Stan tells me, when they weren't getting enough rice, or when they wanted a sick prisoner to be taken to the hospital. It feels new to me. To *not* move, and to do it on purpose, and to have that be powerful somehow.

The judo teacher, Mr. Morimoto, asks that the prisoners in the bullpen be released, since there was no reason for them to be there in the first place.

Lieutenant Swinson tells him that if we clean up the stockade, he'll let the men out of the bullpen.

Mr. Morimoto says we can do that, if we have supplies like mops, buckets, rags, and soap.

We don't get them.

But Mr. Morimoto begins cleaning all the same. Taking one of his own undershirts, he leaves the barrack to begin wiping down the latrine.

Those who are healthy—or the ones who aren't slinging the bull, gambling, or lying around, at least—join him. After making sure Stan is resting, because he's still weak, I help clean the sinks. In the frigid water that flows from the taps, my fingers quickly go numb.

Mr. Morimoto's hands are cracked with cold and the dry air. It must be painful for him, I think, scrubbing grime from the drain, but he doesn't complain. His face is placid, even though there is a deep anger in his eyes that I've also seen in Stan's.

"Why are you doing this, sir?" I ask after a while.

He grunts. "What do you mean?"

"Lieutenant Swinson didn't get us the cleaning supplies."

"If someone always said, *You have to do this for me before I do this for you,* then nothing would ever get done," he says. "If I say I will do something, then I do it. Acting in a forthright and honest manner is the only way to retain one's dignity."

I glance around the latrine with its three malfunctioning toilets, and at the soiled rags in our hands. I think about the men being arrested and the men being released; the bullpen and the interrogations; and the letters we receive or the letters we don't. I think about the unpredictability of it, the dreadful whimsy, as if our lives are no longer governed by sense or patterns, and so we cannot rely on anything, not on food, or warmth, or security, or freedom. "Even here?" I ask.

Mr. Morimoto nods. "Especially here."

FRI., DEC. 31

Although we spent all yesterday cleaning the stockade, the prisoners in the bullpen aren't released. Mr. Morimoto doesn't look surprised, just weary.

"What do you think is going to happen?" I ask Stan.

"I bet Swinson's gonna want us to sit in a circle and braid each other's hair or something. Maybe a tea party."

I grin and give his bald head a rub. "You'll be left out, then."

He shoves me off, grimacing. "Tea with Swinson? I'd rather eat my shoe."

At the mention of food, my stomach growls. We had only two slices of bread for breakfast this morning. "You might have to," I say, "if things continue as they are."

Like yesterday, when it's time for roll call, no one leaves the barrack. One of the MPs comes to yell at us, but no one moves. No one is even tempted.

I keep thinking about what Mr. Morimoto said about acting according to his beliefs. We don't all believe the same things in here, especially about whether we're Japanese or American, whether we want to stay in this country or go, but we all know that our treatment in this place is unjust, and that makes it easier to act as one.

Soon, however, we hear the gate rattling open, the sound of boots hitting the frozen ground. Soldiers march around the exterior of the barrack, banging on the walls with bayonets, shouting, "Get up, you lazy Japs! Time for roll call! Come out on your own, or we've got ways to make you come out!"

I lean over to Stan, whispering, "Are they talking about gas? There are sick guys in here."

He shakes his head. "You don't think a little tear gas will clear up their sinuses?" He sounds like he's joking, but he's so angry, I can almost feel it coming off him in waves, like heat or cold.

Mr. Morimoto sighs and draws a hand down his face.

And we obey.

The air is frigid as we file out of the barrack. It hits the back of my throat like a thousand needles. Behind me, Stan starts coughing. I turn around to help him, but someone shouts at me to keep moving.

When I hesitate, Stan gestures me onward.

Slowly, we line up, standing there with the cold seeping into our bones as they count us.

One Jap, two Japs . . . eighty-eight, eighty-nine Japs . . . one hundred thirty Japs . . . one hundred ninety-nine, two hundred Japs . . . in a stockade meant for less than a hundred.

I can't feel my fingers anymore. In my shoes, my feet have gone thick and solid as ice. All around me, men are coughing and sniffling. Two rows ahead, I can see one of them shivering so hard in his coat, he looks as if he's going to shake apart. I hope it's over now; I hope we can go back inside.

But Lieutenant Swinson isn't done with us. He paces up and down in the yard, sneering like he's won a contest. Then he stops. "You." He jabs a gloved finger at Mr. Morimoto. "To the bullpen."

For a second, Mr. Morimoto does nothing, but he is not frozen the way I freeze sometimes. He is thinking. You can see it in his slow breaths, his steady gaze, the opportunity he gives Swinson to reconsider his stance, to change his mind, to stop this senselessness. This not-moving, this small space of disobedience, is not out of fear but out of defiance.

Then, with a sigh, Mr. Morimoto leaves his place in line.

People start muttering.

"What about the rest of us?" Stan's hoarse voice rises above the others. "I could use a change of scenery!"

"Yeah!" someone shouts.

Before, I might have wanted Stan to be quiet. I might have thought that would keep him safe.

But that only works in a world that makes sense, and the world of Tule Lake does not make sense. In the world of Tule Lake, you are a citizen and you are an enemy; you are an alien and you are a traitor. You have rights; you have no rights. You have a knife; you have a jar of pickles; you have contraband. In the world of Tule Lake, you are fed and you are starved; you are arrested for rioting, for seeing a movie, for curfew violation; you are guilty until you're proven innocent, and you're never proven innocent because you never get charged; you are guilty, and you have committed no crime . . .

"Enough!" Lieutenant Swinson barks. He jerks his thumb at Mr. Morimoto. "If anyone else wants to join him, you can step right up."

Everyone shuts up.

The air strains under the weight of our silence. A green leaf. A nest of feathers. A groaning branch.

All it takes is one move, and Lieutenant Swinson will snap. He'll have someone hauled off by their ankles. He'll beat someone into the ground. He'll loose his MPs on us like dogs.

In the world of Tule Lake, they want you to obey, they want you to be a troublemaker, they want you to admit to things you haven't done and allegiances you never held, they want you to accept these injustices with a smile. In the world of Tule Lake, you are shot at the gates for trying to get to work on time, for moving too fast, for scaring the Caucasians.

You move, or you do not move; you freeze, or you act; it doesn't matter. You are too dangerous anyway, too yellow, too slow, too stupid, too weak anyway. You are arrested anyway. You are beaten *anyway*.

So I move.

The frost crunches as I take a step, a single step, one step forward.

In the silent yard, the sound is like an avalanche.

Or a breaking branch.

Or an eggshell.

It takes a second for Lieutenant Swinson to notice, but when he sees me in the fifth row, his eyes bulge. His cheeks inflate. A vein in his temple pops, blue as a fragment of sky.

But before he can say anything, before he can shout and rail and thunder, before he can have me dragged away, the other prisoners, every one of them, all around me, step forward. The earth trembles under our weight, the weight of all of us, more than two hundred Japs, moving and immovable.

But it doesn't break.

And neither do I.

Saturday, January 8, 1944

Dear Mas,

I bet you thought you'd heard the last of me, huh? Sorry to break it to you, but you can't get rid of me that easily. You know Tule Lake's been under martial law since November? Well, I guess the MPs thought I was mixed up in some kind of trouble, because they picked me up one night like a sack of potatoes and dumped me in the stockade to rot.

That's why I haven't written all these months. It wasn't you. It was me!

Well, it was the army, anyway.

It's been kind of a rough time, but everything changed about a week ago when the guy in charge of the stockade, this blond-wolf type named Swinson, lines everybody up and starts picking people out at random for extra punishment. "You! You! You! I'm an insecure asshole who needs to subjugate others so I can feel better about myself! Wah!" And when we kick up a fuss about it, he says anybody who doesn't like it can step right up and try him.

So this new friend of mine, Yosh, he does. And then we all do! You would've gotten a kick out of it, Mas. All the little guys standing up for what's right.

Of course, Swinson had no idea what to do. I guess he didn't know how to punish all two hundred of us, so he just kind of left us there, standing in the snow for three hours, while he went to get orders from his superior or something. When he finally came back, he said we'd all be on bread and water for the next twenty-four hours.

But we'd had enough.

They'd imprisoned us, isolated us, made us sick with poor quarters and treatment. Now they were going to starve us too? You've got to be kidding me.

So we did the only thing we could. If all they were going to give us was bread and water, then we weren't going to eat <u>at all.</u> Not until they told us why we were there. Not until they gave us fair trials. Not until they stopped treating us like we were less than human.

I'm telling you, Mas. They were torturing us. We were god-damn Americans on goddamn American soil, and they were tortur-ing us. I know you're an army guy now and everything, but you wouldn't have stood for it, either. No one in their right mind could.

We were on hunger strike for a week, and surprise, surprise! At the end of it, nothing had really changed, although they did let me, Yosh, and some other guys go yesterday. Why? Who knows? Who can fathom the perverse inner thoughts of a guy like Swinson?

There are 187 prisoners still in the stockade, and I don't know when they're getting out, but I hear the army is going to give con-trol of the camp back to the W.R.A. any day now, so maybe things will change.

Or maybe they won't. Who knows? It'll be another surprise!

I know you said you were joining the combat team to show them what the Nisei are made of, to show them we're as American as any blond-haired, blue-eyed keto.

Now I just hope you can make them see us as human.

Fight hard and come home safe, Mas. We're counting on you.

Sincerely,
Stan

XI

TWICE AS PERFECT

MAS, 22
JANUARY–MARCH 1944

MONDAY, JANUARY 10, 1944, 2145 HOURS
CAMP SHELBY, MISS.

Dear Dad, I try to be the kind of guy other people go to for help. A rock, a support, a foundation. In Japantown, I bailed Frankie out of fistfights. I taught Shig to drive. I fixed Twitchy's bicycle when he banged it up jumping over those trash cans. I sat with Minnow at the kitchen table, doing math problems long into the night while the rest of the house dreamed—nothing but the scratching of the pencil and the dogged certainty of algebra. Steadfast, reliable. That's the kind of guy you taught me to be.

But I couldn't help Stan.

November: I went to my sergeant as soon as Tommy told me what was going on at Tule Lake. Knew it was a long shot. They don't like you doing stuff like that in the army. They want you focused, soldier! They want your head in the game! Know what happens if you're not paying attention? You and the guy next to you—dead. Forget what's happening on the other side of the country.

But *everything* we're fighting for is on the other side of the country, you know? Shig, Minnow, Ma . . . behind the barbed wire. And it was *Stan,* Dad. I had to do *something.*

I've told you about my sergeant before, haven't I? Caucasian guy? Short as some of the Nisei boys, but with a Napoleon complex like you wouldn't believe? Around the barracks, we call him Little Emperor, and if he ever finds out, we'll never hear the end of it. He said: *Get your head out of your ass, soldier. You've got a war to fight, and it's not in fucking Tule Lake.*

TUESDAY, JANUARY 11, 1944, 0630 HOURS
CAMP SHELBY, MISS.

4x4x4s, punishments, holes. The motion: dig and heave. The earth rattling from the spade. The memory: you, coming home with dirt in the lines of your palms. You, and the smell of loam. I think of the times you brought Shig and me to work with you, of us pulling weeds from the hedges. Those damp clods of soil and roots and earthworms. Did you know I once dared him to eat one? He slurped it right down like the last of a milkshake. Laughed until we piled into the Chevy.

Next time, I went over the Little Emperor's head. (Get it?) Boy, did I catch hell for that one. Two weeks of extra detail, two weeks restricted to post. They learned my name, my face. I wasn't just another Jap anymore. I was Mas Ito, and every time they needed someone for kitchen patrol, for latrine duty, for any of the unsavory jobs they give to army grunts, it was me. My fingers stinking of cleaner. My palms blistered from shoveling. Times like these, I try to remember what you taught me. Chin up. Back straight. Turn the other cheek. One day, they're going to see they were wrong.

SUNDAY, JANUARY 23, 1944, 1000 HOURS
CAMP SHELBY, MISS.

Dear Dad, Sunday KP isn't so bad. It's two meals instead of three, and a break between them if you finish up after breakfast quickly enough, which, of course, we did. I've gotten KP duty so many times now, I can scrub a pan spotless in two seconds flat. Boy, I think of all those times Ma made Shig and me wash the dishes again because we'd left grease on the pots. If only she could see me now.

Maneuvers start Friday. The whole unit will be in the field, all four thousand of us. We've done smaller problems before: a squad of five or six guys, then a platoon of three or four squads, the units getting bigger every time, a company with all its platoons, and finally a battalion of eight hundred soldiers. But this will be the first time the entire 442nd Regimental Combat Team (three infantry battalions, the field artillery battalion, all our supporting companies) will be fighting together. I gotta tell you, Dad, I'm looking forward to showing everyone what a bunch of Nisei boys can do.

THURSDAY, JANUARY 27, 1944, 2100 HOURS
CAMP SHELBY, MISS.

A letter from Tommy: The army has started drafting Japanese-Americans. That means Shig can be drafted. Can you imagine? Shig, in the army? Or Stan, or Tommy, or any of the No-No boys at Tule Lake? Boys who said they wouldn't fight? Boys who were beaten? Imprisoned? *I* volunteered. I *wanted* to serve. They didn't — don't.

I think a lot about your flag, the one you flew every morning before you left for work. Those red and white stripes rippling over our steps. When I think about home, I think about that flag as much as I think about the building, or the street, or the city. The way you folded it every night before sundown, that starred triangle in your arms. I think of you when I carry the flag, when I put on my uniform. Not a thread out of place.

I heard that it was our performance at Shelby that convinced the army to open the draft to the Nisei. In rifle qualifications last year, we had sixty experts and ninety sharpshooters in my company. It was a Camp Shelby record. But it wasn't enough, not for us. We wanted to be perfect. We had to be perfect. No, we had to be twice as perfect to be considered half as good.

Looks like all we proved was that the Japanese-Americans still in camps could be useful to the war effort.

Maneuvers start tomorrow, and if all goes well, we might be deployed soon after. Maybe if we fight hard enough, we'll end this war before any of the draftees see action.

SUNDAY, FEBRUARY 6, 1944, 1930 HOURS
DESOTO NATIONAL FOREST, MISS.
Dear Dad, we wrapped up the last of our first three problems today.

Out here, umpires run around with flags to simulate fire. A mortar, a red ribbon. *You, you, and you, KIA.* But there aren't enough umpires, and the ones we have are overworked, so the guys keep picking fights about who won which engagement. Frankie said his company (Item Company over in 3rd Battalion) started a fistfight yesterday because the enemy wouldn't admit their position was lost. Can you imagine? Good old Frankie, throwing down his rifle to sock a guy in the face. If only all our problems could be solved so easily, huh?

Sometimes, I think about how we used to play at war. It was Buchanan Street, and it was No Man's Land. Remember Frankie leading banzai charges up the sidewalk? Remember Tommy hiding behind Mr. Hidekawa's steps? Shig and Twitchy manning the cannons, their cheeks inflated with the sounds of imaginary explosions. *Ka-pow!* Stan coordinating operations from the fire escape. And you, waiting on our steps with apricots from Katsumoto Co. and the American flag waving overhead. It feels the same, and it feels different. We were soldiers, and we were children. I mean, we are.

WEDNESDAY, FEBRUARY 9, 1944, 2345 HOURS
DESOTO NATIONAL FOREST, MISS.

A guy got killed on maneuvers today. We were crawling under machine-gun fire, the bullets loud above us, loud as a storm in the desert: the thunder crashing, the hail falling on the sand, the barbed wire twitching and jumping in the wind. Except in this case, you didn't look up to watch for lightning. Except in this case, the bullets were hot. You keep your head down, you keep moving forward, and whatever you do, you don't look up.

He was in my platoon. Johnny Tsujimura from Seattle. Good kid. Always got chocolates from his sweetheart in Detroit. Always shared them with anybody who was around. He wanted to study radio engineering after the war. You'd have liked him, I think. Good kid, but not all there. Here's what I want to know: Where did he think he was? Not in the middle of the Mississippi wilderness, but back home? Back in Minidoka? I wonder if he heard someone call his name, and he looked up to see if it would be his mother or his brother or his sweetheart standing there, with the storm thrashing overhead?

Sometimes I think I hear you. I know you aren't here, but sometimes when I'm down at the Service Club or walking across the parade grounds, I think I hear you calling my name. Four years since you died, and it's getting hard to remember your voice, but I'd know it if I heard it. I mean, you. And, just for a second, I think if I look up, I'll see you standing on our steps in Japantown, holding a bowl of apricots, glowing like a sun in your hands. Only I don't. Look up, I mean.

I don't remember a lot about your funeral, but I remember this. The smells: flowers, incense, something chemical and strange. The unbalanced equation: your body in a pine box, and then your body was gone. I know you were cremated, but how could an urn really hold you, I mean, all of you? Your dreams, your loyalties, the future you should have had with us? Or were you somewhere else, somewhere like an ocean current, or a wind, unseen, billowing in the fabric of an American flag?

• • •

Dear Dad, we've got less than a week of maneuvers to go, but it's gotten colder, wetter, and everyone is counting down the days until we head back to Shelby. Last night, falling asleep to the sound of the rain on the pines, I dreamed of that trip to Big Sur when Minnow was six. The smell of the redwoods. The salt in the air. I dared Shig to lick a banana slug, which made his tongue go numb. Ma scolded me; you laughed, wide. On the hike back to the car, you stopped to look at something: a fungus, a leaf, or the rain falling through the canopy like applause in a cathedral. We didn't know. We kept going. And when we looked back, we couldn't find you. Dad? *Dad!* For a minute, five minutes, you were gone. That deep drop of panic, like a fall from a great height. A world where you were missing, where you were not with us? Shig's legs pumping as he ran back along the trail, his shriek of joy, of relief, and anger, when he found you. *Don't scare us like that!*

I was there when they took off Johnny's helmet. Brains everywhere. The only good thing I can think about it is that there was no fear, no pain, no time for his mind to signal the rest of the body, *You're going to die,* before the bullet turned everything off, like lightning striking a power line.

I started writing to you the day after your funeral. I wanted to believe that if I wrote to you, I wouldn't lose you. You weren't gone. You were here, reading, your eyes crinkling at the corners, or your smile appearing or disappearing, as if you were at the kitchen table looking over my report card. A in Mathematics. A in Civics. A– in English. S in

Citizenship. This morning, I woke up looking for you in the rain, in the water coursing out of the branches, as if you were stooping to examine a footprint, a downed branch, a drowned beetle, and if only I turned this bend, if only I climbed out of this dell, I'd find you.

TUESDAY, FEBRUARY 15, 1944, 2015 HOURS
CAMP SHELBY, MISS.

I remember the day we found out I was going to UC Berkeley. I got the letter in the afternoon, but I waited to open it until you came home. I remember you, in the doorway, with your flag behind you. I remember you, smelling of grass cuttings. I remember you, telling me, for the first time, for the only time, that you were proud of me. You told me I was your American dream.

The dream: a gardener's son, a college graduate, an engineer, a doctor, a boy, a man who builds things or fixes them. The promise: five times what you can make in Japan. Opportunity, equality, freedom, prosperity. You know you'll be discriminated against. You know you won't be accepted as one of them. Your name is too foreign. Your skin is too yellow. Your tongue skips too lightly over their language. You still go. You won't have citizenship. You won't have property. You might not even have safety. But you still hope. This is the dream. A better life for your children and your children's children and their children. For Shig, and Minnow, and me.

Maneuvers ended this afternoon. Now we're resting our feet. We're cleaning our rifles. Soon we'll be reviewed, and if we're good enough, if we've proven ourselves, we'll be going to war.

SATURDAY, FEBRUARY 19, 1944, 2200 HOURS
CAMP SHELBY, MISS.

By some miracle, I held on to my weekend pass this week, so today I went into town, where the theater was playing *Blood on the Sun* with James Cagney. I don't know what I was expecting. I knew it was a propaganda film, but I guess after everything, I'd dared to hope.

Blood on the Sun: An American journalist in Tokyo uncovers a Japanese plot to take over the world. The boys would have hated it, Dad. I hated it. As usual, all the principal actors were Caucasian, even the ones who were supposed to be Japanese. (How could they have Japanese actors? We're all in camps.) I had to watch them parade across the screen in their fake eyelids, butchering both of my languages every time they opened their mouths. The sounds in the theater: the actors' tongues heavy as axes, the rapt silence of the audience absorbing every hateful scene, one guy behind me muttering "dirty Nips" again and again and again.

I looked around at the people in the audience, their faces almost translucent in the projector light, their hate bubbling inside them like boiling water.

The morning after you died, Ma didn't get up, and we didn't ask her to. I made breakfast for Shig and Minnow. The sounds of the kitchen: foghorns on the coast, Yum-yum practicing Beethoven a block away, cereal tumbling into white glass bowls, Shig letting the milk fall from his spoon. "Dad's flag," he said, and the three of us looked toward the front hall, where your triangle of stars was laid on the table by the door.

I flew it after you were gone. I had to learn to fold it after you were gone. Halved lengthwise and halved again. Turned at the corner, over and over and over, until all that was left was a wedge of blue and white. I followed the creases you had left, or at least, I tried to. I wanted to keep your flag when we left San Francisco, but there wasn't enough room.

SUNDAY, FEBRUARY 20, 1944, 1945 HOURS
CAMP SHELBY, MISS.

Today I strolled around town for a while. Did you know they have separate drinking fountains here for "white" and "colored"? Separate entrances, separate seating sections, nothing equal? Back in Japan, did you know, when you dreamed of America, that it was *never* equal? Did you understand? Did I?

I met another soldier, Leonard Thomas, a Black guy from Los Angeles. Small world: He knows Stan's friend Yosh's sister, Kimi. He used to share his lunch with her when they were in elementary school. She liked cherries, he said, laughing. "We used to throw the pits at our kid brothers." He and I were standing on the curb, talking, as a group of Caucasian guys approached us, walking three abreast, like they were a great white plow rolling down the sidewalk. Without even thinking about it, I stepped aside, Leonard stepped aside, and I wondered at how we'd been trained to do this, to recede, to shrink, so that Caucasians can have more space. As they passed us, one of them brushed up against Leonard's arm, where the American flag is stitched.

The Caucasian guy, snarling: *Out of the way, boy!*

...

I'm still thinking about that. Leonard is a grown man, a man in uniform, a soldier, an American soldier, and to them, he was still "boy." He stiffened, but only for a second, so fast that if you weren't watching closely, you'd have missed it, like for a moment, he was electrified, hot and angry. Then, a second later, he had averted his eyes, as if by doing that, he could make it so the Caucasians would walk away, would not demand an apology, would not pursue him further.

I've seen people do that before. I've done it before, many times. A month after you died, I pruned the Aldermans' flowering plum trees, the way you'd done for two years. They watched me clip branches for hours, and when I was done, they told me they wouldn't pay me because I wasn't the Jap they hired. In January 1942, I was followed back to the Chevy, to your Chevy, by four Caucasian men, who told me Nips weren't wanted in their neighborhood. I watched half of Japantown on the sidewalk with their luggage, with all the things they had left in the world, while armed soldiers herded them onto buses to be shipped away from the only homes they had ever known.

Leonard and I said nothing about it until it was time to return to Shelby, and he was forced to sit in the back of the bus while I hesitated, like I always do, on the border of the "colored" section, before sitting down in a seat marked "white." Although I am not white, never have been, not in America. I thought of Stan and his friend Yosh standing up to the army in Tule Lake, the same army whose uniform I wear, that Leonard wears. "This isn't right," I said to him, in the seat behind me. We were surrounded: white faces, white ladies, white gloves, white men. We were soldiers, and we were enemies, and there are so many fronts on which to fight. Leonard shook his head, murmuring, "You just figuring that out?"

I felt the air go out of me, like a flag that's suddenly been deprived of wind: no longer a high-flying beacon but merely cloth, beaten and limp. I knew, I had known it a long time, I had just never wanted to admit it, like you had never wanted to admit it, you with your dreams, what this country was and has always been.

MONDAY, FEBRUARY 21, 1944, 2130 HOURS
CAMP SHELBY, MISS.

Dear Dad, I try to remember what you taught me. Chin up. Back straight. Turn the other cheek. But if we never say anything, will they ever know they were wrong?

We received forty replacement officers today, lieutenants and up, all Caucasian. All of our officers are Caucasian. (The 100th Battalion had a Korean-American officer before they were deployed, but now they're fighting at Monte Cassino in Italy.) How long have Caucasians been telling us what we can and cannot do, where we can and cannot live, who we can and cannot love, who we are and cannot be? You wanted me to be able to choose: a gardener's son, a college graduate, an engineer, a doctor, a boy, a man who builds things or fixes them.

Minnow is on the high school newspaper staff in Topaz now. Can you believe it? He's already in the eleventh grade. He sends me a copy with every letter he writes, pointing out which comics he drew and which articles are his, and I think of you and me at the kitchen table, reviewing homework, quiz scores, report cards. I think you'd be proud of him, Dad. He says he's thinking of becoming a journalist, of telling things like they are to the people who need to hear it.

Is that what I'm fighting for, Dad? Minnow's right to decide what he'll become? His right to tell the truth? To *say something* without fearing for his safety? I thought I knew why I was here, why I volunteered: to prove we deserved freedom, liberty, and justice, like everybody else.

But only a few, a Caucasian few, have ever had those things.

Everyone says the new officers mean we're going to be deployed soon. The question: Atlantic or Pacific? Europe or Japan? People who look like our officers, or people who look like us?

SATURDAY, MARCH 4, 1944, 2100 HOURS
CAMP SHELBY, MISS.

We were reviewed today. They lined us up on the parade grounds to be examined by the Chief of Staff. You should've seen us, Dad. We looked like soldiers: rigid, focused, not a thread out of place. A+. The Chief of Staff didn't say much as he walked down the line, asking a question of this man or that. The sounds: a murmured comment, a "Yes, sir," the American flag snapping in the wind, *crack! crack! crack!*

Later, at the Service Club, I told Leonard that the Chief of Staff was pleased. Leonard sighed and lifted his glass. "Then you'd better kiss your ass goodbye."

Twitchy ran up, clinking Leonard's mug with his own. Lucky boy, his furlough came through. He's going back to Utah. He's going to say goodbye to his family, to Shig, to Keiko, whose picture he carries in his pocket.

They say it's going to be soon now. Less than a month, probably, before we get our orders. Leonard and I raised our glasses again. "For Mom," he said. His mother, who didn't want him to go, who said this country wasn't worth giving his life for; and my mother, who knew it's what you would have wanted. "And apple pie," I added softly.

We didn't say: *For honor, for the paychecks, for the knowledge that we rose above.* We didn't say: *For the insults we had to swallow, for the times we had to avert our eyes, for all the ways they've found to hurt us, for the curfews and confiscations, for the thousands of evacuations, for the camps, the lynchings, the segregation, for the grandfathers who were enslaved, for the mothers who pray for better, for the fathers who came with dreams of freedom, for the fathers whose dreams are unfulfilled, for the way it is and has always been, for the future, and the way we hope it to be.* We didn't have to. We're fighting for those things, whether we want to or not.

In the background, the Nisei boys were singing "You're a Grand Old Flag."

SUNDAY, MARCH 12, 1944, 1115 HOURS
CAMP SHELBY, MISS.

Shig's applying for resettlement in Chicago. He's been yakking about it since last year, but I never thought he'd actually do it. The work involved and all. Dumb kid doesn't even have a job lined up or a place to stay. You know Shigeo: jump first, think later. I told him to write to the WRA field office in Chicago to set himself up, but he says he's going to stay in one of the hostels they have for Japanese-Americans and get the lay of the land for a while. You can't tell that boy anything, can you?

I'm worried about him, Dad. I'm worried about the Jap hunting licenses, the Niseis who have been attacked in train cars, the windows that have been smashed in Japanese homes, the fires that have been started on old nihonjin farms in the West. I'm worried about him out there in America.

I want to believe in right and wrong. Here is what's right. Here is what isn't. Here is the line. Here is the question: If I go to war for America, if I kill for America, if I support an America that doesn't support me, am I supporting my oppressors? Am I killing their enemies so they can later kill me? I *volunteered*. I wanted to serve. But who am I serving, Dad? What am I doing here?

WEDNESDAY, MARCH 15, 1944, 1630 HOURS
CAMP SHELBY, MISS.

Dear Dad, we got our orders last night: POM. Prepare for Overseas Movement. We're going to clean the equipment, send out for new uniforms, crate the guns, the jeeps, the mortars. We're going to shutter the barracks and nail the latrine doors closed. We're going to scrub our mess kits so we don't get sick in the field. Not long left in Shelby, and then . . . your son is going to war.

Right now, the whole barrack is crackling with nervous energy, like static. A guy runs past you, and you get zapped. It reminds me of the evacuation. Someone tells us we have to go, and we go. No one knows where. No one knows what it's really going to be like. The only familiar things are what you can fit on your person: a letter, a snapshot, a piece of home. The rest, you leave behind. The rest of *you*, you leave behind.

I left the best of me behind, I think, with Shig and Minnow, with Stan and Tommy, Frankie and Twitchy. It's like pieces of me are scattered across this continent: Topaz, Tule Lake, Shelby, Chicago. I tried to be a rock, a support, a foundation. But I'm crumbling without them, Dad. I told you I started writing to you the day after your funeral, believing that if I wrote to you, I wouldn't lose you, but I think I've lost you. I think I've lost myself.

Would I know your voice if I heard it?

I wish I'd gotten my furlough, like Twitchy, who's leaving in a week. He's going to get Minnow to sign something for him, I think. A drawing. Minnow's a great artist, Dad, really great. I wish I'd seen it sooner. I wish I could've told him I was sorry for being so hard on him. And to disregard my dreams for him, because they're not as important as his own. I wish I could tell Ma I love her . . . and not to worry, even though I am worried. I'm scared, Dad, not just of dying, but of dying for the wrong cause.

Did you know Shig dared me to flunk a math test once? I couldn't do it, couldn't give it anything less than my best, couldn't bear to watch you read the F at the top of my paper, your smile disappearing. I volunteered for this. I said I would fight. So I will.

• • •

I wish I could tell Shig I'm proud of him for being braver than me.

Dear Dad, if I die out there, they'll give Ma an American flag just like yours. My very own triangle of stars. But I don't know if I'm going to want that, when the time comes.

I don't know if I want it now.

Hey, Keiko, I'm sending you one of our 442d RCT patches, like we wear on our uniforms. See how it's got the torch of liberty and the national colors? You better keep it safe, huh? Keep it in your pocket or under your pillow so you dream of me at night, ha ha.

Be home to you soon.
Twitchy

XII

THIS IS THE MOMENT

KEIKO, 18
MARCH 1944

13 HOURS

GATECRASHERS

It's Twitchy's last night in camp before he returns to the army, so to celebrate, you crash a wedding.

This is a moment. This is a memory.

Now the vows.

Now the rings.

Now four dumb kids sneaking in the back while everyone stands for the kiss.

Picture this: The recreation center decorated with the same fake flowers and crepe-paper streamers they reuse for every Topaz wedding. The stained white tablecloth on the Ping-Pong table. The refreshments arranged around the wedding cake like acolytes.

Sidling up to the cake, Twitchy takes a scoop of icing on his forefinger and pops it into his mouth. Seeing you watching him, he winks.

He wore his uniform for the occasion, damn him. The boy has got to know he looks good in khaki.

12 HOURS
FLOWER BOY

Now this: The single gals are huddled on the dance floor. The bride is throwing the bouquet. Twitchy Hashimoto is leaping in front of all of them, snatching the flowers out of the air like a football player intercepting a pass.

"Look, Keiko!" He waves at you, in the back. "I'm next!"

You cock an eyebrow at him and cross your arms.

He takes off running. The girls chase him around the room, over the chairs and around the Ping-Pong table, where they pin him against the wall, squealing and grabbing at him.

And why wouldn't they? In that uniform? With those dimples you could dig your fingers into?

This is a moment turning into a memory. Things happen quickly. Things are always slipping away faster than you can hold on to them.

"Shig!" Twitchy shouts. "Go long!"

He lets the bouquet fly.

Now a scream.

Now a scattering of petals.

The bouquet hits the floor, and Shig jumps back as the girls scramble for it. You watch them climbing over one another.

In the commotion, Twitchy parades to the back of the room where you're standing with Yum-yum and presents you a flower with a flourish and a bow. "Saved one for you," he says proudly.

It's a bruised white carnation, its petals creased, its blossom swinging precariously from a broken stem.

"Nice, Twitch," Yum-yum says.

Look, you didn't ask for Twitchy Hashimoto to fall in love with you. You're not the kind of girl who gets her wishes granted, and if you were, you wouldn't spend them on stupid things like wishing your prince will come.

Not that Twitchy Hashimoto is a prince.

But you can't help yourself. Look at those eyes. Look at that dopey smile.

You snap the flower's head off and tuck it behind your ear. "You're a damn fool, Hashimoto."

You don't say: *And I'm a damn fool for indulging you.*

11 HOURS
CAKE

You watch the bride and groom cut into the cake. The knife is gleaming. The groom's hands are trembling. Both of them grit their teeth nervously as the camera flashes—once, twice. All you can think is they're going to have a photo of them, their wedding cake, and Twitchy's fingerprint in the frosting.

This is a slice of time. This is a cross-section of lives. The happy couple. The photographer. Twitchy Hashimoto, whose name none of them know.

Twitchy nudges you with his elbow. "That could be us one day, huh? You'd look real good in white."

You smirk at him. "I look good in everything."

He grins, and those damn dimples appear in his cheeks. "Careful, Keiko, or your veil won't fit that swollen head of yours."

You don't want to think about that. A wedding requires a groom requires a fiancé requires a boyfriend requires a bouquet of roses or a box of chocolates or you wanting a boyfriend.

And you don't want a boyfriend. Especially not one who's leaving in the morning.

"Keep dreaming, Hashimoto. We're just friends."

"Yeah." He winks. "Like Katharine Hepburn and Spencer Tracy are just friends."

You find him infuriating. You find him charming. You find your heart a traitor.

Shig and Yum-yum squeeze out of the crowd, bearing slices of cake. Leaping up, Twitchy takes one and sashays out the door, calling, "Just admit it, Keiko! You've got it bad for me!"

Shig and Yum-yum exchange a long-suffering look.

You ignore them. You hike up your skirt and go stomping down the steps after Twitchy. "Me? You've been in love with me for months! Don't try to deny it!"

10 HOURS
P IS FOR PACKING

Shig's taking the train to Chicago the day after tomorrow, after Twitchy goes back to the army. If that seems like coincidence, it isn't. He postponed his resettlement so he could see Twitchy one last time.

Those boys. If you hit one of them hard enough, the other would feel it.

Shig's always been kind of lazy, so naturally he hasn't packed a thing. When you get back to the Itos' barrack, you, Twitchy, Yuki, and Minnow sit on Mas's empty cot, watching Shig pull clothes from his dresser. You share a bag of peanuts because watching Shig trying to pack is like watching a tornado trying to make a field goal. Half the barrack is destroyed before he's even filled one suitcase, because

Yum-yum keeps taking his shirts and pants out and throwing them back at him until he folds them like a goddamn grown-up.

This is the last night you'll be together. This is not the first time you've thought that.

You ate oden the night before Pearl Harbor, the perfect meal for a winter evening. Your mother was wearing a pink dress. Your father was grading papers at the table while you read Gertrude Stein and tried to figure out what the hell she was trying to say.

You drank spiked punch in this very barrack the night before Mas, Frankie, and Twitchy left for basic training. You threw up behind the latrines while Bette held your hair.

When the Katsumotos and the Haranos were packed off to Tule Lake, you walked Aiko back to her barrack while she tried not to cry.

You're sick of goodbyes.

"Hey, Shig," Yuki calls, "what's the first thing you're going to do when you get to Chicago?"

He grins. "Probably pee."

Yum-yum smacks him with a pair of pants.

"Ow." He makes a big show of rubbing his shoulder. "D'you hit your students like that, Miss Oishi?"

She sticks out her tongue at him. She's taken over teaching second grade at one of the elementary schools. You haven't seen her in action, but you bet she's perfect for the job. She got enough practice having to deal with her younger brother, Fred, all these years.

"*My* students know how to behave," she replies tartly.

9 HOURS
MUSIC
Shig isn't done packing yet, but you're all done watching him, so Yuki

cranks up Mas's Silvertone radio, filling the barrack with sound. It floods over Mas's unused dresser, spilling across the floor, pooling in Shig's open suitcases. You wonder if Mas knew, if that's why he lugged that damn radio all the way to camp, if he turned up the volume when there were no words left to say, if that's how he kept everyone together all these years.

Music is a connection, binding you all, everyone who hears it: you, Yuki, Yum-yum, Shig, Minnow, Twitchy, the neighbors in their beds, grimacing at the noise as they press their pillows over their ears.

You perch on the edge of the table next to Twitchy and you listen to Shig go on and on about Chicago. There's a good amount of Nisei out there, he says, and almost all of them are from the camps. They've got hostels, Japanese groceries, churches, youth groups, everything you need to set you up. Dances every Saturday. Movies every night.

"Boy, I've missed the city," Shig says.

"Eh." Twitchy shrugs. "Chicago's no San Fran."

He's not talking to you. He's not even looking at you. But somehow he's everything to you. You're not touching but you can feel him, his hand resting next to yours, and that distance is less than an inch and it's hundreds of miles. It's gravity. It's catastrophic. If you extended your pinky, you'd bring him crashing into you.

The song on the radio changes. Jimmy Dorsey croons "Bésame Mucho" from the speakers, and you wonder if, whenever you all hear it again, wherever you are, when Twitchy's in some little French hamlet or Shig pops open his suitcases in a dank Chicago hostel, you'll still be bound together.

This song, this memory, this night.

The last night.

8 HOURS
DANCING

Sometimes with Twitchy. Sometimes with Shig, with Yum-yum, with Yuki, with Minnow, who steps on your toes. Now the jitterbug. Now the Lindy Hop. Now the West Coast Swing.

Sometimes you all dance together, no one really knowing the steps and no one caring, legs kicking, arms pumping, skin slick and throats exposed with laughter.

Sometimes you dance alone, because hell if you need a partner. You dance under the bare bulb, hips swaying, limbs like liquid. You feel undulant. You feel powerful.

You feel Twitchy watching you.

This is a moment. This is your moment. You don't have to share. Especially not when sharing means you have to split yourself the way you've split yourself so many times before.

Mom.

Dad.

Mas.

Frankie.

Stan.

Mary.

Tommy.

Aiko.

Bette.

Now Shig.

Now Twitchy.

You've lost too much to give more of yourself away.

7 HOURS
GOODBYES

It's midnight, and the carriages are turning into pumpkins.

Now is the time. Now is the last time.

Twitchy takes a folded square of paper out of his pocket. The creases are deep as canyons, like he's folded and unfolded it so many times, it's going to rip apart.

He hands it to Minnow. "Sign it for me, will you?"

You catch a glimpse of a drawing: a stoop like the ones in Japantown, a boy.

Then Minnow bends to scribble something along the bottom, and you can't see anything more. When he folds the paper back up and returns it to Twitchy, there are tears in his eyes.

Twitchy tucks it into his shirt pocket and pats it once as if to make sure it's still there. "Hey, kid," he says gently, "don't cry."

Nodding, Minnow wipes his eyes.

Twitchy ruffles his hair. He says goodbye to Yuki and Yum-yum.

Now Shig.

Picture this: They stare at each other. From this angle, you can almost see how they fit together, these boys, like puzzle pieces, their elbows and shoulders molded to one another by the years, the adventures, the skinned knees and afterschool detentions.

Then Twitchy tackles him. They're half hugging, half wrestling around the room, knocking into chairs and bed frames.

Until they're not.

Until they're just hugging, standing still in the middle of the barrack, while the world spins on around them, time slipping away from them, faster and faster, out of their control.

Two boys who love each other, and one going off to war.

6 HOURS
WALKING

Twitchy offers to walk you back to your barrack, and you're not going to say no.

This is the way you hold on. This is the way you dig your fingernails in.

If you'd known to do this before, you would've helped your mom wash the dishes. You would've put down the book. You would've told your dad the papers could wait.

You would've held Aiko as she cried.

Four blocks left. Three blocks. Two.

"Are you scared, Twitch?" you ask. "Of what's going to happen?"

You don't say: *Because I am.*

"Eh, I try not to think about it."

"Why not?"

He kicks at the dust and doesn't look at you when he speaks. "'Cause it's outta my control. My future isn't mine anymore. It's the property of the U.S. government, and so am I."

You know it's stupid, but for a second, you feel a flash of jealousy for your own government.

"I'm gonna go where they want. I'm gonna fight who they want, kill who they want, die . . . if they want. So there's no point in thinking about the future, see? There's only right now. That's the only time that's really mine."

You want to take *right now* like a bull by the horns, but the bull is charging forward into the future and now is already slipping through your fingers.

You're almost there.

Now the latrines.

Now the showers.

Now the laundry.

Now your door.

You clench your hands. You dig your fingernails in.

This is your moment, and you're not letting it go.

You keep walking, past your barrack.

You pause when you notice Twitchy's not with you. You glance over your shoulder, and he's standing by your steps, watching you. You know he'll be etched into your memory like this: him and the barrack and the stars behind. But this is not a memory.

Not yet.

You tilt your head at him. You don't say: *Well? Are you coming?*

He smiles. He trots up to you.

You extend your hand, and he takes it. His fingers are smooth as they weave into yours, and you didn't know holding someone's hand could feel like this, like you're plugged into a socket, like you're bright and alive and tethered and home.

You don't go back. You don't go anywhere, really. You just keep going. You keep holding on.

5 HOURS

STRAWBERRIES

Twitchy emerges from the commissary icebox with a carton of strawberries and the bottle of Jack Daniel's he hid under the floorboards after he got it smuggled into camp. He shakes the bottle, frowning, and a couple of inches of gleaming bronze liquid slosh inside.

"Damn Shig. This was half-full when I left."

You take the bottle from him. "How d'you know it was Shig who drank it?"

"I've been blaming Shig for everything since I was four. Shigeo's the one who pulled Bette's hair! Shigeo's the one who cheated off my test! Shigeo's the one who didn't clean my rifle! Works every time." With a laugh, he plucks a strawberry from the carton and sinks his teeth into it.

You don't know why, but all of a sudden, you're sure you've never wanted anything as bad as you want to be that strawberry. To be tasted. To be on his tongue, between his teeth.

Twitchy grins at you, like he can read your thoughts, like he knows all your dirty secrets. Dimples again. "C'mon." He offers you his arm like he's a goddamn prince. "We've got plenty of time."

4 HOURS
STARGAZERS

You're tipsy with liquor and lack of sleep when you clamber over the barbed wire and stumble to one of the abandoned guard towers. You climb. You leave the earth. You feel free. You feel interplanetary.

The wind, blowing from some distant mountaintop, smells of snow.

You're not that high off the ground, but you're high enough, and when you sit with your backs against the guardhouse, you can't see anything but sky.

Now this: the desert silver with moonlight, the stars tumbling out of the darkness.

Now you drink.

Now you talk. About songs you like and books you've read or, in Twitchy's case, haven't read, letters you've gotten from Bette or Stan or Tommy, plans you made and never went through with, what you think about angels and the universe.

Now: "You were right, Keiko."

"I know." You laugh. "About what?"

"How I feel about you."

Your laugh twists into something desperate. "We're just friends."

"Yeah, like Katharine Hepburn and—"

"Stop." You cut him off. You tumble out of the darkness. You hate him for this. You were free of time. You were free of the future, and now all you can think about is a future without him.

"Look," you say. You try to set things straight. "I'm not going to spend the next six months pining after you."

You're lying to yourself, and you won't admit it.

He raises an eyebrow. "You think this war is going to be over in six months?" As if in afterthought, he smiles sadly.

You don't want to think about what could happen in six months, or a year, or two, or *whatever,* so you seize the empty bottle of Jack and fling it over the railing. It goes sailing into the air, spinning end over end, until it drops out of sight. In the distance, there's the sound of splintering.

"Keiko?"

"Shut up."

He gulps, his Adam's apple bobbing, a shadow on his throat. "Okay."

"I mean it."

He's watching you. His gaze flits to your face, your lips. "Okay."

You lean in.

For a moment, the world is a kiss that tastes of whiskey.

Then you part. There's a gasp like the air is being sucked out of the atmosphere. The world is a vacuum. The world is lacking. The world is empty, and you are wanting.

You allow yourself to want. You want him with you. You want him to stay. You want the earth to stop turning. You want tomorrow to never come. You want and you want and you want, and no amount of wanting will return the moments you have lost and the people you have loved, but you have not lost so many pieces of yourself that you don't want to give away one more.

So you kiss him again.

3 HOURS
TIME IS NOTHING

You kiss. You touch. You're looking out at the desert. You kiss. His fingers are in your hair. You're looking up at the sky, and his lips are at your throat. You kiss. He's lying beside you. You kiss. You kiss.

You slip out of time. You exist right now, and right now exists forever, so you exist forever.

This is the infinite moment.

Now a kiss.

Now a wanting, deep in your core.

Now you tell him you're not going to do more than kiss tonight, and he chuckles. "What, you don't want a nice, fat nihonjin baby?"

"No." You laugh. You're lightheaded. You're lightness itself. "Especially not *your* nice, fat nihonjin baby."

He touches your face, above your right eye, like every beautiful thing in this world is there in the arc of your brow. "Okay."

Grinning, you pull his mouth to yours.

2 HOURS
PROMISE

You're curled in the darkness. You drift in and out of sleep. You are together, and this moment is fleeting, and this moment is endless. You're up there forever, and you live on air. You come down from the tower, and the gravel crunches under your shoes.

You have all the time in the world and no time at all.

You don't say: *I love you.*

Neither does he.

Now this predawn lightness.

Now this quiet.

Now this shared stillness.

The seconds pass. The seconds linger.

Now this: the smell of greasewood, a kiss by the fence, in the street, in front of your door. Lights are appearing in windows all up and down the block. Eyes opening. Dreams fading. The glass slippers are turning to sand.

It's almost time. It was never enough time.

Twitchy cups your face. He's not smiling now, but somehow he looks happier than you've ever seen him.

And he's Twitchy Hashimoto, so that's saying something.

"Don't go," you say.

He puts his forehead to yours. "Okay."

"Don't," you warn him.

"I won't," he says.

But he does.

1 HOUR

CORN FLAKES

This is the memory: a muddle of paper flowers, cake crumbs, the music of Jimmy Dorsey, the smell of whiskey, a climb, a bottle breaking, a kiss, a thousand kisses, the taste of a strawberry.

Dry-eyed, you stir your cereal, watching it grow soggy, watching the milk turn gray.

You wish you could remember everything, but that's the nature of forever, isn't it?

That you forget.

You've forgotten what your parents were wearing when they were taken by the FBI. You've forgotten your final words to Mas and Frankie before they boarded the bus last May. You've forgotten the way it felt to hug Stan and Mary and Tommy and Aiko goodbye. You forget. You forget.

Picture this: Twitchy eating breakfast with his family. Twitchy packing the last of his things. Try to imagine. Try to remember. He's shouldering his duffle bag. His footsteps are echoing on the barrack steps. His neighbors are turning out to wave goodbye.

You're not ready. You were never ready. You'll never be ready.

0 HOURS

NOW AND FUTURE

At the gates, Twitchy says, "Write me."

Maybe it's the lack of sleep, maybe it's that you're having to do this again and you knew it was coming and didn't want to face it, but you're feeling slow and stupid and stubborn. Things are moving too fast. Things are slipping away from you. Things are ugly and bright, and one second is always followed by the next.

Now boarding.

Now the engine sputtering to life.

Now the driver on the horn.

"*You* write me," you tell him.

This isn't your cleverest moment, but it's one he'll remember.

He chuckles and kisses you one more time, in front of all his family and friends. Shig whistles. Mr. Hashimoto scolds him in Japanese.

"I will," he says.

They're unremarkable last words, except they're Twitchy Hashimoto's last words, in Twitchy Hashimoto's voice, and they're about the future and they're about you.

He winks and grins and lets you go.

This is what you have. This is all you have.

His words, his wink, his grin.

Those dimples you want to dig your fingers into.

He's going to board the bus. He's going to open the window. He's going to lean out as far as he can. Stupidly far, because he wouldn't be Twitchy Hashimoto if he weren't doing something stupid. He's going to wave as the bus drives off. It's going to be charging forward into the future, and he's going to be looking back at you, waving, waving, waving, waving—

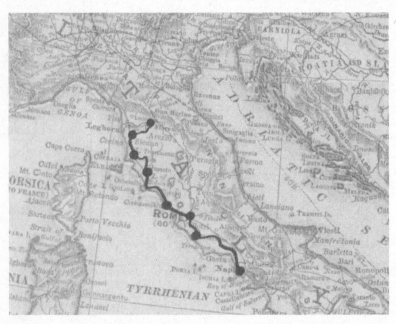

442nd Regimental Combat Team, Italy

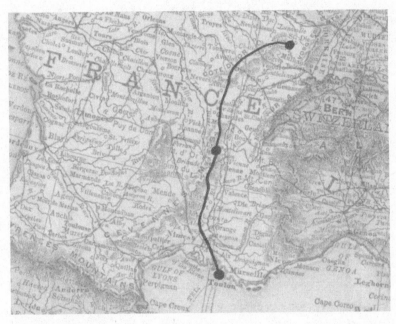

442nd Regimental Combat Team, France

XIII

COMPANY OF KINGS

TWITCHY, 19

JUNE–OCTOBER 1944

ITALY

NAPLES

JUNE 2

It's the first time I've set foot in another country, and don't get me wrong, I know what I'm here for—I saw those sunken destroyers in the harbor, the burned-out hulls pitted by shrapnel, I see the buildings collapsed by artillery fire—but goddamn, I'm excited. Everything's different in Italy—the smells are different, that stink of sea and sewage and sweat, the sounds, the way the language kinda sashays like every conversation is a dance or a knife fight, even the weeds growing out of the rubble are different—and I want to see everything, hear everything, know everything.

My buddy Bill Hayami—he's the only Hawaiian guy in our squad —says he's gonna try to get a pass to see the ruins of Pompeii.

And I say, "What the hell is Pompeii?" because it sounds like some dried flowers and shit white people would put in their bathrooms.

He laughs and calls me a stupid kotonk, you know, the sound a coconut makes when it hits the ground, but he also tells me all about how this real old Roman city got buried under a ton of ash when this old volcano erupted, and all that ash protected it from erosion or whatever until archaeologists dug it up thousands of years later.

Bill may be a buddhahead, but he's a real nice fella 'cause he always takes the time to explain shit to a dumb kid like me.

Funny how a place can be so old and so new at the same time, huh? New to me, but some of these buildings are older than the country I'm fighting for. All those cathedrals and palaces and stuff brought to their knees, piazzas jammed up with jeeps and GIs and bullet casings and trash.

ANZIO
JUNE 7

We get our first taste of war when the Germans decide to raid the supply dumps at Anzio, and me and my pal Kaz Okuda run to watch. Kaz's a funny guy. He kinda reminds me of Frankie, who's in Item Company, 3rd Battalion, so I don't see him much, but more than I see Mas, who's all the way over in 2nd Battalion, but smaller and wiry like a fighting weasel or something.

When we met, he told me, "No offense, but you better be in another company because I sure as hell don't want a guy named *Twitchy* covering my ass." Turns out we're both in the same platoon in King Company, and the first time we get to handle live grenades, Kaz fumbles his. Lucky for him, I snatch that thing right up and toss it before our platoon sergeant's any the wiser. Kaz liked me fine after that.

Now German planes are roaring through the sky, red tracer fire streaking through the darkness. Flames explode over the supply dumps. On the ground, the antiaircraft guns are flashing, flak bursts rat-a-tat-tatting through the air.

"It's like the Fourth of July!" Kaz shouts. His eyes are lit up like he's a kid seeing firecrackers for the first time.

"Except they're a month too early!" I say.

He laughs. Kaz has got this big laugh, all teeth and gullet. "Someone's gotta teach those Germans some goddamn U.S. history!"

BELVEDERE
JUNE 26

You can say a lotta things about me, but you can't say I don't admit it when I'm wrong.

And boy, am I wrong.

I *didn't* know what I was here for, and that raid at Anzio *wasn't* war.

No matter how much you march or how many targets you shoot or how many maneuvers you do, you can't really imagine it till you're in it. Till you've got orders to take some city in the middle of Tuscany you've never heard of and your buddy Bill hasn't either, and that's saying something 'cause Bill's gotta be the smartest guy in all of King Company, and you're charging up the road and your ears are ringing with the sound of artillery fire you can't identify yet and your weapon's slippery in your hands and you're running with the rest of your squad or who you hope is the rest of your squad—you can't tell 'cause it's so fucking chaotic—and you reach a shed or something and you look around for the guy next to you and suddenly the guy next to you isn't there, he's on the ground in that field you just crossed and there's a hole in his helmet where an MG got him and he's dead, shit you've never seen a dead guy before, but there he is.

Bill runs up and he's got this panicked look in his eyes and he's yelling, "That's Ted Araki! He's dead, Twitch!" and you're screaming,

"I know! I know! I saw!" Actually, you can't stop seeing it, even when you're not looking, and your sergeant's grabbing you by the jacket now, he's pulling you forward, shouting, "Keep moving! Get going!" and you want to obey 'cause you know you're supposed to obey but god-damn, Ted Araki is dead and you don't wanna fucking die, you wanna hunker down somewhere safe and quiet, except the last time you felt safe and quiet was in the arms of a girl in a desert and now she and the desert are half a world away and they're *shooting* at you, those bullets are *real,* those guys are really falling, dying, and holy shit, I mean holy motherfucking shit, this is really it, this is *war.*

3rd Battalion, that's Item, Jig, and King Companies, makes it fif-teen hundred yards or something before we're held up south of our objective. It's not even noon, and we're stuck. There's those big explo-sions our sergeant says are from German 88s and some automatic fire coming straight at us from Belvedere every time we show our faces.

Me and my buddy Bill are next to each other in the shelter of a road embankment, and he keeps taking off his glasses and cleaning 'em and putting 'em back on only to take 'em off again.

I lean back. "Shit, Bill, I didn't come all the way to Europe to sit in some ditch. When do we get a move on?"

Then they call the 100th Battalion outta reserve. Yeah, the same 100th that's made of Hawaiians who joined up after Pearl Harbor and replacements we sent from Shelby. The 100th that's been fighting in Italy for nine months. The 100th that almost took Monte Cassino with the 34th Division. The 100th they call the Purple Heart Battal-ion 'cause they've had so many guys wounded or KIA.

These guys are veterans now and goddamn heroes 'cause they go charging right up the middle between 2nd Battalion and us in 3rd, take the high ground, Belvedere, and another nearby village. I mean, you think you know something, and then some guys come along and show you that you know nothing and you'd better shut up, watch, and learn fast.

By the time 1700 hours rolls around, we're advancing again, driving the Germans right into the sweet embrace of the 100th. It feels different this time, knowing that the gunfire's gonna be all around us, knowing that after the 100th's lightning strike on Belvedere, we can't let them show us up, knowing that this is what we came here to do, this is really it, and we can't choke now.

MONTEVERDI
JUNE 30

After three days of fighting around Belvedere, they pull us back to Monteverdi. It's a pretty little hilltop town of red shingle roofs, green shutters, and stone the color of orange sherbet. Best of all, on the second day, me and Kaz are poking around, looking into storage sheds for eggs or some of that good Parmesan Mrs. K. likes to use on Italian night at the Katsumoto house, and Kaz is scuffling around, griping about something or another, when he knocks over a sack of grain. The thing hits the floor, *whump!*, and the burlap splits, spilling seeds like a little waterfall.

Kaz curses and kneels to scoop it back into the bag, but he stops. The grain's going right through the floorboards, and in the silence you can hear it falling, *sssssss,* down a long ways.

Quickly, we move some barrels around and pull up a trapdoor like the one my dad uses in Topaz to hide his sake still, and we look down this hole with a ladder leading into cobwebby darkness.

Kaz whistles. "Think it's a crypt or something?" he asks.

It isn't.

It's wine. Barrels and barrels of the stuff. Must be ten thousand gallons at least, all holed up below this old storage shed. Some of it's bottled, and Kaz is quick to taste it. "Gotta see if it's poisoned, am I right, Twitch?" He takes a big gulp, and his eyes go real bright. "Hell, if that's poisoned, I'm gonna die happy!"

Except we don't get a chance to enjoy it. Half an hour later, we're ordered out of Monteverdi and on to Bibbona, and I swear to God, Kaz couldn't've been sadder if he'd gotten a Dear John letter from his sweetheart back in Minidoka.

"All that wine!" he moans as we load into the trucks.

"Yeah," I say. "It's a crying shame."

"Don't gimme that," he says. "*You* didn't taste it. You don't know what you're missing."

"I'm not missing anything." With a grin, I flip open the top of my pack. Inside, I've got four bottles of wine for our squad.

He lets out a whoop that echoes off the Monteverdi walls. "Twitchy Hashimoto, you sly son of a gun!"

HILL 140
JULY 6

Guys who were injured at Belvedere start going AWOL from the hospitals and the aid stations, trying to get back to the line. They reappear at the company command post, grinning like nothing happened, maybe they've got a limp or something, but they say as long as they've got a working trigger finger, they wanna keep fighting. I mean, can you believe that? White boys go AWOL 'cause they're scared. Nisei boys go AWOL 'cause they wanna keep fighting.

You know what's funny? If a white guy abandons his post, he's a coward. It's a shame. But he's just one guy. But if a Nisei did that? Hell, it wouldn't just reflect on him, would it? Nah, we'd *all* be cowards.

I think that's why the 100th tackled Monte Cassino so many times last winter, even though it was hopeless. That's why they struck so hard that first day in Belvedere, doing in one afternoon a job that everyone else thought would take days.

Mas says it best, I think: We gotta be *better*. We gotta fight *harder*. We gotta be twice as perfect so they can't overlook us.

And we are. Fucking perfect.

We're on the western slopes of Hill 140, this ridge so long that in the distance you can see all the way down to the ocean, and the going's hard. The whole hillside's riddled with caves, and it seems like the Germans are holed up in every one of 'em, but we're protecting 2nd Battalion's left flank, and if they've got any hope of reaching the summit, we gotta be there for 'em.

We're under cover in this dry creek, but at any second the Germans could come striking at us from above, and our sergeant, Toshi Tamura, he peers over the lip of the wash. *Sprat-a-tat-tat!* Some machine-gun nest to our left goes after him. He ducks back down and he grabs his Thompson. "Cover me!" he says.

Then he runs out.

"What the hell!" Bill says. We're laying down covering fire, *bang bang bang bang,* shells flying. Sgt. Tamura is running across the slope, his Tommy gun chattering, Germans firing on him left and right, but he takes out the machine-gun nest. Lots of blood. Germans falling. He turns, fires again, takes out another bunch of guys we didn't even know were on our right.

"Holy shit!" I say. "Are you seeing this?"

The sarge is outta ammo now, so he tosses his Thompson, grabs a potato masher, you know, a German grenade, and chucks it into one of those goddamn caves. The machine gun's after him while the other Germans try to get his grenade out of their nest. Dirt's spraying up at his heels. He skids in the dust.

I'm screaming, *"Get outta there, Sarge!"*

Then *boom!* The cave explodes. He hardly stops. He gets right back up, and he's motioning us all outta the wash. "Get moving, boys! We got a hill to climb!"

And I look at Bill, and Bill looks at me, and we grin at each other and grab our guns and go charging out, out and forward, up the hill.

LUCIANA
JULY 16–17

Day one in Luciana, and we already know it's a different kinda fighting here.

Luciana's a small village, barely even a village, a dozen buildings, maybe, a couple blocks, it's even smaller than Japantown back home. But you take Luciana, and you've got the high ground on the port city of Livorno, which they call Leghorn but I like the rolling sounds of the Italian, *Lee-vorrrr-no,* and everybody knows that. Us and the Germans both.

So they don't give it up easy.

First thing, we're met with a barrage. They throw everything at us. Tanks. Artillery. Automatic weapons. Our first command post is a little house on the edge of town, and it's shelled so hard, we have to abandon it. Seconds later, the thing is totaled. Direct hit.

In the fighting, we lose most of our officers, including our company CO.

But we keep going. Our radioman's calling in enemy positions in Japanese and the 522nd Field Artillery is delivering, *boom! boom! boom!* A tank, gone. A machine-gun nest in a second-story window, destroyed. Our bazooka guys are blasting through walls and shop windows. Mortars are falling on the rooftops, in the streets.

That night, you hear patrols skirmishing in the darkness. The quick fire of machine pistols, Tommy guns. The guys on guard duty with you jumping at shadows. The guys who were sleeping or who were trying to sleep starting out of their dreams and grabbing for their rifles.

Day two's worse, if you can believe it. We're going house to house, room to room, smashing windows, throwing grenades. We kick open doors. We storm up creaking staircases. A guy at the window with a rifle. *Pop! Pop!* He gets two rounds in the chest and then I'm gone again, down the creaking steps, past the blown-out parlor and the dead bodies on the floor.

Every street crossing is a hazard, every street corner is a deathtrap. They've got snipers in every window, MGs — you know, machine guns — on every floor. Our squad has gotta cross this intersection, but we're too spread out. An MG's got some guys held up behind a pile of stones and warped iron from a collapsed balcony. Me and Bill are pinned in a doorway. The rest of our squad is somewhere farther down the street, trying to get to us, but if we don't hurry up, the Germans are gonna call in our position, and I don't wanna be around when the mortars start falling.

Me and Bill peep around the doorframe. There's a flash from

across the intersection, and we duck back as a bullet chips the wall where my head just was.

"You see where it came from?" I glance at Bill.

He clutches his rifle. "Don't do nothing stupid, Twitch."

I laugh. "Don't you know me by now?" And I dash out the doorway, into the street. Bullets ping against the stones behind me. I can almost feel them, they're so hot, and I think I could die, I could die right now, but I'm not afraid. I've got Bill backing me up.

There's a *bang* of Bill's M1 as I hurl myself against the wall on the other side of the road. The sniper fire stops. But I don't. I'm in the MG's line of fire now, and I'm scrambling for the nearest cover and I'm really scared this time, fingers digging at the cobblestones, trying to run faster, go faster, except you can't outrun a bullet.

But good old Bill's still watching out for me. While the Germans are shooting, he pulls the pin on one of his grenades and runs right up to that machine-gun nest. He flings a grenade through the window, but not before one of them gets him. *Crack!* He goes down. The walls explode outward.

"*Bill!*" I run for him.

The guys are all around me. They're shooting out windows as I drag Bill outta the line of fire, but my hands are slick. I don't know where he's bleeding from. I'm screaming, "Medic! Medic!" as I get him behind the rubble again.

The rest of our squad's passing us, and he's patting me, saying, "I'm doing fine, Twitch. I'm doing fine. They just got my arm. I'm doing fine."

Sgt. Tamura's leading the squad across the intersection and the medic's heading for us and by God I can't believe we made it but we did, and all I had to do was a bit of running.

I let out a chuckle and fix his glasses, which were knocked crooked when he got hit. "You're one crazy motherfucker, Bill."

He grins at me. "Yeah, yeah. Stupid kotonk."

By midafternoon, we're running outta ammo and there's jeeps coming in at the edge of town, but half of them are shelled on the way in and don't make it. Luciana's in ruins. This little village. Roofs collapsed, rubble falling into the streets, shrapnel flying, shells exploding, guys crying "Medic!"

Then someone calls in an artillery barrage. We find cover as hundreds of rounds rain on Luciana. The noise is deafening. That sound of breaking rock, wood splitting, rockets exploding, glass showering the chewed-up ground.

And I'm watching this and I'm rubbing my knuckles, waiting for the barrage to end, waiting for orders to push on, and I'm thinking about Japantown. The Toyo Hotel demolished, all the bay windows on Post Street shattered, Uncle Yas's tailor shop blown to pieces by a grenade, dummies and sewing needles on the floor, the churches turned into rubble, Katsumoto Co. raided, corpses in the aisles, Yum-yum's piano in the middle of the street, splintered by shell fragments, its innards showing.

Then Sgt. Tamura is telling me to move, and I'm back in Italy, I've got my rifle and my orders, and by dusk we're chasing the last resistance out of Luciana and my hands are so black I don't even remember that part of it's blood, German blood, Bill's blood, until I start trying to wash 'em clean again.

VADA

We get as far as the road between Livorno and Firenze, which they call Florence, when they pull us back to Vada for hot showers and a couple nights of rest. Me and Kaz even scrounge up some pretty good grub. There's some ceremonies. The 100th Battalion gets its Distinguished Unit Citation for the job they did at Belvedere. In 2nd Battalion, Mas gets to meet the king of England, who's in Italy to review the troops or something.

A couple days in, Frankie comes over from Item Company to find me. He's got a butterfly knife, like the old one they took from me back in San Fran.

"Jeez, Frankie," I say, flipping the blade open and shut, open and shut, finding the rhythm of it again after over two years, the familiar *click click click click* of handles coming together. It's like a little piece of home, right here in my hands. "Where'd you get this?"

He shrugs and takes a swig of the cognac I liberated from an enemy observation post near the river. "Got it off some dead German."

"What's a dead German doing with a butterfly knife?"

"Nothing. That's why I took it."

Click click click click.

"How're you doing out here?" he asks.

"You know me." I grin at him. "Having a ball."

He gives me a look. He's got this mean-looking scar on his chin now from a grenade fragment. "You hear from any of the folks back home?"

"I write 'em all the time."

He wipes his mouth with the back of his hand. "I don't."

In the evenings, we spend a helluva lot of time slinging the bull about all the things we've seen and done. Guys talk about the grateful Italian women. Kaz tells the Monteverdi story over and over, embellishing it a little more every time. Sgt. Tamura's too modest to say anything about his run on Hill 140, so I tell that one and I tell it pretty good. During the day, we even do a bit of training with the replacements to get them ready to go into the field. No one who's been out there already really wants to go back, but we all laugh about it and say, "Yeah, get us back on the line. We'll push those Germans outta Italy. Lemme at 'em. I'm ready. Hitler's got another thing coming. I'm ready. I'm ready. I'm ready."

ARNO RIVER
AUGUST 20–SEPTEMBER 5

Course we do end up back on the line, on the Arno River, west of Firenze, trying to throw the enemy off-balance. But we're veterans at this now. We patrol the hedges, we skirmish in the vineyards, our OPs get hit by artillery, our guys by small-arms fire, our guys go to the aid stations, our guys get up again, our guys keep patrolling, skirmishing, fighting. We're all looking for prisoners 'cause we wanna know what the Germans know, and some of us get lucky and capture some troops from the Panzergrenadiers.

We cross the river. We cross a minefield with the help of some Italian partisans. We occupy San Mauro, where I'm on guard duty with Bill, who went AWOL from the hospital to get back to us, and split a tube of Limburger cheese as we watch the sun go down on the river, turning the waters red.

NAPLES
SEPTEMBER 27

As soon as we're relieved, there's talk of sending us to France. For a while, we're shuffled around. Castiglioncello, the 88th Division, Piombio, the Seventh Army, Naples again.

Naples is different, somehow. There's still the sunken destroyer in the harbor. There's still weeds in the rubble. But it's dirtier, more crowded, replacements yakking and patting their rifles, saying shit like, "Berlin by Christmas," guys with their legs blown off getting wheeled over the cobbles, everything looted and stripped down, the fountains clogged with dead leaves. I dunno if it's me or the city or both that's changed, but when we finally board the assault boats that'll take us out to the navy transports, I watch the collapsed buildings and cathedrals and palaces and piazzas disappear, and all I can think is I'm glad to be leaving them behind.

FRANCE
LYON
OCTOBER 11

Once we get to France, most of the 442nd Regimental Combat Team departs for the line in a bunch of old trucks, but us suckers in 3rd Battalion have to wait another couple days before we're crammed into ancient 40x8 boxcars—that's forty guys or eight horses—and sent by railroad like cargo.

We're chugging up the Rhone Valley in these rickety old trains and we pull to a stop in Lyon, where we hop out to stretch our legs. It's a rail yard, so there's not much to see, just some woodland and some tracks, but I'm poking around the other cars when I slide open this door and find crates upon crates of C rations, all those beautiful cans, ham, turkey, stew, franks and beans, powdered coffee, graham crackers, and it may not seem like much, but we've been on a steady diet of pork loaves and fighting biscuits from our K rations and whatever we can scavenge, so right now a can of stew is a real sight to behold.

I whistle. "Hey, Kaz, Bill, c'mon!"

And we just start taking stuff. We're carrying boxes back to our 40x8 by the armful, and as soon as Sgt. Tamura catches on, he organizes a supply party and before you know it, the whistle's blowing and we're all clambering back into the boxcar with twenty new cases of nutritious combat meals.

There's things I'm never gonna forget, like the sight of the Japantown boys running down Buchanan Street or the first time I saw Keiko laughing in the snow, and I know this is gonna be one of 'em.

The whole squad's perched on the C rations, all of them, Kaz and Bill and Sgt. Tamura and the rest, and they look damn good up there, laughing and talking and passing around a pack of cigarettes.

These guys, I'm telling you. These tough sons of bitches, these Nisei warriors. Some of us have been together since Shelby, and that means we're real fucking close. We can recognize a guy by the way he walks in the dark, by the way he *breathes*. We're in the shit together when the shit hits the fan and there's no one in the world we'd rather be in the shit with 'cause there's no better bunch of guys in this or any other army.

No wonder they call us King Company, huh? We're like goddamn royalty out here.

I'm just scrambling into the car when this colonel appears. He's a hairy guy, he's got so much hair, you can see it sticking out his nostrils when he looks up at us and starts yelling.

"What do you think you're doing? Put those crates back!"

The whistle's blowing again and the train's starting to roll and we're all waving from our C-ration thrones. Someone tosses him a packet of instant coffee that lands inches from his polished boots.

"You're all going to be court-martialed for this!" he's saying. "I'm a colonel!"

Laughing, Kaz salutes him as we roll the door shut. "Thanks for the grub, Colonel!"

BRUYÈRES
OCTOBER 18–24

And that's a lot of fun, but it's the last bit of real fun we're gonna have for a while, because as soon as we get to the assembly area at Charmois-devant-Bruyères, it starts raining, and it doesn't let up. After an hour it doesn't even matter that it's raining 'cause we're already soaked through, and then it's the cold that gets you, the cold that's almost freezing but not quite, and you're shaking so much, you don't even notice it until you're trying to hold your rifle and you can't keep the damn thing still long enough to shoot.

Thanks to the 100th and the 2nd Battalions, who've been fighting it out on the hills around Bruyères, it only takes a day and an artillery barrage to clear the town. By evening, we're going house to house with the 143rd Infantry, rounding up prisoners, and me and Bill are marching a German out of a blown-out townhouse, and one of the boys from the 143rd says to me, "I wanna ask you something."

I glance at Bill, who shrugs. "Yeah?" I say.

"How is it you 442nd boys don't got an ounce of fear?"

"Oh, we're afraid, just like you and anybody else and this guy

277

here." With a laugh, I poke the prisoner, who kinda glances back at me over his shoulder. He doesn't look much older than Minnow. Jesus.

"You're shitting me," the guy from the 143rd says. "What's your secret? Some kinda Oriental meditation thing?"

I wanna say, *Hai, hai. It ancient Bushido technique called kusottare. You want know how?*

But then I think of Ma and Pa and my siblings back in Topaz and I wanna say there is no secret. There is no secret, you just gotta do the job, you just gotta get out there and do the thing you were trained for, the thing you volunteered for, because there's a bunch of people back in America counting on you, and they're in camps, they're in fucking camps, they were forced outta their homes, they were put in stables like goddamn animals, they had their jobs taken, their families, their liberties, and you're here as evidence that all that shit was wrong because the ketos won't see they've fucked up until they see Nisei boys spilling blood over it.

I think of Shig and his origami and I wanna say, *Gaman.*

Instead I say, "Yeah, and it takes a year of silence to master, so you better start now." And me and Bill walk away with that prisoner who reminds me of Minnow.

That night, I'm jarred out of a dream when the 232nd Engineers blow a roadblock, and all the windows in Bruyères are shattered. My ears are ringing for a long time afterward, and I dunno why, but in that ringing, I keep thinking I hear the distant sound of a piano. Some faint melody like when you'd walk past Yum-yum's block and you'd hear her practicing, the notes floating like soap bubbles down the street.

• • •

In the morning, we jump off against Hill D east of Bruyères, and it's like we're fighting in a dream, in a nightmare, with a cold fog on the slopes and the pines breaking under enemy fire, crashing all around us.

The Germans are all dug in here and they've got such good cover, we pass 'em right by and don't even know they're there until they pop up behind us.

We hit the ground. We try to find some cover. A fallen tree. A broken stump. A low place in the terrain with the rainwater pooling in it.

Me and Bill are trapped behind a log with a few limbs for cover. There's a machine-gun nest only twenty-five yards off, and they're peppering us with fire, splitting the log, breaking the branches, making the air smell stronger and stronger of pine, and me and Bill are doing our best to return fire when my rifle jams.

We can't stay here, but there's a dead German nearby and *he's* got a weapon he isn't using, so I lunge for him. Dirt sprays up around me as I take his weapon and roll into a little divot of earth that's not much cover but it's some. Even better, I've got that machine-gun nest in my sights and as Bill gets their attention with his Thompson, I shoot. It's a German rifle, but it's not that different from my M1. Aim and fire. Aim and fire. I get four of them with their own bullets, and me and Bill continue the advance.

By noon, we've taken Hill D and we've got orders to move on to the railway embankment near La Broquaine, so we go dig ourselves in a hundred yards from the German line. Only problem is, and we don't find this out till we get there, that us suckers in King and Item Companies are bivouacking in the middle of a goddamn minefield.

The Germans got all sorts of mines—teller mines to take out

tanks, S-mines or "Bouncing Betties" that pop twice, once to jump into the air and a second time to blast you with shrapnel—and until the 232nd Engineers can get here to sweep the place, we gotta clear our own paths.

So it's near dark and it's still raining and my job is to find a way to the observation post so we can relieve the forward observers, and I'm belly-down in the mud, poking around with my bayonet, hoping not to trigger a tripwire or a shoe mine, 'cause one of those can be set off by the pressure of a single step, and my face is so close to the ground right now, it wouldn't be a pretty sight for the folks back home if I got hit.

Every time I find something, I wrap a bit of toilet paper around a rock and place it so the guys behind me know where not to step, and I think about how something you use to wipe your ass is the only thing keeping you alive, and I can just picture Shig laughing over that in some dinky room in Chicago, good old Shig, who writes pages of nothing 'cause he knows anything written in his chicken scratch is better than anything here, descriptions of the hostel where he's been staying, the crummy all-nihonjin dances that're no fun without Yum-yum, the shit jobs he gets and quits 'cause he's always been a lazy bum and he's not gonna change now, and I wonder if I'll still be alive when he gets my letter, or if I'll have been taken out because the toilet paper disintegrated in this goddamn rain and I didn't step carefully enough.

The next morning, me, Bill, and Kaz are crouched in a foxhole when Sgt. Tamura comes to tell us we've been attacked from the rear. "Germans on Hill D," he says grimly.

"We just took Hill D," Kaz says, poking at the layer of ice that's formed on the puddle at the bottom of the foxhole.

"Guess they took it back," Bill says.

With his finger, Kaz submerges a chip of ice, which bobs to the surface again as soon as he's released it. "Why'd we take it in the first place if we couldn't keep it?"

Three companies are sent back to retake Hill D, and the rest of us push on. It takes us all day to cross the embankment, but once we're on the other side, it's another long fight to push the Germans back to the Belmont forest.

The fighting seems like it's dying down when we stumble onto a German squad in their slit trench. The sudden fire. The scramble for cover. We're ducking behind trees and returning fire, and Sgt. Tamura gets 'em with a rifle grenade. There's an explosion of earth and wood, and in the smoke, we're shooting at silhouettes, which fall one by one until there are no more.

I'm breathing hard. I've got my rifle to my shoulder. I'm blinking rain out of my eyes.

A guy gets up, gray uniform almost black in the downpour.

I shoot him straight through the helmet.

He falls.

We move forward. If those Germans are alive, we've gotta capture 'em. "Shit, Twitchy," Kaz says, starting forward, "I think you got an officer!"

I'm so close, I hear the first explosion of the S-mine, that soft *boom* of the Bouncing Betty as she takes off into the air, and I fling myself face-down in the dirt as the second charge detonates, and it's deafening this time, so loud it knocks the sound outta the world, and for a second I'm lying on the ground and my ears are ringing again with that piano song I can't quite remember, but then the ringing fades, and someone's groaning. Someone's gibbering and whimpering.

"Bill?" I call.

"Doing fine," he says. "I'm doing fine."

"Kaz?"

No answer. Just a moan. Just a cry. He's ten yards away from me and his uniform's all ripped to hell and I'm running to him even though there could be another mine around here. I'm turning him over and he's bleeding from so many places, I can't count 'em all. Sgt. Tamura is shouting for a medic, and Kaz is looking up at me, and half his face looks like pulp.

"I got you," I say. "I got you, Kaz. It's gonna be okay."

He gulps and looks up at me out of the one good eye he's got left. "We got an officer, huh?"

I have no idea, but I'll say anything to keep him calm at this point, so I say, "Yeah, we got him." I'm trying to apply pressure, but I've only got two hands and there's just so many holes in him.

He grins. Kinda crooked. I dunno why he's grinning, but he's still got that dumb look on his face when the medics take him away on a stretcher.

Turns out we did get an officer, and he had plans for the defense of the whole sector on him. They make a task force. They send 'em out in the dead of night to outflank the Germans on Hill 505. I wonder if Kaz knew if it would happen like that. If that's why he was grinning like a damn fool.

The next few days are senseless. They send us at this hill, at that hill, clear out that enemy pocket, flush those Germans from cover. We do what they say, we take our objectives, but a day later, the areas we just cleared have been taken again. *Take Biffontaine. Defend Biffontaine. Get supplies to the 100th at Biffontaine 'cause now they're cut off.* I write home. I write to Keiko. I tell Shig about that toilet paper stuff. I hope that in writing, things will make sense again.

They don't.

BELMONT
OCTOBER 25–26

When we're finally pulled back to Belmont for some rest, I find out that Kaz is gonna live. They're sending him to a hospital, then back home, and it's funny because I know he's lying on a cot somewhere with a roof over his head and some nurses checking his bandages or whatever, waiting to get well enough for the ship back to America, but to me it's like he's dead because—home? Thinking of home? It's like thinking of heaven. Some place you hope you'll end up one day, but good luck, buddy, because you're a soldier, not a saint.

I dunno what happened. Two months ago, three months ago, home seemed so close. A little fighting, and the war would be over. A little fighting, and we'd be sent back to our families. A little fighting, and we'd all be reunited in San Francisco, with those beautiful red towers rising out of the fog. Me, Shig, Keiko, my folks, my siblings, Minnow and Mas and Frankie and Stan Katsumoto and Tommy and Yum-yum and Bette Nakano and all their kid brothers and sisters . . .

Now I'm in this little village in the Vosges Mountains, stripping off my clothes in a shower tent with the sounds of shells falling on the main road junction, and my skin is white and wrinkled from the rain and cold to the touch and I look like a corpse, and home is like one of those dreams that seem so real when you're asleep, but when you wake, you can barely remember them. Because in the dream, things made sense, they had that dream logic, only when you wake to this, to the chatter of a machine pistol, to a guy crying for a medic, to new orders, *Take this hill, take that hill, keep moving forward, keep pushing 'em back,* nothing makes sense anymore. What's peace? you wonder. What's it like to walk down the street, to walk from one building to another and not run for cover at the sound of a German howitzer? What's it like, you wonder, to dance to the sound of the radio? To eat rice out of a bowl with a pair of hashi? To close your eyes and get some shuteye and not be afraid of waking?

Tossing everything but my dog tags, I stand under the hot water and wait to thaw.

FORÊT DOMANIALE DE CHAMP
OCTOBER 27–29

We're hoping for a week of rest at Belmont, but of course we don't get it. They've got something that needs doing, another objective that needs taking, and who're they gonna send in but the boys in the 442nd? 2nd Battalion is ordered out on the 26th. Us and the 100th follow the next morning at 0400.

There's no light, no light at all, just us and the rain and the dark. We're marching in columns, but it's so black out here, I can't see the guy in front of me, the only way I know he's even there is by the sound of his footsteps and the creaking of his gear. I feel like I'm marching into nothing, we're gone, we're going nowhere, we're dead already.

Then the guy behind me grabs onto my pack, this heavy tug, like a weight, like an anchor, and all of a sudden I'm connected to something. I grab the guy in front of me, the strap of his pack in my fist, and I feel him grab the guy in front of him, and we're all links in this long chain, and we're walking through the darkness, but we're not walking alone.

•••

I dunno what to tell you. We lose a lot of guys in those woods.

Their legs are blown off by mortars. Their bodies are undone by machine-gun nests. Their skulls are punctured by sniper fire. A tank takes out our platoon leader and all the guys that are with him.

Still, we move forward. A yard at a time. A tree at a time. We move forward.

Guys get wounded, little wounds our medic patches up, 'cause there's no going back. If you can walk, you stay on the line. Part of it's 'cause we have to. Part of it's 'cause our supply lines are in danger and half the stuff we ask for, ammo, supplies, replacements, doesn't make it to us, so even if we wanted to go back, we couldn't.

But we don't wanna go back.

I dunno why. It's like a compulsion now. It's not just our duty. It's not just our orders. It's like we're detached from reality somehow, like we're a thread that's come loose, and the only thing we've got to hold us together is the mission. The moving forward. The next yard. The next tree. We dunno why. We don't have to know why. We just keep moving forward.

It's the first night and no one's getting any sleep, but at least they got us some replacements and some coffee, and me and Bill have got a cozy setup in our foxhole with a little fire and a tarp for light discipline when our new platoon leader, Lieutenant Parker, comes around to check on us.

"Hey, Lieutenant, how's it?" Bill offers him some coffee, which he waves off.

"How're you boys doing out here?" he asks.

"We're doing fine, sir," Bill says.

"Snug as a bug in a freezing pit of water, sir," I add.

Lieutenant Parker laughs like he hasn't heard a joke in weeks, which maybe he hasn't. I think I'm gonna like this guy.

"Say," he says, taking an envelope from his pocket, "I've got a letter for some guy called David Hashimoto. I've been asking around and no one seems to know who he is. You don't think the mail guys made a mistake?"

I'm taking a sip of coffee and I almost spit up all over our new lieutenant, but I hold it back. "I'm David Hashimoto," I tell him.

He cocks an eyebrow at me. "You?"

"Me, sir."

"They told me your name is Twitchy."

I shrug. "Just a nickname, sir."

As he hands me the letter, he looks me up and down. "David, huh?"

"Yes, sir."

He laughs again and shakes his head. "You don't look like a David."

I grin. "Thank you, sir."

He nods at us. "All right, well, I'm gonna check the line. You boys keep your heads down and don't get hit, huh? We've got fighting to do tomorrow."

"Yes, sir," I say as he lifts the tarp and crawls out into the darkness.

"Shit." Bill takes the cup from me, and his hand is shaking so bad with cold that the coffee sloshes onto his gloves. "I forgot your name was David."

The letter's from Keiko. She says Shig's gotten a new job as a dishwasher at some place in Chicago. She says my folks are well. She says she's been stealing fruit from the iceboxes in my honor. She says there's talk of lifting the exclusion order that's kept us from the West Coast, so they could be going home any day now. She says she misses me. I'm reading it for a second time when we find out that Lieutenant Parker was killed as he was checking the line. Another officer gone. Another guy dead. I sigh, fold up Keiko's letter, and try to get some sleep.

The next day we run into a manned German roadblock, and these things are no joke. A whole company of infantry with a nice fat supply of automatic weapons, and we can't keep moving forward unless we get rid of 'em, so it's us and whatever we're carrying against these well-armed, dug-in soldiers, and I'm not a gambling man, but those aren't great odds, except us and whatever we're carrying have taken every objective they've asked of us for five fucking months and we're not about to stop now.

Guys are advancing alone, killing snipers, knocking out machine guns. Guys are using bazookas and stolen pistols and their Thompsons. Me and Bill blow a machine-gun nest with a potato masher and go jumping in after to take out the gunners. I get one of 'em with my butterfly knife, *click click slash,* and then we're moving on, we're moving forward again, me and Bill.

We're on the far left flank with the rest of our squad when there's a rustling in the underbrush. I don't even have time to look before Bill yells, *"David, get down!"* and tackles me as the rattle of machine-gun fire breaks over us. I hit the dirt with him on top of me, and the guy's heavy, so I'm balled up on the ground with that *rat-a-tat-tat* all around me and I can't see anything but twigs and mulch, but then there's the *boom* of a grenade and the MG stops.

I kinda catch my breath for a second. "Bill?" I shake him a little. *Doing fine.* That's what he's supposed to say. *I'm doing fine.*

"Bill!" I say again. I'm struggling out from under him, and he's *too* heavy now, he shouldn't be this heavy. *"Bill!"*

But he doesn't answer, and when I turn him over, he's all shot through and there's blood coming from his mouth and his glasses are gone and he's staring at nothing. To our left is the smoking remains of a hidden machine-gun nest, and ahead of us the rest of our squad is moving forward, and Bill's dead.

"C'mon, soldier," Sgt. Tamura says, hoisting me up. My legs are like rubber. *Bill's dead.* "We can't stay here."

The rain's striking Bill's upturned face as we leave him on the slope, as we keep moving forward, pushing forward, 'cause there's a hill to be taken and it's our job to take it.

We gain five hundred yards that day. Bill's life for five hundred yards.

That night, I'm sitting down, staring at the puddle forming at the bottom of my foxhole, the rain pattering its surface the way it pattered Bill's dead face, small, never-ending drops, and I'm thinking about how he called me David. Funny, right? I don't think he's called me David once since we've known each other, it's always been "Twitchy" or "stupid kotonk," but almost the last thing he says to me is my given name. I can almost hear him now, saying how funny it was, how he didn't even think about it, must've been that stuff with the lieutenant and the letter last night. Funny.

There's movement between the trees, and wouldn't you know, it's the commander of the whole division walking by with his aide-de-camp. I guess they want to see the front. I guess they want to walk those five hundred yards they bought with Bill's life.

They're so clean. That's the thing I notice, how clean they are. I wonder if they smell clean too, like shaving cream or cologne or whatever, or if they smell like mud and sweat and damp like the rest of us.

I dunno how long I think about that, but sometime later, there's the report of a rifle, and I'm crouching in my foxhole, searching the darkness for signs of movement, and someone's calling for a medic, and soon the Division Commander's walking back in a hurry. He's missing his aide and he's got blood on his hands and his uniform, which means he's not so clean anymore, and he looks at me looking at him without his aide, those pouchy eyes beneath his helmet, and he doesn't say anything.

Maybe I drift off. Maybe I dream of Bill, of Kaz, of Keiko, of Shig, and when Sgt. Tamura slides into the foxhole with me, for a second I'm disappointed because for a second I thought for sure he'd be Bill.

"The general's aide okay?" I ask him.

Sgt. Tamura looks tired. "He'll live."

"Huh."

"They say one of our battalions from the 141st is out there." Sgt. Tamura nods toward the front, toward the rest of the hill we've yet to take. "That's why we're doing this. There's two hundred guys out there with Germans on all sides, and no one's been able to get through to them for days. They're going to die out there if we don't get to them."

I look out into the woods, like I'll be able to see the silhouettes of the lost soldiers out there, helmets and M1s, or peeking between the trees with their pale, rain-washed faces, like I'll be able to see Bill out there.

And even though I know we won't find Bill, even though we might lose a lot more guys tomorrow, I somehow manage a grin. "Then I guess we'd better go get 'em, huh, Sarge?"

•••

The ridge up to the Lost Battalion narrows until there's only room for King Company and Item Company to advance, and we're chipping away at the German defenses, gaining a yard here, a tree there, when we're held up by mines and artillery fire. It's death from above and death from below, and guys are falling all around me, dead, wounded, wounded, wounded, dead.

So we try to flank 'em on the left side, but it's so steep and they're so dug in that we come out with half the guys we started with.

Then we try to hit 'em with tanks and artillery and maybe we get a little farther this time, but we're stopped again by machine guns and mortars, and, Jesus, we're down to a third of our fighting strength, and I know I said we've taken every goddamn objective they've asked us to, but this hill, this one hill, this fucking hill in France, this one hill and two hundred stranded guys from the 141st, two hundred guys to save and we've already lost more than that, double that, triple that by now, dead, dead, wounded, dead, dead and wounded Nisei boys, and this one hill might finally have us beat.

So we're driven back after two failed attempts and we know that if we're gonna do this thing, if we're gonna do what we always do and that's take our objective, if we're gonna break through to the Lost Battalion, we're gonna have to go through the Germans, those Germans on their high ground, in their machine-gun nests and slit trenches, those Germans with their guns and mortars, who've been told to hold to the last man 'cause we're on the edge of their border and they're what stands between us and their homeland.

And the orders come down.

Take the hill.

We look at one another. The rest of the platoon. The last of the platoon. No more officers. No more Kaz or Bill. Just us clutching our weapons and Sgt. Tamura to lead us, if he wants to lead us, if we wanna follow him, up that hill.

All up and down the line, no one moves.

There it is. No one wants to go. No one wants to move forward now because moving forward means throwing yourself into the paths of the MGs, means leaping toward the artillery fire, means launching yourself at death with your rifle in your hand and your heart in your throat.

Sgt. Tamura looks around at us and he sighs and he takes up his pistol. "Well, boys?" he says. "Let's go."

He's first. First out of the foxholes. First into the line of fire. I dunno how they don't get him right away, how the bullets don't find him, how the shells miss him by what seem like miles on this narrow ridge, but they don't. He keeps going, keeps moving forward.

And as we watch him, charging up that slope, we, too, break from cover. We keep moving.

I go pretty fast in life, but for some reason this part's real slow. Trees are exploding all up and down the hillside. Dirt's flying. Guys are lunging forward, shooting from the hip. The ground's muddy. The earth's torn. There's fire all around us, and we know we don't have a chance in hell of making it, but for a second it seems like we're invincible, unstoppable, kings of this godforsaken hill.

The guy next to me opens his mouth. He looks scared. I guess we all look scared. Scared and determined and fucking *magnificent*. And he shouts, *"Banzai!"*

Banzai.

The word rushes over me like a river. A memory of what we used to say on the streets of Japantown when we played at war. A memory we inherited from our fathers and their fathers, this word, this history, this giving of ourselves for the nation, for the emperor.

Except now it's not for the emperor.

I don't think, in this moment, that it's even for our nation.

It's for us, for our brothers, here, who have died on this hill and in dozens of battles before, for our families back home, in that dreamworld of deserts and barbed wire, for our folks who had everything taken from them and still were asked for more: compliance, obedience, money, blood.

And I look around here, and we're not invincible, guys are dropping all around me, and I'm pulling that trigger over and over again, screaming, *"Banzai!"*

We're not invincible.

But we are unstoppable.

"Banzai!" The cry echoes around me. So Japanese and so American at once, this one cry in this one moment, this last cry, this last moment. *"Banzai!"*

We move forward.

Up the hill.

We're almost at the enemy line. We're almost to the Germans, and we can see them running. What's left of a hundred guys, running from these Nisei boys, these scattered, scared, determined, magnificent boys, who take every goddamn objective that's asked of them.

But not all the Germans run.

One gets me. I don't know from where. It's so loud, it's so quiet, I don't even hear the shot.

I feel it, though, *wham,* right through my thigh, and I crumple. I grab the earth.

At first I think I'll be all right, it's just my leg, a couple stitches and I'll be all right, maybe it got the bone, maybe I won't be so fast anymore after this, but I'll be all right.

I try to crawl, I try to keep going, but for some reason I can hardly move, the blood's going outta me so fast, rushing outta me onto this hill, onto this wet earth, and I'm collapsing, I'm sliding down that slope, back, back, until I'm stopped by something, another body, another buddy, I think, and I know it got something important, that bullet.

I'm fumbling for my leg. I'm trying to stop the bleeding, but my blood goes so fast through my hands, fast like me, faster and faster, and I'm cold, and I'm scared, and I don't wanna die.

I can't apply enough pressure. My hands are shaking too hard, my fingers are too weak, and I'm lying back now, lying back against my dead buddy on that bloodstained hill, and I turn my face to the sky like my pal Bill.

It isn't raining anymore. The rain has become soft and light and cold.

It's snowing.

Snowing.

I'm thinking of Topaz and the first snow I ever saw, flakes tumbling lazily out of the sky and settling on the barracks and the dusty roads, so quiet.

And the guys throwing snowballs. That numbness in your fingers, that wet slap in your side, Shig and Tommy and Minnow and Stan Katsumoto . . .

Everyone running and shrieking with laughter. Mas, Frankie, Bette, Yum-yum . . .

Keiko laughing. Prettiest girl I ever saw, with snow like stars in her hair.

I close my eyes, and I think I can hear us, all of us, running. The Topaz roads are turning into pavement, the barracks are turning into San Francisco apartment buildings, the desert air is turning wet and salty, and we're running, running, running until we hit the ocean, that roaring blue expanse, and all of us, running into the waves.

Laughing.

WESTERN
UNION

| A. N. WILLIAMS | NEWCOMB CARLTON | J. C. WILLEVER |
| PRESIDENT | CHAIRMAN OF THE BOARD | FIRST VICE PRESIDENT |

The filing time shown in the date line on telegrams and day letters is STANDARD TIME at point of origin. Time of receipt is STANDARD TIME at point of destination.

WASHINGTON D C 11/23/44 814P

MRS KAORI HASHIMOTO
TOPAZ UTAH

THE SECRETARY OF WAR DESIRES ME TO EXPRESS HIS DEEP REGRET
THAT YOUR SON PRIVATE FIRST CLASS DAVID HASHIMOTO WAS KILLED
IN ACTION IN THE PERFORMANCE OF HIS DUTY AND SERVICE OF HIS
COUNTRY 29 OCTOBER 44 IN FRANCE LETTER FOLLOWS

ULIO THE ADJUTANT GENERAL

XIV

WE HOLD OUR BREATH

ALL OF US
NOVEMBER–DECEMBER 1944

We hear the news, but we don't believe it at first.

Twitchy? Not Twitchy. Not that boy of light and speed and laughter. It can't be. We were just reading his letters. We were just tracing his words:

> *Hey, Keiko, you know what I like about the French language?*
> *How the words kinda drift off at the ends, like people are so lazy*
> *they can't be bothered to finish them. It's a Shig kinda language,*
> *ha ha . . .*

He was just alive. He was just telling us about the smell of bullets and chipped stone. He was just describing how much he's looking forward to a hot shower. He was just wishing for some nabe. *It's so cold here, Stan. I sure could use some of your mom's cooking . . .* He was just signing his name. He was just licking the envelope. He was just sitting in his foxhole, scribbling down our address. He was just . . .

He can't be dead.

On one of the Topaz baseball diamonds, Yuki laughs when we tell her. She says we're joking. She says that's a good trick. She says, "Very funny."

We say nothing. We don't want to believe it either.

We hold our breath, waiting for her to understand. Waiting for the news to strike like a lightning bolt. We watch the laughter drain out of her face. It leaves her eyes first, leaves them startled and black as moonless nights, then her cheeks, which go pale, and her lips, which go slack.

We're not joking. We wish we were.

We get a telegram.

The Secretary of War desires me to express his deep regret . . .

We forget how to breathe.

The news hits Minnow like a truck. He collapses in the middle of the Topaz high school newspaper office, pens and papers flying up around him like disturbed gulls, only to come crashing back down again. The sound of things hitting the floor: knees, hands, pencils. The sound of sobbing, of loss, that wailing that's dredged up from the deepest parts of your soul.

They send for his mother, who finds him curled in a pile of drawings like a soft blanket of snow, crying.

We send out letters. We share the news.

In Tule Lake, Stan punches the outer wall of his barrack. Hard. His breath steams. His eyes burn. He hits the wall again and again —the wall, the wall—until the flesh peels from his knuckles and the wall bleeds.

Tommy finds him in the shadow of the barrack, spread-eagled on the ground, like he's willing himself to sink into the earth, through the crust and the mantle and the core, where the breath will be crushed out of him, and to the other side, where he'll finally breathe again, face-up beneath the gray French clouds, beside Twitchy's body.

We hear the news. We hold our breath.

We make a wish—the way we wished when we drove through a tunnel, the roar of the black road swallowing every other sound in the universe as we fought for air.

"He's in a better place now," Bette, back from New York for Thanksgiving, dabs her eyes with an embroidered handkerchief.

Yuki crosses her arms. "You don't know that."

"Of course I do." Bette smiles. She even looks pretty in mourning, the tears on her lashes like jewels. Like snow. "He was one of the good ones."

Yuki hates how certain her sister is, how calm, how easy this is for her. Death shouldn't be easy. She wants Bette to feel this loss like *she* feels it, right down to the bone. So she says, "He killed people, Bette. You go to hell for that."

Bette slaps her.

It stings, but Yuki welcomes the pain, the heat spreading across her cheek like ice hissing on a hot stove, because it's an easier pain than that raw, cutting grief inside her.

Yuki leaps to her feet. "Don't be stupid, Hiromi!" She's screaming now. She's sobbing and spitting. "He's gone! He's just *gone!* You don't know where he is any more than the rest of us!"

And she runs.

She runs out the door. She runs down the steps. She runs through the streets until she reaches the fence, but she doesn't slow down. She leaps the barbed wire, quick and elegant as a deer, and races into the desert.

She runs. The sand dimples under her feet. She runs until she can't breathe, until the air is caught somewhere between her lips and her lungs, and she bends over, hands on her knees, trying to scream.

We hear the news. We hold our breath, imagining the weight of his soul being lifted from the earth. We try to remember what we were doing on October 29.

Did you know, when it happened?

Did you feel it?

Did you see him streaking across the sky, open-armed for the angels?

Mrs. Hashimoto swears he visited her at Topaz when he died. She was powdering her face, she says, and in her compact mirror, she saw him. He was standing behind her, just there, by the stove, grinning. You know that grin of his: straight, white, blindingly handsome. She saw him only for a second, because when she adjusted her compact again, he was gone.

But she saw him.

Keiko, who's sitting with Mrs. Hashimoto, looks at the place, just there, by the stove, looks and imagines him grinning and hopes it's true.

But she doesn't believe it.

We make a wish. We read the letter again and again. It's from Frankie, who was there to see Twitchy brought in on a stretcher. Frankie, who never writes.

Jesus, he says. *Jesus Christ. I'm so sorry.*

My company walked out of there with seventeen guys, you know? Seventeen guys. Out of two hundred. King Company . . . Twitchy's company . . . they walked out with eight. But Twitchy wasn't with them.

Frankie tells us he found three things in Twitchy's pocket.

The first was a photograph of Keiko.

The second was one of Minnow's sketches. It's of the boys, Frankie says, sitting on Mr. Hidekawa's stoop. *Everyone,* he says. Mas, Shig, Minnow, Frankie, Stan Katsumoto, Tommy . . . and Twitchy, leaping down the concrete banister. It's signed: *To Twitchy. Love Minnow.*

The third was an unfinished letter to Mrs. Hashimoto.

Hey, Ma, remember how you used to yell at me for climbing stuff? The fridge, the fire escape, the trees? Well, they want us to climb this hill tomorrow to rescue a buncha guys who got themselves stuck up there, so it's a good thing I got in all that practice when I was little, huh? Guess it goes to show

But we never learn what it goes to show, because he never got to finish the letter.

He never got to finish a lot of things.

We want to say he died like a hero. We want to say he was brave until the end. And maybe he was. Maybe he was.

But he was also just a kid. He was a scared kid who died far from home, in a country that wasn't his, a country that took his blood and his weight and his tears and didn't give him back to us.

"It should've been me," Frankie says to Mas in an assembly area outside of Nice. "I'm the delinquent. I'm the asshole. I'm the one who should've died."

Mas runs his thumb along the handle of Twitchy's butterfly knife. Frankie didn't feel right keeping it, he said, so it went to Sgt. Masaru Ito, Easy Company, 2nd Battalion, 442nd RCT, who didn't cry when Frankie told him the news, who went cold and hard as a stone or a fossil.

"It should've been *me*," Frankie repeats, rubbing tears out of his eyes. "Not Twitchy. He was a good kid. He was the best kid. He loved this world so fucking much, and now he's not in it anymore. That seem right to you?"

There's a flash of silver as the light glances off the knife handle, and for a moment, Mas is blinded. For a moment, he thinks of Twitchy's smile. "No," he whispers.

We hear the news. We close our eyes. We make a wish.

Give him back to us.

We hold our breath.

In Topaz, Yum-yum plays the pianos at the music school. She plays Twitchy's favorite songs, the fast ones, her fingers moving so quickly over the keys, they barely touch. She skips notes, more and more of them, the faster she goes, leaving so many holes in the melodies, the music collapses, and she's left with silence.

She plays songs backwards, like reversing them will somehow make time run in the opposite direction. The sun will rise in the West. Streams will flow uphill. In the elementary school yard, children will bound backwards, and on that battlefield in France, Twitchy will get up. He'll get up, and he'll sail back home, guided by a long, white wake. The camp gates will open. The bus will back up. He'll appear in the doorway, grinning and waving, like he never left.

But it's not Twitchy who comes back.

It's Shig, who's taken the train from Chicago. Shig is back. He's home . . . as much as it can still be home, after so many people you love have left it.

He and Yum-yum hold hands as they walk to the Itos' barrack, and she taps out Chopin on the edge of his palm.

As soon as he steps through the door, he drops his suitcase.

Minnow hasn't gotten up for days. Why should he get up? Why eat? Or wake? Or care?

Above him on the barrack wall are dozens of drawings of Twitchy: Twitchy running, Twitchy laughing, Twitchy doing tricks with his butterfly knife. He idolized Twitchy, we think. He would have worshipped at Twitchy's feet if that boy had ever slowed down long enough.

Dropping his suitcase, Shig goes to Minnow's cot and falls on him. The weight of a brother. For a second, the breath goes out of Minnow's body. Tears leak from the corners of his eyes.

If Twitchy were here, he would have dogpiled on top.

The missing weight of a brother.

Yum-yum sits on Mas's empty cot, and on the edge of the mattress, she replays the Chopin in reverse.

The news still doesn't seem real. We don't want it to be real. We want it to be a nightmare, because nightmares you can still wake from.

Sitting on his cot in Tule Lake, Tommy cuts a map from an atlas and, using Twitchy's letters to guide him, traces King Company's path through Europe. Anzio. Belvedere. Monteverdi. Red X's in every place Twitchy ever mentioned. A boat from Naples to Marseille. A train to Lyon. To Charmois-devant-Bruyères.

Some of the villages are so small, he has to hunt down their names on the library shelves, and many of the locations, he can't find at all

— the hills, the numbered peaks, the railroad crossings — so he has to guess, X-ing unmarked countrysides and green woods.

"This is where he went?" his sister Aiko asks, her finger tracking a red line up the Italian coast.

Tommy nods. He closes his eyes and imagines what the trees smelled like, how the air tasted, because these were the last things Twitchy smelled, the last things he tasted, the last memories he made before he couldn't make any more.

In Topaz, Keiko walks to the post office, hoping for mail.

She knows he's dead. Of course she knows that. But she still got letters after he was gone. On November 1, she received a letter from PFC David Hashimoto, postmarked from Marseille. He was dead, even though she didn't know it yet, but somehow, he was still writing.

On November 6, another letter arrived.

On November 8, another.

The day of the telegram — *The Secretary of War desires me to express his deep regret . . .* — she got another.

So she walks to the post office every day, even Saturdays and Sundays, even national holidays, when she knows the building will be closed, the doors shuttered, hoping they'll keep coming, those battered envelopes, bearing dates from a month ago: October 21, October 25, October 26 . . .

She hopes the post office has misplaced letters. She hopes they'll discover them a year from now, ten years from now, the letters finding their way to her, across oceans and continents, wherever she might be, so he can keep writing. Just like he promised.

The news connects us. We hold it in our hearts, and although we are scattered like windblown seeds, like we are a wish made on the head of a dandelion, we are still together somehow. We are joined in our missing him.

In Topaz, we sit with Mrs. Hashimoto—Yuki, Yum-yum, Keiko, Shig. Especially Shig. We sit with her and hold our breath, because breathing feels like a betrayal there, in that silent barrack, with that grieving mother, whose boy isn't breathing anymore.

In France, Mas sits alone. He still has the butterfly knife, but he doesn't use it. He doesn't practice with it, and the blade remains still and cold in his pocket. It just doesn't seem right to use it with Twitchy gone.

Sometimes at night, in his slit trench, he feels like he's underwater, like he's at the bottom of a river, everything coursing over him, so fast and so strong. He used to think he was strong, but now, at the bottom of the river, staring up at the watery white moon, drowning, he knows that he's not strong enough for this.

In Tule Lake, Aiko has started folding paper cranes, one after another until her fingertips are sore. A dozen cranes made out of comic-book pages and candy-bar wrappers. Thirty. Fifty.

There's a legend that if you reach a thousand, you are granted one wish.

We join her—Tommy, Stan, Mary, even Kiyoshi. No one talks about the wish, as if talking about it will jinx it, as if our silence will make it come true.

So we fold. Again and again, we fold.

A hundred cranes. A hundred and one. A hundred and two.

We keep wishing.

Time passes. The heaviness on our chests eases. The news is no longer news.

In the Itos' barrack, Minnow finally moves. He tears down his drawings. He peels them from the walls, the ceiling, and they fall in long, wide ribbons, like wakes.

Keiko finds him in the middle of the barrack, pulling pages from his sketchbook: bridges, windmills, Ocean Beach. She joins him, the paper crinkling beneath her as she sits.

They are surrounded.

Twitchy's dimples, Twitchy's ear. Twitchy's arm. His calf. She thinks for a minute that they could reassemble him here, out of paper.

"I loved him," Minnow says.

"We all did," she murmurs automatically.

Because it's expected.

Because what do you say?

What *can* you say? What do you have but platitudes? *We're sorry for your loss. He was a good boy. We loved him.* The words mean nothing, and that's why you say them. Because you need that fog, that barrier of obscurity, between you and everybody else, or your grief will blind them in its rawness, in its brilliance.

"No," Minnow says. He looks frightened. He swallows. "I mean, *I loved him.*"

To Twitchy. Love Minnow.

Keiko doesn't mean to start crying, but she does. Someone who loved him like she loved him? Acutely? Passionately? Bodily? Someone who misses him like she misses him? With blood and bones and desire? The fog around her burns away, revealing her in all her rawness, all her bright, bleeding sorrow.

Because he knows. Minnow *knows.* He knows the way her skin aches. He knows the way she wakes, choking, in the middle of the

305

night, remembering Twitchy is dead. And it is a relief to be known. To be seen. To be not-alone.

She cries, and Minnow gathers her to him. They put their arms around each other, and they know these aren't the arms either of them need, but these are the arms they have, the only arms they have.

They hold each other among Minnow's drawings, among pieces of Twitchy Hashimoto, and they don't let go.

We cling to one another. We are the roof we touch when we drive over the railroad tracks. We are the breath we hold when we go through the tunnel. We are our own wishes and our own answers.

Back in New York City, Bette writes a letter to Frankie.

Dear Frankie, she says, *don't you ever let me hear you talking like that again. Twitchy would not want to hear you complaining about how you're not good enough to be here. He'd want you to do better. Love better. Love harder. Love more. He'd want us all, I think, to love the way he would have loved, to live the way he would have lived. If we can do that, for him and for us, I think that'll bring some light back into this world.*

In sum, she writes, *don't be an ass. I won't stand for it.*

But she signs it *xo.*

In the Katsumotos' barrack, we scrape together our food stores and hold a feast in Twitchy's honor. We eat. We drink contraband sake. We toast. We tell stories.

See, Kiyoshi never got the chance to meet him, but we make sure he *knows* about Twitchy Hashimoto.

The time Twitchy and Shig tied up Minnow and left him in the bathtub for Mr. Ito to find. The time Stan dared Twitchy to chug a gallon of milk and it all came back up in minutes. The time Twitchy got Frankie out of detention by pulling the fire alarm, which got them both detention again the next day. The time Twitchy gave Mary her first softball mitt.

We laugh.

And for the first time in a while, we don't feel guilty about it.

It's been weeks since we got the letter, the telegram, the news, and the camp rings with Twitchy's absence. The loose floorboard in the commissary icebox where he hid that bottle of Jack. The rocks he threw over the fence, now lying still in the desert. The firebreak where he hit Bette with the first snowball of his life.

We are still splintered. We are still rough-edged. But we are also knitting together in the places where we were broken; we are finding each other in the darkness; we are holding fast.

We eat.

We sleep.

We breathe at last.

EXTRA   EXTRA

COAST BAN LIFTED

EXTRA   MEWELL, CALIFORNIA   DECEMBER 17, 1944

WAR DEPARTMENT REVOKES EXCLUSION ORDER SUNDAY

(Although the regular issues of the NEWELL STAR were to be discontinued in preparation for the special New Year issue, a major announcement by the Western Defense Command lifting the West Coast ban has necessitated this issue to acquaint the residents with all-important information.--Ed. Note)

The Commanding General of the Western Defense Command has today issued the necessary orders to terminate mass exclusion of persons of Japanese ancestry from the Pacific coastal area. In the future only those individuals whose records indicate that they are potentially dangerous to the military security are to be excluded.

The new system will permit the great majority of persons of Japanese ancestry to move freely anywhere in the U. S. that they may wish to go. The military authorities have now classified Japanese Americans in three groups:

1. A group of those persons who will be free to move about or reside in any part of the U. S. The vast majority of persons of Japanese ancestry will be in this group.

2. A group of those who have definitely indicated that they are not loyal to the U. S. or are considered as potentially dangerous to the military security. These individuals will continue to be excluded.

3. A very small group of individuals whose cases have not yet been determined.

The Project Director of the center has been supplied with a list of those individuals who are to be permitted to move freely throughout the U. S. will take appropriate steps to inform those who are on that list. Those on the list who wish to have identification cards from the Western Defense Command their possession may secure them by applying thru the Project Director, to the Western Defense Command.

Representatives of the Western Defense Command have arrived at the center and starting tomorrow will individually notify any individuals who are to be excluded. They will also notify those individuals whose cases have not yet been determined and will interview such individuals in order to determine their final status.

It is not contemplated that any list will be published to the general public of those whose exclusion is to be continued.

XV

JAPANESE/AMERICAN

TOMMY, 19

DECEMBER 1944

JAPANESE

In the mornings,
we wake before dawn
to run the dusty roads of Tule Lake.

We are no more
than the whisper of gray cotton sweats,
our frozen breaths.

Through the snowfall,
the bugles call, red as suns
on white flags.

At sunrise, we assemble
in front of the administration building,
and bow to the East.

AMERICAN

I don't always bow.

When we were little,
and the other kids
pledged allegiance
to the flag
of the United States of America,
Shig and I would cover our hearts
and sing "I'm Popeye the Sailor Man."

And to the republic—
I'm Popeye the Sailor Man!
for which it stands—
I'm Popeye the Sailor Man!

Our teacher's frigid glare—
our pyrotechnic laughter.

We were indivisible
then.

Now
I watch everyone bend
like waves collapsing,
breakers red with daylight.

Now
I am surrounded,

waist-deep in their rising sea.

JAPANESE

To understand the origins
of Hokoku Seinen Dan,
the Young Men's Organization
to Serve the Mother Country,
one must first understand:

They were American boys once,
fearless, patriotic, wholesome, polite,
but then the evacuation,
then the camps, then segregation,
and if these things did not happen
to American boys, then they could not be
American boys, but they wanted to be
something. Not American?
Okay, then, Japanese.

They were going to prove themselves
dutiful, loyal, courageous, good,
healthy, strong, and mentally sharp,
if not for America, okay, then.

For Japan.

AMERICAN

After the announcement that the camps are closing,
the army sends interviewers to Tule Lake.

Will you renounce
your American citizenship?

Will you renounce
and stay in Tule Lake?

Cut off from civilization,
we don't have many sources:
gossip, propaganda, hearsay.
So when we get a piece of news
(like that slippery word *and*),
we seize upon it feverishly
and circulate it like a disease.

Choose a side, Tommy.

Renounce *and* stay.
Be American *and* go.

You cannot have both.

JAPANESE

But why be American? We hear
America only promises
wholesale bloodshed and violence—
nurseries burned, barns bombed,
wounded soldiers, back from Europe,
shot in train cars. In America,
it's still open season on Japs.

In here, we are safe,
as long as we're disloyal
Japanese.

So my parents request repatriation.
My mother ties obi made from wire.
My father wears the fence like armor.
My parents pin barbs in my sisters' hair
like chrysanthemums and stare expectantly
at my bowed head, my frozen hands.

A son should remain with his family.

He should knot the barbed wire at his waist
like a sword belt.

Make a decision, Tommy.

In here, we can be together,
though we will not be free.

AMERICAN

Frisco, 1939: I was singing
"Over the Rainbow"
to get baby Fumi to sleep.

I know it's stupid, but I wanted to believe
if I kept singing, I'd fill her dreams
with bluebirds, stars, and lemon drops,

so when she closed her eyes,
I didn't stop.

I didn't know our father was lurking
in the doorway, staring at me,
like I was an intruder in his home.

"Cut that out," he said,
and I did,

but he had already turned away,
his back and hunched shoulders
disappearing down the hall.

He never could stand to look at me
for long.

I kept flunking Japanese.
I broke my arm in judo.

I flinched when he hit me.
I sang a lullaby to my little sister
like a woman.

If I renounce my citizenship to prove
I am not American, I am disloyal,
I am his son,

will he turn around again
and see me?

JAPANESE

In the dream, my parents like me.

On the table, my mother births me,
red and wrinkled as a pickled plum.

There is no screaming in the dream,
no crying.

My father holds me in his arms,
studies my puckered mouth, my nose,
declares, "He has my eyes!"

A blanket enfolds me
like a furoshiki.
My mother cradles me
like a gift—
warm,
silent,
wanted.

AMERICAN

Kiyoshi and Kimi are teaching their mom to swing
to Ella and the Duke, duetting on a borrowed radio.

They scuff the floorboards,
heels kicking,
hands waving,
their mom saying,
"What is 'doo-wah'?"
and scatting inexpertly
when they explain it to her:
"Doo-wah, doo-wah, doo-wah . . ."

I used to own this record.

I used to dance like this
with my sister Aiko,
hopping and jiving
on weekday afternoons
before our parents
returned from work
and yelled at us to stop.

The snare pops. The trumpets squeal.
Laughing, Kiyoshi's mom embraces him
as the next song begins.

I try to imagine my parents swinging,

but it's like trying to imagine boars
clodhopping to a shamisen.

Some things are too painful to watch.

JAPANESE

My mother believes in Radio Tokyo
like some people believe in the gospel.

Japan has taken Formosa,
Leyte, Morotai; Japan shall cover
all the world under one roof—
forever and ever, hakkō ichiu.

She doesn't believe it when the papers say
the reports are false. Japan is losing.

"American propaganda. You fool."

She sweeps imaginary dust
from the doorway.

"Whose side are you on?"

My mother believes the rumors:
If true Japanese return to the homeland,
they will be endowed with property,
jobs, accolades, gestures of gratitude
from the emperor himself.

"But the homeland will have nothing left,"
I say, "when the war is over."

Crack! A red handprint
burning on my pale cheek.

"If you were a good son,
you wouldn't doubt your mother."

AMERICAN

"Mom's losing it."

Aiko has callused fingertips,
nearly a thousand cranes, and a wish
she was going to spend on Twitchy.

"She's just confused," I say.

"You always make excuses for her."

Aiko folds cranes from comic books
Hokoku would frown upon — *Superman*
and *Captain America* — cranes that punch Nazis
and Japs.

Taking a fresh page, she turns it
into a triangle, a square, a kite,
the paper transforming under her hands:
not a blue-eyed hero but an origami bird.

I wait for it to breathe.

"She's our mother," I say.

Nearly a thousand cranes —
I can almost hear them

rustling in that old shoebox,
scratching, restless, at the lid.

"Since when has she ever
been a mother to you?"

JAPANESE

This was not how Hokoku began,
but this was what Hokoku became.

Tule Lake, 1944: The camp swells
with misinformation. Stewing
in our own fear, our confusion,
our anger, we tear ourselves to pieces
over a rumor, speculation.

Pick a side, Tommy.
Grow a backbone, Tommy.

Under enough pressure,
everything

warps—

True Japanese
speak Japanese,
study Japanese,
wake at dawn,
run the camp,
serve the emperor.

True Japanese
obey their parents

when they're told
to join Hokoku.

And my parents always dreamed
of having a good Japanese son.

AMERICAN

Stan Katsumoto said no

at first.

But under enough pressure,
everything splits—

If you're not in Hokoku,
you're not true Japanese,
and if you're not true Japanese,
you and all your family
could be inu.

You know, dogs.
Spies.

American.

So when one of the cooks was arrested
(he was an officer in Hokoku)
and Mrs. K. took his job in the mess hall,
people said she was sicced on them like
a little bitch.

True Japanese spat
in her food, hounded
her daughter, attacked

her husband, beat
her sons, threatened
her life.

Two days ago,
Stan became a true Japanese
like me.

JAPANESE

A thousand voices ricochet through camp.

"Washo! Washo!"

We touch our toes — stretch — clap.

"Washo!"

On my forehead is the rising sun
worn by the sons of Japan.

"Washo! Washo!"

Four rows down, Stan's a grim scarecrow,
glasses fogging.

"Washo!"

Under his eye, a week-old shiner,
yellow as miso.

"Washo!"

We lock eyes. Our silence,
a shrieking kettle.

"Washo!"

AMERICAN

If Twitchy could see me now,
he'd be laughing his ass off.

I can just picture him,
arms flapping, screeching,
"Washo! Washo!"
like a demented albatross.

"What're you doing, Tommy?

You don't believe in this shit,
do you?"

JAPANESE

My mother loves the idea of me
more than she loves me.

She clings to the dream of me
like she clings to the dream of Japan:
silk kimonos, rice-paper screens,
cherry blossoms she hasn't seen
since she was sixteen years old.

In her dream, her son is obedient,
speaks Japanese without an accent,
is stoic, good with money,
going into engineering or
another profession of equal pay.

She dresses me in his clothes:
shoes, suits, overcoats so big,
they swallow me.

What is the sound
of one boy drowning
in his mother's dreams?

AMERICAN

Upon their departure from Tule Lake,
every evacuee will be compensated
with twenty-five dollars and a train ticket.

In my head, I'm composing a song
featuring Benny Goodman on clarinet:

Twenty-five dollars and a train ticket.
Twenty-five dollars for a ride outta town.
Twenty-five dollars for your trouble, sirs.
Japs, get moving! We don't want you around.

Stan's writing again, like if he can write
enough letters, the ink will carry us back
to each other, like rivers carrying souls
to the sea. Even though he knows,
with Bette in New York, Shig in Chicago,
Mas and Frankie somewhere in France,
Twitchy gone like a flashbulb,
there's no going back to Japantown
the way it was before Pearl Harbor, 1941.

"Twenty-five dollars—"
Stan's voice, a rock tumbler.
"—to start Katsumoto Co. from scratch."

"Or rent a room," Aiko adds,
with a glance in my direction.

Twenty-five dollars and a train ticket . . .

If Twitchy were here, he'd sing it with me:

Twenty-five dollars and a ticket in your pocket.
Golly, boys, it's the American Dream!

JAPANESE

My mother slaps
the renunciation form
in front of me.

"You must renounce,
or we will be separated."

I stare at my name, my desire
to give up my country,
transcribed in my mother's hand.

"You must renounce."

My father shoves
a pen across the table.

"No son of mine
abandons his family
for a country
that's given them nothing
but disrespect."

Across the barrack, Aiko makes a crane
out of a candy-bar wrapper
and extends its wings for flight.

Do something, Tommy.

"You must renounce."

"You must keep
the family together,
son."

AMERICAN

From Topaz, Minnow writes to tell us
he's moving back to San Francisco.

"It's time to go home, Tommy."

Taking the letter, Aiko folds a final crane,
which she places in my hands.

A gift.
A wish.
A demand.

"This is your chance, Tommy."

I think of Frannie and Fumi, only five.
If they leave America, will they forget America
the way our mother forgot Japan?
Forgetting the fences, the word "Jap,"
the horse stalls stinking of manure?
What will they have left of America
besides Aiko's bedtime stories of softball,
Charleston Chews, comic-book heroes,
and boys from San Francisco?

If they dream of me, what will they dream of?

A fragment of a song they barely remember—
something about wishing stars and rainbows?

"I don't want to leave you," I say.

"Yeah." Aiko shrugs.
"But do you want to stay?"

JAPANESE

The renunciation applications of Hokoku members
float through the system like dead leaves in a current.

Renunciation approved.
Renunciation approved.

Want to be Japanese? Renunciation approved.

Want to stay with your family?

On December 27, seventy Hokoku officers are arrested
for being "undesirable enemy aliens." No longer American,
nor truly Japanese, these sons of the Mother Country
are bound for a prison camp in Santa Fe.

Dead leaves caught in a net.

Upon their departure, they are accompanied to the gates
by forty armed guards and a parade: buglers, banners,
people calling *"Banzai!"* like it's a summer holiday,
a time for picnics, fireworks, and swimming in the river.

AMERICAN

The signature line
of my renunciation—

untouched as new snow.

JAPANESE

Offering our sympathies to the parents
whose sons were sent to Santa Fe
begins with a walk beside my father.
His silence, a cold fire, a coal bucket,
a chore undone.

In her barrack temple, a Hokoku mother
sits by the fire, serene as a toad.

Her son, a martyr. His portrait, a shrine.

"You're sorry?" she croaks.

Her umbrage. Her throat bulge.

"*My* son has proven his loyalty.
My son is a true Japanese.
My son is the pride of this family.

Offer your congratulations, not your pity."

"Son" — a sore subject for my father.
His mouth twists, as if she's prodded him
in an open wound. He bows —
a gesture of shame. "Congratulations."

"And you?" Her eyes swivel to me.
"Have you renounced?"

Man up, Tommy.
What's it going to be, Tommy?

My existence, a wart. I say nothing,
undeniable as a bitten tongue.

An amphibian smile.
"You have my sympathies, Mr. Harano."

AMERICAN

Returning to the barrack
is an ice-age migration.
My father's silence yawns,
black as a tar pit, waiting
for me to stumble in.

Mounting the step, he looks back —
it's 1939 again. He's staring at me
like I'm a stranger again, unwelcome
as always.

"You've got one more day
to sign that application."

He turns away — I'm thirteen again,
wishing he could see me again.
Hear me. Want me. Just once.

I take a breath.

But he's already leaving,
his back and hunched shoulders
vanishing into the barrack.

Well, Tommy?

I think of Aiko.

"This is your chance, Tommy."

I turn away, to the empty street,
where the silence rings with possibility:
stillness waiting to be broken,
songs waiting to be sung.

At the edge of the camp,
the barbed wire hums—

JAPANESE-AMERICAN

In the morning,
I wake before dawn
and run the dusty roads of Tule Lake.

I am everywhere — in the air,
beyond the fence, fast as a crane
or a boy named Twitchy.

Removing my headband,
I leave it in the snow
like an old bandage.

A message for my parents:

I am not the son you wished for.
But I am the son you have.

In the assembly, I find Stan
and take him by the shoulders.

"What're we doing, Stan?
We don't believe in this shit,
do we?"

His laughter, a swinging gate.
My singing, an ocean breeze.

We peel away from the sunrise,

turning, on the final day of '44,
west toward San Francisco.

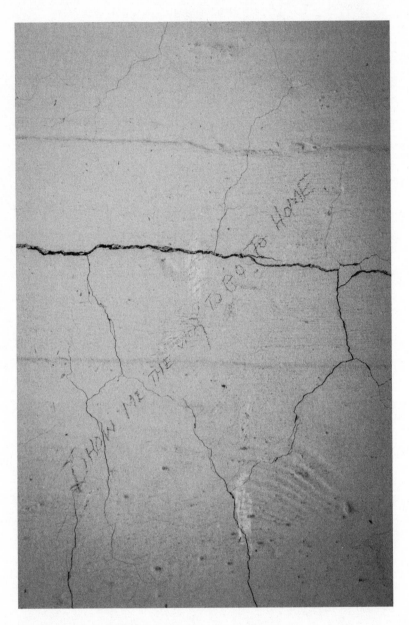

Graffiti, Tule Lake Segregation Center, California

XVI
HOME

MINNOW, 17
FEBRUARY–MARCH 1945

I wake to the murmur of voices, the sound of someone snoring, and the creak of army cots. For a moment, it sounds so much like Topaz that I think I'm back in camp.

But when I open my eyes, it isn't the low ceiling of our barrack looming over me but the high rafters of the Buddhist church gymnasium, and I remember.

I'm back.

It's my first morning in San Francisco after almost three years.

Nearby, someone snorts and rolls over as I sit up, rubbing my eyes. Since the camps are supposed to close before the end of the year, most of the men are here alone, looking for work or apartments to rent so that when their families come to join them, they'll have somewhere to go. In the light filtering through the gym's slatted windows, the men shuffle back and forth from the restroom at the far end of the gym, towels draped over their shoulders and toiletry kits in their hands.

Sliding my suitcase from beneath my cot, I lift a stack of sketchbooks into my lap. I've filled four of them since 1942, and each one is overflowing with extra doodles I drew during class, comics I did for the *Rambler,* studies of the mess hall, the guard towers, my mom. Carefully, I open the topmost book, leafing through my old drawings.

Light on the distant mountains.

Kids playing in the coal piles.

Twitchy and the fellas horsing around on the back of the commissary truck.

It all seems so far away now: the war, the evacuation, Tanforan, Topaz, the loyalty questionnaire, the way everyone left, one after another, drifting away like ash on the wind until no one remained but me.

In one of his letters, sent just after Twitchy died, Mas said that us being separated over the past few years was like having the best, most alive parts of him slowly stripped away. It feels like that now, like if I drew a self-portrait, I'd draw myself sanded down to the bones, my friends and family peeling from my skeleton.

Mas, my head. Frankie, my fists. Twitchy, my arms and legs.

Stan, my guts. Tommy, my lungs.

Shig, my heart.

I hope for a second that none of it happened, that I'll walk out onto Post Street and nothing will have changed. Tommy will have a new record to play for us. Yum-yum will be practicing arpeggios, the notes wafting through her window onto the block. Twitchy will be doing tricks with his butterfly knife while he waits for Shig and me to emerge.

We'll be together.

I'll be whole.

I tap my pencil twice on a blank page and do a quick sketch of the gymnasium: the men, the rows of military cots, the trunks and suitcases, the nightstands made out of produce crates, nothing permanent, everything able to be packed up and moved and abandoned, all of this, on and on, stretching into the distance, like if you looked closely enough, the beds and the men and the luggage would reach all the way back to Utah.

At the bottom, I write, *Miss you, brother,* and seal the drawing into an envelope addressed to Shig.

In the bathroom, I lock the stall door and stare down at the toilet with its clear bowl of water. Out of everything here, this seems the most out of place.

Or I seem the most out of place, here.

To wake up. To walk to the bathroom without stepping outside. To stand before a flushing toilet instead of a latrine. It feels like a dream.

Tentatively, I press the handle and almost jump back as the pipes roar. The water circles the bowl, around and around until it disappears down the drain in a single, violent gurgle.

We can't stay in the Buddhist church hostel forever, so after breakfast, Mom and I set out in search of an apartment. Something small, for the two of us. No Mas, no Shig, who returned to Chicago after Twitchy's funeral.

Although we have some money for an apartment — Mom's twenty-five dollars from the government and a little savings besides — it's not enough to splurge on bus tickets, so Mom and I walk through the old neighborhood in our Sunday best, clutching a list of addresses and knocking on doors.

I guess I should have known things would be different when we came in on the ferry last night. The fog-thick air had a surreal quality to it, the lights of the Bay Bridge like spirit lanterns, the streets like a labyrinth. I didn't even know we'd reached Japantown until we got off the bus in front of the Buddhist church.

But in daylight, I realize it wasn't a dream. The neighborhood really has changed. Most of the old Japanese-owned businesses have been turned into nightclubs and saloons that cater to the sailors who stop in San Francisco on shore leave. "That used to be Mr. Fujita's tailor shop," Mom says as I help her over a splatter of vomit on the curb. "That used to be a laundry."

We pass the old Katsumoto Co., and at least it's still a grocery, but the name *Katsumoto* has been scraped from the windows, and the only remains of the I AM AN AMERICAN sign are the painted-over nail holes above the doorway.

We walk all morning, but no matter where we go, it seems there are no rooms available. Every place was rented last week, or yesterday, or an hour ago.

At one apartment building, a hakujin man in a white undershirt says, "No rooms available," and puts his hand on the doorframe like a skinny Japanese kid and his five-foot-tall mother are going to try to enter by force. His undershirt is stained at the armpits, the color of urine when you haven't had enough to drink.

For a second, I feel like I'm fourteen years old again, being hounded by ketos just because of the way I look. For a second, I want to crawl into the gutter. I want to run home to Mas and Shig.

But Mas and Shig won't be there.

And I have nowhere to run.

"There's a 'For Lease' sign in your window," I point out.

"Yeah." The man sucks his teeth. "I've been meaning to take that down."

I stare at him. Long enough to let him know I know the truth: that he won't rent to us because of the slant of our eyes.

But he stares back, daring me to say it.

"So sorry," Mom says in her accented English. She starts to bow, but seems to think better of it halfway, and she kind of bobs up again before turning away, stiff-backed like she's trying to remain dignified, even though it's hard to be dignified when you keep getting rejected.

Gaman again.

Sometimes I'm so sick of gaman.

I'm sick of the distrust in these hakujin faces, the cowardice in how they won't admit it, the way we have to swallow their lies with a polite nod, the way Mom has to say, "So sorry," even though she has nothing to be sorry for. She's allowed to be here. We all are, now.

We're supposed to be, anyway.

When we reach the street corner, I turn back to see if the sign's still there.

It is.

For lunch, Mom and I stop at a diner where we used to go when Dad wanted to take us out for a treat. The five of us would cram into a vinyl booth—Mom and Dad on one side; Mas, Shig, and me on the other—and Dad would order us a milkshake, which he'd split evenly among five cups. We'd have to take turns picking the flavor, but Dad would always give Mom the cherry on top.

Now we sit in a booth that feels uncomfortably large, waiting for one of the servers to notice us. A minute goes by, then two, then five, the waitresses passing our table without so much as a glance, the cooks glaring at us from the kitchen, the other diners watching us furtively as they tuck into their hamburgers and scoops of pie. For what seems like the tenth time, Mom straightens the silverware on her napkin.

Reaching across the table, I take her hand. Her skin feels thin, like tracing paper. "Come on, Mom. Let's just go."

As we leave, I look back at the other diners and wonder what they're waiting for. Do they think we're going to loose some mustard gas and shout "Banzai!" as we run out the door? Do they think we're going to scream at them for not doing anything when we were forced from our homes, shipped to racetracks and fenced enclosures like animals? For not doing anything now?

Most of all, I am struck by how almost none of their faces look like mine, how alien I feel in this diner I used to love. I guess I took it for granted, seeing people who look like me every day. When we were evacuated, we lost our homes, but we were still surrounded by our families, our friends, our traditions. We kept them, tried to hold on to them, even as we were sent across the country, across the world, our community dissolving, little by little, as pieces of it moved farther and farther from home.

Now I *am* home, but without Mas and Frankie and Stan and Tommy and Twitchy, without *Shig,* my older brother who was always there to bail me out, to cheer me up, to wake me from my nightmares, this is just a building, these are just streets, this is just a city that doesn't belong to me anymore.

Late that afternoon, someone finally tells us, "No Japs," and to be honest, it's almost a relief to know I wasn't imagining things. I wasn't getting worked up over nothing.

At least now I know if I hate them for hating me, I'm not wrong.

Defeated, Mom and I trudge back to the hostel. My feet are

throbbing from walking all day in my dress shoes. Mom's even worse off, leaning on me for support and wincing every time she puts her left foot down.

Limping along together, we pass Mr. Hidekawa's steps, where I sat with Mas and the fellas after they rescued me from the ketos. The turtle-shaped bell over the door is gone.

"Do you know when Mr. Hidekawa's coming back?" I ask.

Mom squeezes my hand. "Mr. Hidekawa passed away in camp."

I stop so quickly, she almost stumbles. I catch her arm, steadying her. "What?"

"He died in one of the prisoner-of-war camps in 1943."

Two years, Mr. Hidekawa's been gone. I didn't know. I wonder how many other people are just never coming back, and we'll stare at their vacant steps or their old businesses and wonder what happened to them, never knowing if they died or just moved.

"But he was so healthy," I say.

"The relocation was a blow to all of us. Some people didn't recover." Squeezing my hand, Mom tugs me onward. "Some people never will."

That night, I sit with Mom in the common room of the hostel, rubbing her arches while she looks over a new list of possible apartments. Shig used to rub her feet for her. He'd do it for Mas, too, after a long day of work. I wish he were here now to rub mine.

"Cheer up, Minnow," she says. "We'll find a place tomorrow."

"What if we don't?"

She frowns. "Of course we will. There are still good people in this city, and more nihonjin are arriving every day. Someone will rent to us."

"What if we didn't stay, though?"

She inhales sharply as I start kneading a particularly tough knot by her heel. "What do you mean?"

I mean I never thought I'd miss being in camp, but after today, I wish I could crawl back into my cot, with my drawings pinned to the walls above me and Mas's Silvertone radio piping quietly in the corner. I want to be welcomed into the *Rambler* offices by guys who have already left Topaz. I want to eat the thin, mess-hall miso soup because I've gotten so used to it, it's the only kind of miso soup I like now. I'm homesick for a place that's already being dismantled, the baseball leagues closing down, the recreation centers shuttering their doors, the schools emptying out like drainpipes, people departing for different parts of the country every day.

I'm homesick for camp the way I used to be homesick for San Francisco, and that makes me want to leave here even more.

"No one says we have to stay," I say. "We could move to Chicago with Shig."

I picture us going to baseball games and walking along the river. Shig showing us the Japanese churches, and community centers, and markets where we can buy kamaboko and mochi rice. The three of us crammed into an apartment with the snow coming down outside in winter, and Mas back from the war, his medals displayed in a frame Mom proudly hangs over the mantel.

A new home. One without so many ghosts.

Mom's lips flatten, and I tense up. She's got that look she used to get when I'd ask for new clothes instead of hand-me-downs, turkey sandwiches instead of musubi, a milkshake of my own because Mas always picked strawberry and I hated strawberry.

"Your father and I moved to this city when Masaru was two years old. You and Shigeo were born here. This is where we raised you. *This* is where your father died, and where I will die too one day," she says. "I will not leave again."

Two days later, we're no closer to finding a place to live, and I'm hanging around the ferry building, waiting for Stan Katsumoto, who's supposed to arrive today. He's coming to find a job and an apartment for his family, who are at Tule Lake until they have a place to stay in the city.

Leaning on one of the pylons, I watch the nihonjin milling around the dock. Some are hoisting duffle bags onto their shoulders. Others are juggling infants who are so young, they must have been born in camp. The whole scene reminds me of the evacuation: the luggage, the harried families, the way people keep snapping at one another in travel-strained voices.

It's like we've been kicked out of camp the same way we were kicked out of San Francisco three years ago.

The only thing that's missing are the ID tags.

When Stan Katsumoto finally comes down the gangway, I almost don't recognize him. I haven't seen him in a year and a half, and he's gotten so thin, you could turn him sideways and he'd disappear. His cheeks are bony, and his black eyes seem sort of sunken behind his taped glasses.

But it's Stan. A little piece of home.

"Minnow!" Dropping his suitcase, he wraps me up in his long arms. "Boy, are you a sight for sore eyes!"

I hug him. To my surprise, my chin fits right on his shoulder. I don't even have to stand on tiptoe and I'm almost his size.

"You've gotten tall!" He laughs, thrusting me back. "You been drinking your milk like a hakujin kid or something? I bet you're taller than Mas now."

"Oh." *Taller than Mas?* I can't even imagine it. In my head, Mas is a towering figure, stronger and smarter than everyone around him, especially me. "I don't think so."

"You heard from him lately?" Stan asks, picking up his suitcase again. Together, we head for the busy intersection outside the ferry building, the people rushing about, the cable cars clanging their bells.

"He's still on the French-Italian border, I think. I guess they're not seeing a lot of action."

"That'll be good for him." Stan's glasses flash in the light. "After what they went through."

I nod. Sometimes I wonder what Mas will be like when he comes back. If he comes back. Frankie said that after what happened to Twitchy, Mas was diagnosed with battle fatigue and sent back from the front.

I can't imagine that, either. Mas coming apart. I write to him often, even though I don't know if it does any good, because my brother is made of stone, and if stone cracks, it can never really be made whole again.

I wish he'd come back. I'd even take him yelling at me about my grades and not joining the football team, if it meant he was the same old Mas.

Stan and I make our way through the trolleys and buses and crowds of sailors in their navy uniforms and crisp white caps. I tell him Mom and I are staying at the Buddhist church, that we haven't had any luck finding an apartment.

"They were afraid of us then. They're still afraid of us now," Stan says.

"But we didn't *do* anything."

"What d'you mean, Minnow?" Stan smirks, but there's a hard edge to his expression, like the blade of an axe. "We exist."

That night, Stan takes me out to see Count Basie at the Golden Gate. We're so far in the back of the theater that we can hardly see him up there at the piano, but the music's loud enough for everybody: Black, white, nihonjin. The band plays hits like "Pennies from Heaven" and "One O'Clock Jump," and the crowd goes wild over every solo, every bright note, every swinging beat.

Boy, it feels good to let loose for a night. Those blazing trumpets. Those syrupy saxophones. They're a riot of color in a world of graphite, like everything for years has been dull, dull, dull, rendered in grays, and all of a sudden I'm remembering rainbows, sunsets, forests, reds.

I lean over to Stan. "Tommy would've loved this!"

Stan's got one of those smiles so relaxed, it's almost one long laugh. "Let's get him a new recording once we've got a little saved up! Give him a head start on his collection when he gets back!"

After the show, we go traipsing back into the fog with the rest of the concertgoers, dizzy with music. People split off in different directions, skipping across the cable-car tracks on Market or heading up Taylor to the Tenderloin district. All these different kinds of people bound for a couple of hours, held by the spell of Count Basie's music, and then . . . *poof.* We disperse again. Is that what life is like? People coming together and drifting apart, coming together and drifting apart, over and over until there's no one left?

Will we come together again, after all that's happened to us? Can we, when we are so broken?

As Stan and I turn toward Japantown, he starts singing, "Between the Devil and the Deep Blue Sea," swinging around streetlights like he's in a Hollywood musical, even though he's got a voice like a raven.

"C'mon, Minnow, sing it with me!"

Three years ago, I would've shaken my head and hung back with Tommy while braver guys like Shig and Twitchy whooped it up, but there is no Tommy, no Shig and Twitchy. So I open my mouth and out comes the most terrible note anybody's ever sung.

Behind us, a couple of Black ladies who followed us out of the theater start laughing, cigarette smoke trailing from their mouths.

I blush, but Stan gives them a bow. "Well, gals, think we can cut a record?"

One of them shakes her head. She's got an easy, lopsided smile that reminds me of Shigeo's. "You can cut one," she says, "but no one's going to pay to listen!"

We laugh. It feels good to laugh with strangers, walking the length of a city block, talking about our favorite songs of the night. Then, at the next corner, we go our separate ways, us strolling toward Japantown, the ladies disappearing in a cloud of smoke, the lit ends of their cigarettes seeming to float between their fingers like distant stars.

Coming together.

Drifting apart.

Since I've been treading these streets, looking for an apartment, picking up Stan, catching a show, I feel like I'm wearing in the city the way I'd wear in a secondhand pair of shoes. It's not mine. It stopped being mine the day we boarded that Greyhound bus for Tanforan.

But for the first time since I've been back, I wonder if it could be mine again, someday.

A week later, Stan and I are sitting on the steps across from the Oishis' apartment building, waiting for a bunch of ketos to emerge from Yum-yum's old place.

Mr. Oishi's been back in town for a few days, trying to evict one of the white families who rented from them while they were gone. I guess the ketos in the lower flat didn't want to surrender their apartment to a bunch of Japs, even though the Oishis own the building.

Yum-yum's dad finally had to get the police involved, and now the ketos are supposed to be out by noon.

I've brought my sketchbook, and Stan's brought a bag of popcorn, and we take turns tossing kernels into each other's mouths. I miss more than I catch, but Stan doesn't seem to mind. We've gone through half the bag by the time the moving truck pulls up to the curb, and the ketos finally start coming out of the building.

Picking up my pencil, I draw them lugging their tables, their mattresses and trunks down the steps, and I think of me and the guys carrying Yum-yum's piano to the sidewalk, the way she played her heart out on the street.

"Good riddance," Stan says, tossing popcorn in their direction like he's at a propaganda show, throwing garbage at onscreen Germans.

They've almost filled the truck when they march back inside. There's the sound of breaking glass. Something heavy crashing to the floor.

"They're trashing the place," I whisper.

Stan clicks his tongue. "Soldiers salting the earth."

"But we're not at war with them."

He laughs. "What, d'you think we were let out of the camps because FDR woke up one day and realized, oh shit, he was wrong? You can't just lock up a hundred thousand people and call it good? C'mon, Minnow. We had to fight for that. We're fighting all the time, whether we know it or not."

I add silhouettes behind the curtains in my drawing. "But we're already fighting a war out there. Why do we have to fight one in our own country, too?"

Stan nods across the street, where there are the sounds of raised voices now, as if in argument. "Do you think *they* think this country belongs to us?" He shrugs.

Before I can answer, a girl comes out of the Oishis' building, slamming the door behind her. She must be around my age, maybe a year or two younger, in her worn sweater and scuffed saddle shoes. Across the road, our gazes meet.

Stan waves at her, smirking.

She frowns, and for a second I think she's going to scream at us for kicking her out, or for being Japanese, but then her fists unclench, and she trots down the steps, crossing the street in a few quick strides.

Up close, her skin is flushed, and there are tears in her eyes. If I was going to do a portrait of her, I'd do it in watercolor—splashes of paint on her cheeks and lashes.

"Is that building yours?" she asks.

"A friend's," I say.

The girl bites her lip. "I'm sorry . . . for what my parents are doing. I tried to get them to stop . . ."

Stan looks her up and down. "Were you the one yelling?"

She nods.

He offers her some popcorn.

Taking a few kernels, she nibbles them fretfully, like a rabbit.

I don't think anyone knows what to say. In the Oishis' apartment, there's the sound of wood breaking.

"She plays the piano," I tell her. "Our friend." Flipping through my sketchpad, I find a picture of Yum-yum as a constellation over Tanforan, stars winking over the barracks and barbed-wire fences.

We're all there, on the infield below. We're all alive, and together.

I swallow the lump rising in my throat.

The girl stares at the paper for a second, her gaze darting back and forth across the page. I watch her carefully, wanting to know that she's seen it, that she understands.

"This is where you were sent?" she asks finally.

I nod.

She lifts a finger, almost touching one of the guard towers. "It wasn't right, was it? It should've never happened."

"Nope," Stan says. "But it'll happen again, if we're not careful."

The girl nods silently. Across the street, her family is appearing again, piling the last of their belongings into the truck.

She glances over at them, then back to us. "I'd better go," she says, slowly backing down the steps.

For a second, I'm scared—not of the girl or her family, but that this moment was too short, too small, that she'll just go away like nothing has changed. She'll go back to her normal life, and in a few weeks, she won't remember ever having talked with the two Japanese boys fresh from the camps. Maybe one day, she'll even be sitting in a diner watching a mother and son wait and wait for service, wait and wait because they aren't white, they don't *belong here,* and she'll keep eating her grilled cheese or her Cobb salad like nothing at all is wrong.

Standing, I tear the drawing of Yum-yum from the sketchbook and offer it to the girl. "So you remember," I say. "So you won't forget?"

This happened. This happened to *us*. This happened to kids like her. This can happen again.

We cannot allow it to happen again.

With a nod, the girl takes the sketch and tucks it into her pocket.

"Keep yelling," Stan adds. "Maybe they'll hear you one day."

A smile flashes across her lips. As she heads back to her family, they glare at us from the other side of the truck.

Smirking, Stan and I wave.

When we get back to the Buddhist church hostel, there's someone lounging on the steps, watching passersby.

I squint.

I recognize that slouch.

It's Shig.

Shigeo.

My brother.

As he stands, I see my drawing of the church gymnasium in his hands.

Am I talking? My mouth is open. Am I running? I'm barreling toward him.

"Miss me?" he asks.

I charge into him so hard, I can feel the air go out of him.

"Easy, Minnow!" he cries.

I finally find my voice. "You're here! You came!" I'm crying and I'm hugging him, and I feel Stan slam into us both from behind.

"You son of a bitch!" Stan's saying. "You sneaky son of a bitch!"

Shig laughs, squeezing us both so tight, I don't think he'll ever let go. "Chicago's for suckers. It's too damn cold there to have any fun at all."

"What about your job?" My voice is wet with tears, but I don't care. Shig is here. He's *here*.

"Eh, it was too much work."

"Why didn't you tell us you were coming?" I say.

"And miss the look on your faces?" Shig laughs again. "Never."

I don't know how he does it, but Shig's return changes everything for us. He, Mom, and I help Yum-yum's dad clean up the mess the ketos left in his building. Since the rest of the Oishis are still in Topaz, we're going to stay with him until we find an apartment of our own.

Shig and I share a room, like we used to. I don't realize how much I missed the sound of his breathing until I fall asleep to it the first night, quicker than I've fallen asleep anywhere since he left for Chicago.

The Katsumotos agree to rent out the upper flat, and Stan's going to see about applying to UC Berkeley in the fall. He wants to be a lawyer, maybe work for the American Civil Liberties Union of Northern California, which fought for Fred Korematsu all the way up to the Supreme Court.

At our new address, we get letters from our friends.

Aiko's considering moving back to San Francisco, since she's going to be seventeen this year, to work for one of the officers' families who live in the Presidio. Until their parents leave for Japan, though, both she and Tommy will be staying in Tule Lake. Although, she adds, with so many Tuleans renouncing their citizenship, who knows when the repatriates will be sent back?

Keiko's going to move back with her parents to get the old Japanese school Soko Gakuen running again.

Bette insists that New York is the greatest city in the world and says we're all welcome to visit her. I bet when Frankie gets out of the war, he's going to take her up on that.

Mas tells me I'd better go back to school ASAP and graduate *or else*. It's nice to hear him sounding like himself again.

So with only a couple of months left in the semester, I re-enroll at George Washington High School. On my first day back, Shig walks me all the way to campus. Together, we pass Mr. Hidekawa's steps, the corner where the ketos jumped me, the new nightclubs, the old Katsumoto Co., the Jewish Community Center, and when we get to school, we stand on the 30th Avenue sidewalk, looking out over the football field, the concrete bleachers, the other students trudging past us — Chinese kids and Mexican kids and nihonjin kids and white kids and Black kids all together.

Shig puts his arm around my shoulders. "Study hard, Minnow, or Mas will have my head." After a second, he adds, "But not too hard, or Twitchy will come back to haunt you."

To my surprise, I laugh. It just kind of bubbles out of me, thinking of Twitchy flying around, a free-floating ghost boy cupping his hands to his mouth and going, *"Woooo!"*

"You know, for a long time, I didn't think I could ever come back from losing him?" I say. "I didn't think I could make it in a world without him."

"I know, Minnow. Me too." Shig squeezes me to him. "But here we are."

I grin at him as the first bell rings, and there's a sudden storm of chatter, doors opening and closing, the other students rushing to class.

I'm about to head in too when the Golden Gate Bridge appears out of the fog, stopping me in my tracks — the red towers, the flaking paint, the sections in need of repair. For some reason, it looks smaller, more fragile, like if we're not paying enough attention, if we're not constantly working to keep it upright, then one day, we could turn around and it'll have collapsed on us.

But it's still my bridge. My favorite view in the city.

Shig gives me a nudge. "Hey, you're gonna be late."

"I know." Turning back, I take a breath, drinking in the sight of it: the school, the bleachers, the bridge, the fog curling into the bay. Beside me, I feel Shig breathe in too.

We made it, brother, I think.

We're home.

AUTHOR'S NOTE

HISTORY, FAMILY HISTORY, AND FICTION

We Are Not Free may be a work of historical fiction, but to me, it is more than either history *or* fiction. In 1942, following the bombing of Pearl Harbor and the subsequent spike of anti-Japanese sentiment in the United States, my grandparents and their families were uprooted from their homes and forced into incarceration camps with more than one hundred thousand other people of Japanese descent. From the beginning, telling this story has always been personal for me, because this history is my history. This community is my community. It happened; it happened to my family; and it has impacted so much about who we are and how we exist in this country.

In the course of researching this book, I interviewed a number of my Nisei relatives, whose experiences have provided inspiration for some of the novel's narrative details, although any particulars as they occur here have been transformed into fiction. A small sampling of these elements includes: My grandmother's blond wig and the story of how she brought it home, which are now immortalized in Yum-yum's chapter, although my grandmother didn't get her blond wig until after she was out of camp and in beauty school. Or, for example, my great-uncle was younger than Yuki when he was shouted out of an ice cream shop, but the words "We don't serve Japs here" are part of his childhood. Two of my grandparents met in Tule Lake when my grandmother's studies were interrupted by a boy walking in through the back door of the classroom, but Mary's sullen disposition is much more like my own than my grandmother's. In 1942, my great-aunt was a junior in high school, and in her civics classes, she was told again and again how lucky she was to be a free American. After she was incarcerated, she would sit in the grandstand at Tanforan, watching all the people strolling around San Bruno, and she would say to herself, again and again, "I am not free"—words that inspired the title of this book. For the opportunity to share these and other pieces of my family's history, I am both honored and grateful.

As I have threaded snippets of family history through a fictional narrative, I have also woven this story through real historical events, including the forced removal of Japanese-Americans (a term I use here to encompass Issei, who were barred from becoming naturalized citizens by the Naturalization Act of 1790, as well as their descendants); the substandard conditions of temporary detention centers like Tanforan; the desolate incarceration camps such as Topaz and Tule Lake; the loyalty questionnaire and its divisive effects on the Japanese-American community; the formation, training, and campaigns of the 442nd Regimental Combat Team; the turmoil at the Tule Lake Segregation Center and its period of martial law; and the return (for some) to the West Coast. Mentioned in these pages are certain public personages, like President Franklin Delano Roosevelt, Mike Masaoka, Dillon Meyer, Ray Best, and Dr. Reece Pedicord, who are historical figures, but all the characters who speak and act in *We Are Not Free* are works of fiction.

Always, I have endeavored to be true to and respectful of the historical events of 1942–1945 and the people who lived through them. However, in the interests of telling a good story, I have occasionally bent the details a little. For example, an Issei man was shot by a white soldier in Topaz, but the shooting occurred in April 1943, not February, as it does in Stan's chapter. Construction on the gymnasium at

Tule Lake was not completed until 1944, although I have written the gym into a scene from late October 1943. *Blood on the Sun* was not released in theaters until 1945, but after reading my grandfather's letters describing his reactions to the film, I could not pass up the opportunity to include it. The Tule Lake jail, in which the graffiti SHOW ME THE WAY TO GO TO HOME appears, was not built until 1945, although I have placed a photo of it between chapters set in December 1944 and February 1945. Any other errors in geographical or historical fact are mine.

While one of my goals in writing this novel was to illustrate some of the depth and breadth of Nisei experiences during World War II, I'd like to note that these fourteen perspectives are a mere fraction of what this generation went through. With thousands of people incarcerated, their experiences varied, sometimes drastically, depending on where they were and what assets they possessed at the time of their forced removal. The story of a teenager from San Francisco, therefore, will be different from that of one from Bainbridge Island or Honolulu, just as stories from Manzanar are different from those from Topaz, Tule Lake, or Crystal City and the experiences of the Nisei in the 442nd are different from those in the Military Intelligence Service or the Women's Army Corps. I have included some suggestions for further reading in the following pages, and it is my hope that we continue to explore our existing literature on the incarceration as well as discover more and more of these stories in the years to come.

LANGUAGE

In recent years, there has been a movement to change the terminology of the incarceration. The words most often used, such as "internment," "evacuation," and "assembly center," for example, are euphemisms originally intended to conceal the truth of the inhumane conditions, poor treatment, and civil rights violations that occurred in the camps. These are the terms my characters, who do not have the benefit of hindsight, use in the text. However, when speaking about the history, I have chosen to base my language on the Japanese-American Citizens League's updated terminology, outlined in the *Power of Words Handbook,* including the terms "incarceration," "forced removal," and "temporary detention center." I would encourage others who are speaking about the camps to do so as well.

After much thought, I decided to include three ethnic slurs in *We Are Not Free,* and I have tried to choose which characters use them and under what circumstances in order to illustrate the racial tensions between the Japanese-American and white communities at the time. I would like to clearly state that these terms are both offensive and outdated, and should not be repeated.

Despite their historical accuracy, I have elected *not* to include other historical terms for race, having chosen instead to use their modern counterparts. There are other words more accurate to the times, but they can also be heavily charged today, and it did not feel appropriate using them without unpacking them clearly and thoughtfully in a way that is sensitive to contemporary readers. It is important to me to note, therefore, that while "Black" was considered a slur in the 1940s, when my characters use the word in the novel, it is anachronistic and not intended as derogatory.

PAST AND PRESENT

As with all historical events, the incarceration did not happen in isolation. Prior to the attack on Pearl Harbor, anti-Asian sentiment in North America had been building for decades, and the unjust, often brutal treatment of nonwhite people has profound and extensive roots in U.S. history. During World War II, the mass incarceration affected over one hundred thousand Japanese-Americans—more, if we consider the people of Japanese ancestry who were deported from their homes in Latin America and imprisoned in camps in the United States. The effects of these events have been both deep and widespread, not only for those who lived them, but also for later generations of Japanese-Americans, like myself, and other communities of people of color.

Although *We Are Not Free* is both history and fiction, I believe it would be a mistake to relegate the racism against and mass incarceration of Japanese-Americans in the 1940s to some bygone era, with no relevance to current events. During my research, the more I have learned about our history, the more I have come to realize that we are part of an ongoing pattern of injustices that have affected and are still affecting millions of people of color on this continent. I don't think it's fair or right for me to compare the various ways minority groups have been and are being abused, oppressed, and denied their human rights in this country, but when I look around, I cannot help but feel that history is repeating itself in new and sometimes more horrific ways.

History is not dead. We have not moved on. Like Minnow and many of my other characters, I love this country because it is my home, and my parents' home, and my grandparents' home, and because I was raised to believe in the opportunity and equality America promises, but this does not prevent me from seeing its problems, seeing all the ways it has failed its people again and again. Rather, I'd like to think that it's because I love this country that I am here, working in the ways that I can toward making it a better, more just, more egalitarian place for *everyone*—a place that, one day, I hope can truly live up to its promises.

ACKNOWLEDGMENTS

Among other things, I think *We Are Not Free* is a book about community—people who come together, even across great distances—and it is a community who brought this book into the world. I am thankful for the assistance, guidance, encouragement, and efforts of more people than I could ever hope to name in these pages. Thank you, always, thank you.

Thank you to my agent, Barbara Poelle, for knowing this was the book of my heart long before I was brave enough to admit it, and for championing it with such ferocity and care. Further gratitude to everyone at IGLA—I am so humbled to be counted as one of your authors.

Thank you to my editor, Catherine Onder, for believing in each of these characters and all of them together. Under your guidance, they've gotten the opportunity to become who they were always meant to be, and I'm forever thankful. My admiration and gratitude to the whole team at Houghton Mifflin Harcourt for bringing this book into the world: Gabby Abbate, Mary Magrisso, Mary Hurley, Tara Shanahan, Amanda Acevedo, Margaret Rosewitz, Alix Redmond, Ellen Fast, and Erika West. With additional thanks to Jessica Handelman, John Lee, and David Field/Caterpillar Media, who created this extraordinary cover; Mary Claire Cruz, who laid out the interior of this book with such great care; and Julia Kuo, who brought Minnow's sketches to life.

Thank you to my readers, Diane Glazman, Samira Ahmed, Tara Sim, Laura Edgar, Averill Elisa Frankes, Mark Oshiro, Masa Motohashi (and James Brandon, who set in motion the events that would put us in contact), Heidi Heilig, Patrice Caldwell, Jane Beckwith, and

Robert Miller. Thanks also to Lucas Sakata for the translation and the crash course in late Meiji–era rhetoric. Thanks to David Harper (and Jesse Dizard, who introduced us) for speaking with me about the intersections between the Poston camps and the Colorado River Indian Tribes, and to Angela Sutton for providing a tour of Tule Lake on such short notice.

Thanks to my friends for the encouragement and fellowship, including (but never limited to) Stacey Lee, Parker Peevyhouse, Jessica Cluess, Evangeline Crittenden, Emily Skrutskie, and Christian McKay Heidicker.

To my family—more love and gratitude than I could ever hope to convey. This book is *from* you, *for* you. Special thanks to Mary S. Uchiyama, Aiji Uchiyama, Osuye Okano, Sachiko Iwata, and Mutsuo Kitagawa for sharing your stories with me, and to Kojiro F. Kawaguchi for putting yours on CD. Thanks to my grandfather, Peter Kitagawa, for writing so many letters to my grandmother, and thanks to my grandmother, Margaret Kitagawa, for keeping them all those years. Thanks to Matt Kitagawa for the grade-school heritage report, and to Gordon Kitagawa for digging it out of storage. Thanks to Don Aoki for the Hamada family tree. Thanks to Chris Iwata for chatting with me about the army . . . and for not noticing when I borrowed my first research book from your study. None of this would have been possible without Pauline Kitagawa and Kats Kitagawa—thank you for everything: arranging interviews; driving thousands of miles across literal deserts; letting me pick through Grandma's old steamer trunks; the trips to Topaz, Manzanar, and Tule Lake; and every time I texted you to check a fact about cooking, slang, J-town, katakana, or our family history. You have been an integral part of this journey, and I will never forget it. As ever, thanks to Cole for your continued love and support.

Finally, thank you, reader. Thank you for seeing this story and not turning away. It happened. It happened to my family. It has happened, in other forms and with other faces, to other communities and other individuals all over the world. It is happening right now, and it will happen again. We cannot allow it to happen again. Love and fortitude to you all.

FURTHER READING

Densho: The Japanese American Legacy Project. (www.densho.org; accessed Aug. 7, 2019)

Houston, Jeanne Wakatsuki. *Farewell to Manzanar.* New York: Random House Children's Books, 2012.

National JACL Power of Words II Committee. "Power of Words." Japanese American Citizens League. 2013. (jacl.org/education/power-of-words; accessed Aug. 6, 2019)

Okada, John. *No-No Boy.* Seattle: University of Washington Press, 2014.

Okubo, Miné. *Citizen 13660.* Seattle: University of Washington Press, 2014.

Oppenheim, Joanne. *Stanley Hayami, Nisei Son.* New York: Brick Tower Press, 2008.

Tanaka, Chester. *Go for Broke: A Pictorial History of the Japanese American 100th Infantry Battalion and the 442d Regimental Combat Team.* Richmond, CA: Go for Broke, Inc., 1982.

Tule Lake Committee. *Second Kinenhi: Reflections on Tule Lake.* San Francisco: Tule Lake Committee, 2000.

Uchida, Yoshiko. *Journey to Topaz.* Berkeley, CA: Creative Arts Book Company, 1985.

IMAGE CREDITS

20: "State of California, [Civilian Exclusion Order No. 20], City of San Francisco, northeast," April 24, 1942, by J. L. DeWitt, Lieutenant General, U.S. Army, Western Defense Command and Fourth Army. Courtesy of the San Jose State University Department of Special Collections and Archives, John M. Flaherty Collection of Japanese Internment Records.

74: "Topaz concentration camp, Utah," October 18, 1942, by Tom Parker. Courtesy of the National Archives at College Park, 210-G-E13.

99: *Topaz Times*, vol. II, Extra, January 29, 1943. Courtesy of the Library of Congress, Serial and Government Publications Division.

159: "Allied Nations 2-cent 1943 issue U.S. stamp," January 14, 1943, by the Bureau of Engraving and Printing. Courtesy of the U.S. Postal Service, National Postal Museum.

172: "Camp new arrivals," 1943 (ddr-densho-37-2797), Densho, National Archives and Records Administration Collection. Courtesy of the National Archives and Records Administration.

243: Shoulder insignia for the 442nd Regimental Combat Team

260–61: "The Rand-McNally new library atlas map of Europe" by Rand McNally and Company. Courtesy of the Library of Congress, Geography and Map Division.

308: "Coast Ban Lifted," *Newell Star,* Extra, December 19, 1944, Densho, Newell Star Collection. Courtesy of the family of Itaru and Shizuko Ina.

346: "Graffiti from Tule Lake jail" by Kats Kitagawa. Courtesy of Kats Kitagawa.